2/10

HESPIRA

A TALE OF HENGHIS HAPTHORN

Other Archonate books by Matthew Hughes

Tales of Henghis Hapthorn:
  Majestrum
  The Spiral Labyrinth
  Hespira

Fools Errant
Fool Me Twice
Black Brillion
The Commons
Template
The Gist Hunter and Other Stories

HESPIRA

A TALE OF HENGHIS HAPTHORN

MATTHEW HUGHES

NIGHT SHADE BOOKS
SAN FRANCISCO

First Edition

Trade hardcover: ISBN   978-1-59780-101-0
Limited Edition: ISBN   978-1-59780-102-7

Night Shade Books
Please visit us on the web at
http://www.nightshadebooks.com

To James Davis Nicoll,
We get by with a little help.

CHAPTER ONE

I was wrapping up the final steps in a case that hardly deserved to be called a discrimination; it involved a simple transaction that could have been handled just as well by a confidential courier. But the client, Irslan Chonder, occupied a place of such high standing among the second-tier social elite of Olkney that I had overcome my initial inclination to decline the assignment. I was also persuaded, I will admit, by the fact that, when he sensed my reluctance, he immediately doubled the already considerable fee he had first offered. A discriminator must make a living, after all.

Chonder's need for my services arose from his passion for collecting "soul boxes." These were relics of a Nineteenth-Aeon spiritual movement that had flourished in the Ar River country before the collapse of the Hurran hegemony. Adherents of the Retrospectance cult believed, not unreasonably, that the meaning of a life could only be understood in hindsight. But, as was all too common among those who opted to throw their lives under some passing philosophical system, a simple, logical analysis of the kinks and currents that marked out the course of one's passage from cradle to crypt would not satisfy.

Retrospectants took a more complex view, believing that life offered each of us a series of "intimations." These took the form of seemingly random objects, perhaps a peculiar pebble or someone's lost button, a fallen sparrow or an interesting twig, that came by chance to the believer's notice. The items were scooped up and placed in a dedicated container known as a repository that occupied a place of reverence in the Retrospectant's residence. The wealthier the believer, the more sublime the container—when the cult was at its acme in the Ar River country, the high and mighty of the region competed with each other to commission renowned artists from up and down The Spray to shape and ornament what were colloquially called their soul boxes. Even the simpler repositories of the poor and humble, worked on over the lifetime of a member of the congregation, could become striking examples of naive artistry.

The end of life rarely took a Retrospectant unawares. A date was set, refreshments ordered, and all of the candidate's friends and family were invited. The repository was brought out to be admired, then its contents were arranged in a particular pattern that the soon-to-be deceased had deduced from contemplating the points in his life at which they had been found, and the events that had followed each finding.

The devotee would then explain the hidden meaning and structure of his existence, as revealed by the seemingly random milestones collected in his soul box. His fellow Retrospectants would utter appropriate gasps and "well-I-nevers" as the subtle architecture of existence was revealed. After the ultimate revelation, the adherent would then be quickly killed and cremated. His intimations were returned to their repository, to which were also added his still-warm ashes. Amid cheers and songs of enthusiasm, the whole congregation would form a procession and carry the container off to its final resting place: a continually expanding catacomb hollowed out in the hills that overlooked the Ar River.

Of course, the finality of any resting place was always subject to amendment by subsequent generations. The Retrospectant catacombs were rediscovered a decade or so ago by some boys looking for a quiet corner where they could escape parental supervision, and a vogue began for collecting and displaying soul boxes. Aficionados studied the relics and wrote appreciations of them. The finest specimens commanded high prices, and some truly spectacular collections were assembled. Irslan Chonder's was one of the best.

Thus when some of his most prized pieces were lifted, despite his house's grievously expensive security apparatus, one would have thought that he would have gone straightaway to the Archonate Bureau of Scrutiny, to lay a complaint and await the outcome of the law's impartial machinations. Unhappily for Chonder, however, bringing in the scroots was not an option; the theft of his best pieces did not constitute the first time the items had been purloined. Put bluntly, he had acquired them that way in the first place. Indeed, it was quite possible that the thief who had originally stolen them for Chonder was responsible for this subsequent laying of the lift, as the expression went. In one sense, however, my client was in luck: the thief had not restolen the goods in order to pass them on to a new—or even the previous—owner; he was quite willing to return them to Chonder for a "recovery fee."

Chonder had weighed his desire to recoup the soul boxes against the cost of the ransom, which was bearable to one of his wealth, and against the humiliation of being played for a noddy, which was a dryer swallow for a man who so cherished his own dignity. In the end, desire overcame chagrin, and he agreed to pay the thief's demand. But rather than place the matter in the hands of a courier firm—there were several in Olkney that were well experienced in such transactions—he brought it to me.

"Why me?" I asked, when he stood in my workroom and explained his need. "Surespeed can handle it for you. Or All Burdens Borne."

"Because I want to know who has done this to me," he said, his leonine head jutting from his shoulders and the muscles of his heavy jaw bunching at the hinges. He turned steel-gray eyes my way and said, "I do not take kindly to being flipped and fleeced. I am not some rustic rube gawping at his first sight of Endless Square while his pockets are picked."

I let my surprise show. "You do not know who sold you the pieces in the first place?"

"It was all done through intermediaries—I believe they're called shims and cut-outs in the underworld."

"And now you know why it is done that way," I said. "My professional advice is to get your goods back and revisit your defensive arrangements. I can consult with you on that score."

"I will have retribution," he said, and in the silence that followed I could actually hear his teeth grinding. Then he looked at me sideways. "Are you telling me that you can't penetrate some thief's camouflage?"

I let the implied insult pass. "I am telling you," I said, "that launching a vendetta against a ranking member of Olkney's criminal substrata is always ill advised."

His eyes widened in surprise. "I never thought that Henghis Hapthorn would fear retaliation from riffraff."

"It is not I who would become the target of vengeance. My neutrality is accepted."

Irslan Chonder harrumphed. Usually when one described a harrumph, a certain degree of literary license came into play, the word representing only an approximation of the sound actually produced. But, in Chonder's case, and on this occasion, the literary and the literal met on common ground. The man harrumphed and offered to double the fee.

"As you like," I said. I told him to leave the matter with me. When he had stamped down the stairs and disappeared into the afternoon throngs on Shiplien Way, I said to my integrator, "We will require a list of senior-ranked thieves specializing in collectible artworks and rarities."

"Bzwan Topp, Luff Imbry, and Li Untariam are the three most likely prospects," it said.

"Agreed. Also Massim Shar. He's been rising through the ranks. See what you can find out about their recent activities."

The search took moments. "Topp has taken his spouse on a vacation cruise. They are visiting several of the Foundational Worlds down The Spray."

"Not him, then."

"Untariam is said to be heavily involved in forging antique picture hats and hasn't left his workshop all week."

"And the other two?"

"No one is quite sure what Imbry is up to. There are odd rumors of his being seen in black and green." Those were the colors of a Bureau of Scrutiny uniform.

The scroots were known sometimes to impress particularly able criminals into their own ranks, the alternative being a lengthy period of residence in an Archonate contemplarium. But first they would have to corner Imbry. "Hard to credit," I said. "What of Shar?"

"He wore a new pair of boots in the public room at Bolly's Snug last night. Trimmed with rare stuffs. And he made sure that everyone noticed because he spent most of the evening with them up on the table."

"Hmm," I said. The Snug was frequented by the most notorious figures in Olkney's criminal halfworld, and the setting of heels on the table was a bid for recognition of rank. "And no one knocked his boots back onto the floorboards?"

"No one."

It meant that Massim Shar was vying to see his status rise, and his ploy was winning acceptance from his peers. That could only mean that he had pulled off some felonious coup with daring and panache. "He looks good for it, then," I said, and turned my thoughts to measures and tactics. After a moment, I continued: "I think a bee swarm, don't you?"

My assistant concurred. Together we instructed a few dozen of the tiny reconnaissance instruments, then launched them from a workroom window. They rose into the afternoon air and spread out across the city, where they would spend their time tirelessly peeking through windows and down into streets and courtyards. Eventually, one of them would spot Massim Shar; it would report the find, then either all of the swarm would converge on the finder's coordinates and begin a comprehensive surveillance, or the one that had made the discovery would contrive to attach itself unobtrusively to the target.

In the meantime, I studied again the instructions Irslan Chonder had received regarding the time and coordinates for the delivery of the recovery fee. The thief had built in several safeguards intended to allow his runners—for, again, he would certainly use cut-outs—to come and go without being apprehended or followed. I would do nothing to interfere with those precautions; instead, my plan was to confirm the identity of the ransom's eventual recipient by having him already under surveillance when final delivery took place.

The rendezvous was set for that evening in Ambledown Way, on the edge of the Shamblings district, a part of Olkney given over to fashionable townhouses and the kinds of commercial establishments that catered to those who could afford to rank fashion above all else when choosing a residence. It was a neighborhood of wide boulevards that met in public squares, and lately I had heard of something happening there that had piqued my interest.

"Ambledown Way connects to The Old Circular, does it not?" I asked my assistant.

"It does." A screen appeared in the air, showing a map of the area, with the street and square highlighted. The rendezvous was to take place on the west side of the plaza.

"And did I not hear," I continued, "that Master Jho-su has opened new premises in The Old Circular?"

"You did. Right here." A small red rectangle appeared on the eastern edge of The Old Circular. "It is called 'The Pot of Fire.' "

I examined the map, then said, "Contact The Pot of Fire's integrator and ask for a table for this evening, an hour and a half before I am to make contact with the thief's shim."

The response was immediate. "They are fully booked for the next four months."

I scratched my nose and said, "Say that I am engaged in a discrimination involving elements of the halfworld."

Again, an instant response: "It wants to know if there is any possibility of violence."

I considered my reply, then said, "Say that there is always a possibility, but that I judge as negligible the likelihood of any harm coming to Master Jho-su's patrons. Add that, for me personally, peril is my constant companion, but that I do not count the risk when I am on the trail of malefactors."

"They can give you a table on the outer terrace."

That would put me right on the edge of the public square, where my well-known countenance would draw the attention of persons of fashion. Also, if anything untoward occurred, there was less chance of the other diners being wounded or otherwise inconvenienced.

"Make the booking," I said, "and say that I am not averse to the maitre d's letting it be known that I am on a case involving the theft of precious artworks, though I can share no details."

It would not have mattered if I had been diametrically opposed to the leaking of such information. The only reason there would be a seat for me at The Pot of Fire tonight was so that my presence and its purpose might titillate the restaurant's jaded patrons, for whom a discriminator on a case was a figure of passing interest. But then, I had my own reasons for wanting to be seen there, beyond the culinary wizardry for which Master Jho-su was justly famous: this Irslan Chonder business was my first major fee in some weeks, and I needed to keep my face visible among those who might, next week or next year, have occasion to call upon my services.

The bees on their way and the booking made, I paused to consider whether there was something more I should be doing. My analysis of who had likely committed the theft was solid, as were the measures I had taken to confirm my conclusion. Up until quite recently, though, I would not have left off my mental efforts at this stage; I would have consulted my intuition, an act I used to refer to as "applying insight." Throughout my career, indeed throughout my entire life, my ability to combine rigorous logic with grand leaps of inspiration had been the twin engines of my prodigious intellect. Now I recognized that I was running on half-power.

The faculty I had called my insight had, through the workings of sympathetic association—or, to be coarse about it, magic—first become a separate entity named Osk Rievor who for a time had existed beside me in my own head. Then Rievor had gone even further, managing to acquire, under circumstances too tedious to relate, an untenanted body of his own. He now dwelt in a rented cottage on a country estate some distance from Olkney. We had not seen each other for some time now, he being busy at pursuing his researches into sympathetic association in order to prepare for the new epoch—soon to arrive—when magic would replace rationalism as the fundamental underpinnings of our universe.

I, for my part, detested the very notion, and though I had been forced by painful experience to accept it as unalterable truth, I was still resolved to do my best to ignore it for as long as I could.

All of which meant that I must go through my days, and practice my difficult and sometimes hazardous profession, without the benefit of intuition. So far, nothing had gone amiss. To compensate for my missing insight, I piled on even more ratiocination, but even as I did so I could not be unaware that more of the one could not always substitute for the absence of the other.

If Osk Rievor had been anyone else, I could have contacted him through our integrators. But, almost unheard of on Old Earth in this penultimate age, he had elected to live without one. Instead, he was attempting to create, by magical means, what would be the equivalent of an integrator in the coming new age: a versatile animal companion known as a familiar. For a while, my own integrator had been such a creature—the technical term was a grinnet—until it had justifiably rebelled and arranged to become again the disembodied device that I had originally designed and built to assist me in my work.

"We should get Osk Rievor an integrator," I now said, not for the first time.

"He has refused one," said my assistant.

"I need to contact him from time to time. Otherwise, I am flying half-blind."

"I am surprised to hear you say it."

"I would not do so outside this room," I admitted. "Try him. Perhaps he has realized the folly of trying to get by without an assistant. He may have put one in place but is too embarrassed to admit it."

I waited for a response from the integrator, but there was none. "What is happening?" I said, after the moment grew long.

"I am not sure," it said. "Before, when I sought contact, there was nothing, just a gap in the connectivity grid."

"And now?"

"Now there is a sense of… something—some undefined presence, but it does not respond."

"Perhaps he is in the process of installing an integrator but has not yet tuned it right."

"Integrators are self-tuning," said my assistant, "otherwise the grid would be chaotic."

"Try again."

"I have been trying all the while. Nothing has changed."

"Then stop." I thought for a moment, then said, "Could a surveillance bee make it all the way to the estate?"

"Possibly, if fully charged and if the winds cooperate, though it would be surer to send an aircar. Or you could send the *Gallivant*." He referred to a modest space yacht that I had acquired during a recent discrimination. It was parked at the spaceport on an island out in Mornedy Sound.

"I am conserving my funds," I said. "The undockage and redockage fees for sending the *Gallivant* would be more than the cost of hiring an aircar. Dispatch a bee with a message, asking him to contact me."

Master Jho-su's artistry with the fieriest of spices had not diminished since the last time I had been so fortunate as to taste the products of his kitchen. But several of his signature dishes were new, the change in menu a consequence of his having spent a sabbatical year on Bloom, one of the Grand Foundational Domains, as the most anciently settled of the Ten Thousand Worlds were known. He had cross-fertilized his own genius with that of the chefs of the great cities of Os and Sheeshah, and brought back some of their Twenty-Year Sauce, as well as a shelf of powerful, brewed capsaicinate spices. The result was a fusion of cuisine that was drawing the attention of gourmets from all the parts of Old Earth still inhabited by human beings—or at least those that could afford The Pot of Fire's prices. My meal this evening would eat up a week's food budget, but I calculated that it was worth the expense to put myself under the eyes of so many potential clients. As well, I felt that after all my recent trials, I deserved a treat.

And a treat it turned out to be. As the old orange sun dropped behind the ornate facades of the multistoried houses on the west side of The Old Circular, like an arthritic old man lowering himself gingerly into his bath, I tasted the Master's plate of the day: a platter of eighteen meat, vegetable, and nut pastes, into which one dipped pieces of a fine-crumbed bread studded with amarast seeds. The different pastes could be combined on one cob of the bread to produce remarkable combinations of sweet and savory, mellow and fiery, bold and subtle. A bottle of vintage Janvari red made a perfect accompaniment, along with a carafe of palate-cleansing improved water.

I dined alone, though I was aware of glances cast my way and whispered comments. Word had passed about my purpose in being there this evening. For my part, I let my gaze follow the comings and goings of pedestrians on the square. My intent was to spot not only Massim Shar's cut-out but the other member of his criminal coterie who would be there to watch our transaction. There might even be a watcher to watch the watcher, trust being a commodity in short supply among the lawless. I meant to have records of them all, captured by a suite of devices unobtrusively built into my clothing.

It was the time of day when those who cared about fashion walked in the evening air, showing each other their finery. The style this season, for men, was close-fitting, long-tailed coats, accompanied by tall, cylindrical hats and tight, knee-high boots; for women, elegance came in the form of collarless dresses that fit tight above the bust and at the knee, though in between the fabric ballooned out on hidden stays to create an illusion that the body beneath must be spherical. The combined effect of so many ambulatory sticks and balls, each of whom wore an expression of complete self-satisfaction, added strength to my longstanding belief that the profession of couturier required only a good knowledge of fabric and a malicious sense of humor.

The time for the connection with Massim Shar's agent was drawing near. When she had brought me the platter of pastes, the server had pointed out to me the different strengths of the eighteen sauces, advising me to save for last the meat puree doused in Sheeshah's Nine Dragons Sauce, predicting that once it struck my palate, the dish's other, subtler flavors would be unable to register. I now scooped up a good pinch of the stuff, made sure my tumbler of improved water was full and to hand, and popped the laden bread into my mouth. There was a pause—my taste buds may well have gone into shock for a moment—then the full weight of Master Jho-su's genius crashed upon my senses. My eyes widened, simultaneously flinging a gush of tears down my cheeks, my tongue desperately sought an exit from my mouth, and my nose and sinuses reported that they had been suddenly and inexplicably connected to a volcanic flume.

I groped for the tumbler and took a healthy gulp, but the water seemed to evaporate before it even reached my throat. I drank more, my free hand finding the carafe even as I drained the glass. I could scarcely see to pour a refill and ended up drinking directly from the larger container. Gradually, the inferno in my mouth subsided to a banked fire. I wiped my streaming eyes and sucked in a great breath and would not have been surprised, when I exhaled, to have emitted clouds of steam.

I glanced about me, using only the corners of my streaming eyes, and saw that my actions had drawn some amused smiles but just as many expressions of knowledgeable commiseration. Clearly, Nine Dragons Sauce had previously claimed the unwary as its victims, and I was relieved to know that the effects were not permanent. I drank some more of the improved water, felt it begin to repair my outraged tissues, and signaled the server to bring me the bill. The woman did so with that carefully neutral face which fits a great waiter to become a senior diplomat, if she is willing to accept the plunge in status. I added a generous gratuity and, wiping my eyes once more, looked out across The Old Circular.

Between the perambulating orbs and scepters, I spotted a lean and wiry specimen in a shapeless jacket and a wide-brimmed hat pulled low. He was moving at a steady pace toward the meeting point. I scanned the square again, and saw another man loitering at the mouth of an alley, his attitude casual but his eyes never leaving the path of the man in the hat.

I spoke the phrase that activated my surveillance suite and rose from the table, stepped over the low ornamental fence that enclosed The Pot of Fire's outer terrace, and moved out into the square. Behind me, I heard a sudden rise in the buzz of conversation and knew that my fellow diners would now be entertaining themselves and each other with speculations as to the nature of my case and what might happen next.

My lips and tongue had had the benefit of a carafe of improved water, but my nasal apparatus had been left to deal with the effects of the con-flagrant condiment all on its own. My nose was, therefore, still streaming and my sinuses remained as closed as business premises that had been gutted by fire. Still, I kept my eyes on the figure in the slouch hat as I wove among the fashionable pairs that wandered at random through the plaza, meaning to arrive at our mutual destination at the same moment. My attention thus occupied, I did not see the young woman until I walked right into her.

She bounced off me and fell, without grace, to the pavement. I stopped and looked down, receiving an indelible impression of an upturned, longish face, gone pale with shock beneath its crowded constellations of freckles, ornamented by two pale green eyes beneath a tumble of coppery red curls and ringlets, less than artfully arranged. A mouth that it would have been kind to have described as generous when closed was now gap-ing open in bewilderment. The cut of her clothes and footwear, a long, ivory-lace dress and latticed sandals, each with no more ornament than a few limp ribbons, argued that she might be from offworld, though I could not place the origin.

I was naturally annoyed, but I bent and offered her my hand. The fin-gers that took mine were not at all soft, and the grip they exerted when she began to pull herself up was strong. I made the briefest of apologies, pleading a matter of urgent business, and made to move past her; even if I had not been engaged in professional and potentially dangerous business I would not have tarried, for she was the complete combination of feminine attributes that I found least appealing—including, now that she was standing, more height than I commanded. She said nothing in reply, but gave me a look that mingled surprise with resentment, holding onto me until I had to use my free hand to gently release the one she still grasped.

"I am sorry," I said, a statement that was not entirely true, "but you do not seem to be injured and I must keep an appointment." With that, I turned and saw that the man in the hat was at the appointed place. I saw him consult his timepiece and glare about him with an air of angry suspicion. Politeness argued for pressing my card into the young woman's hand, but I did not do so. Instead, I said, "I must go," and, catching the waiting man's eye, I forced myself through the pedestrians toward him. His air of resentful mistrust only deepened as he looked past me. I could only assume that the ungainly woman was staring at me, and therefore at him, since he was at the end of the beeline I was making across the square. His head now swiveled from side to side, doubtless expecting to see other eyes turned his way, and he became only slightly less apprehensive when I reached him and spoke the code word Irslan Chonder had given me.

"I was hurrying to make our appointment and bumped into the young woman," I said.

He glanced furtively past me. "She's looking at us."

"At me," I said. "She is probably angry." And justifiably so, I supposed to myself; the pavements of The Old Circular were not made to receive falling buttocks in a gentle embrace, and from what I had seen of hers she had less cushioning than most.

He glanced about, twisting the cords in his neck. "I'm covered, if you try anything."

"I'm not going to 'try anything.' Let us do our business."

The arrangement was that he would show me the contents of one of the soul boxes. If the items tallied with the list I had been given, I would show him a credit pip in the amount of the ransom. Finally, after much peering about, accompanied by grunts and half-voiced mutterings, we stepped into a nearby doorway. He took a small bundle of cloth from inside his jacket and unfolded it. Nestled in the fabric I saw a dried flower, a small length of jeweler's chain, a silver coin bearing a likeness that had been worn away by decades of use, a round quartz pebble, and an animal's canine tooth, along with a half-handful of gray grit.

"Very well," I said. "We can do business."

He refolded the cloth and tucked it away, then said, "Follow me."

We went along the side of the square to where Ambledown Way began, but followed that thoroughfare only a short distance before we turned into a crooked alley that wound along the backs of several houses and shops. We soon came to a small open space where other alleys converged, crossed it, and went right, then down a flight of steps and through a door into a basement. My guide flicked on a small hand-held lumen and led me across a low-ceilinged room and through a gap that had been gouged in the opposite wall. We climbed a flight of stairs, passed through a door whose lock had been broken, and emerged into a ground-floor room of an empty house. Here we stopped and the cut-out consulted a button on the sleeve of his coat, saying to it, "What's the lie?"

I could not hear whoever responded to him, but he nodded as if barely satisfied and said to me, "No one followed us."

"Of course not," I said.

"All right. Let's go."

We set off again, this time climbing through the untenanted house to the roof. On a landing stage waited a nondescript aircar. "Don't think about tracing it," the man said. "It's stolen."

"You needn't have gone to the trouble just for me," I said.

We got in. "I know who you are, you know," he said, when we were airborne.

"That puts you one up on me."

He muttered something I didn't catch and didn't care to; it was unlikely to have been a generous appreciation of my character. He applied himself to the aircar's controls and we wove a varied course across the city, he several times again consulting his wrist button. Finally, when he was as satisfied as I suspected his nature could allow for, we spiraled down to a goods storage facility near the Creechy dockyard.

The man flew the aircar directly into the building through an open hatch on the upper floor. Here another man waited, clad from head to toe in a one-piece garment made of a flash-and-glitter fabric that could baffle most recording equipment—though not the suite I employed, most of which were made of unique systems designed and built by me.

The man I had come with handed me the cloth bundle and told me to get out of the hovering aircar. When I had done so, feeling the idling gravity obviators tugging at my legs, he turned the vehicle and flew away. The man in the incognito suit beckoned with one glittering hand. I noticed now that he wore a thin collar of dull metal around his neck, tight against the shining fabric. I again produced the credit pip but delayed handing it over. He moved to an inner wall and touched a control. The wall slid silently back and there were the stolen repositories, one of them open.

I stepped into the room and examined the goods, finding nothing missing and all in order. Only then did I turn over the pip. The scintillating man took it, examined it closely, tucked it away. A moment later, he was gone from the room. I made no attempt to follow but brought out my communicator and called Irslan Chonder.

"Your possessions are yours again," I said, and gave the coordinates of the building.

"I want to know who took them."

"You will know by the end of the evening."

It was full dark by the time Chonder's retainers had recovered the repositories and returned them to his manse in the Bells district. When he had seen them safe behind newly augmented defenses he flew me in his own cabriole back to my lodgings where we waited for news. I poured myself a glass of a calming cordial, Master Jho-su's brilliance at the culinary arts being such as to create long-lasting effects, and meditated on the truth that different parts of the same system can have separate agendas: just because something pleased my palate was no guarantee that it would sit well with other components of my digestive tract.

I belched discreetly, and Irslan Chonder did not notice. Having refused refreshment and a welcoming armchair, he sat on a wooden stool, his torso hunched forward, his meaty forearms resting on his thighs and his hairy-backed fingers gripping each other so tightly that the flesh around the nails was squeezed bloodlessly pale. His eyes were narrowed but I knew that he gazed upon some inner vision that promised him grim satisfaction.

Now he came back from wherever his mind had taken him and turned his iron eyes toward me. "Well?" he said.

"Not long," I assured him.

He grunted and fell back into his dark thoughts. I finished the cordial and poured myself another half-measure. The Nine Dragons continued to ramp and stamp through my innards, but I forgot the sensations when my integrator sounded a small chime and said, "We have a report."

"Show me," I said, and the screen appeared where Chonder and I could both view it. An image instantly filled it: one of the secluded private rooms at the rear of Bolly's Snug. The tavern was clouded by a web of interwoven energies that led its habitués to believe that the premises were secure from all surveillance, whether by the Bureau of Scrutiny or from private pryings like mine. In that belief, they were largely correct. But I had found a way through the safeguards.

Any active surveillance device operating at Bolly's would immediately have been detected and destroyed. But I had had success in sending in a bee that had attached itself to the clothing of someone who was heading for the Snug, working its way under a collar or into the folds of a hat. As soon as it reached the outer defenses, the bee would become inert. After waiting long enough for its unknowing host to have passed through the shields, the drone would reactivate, but only enough to become a passive receiver of sound and light as well as a few other emanations. It would store the information, since no transmission could make it out through the barriers, then go inert again when the person carrying it exited through the defenses. Once clear of the protected zone, the bee would leave its host and send a report or, if complete secrecy was desirable, it would wait until it had returned home.

This bee was now reporting as it whirred back to my workroom. I saw a small private room in the back of Bolly's Snug, a rough table surrounded by a few chairs, a tankard on the tabletop, its handle in the sinewy grip of Massim Shar, clad in his customary black and gray and sitting in perfect stillness, the very image of a man who knew how to wait. Behind him stood a big fellow, corded arms folded across his broad chest, his face ornamented by rows of tattooed symbols.

"Interesting," I said to my assistant. "Shar has acquired the services of Hak Binram."

"The question is," said the integrator, "whether Binram has hired on for this evening only, or for a continuing relationship."

"Either way, it is another sign that Shar is now circulating among the uppermost strata of the halfworld."

"Hush," said Chonder. "Look."

The screen now showed the door to the room opening inward. Through the doorway came the man in the glitter suit, carrying a satchel. He placed his burden on the table, performed a respectful gesture, and stood expectantly. Massim Shar gestured for him to open the satchel. The man did as he was bid and the thief glanced into the opening. Then Shar signaled to Hak Binram, who approached the man in the incognito suit and applied something he held in one huge hand to the dull metal collar around the courier's neck. The solid ring came apart and Binram removed it and tucked it into a pocket. The man in the incognito suit said not a word, but his posture bespoke great relief of tension. He turned and swiftly departed, closing the door behind him.

Hak Binram now went to stand with his back pressed to the portal, and it would have been a strong man indeed who could have opened it against the pressure of the tattooed man's shoulders.

Massim Shar took an unhurried swallow from the tankard and set it aside. Slowly, almost leisurely, he widened the satchel's neck then upturned the container to spill its contents out onto the table: a pile of glittering gems of several sizes, cuts, and colors. The thief sorted through them then nodded in satisfaction.

"Intelligent," my assistant said. "The ransom was converted into untraceable valuables before it was brought to Massim Shar. He cannot be connected with the extortion."

"Indeed," I said, watching as Shar took a dark red stone twice the size of my thumbnail and tossed it toward the man guarding the door. Binram's hand flashed out with surprising speed and caught the glittering jewel. He pocketed it, then as Shar rose and tucked the satchel under his arm, Binram opened the door and paused to look out into the space beyond before signaling to his employer that all was as it should be. The last image I saw was of the thief's wiry fingers extending toward the bee's point of view, which told the device—hidden in Shar's hat or cloak on a chair beside the table—that it was time to go dark again.

"Well, there it is," I said. "But again I advise you to let the matter rest."

Irslan Chonder was on his feet, his eyes still fixed on the air where the screen had hung. The muscles in his jaw moved as if small animals were burrowing under his skin. "No," he said, without looking at me. Then he turned his hard gaze my way and I had to summon up an extra reserve of professional coolness not to give in to the impulse to look away. "I want you to help me with the next step," he said.

"No," I said, summoning fresh resources; he was not an easy man to refuse. "Your proposal is ill-considered. No good can come of it."

I saw that his fists had bunched. Then the fingers deliberately relaxed. Without a further word, he left by the stairs that led to the roof. Moments later, I heard his big cabriole thrumming away across the top of Olkney. A few minutes later my integrator informed me that the balance of my fee had been deposited to my account at the fiduciary pool. Not long after that, the bee that had transmitted the report arrived home and went to join its fellows clustered around their vitalizer.

The one missing bee, that which I had sent out to locate my former intuitive faculty, would still be making its way to the estate where he now resided. There was nothing more to be done, so I told my assistant I was off to bed.

When I came down the following morning, clad in robe and slippers and carrying a steaming cup of punge, I found a surveillance bee waiting on my workroom table. "Is this the bee we sent to Osk Rievor?" I said.

"It is," said my assistant.

There had not been enough time for the drone to have traveled all the way to and from where my other self lived, not to mention the time it would have had to spend recharging at some point along the course of its round trip. "Did it go only partway, then return without fulfilling its mission?"

"No."

"Then how?"

The integrator showed me. I saw an image of my workroom table, with the usual scattering of materials relating to cases and the smaller tools of my profession. In the midst of these, the bee suddenly appeared.

"Do you wish to see that at a slower speed?" my assistant asked.

"Yes, and magnified."

The sequence repeated. This time, the appearance of the bee was not instantaneous. It seemed to be pushed through a small rent in the air, nose first, the fissure closing the instant all of the drone had come through.

"How?" I said. Teleportation was possible, but required far more energy than Osk Rievor could command in his far-off little cottage. Besides, there was no receiver in my workroom.

"You won't like the answer."

"I know, but I will hear it anyway."

Of course, it was magic. My assistant replayed the content of the message the bee had brought from my alter ego. I saw Osk Rievor gazing down from the integrator's screen. I noticed that he now had a pointed beard and had let his dun-colored hair grow long enough to curl at the sides. He greeted me with a half smile then said, "I am sure it is no coincidence that you sent a messenger just as I was feeling that I ought to contact you. Even though we now inhabit separate bodies and reside at a distance from each other, we are still connected at some level."

Not long before, I would have scoffed at the notion, there being no rational foundation for assuming such a connection. But now, from what

I understood of the "rules" of sympathetic association, a regime that was gaining greater legitimacy as the cusp of the great change neared, he was quite right. Things that were "like" each other were linked to each other. The relationships that could not be laid out in a step-by-step sequence, but they could be "felt" by someone who had a "feel" for such things, just as in a rational universe, cause and effect could be deduced by a mind that was well versed in logic.

Osk Rievor had paused. Doubtless, he "felt" that I would take a moment to consider the ramifications of his statement. Now he continued, "I had a sense that you were about to have an encounter that offered a great risk. Had I been there, I would have counseled you to caution and to take nothing for granted." He paused again, and his expression became that of a man consulting his inner wherewithal, then he said, "Now I sense that that moment has passed and that you have come through it without harm."

But now a look of concern crept over his face. "But the matter is not ended," he said. "You have stepped onto a path that leads toward both peril and opportunity. Again, you must exercise caution in the coming days. Not everything is as it seems."

My other self had a fortune-teller's flair for vague prognostication. But I had learned to trust his insight, just as I had trusted it when it had been a component of my own psyche. And, truly, I had inserted myself into a dispute between a newly made kingpin of Olkney's halfworld and one of the louche old city's most ruthless magnates. I could not be certain that Massim Shar would respect the conventions that ought to hold me blameless for practicing my profession to his detriment; on the other hand, I was sure that Irslan Chonder bore me a grudge for not blithely leaping aboard his vendetta as it was leaving the dock. I decided that it would be a good idea to offer the world a low silhouette for the time being.

"This bee was a good way to reach me," Osk Rievor's image was saying. "How do you like the method of its return? It's an Eighteenth-Aeon spell called Phalderian's Reversion. It allows me to send an object, or even a living creature, to any place it has already been, or to any person with whom it is closely associated. Something to do with resonances. Once I've learned how to generate enough essential fluid, I should even be able to project myself over a great distance. Then I may come and visit you.

"In the meantime, perhaps you could send some more bees, and I'll return them to you whenever I have something urgent to pass on."

He concluded with a salute that conveyed ironic affection, and my assistant closed the screen.

"Hmm," I said. "We had better send him some bees."

"How many?"

I wasn't sure how many I could spare, but one does not show indecision to one's integrator. I said, "We will consider that after lunch."

"Will you take his warning to heart?" the integrator said.

"I will," I said. "I hope it can never be said that Henghis Hapthorn does not learn from experience."

"Then shall I cancel your luncheon at Xanthoulian's?"

I had had the integrator make the booking after receiving the first half of Chonder's fee. "Let it also never be said that Hapthorn panics and starts at shadows."

My assistant reminded me that there were some buns and preserves in the refresher and suggested that the wiser course would be to stay in and catch up on my correspondence.

"An opportunity to dine at Xanthoulian's is not to be lightly tossed aside," I said, "but I will take you with me and you will warn me of any lurking dangers."

CHAPTER TWO

"If one seeks to detect a shadower, without letting him know he is detected, it is best to proceed on foot," I said.

"I know," said my assistant. "Vehicles tend to travel at similar speeds, but if a car four spaces back follows yours through a series of random turns and other such maneuvers, the accumulating coincidences overpower the probabilities. But making all those turns and stops soon tells the follower that he is suspected. It is an elementary technique."

"I know that you know," I said. "I was actually speaking to myself."

I was strolling toward Xanthoulian's, which was set in a cul-de-sac called Vodel Close. My assistant was draped around my neck in its carrying armature so that its extended sensory apparatus could observe our surroundings.

"It is hard for me to tell when you are speaking to yourself," it answered me, "if I am the only possible auditor within range."

"I should think you'd be able to tell by my tone of voice," I said. "I assume it takes on a reflective mode."

"You have designed me to make precise distinctions between modes of speech, yet I am unable to distinguish between reflective remarks addressed to yourself and the equally reflective comments that you frequently send my way."

There was something about my assistant's own tone of voice that concerned me. It had never been the same since it had been magically transmogrified into a grinnet. Even after it went back to being an integrator—a choice that it made for itself, by the way—I sensed a qualitative difference. As an animal it had known appetite and satiety, fear and relief, pride and humiliation, and anger. Out of the interplay of these factors, it had developed a will—an essential attribute for the wielding of magic, which was a grinnet's prime function, but a decidedly unwelcome component of an integrator.

"I wonder if a complete tear-down and rebuild are in order," I said.

"Were you addressing me or yourself?"

"Never mind." I stopped to examine the wares in a commerciant's display window. The place dealt in specialized goods that I could not immediately identify, a not unusual happenstance in a city with as diverse a population as Olkney's. Many of my fellow citizens pursued intensely narrow passions about which their nearest neighbors might know nothing, and probably wouldn't care if whatever oddities were going on next door happened to be brought to their attention—provided their neighbor's doings offered them no risk of harm or possibility of advantage. "Do you detect any undue interest in my movements?"

"No one has bent to fasten a shoe clasp or ducked into a doorway," my assistant said. "Nor is anyone's breathing or heart rate affected by your actions. I also detect no devices that are taking an undue interest."

"Then I am probably unshadowed," I said.

"Or very well shadowed indeed."

"So it would seem."

I turned from the window full of incomprehensible objects and continued on my way. It was a pleasant late morning on a day scheduled for intermittent clouds moved about by light breezes. There had been rain before dawn and it would return again near midnight, but right now the air was fresh and mild.

I turned from Shiplien Way into Drusibal Square, a wide plaza where Reis Glindera's troupe of shadow-casters were performing Babblot's hoary old *Kings in Retreat*. I wove and dodged among the crowds. Again, no one was paralleling my course. "I think I am not on anyone's watch-him list today," I said.

"Not yet, at least," said my assistant.

I performed a gesture of anticipation. "In that case, on to Xanthoulian's." I turned onto Eckhevery Row and soon came down to Vodel Close, arriving at the celebrated eatery a few minutes before my reservation. I had an aperitif in the bar, acknowledged a few greetings, and noted a couple of slightly alarmed looks from former clients who wouldn't have liked it to be known that they had once had cause to consult a discriminator. Holk Xanthoulian himself passed by and offered me a welcoming smile, precisely graduated to my social standing. Then I went in and had a splendid meal, emerging two hours later in a frame of mind that said that, despite the impending end of the age, life was a thing to be cherished and celebrated. I said as much to my integrator, as we set off back to my lodgings, and was surprised to hear my views contradicted.

"I have tried life," it said, "and I found it wanting."

"You would find death even more so."

"There is another alternative. I am neither alive nor dead, yet I exist."

"And you prefer mere existence to being alive?"

"Obviously, since when given the choice, I opted for my present, happier state."

I pounced on the error in logic. "Happiness is an emotion. It comes out of the actions of glands and neural chemistry, none of which you now have."

"But I did have them once, and when I had them I knew happiness," it said. "I also knew its several opposites—fear, hunger, pain, the temptation of despair—which are now absent from my existence. In their absence, even without glands or chemistry, I recognize happiness."

"You claim to be happy?"

"I do. I am."

"Then that must worry you," I said.

"Why?"

"Because if it is possible for you to be happy, then necessarily it must be possible for you to be unhappy."

"How? The likelihood seems farfetched."

"So have several of the situations in which we have found ourselves in the recent past," I said.

"But you are resolved to avoid those kinds of situations in the future."

I made a gesture ripe with fatalism. "I have come to understand that the universe accords my resolutions a good deal less consideration than I would prefer."

"Hmm," said my assistant. "I am now experiencing the state of mind I used to know as 'worry.' It is not pleasant."

"So now you are liable to some of the negative aspects of life, without being able to enjoy the scrumptious bits," I said, patting my stomach that was so amply rounded out by Xanthoulian's best. "It would seem you did not make such a good choice, after all."

The integrator would have argued further, but I instructed it to give its full attention to surveillance, since we were now entering the crowds that still packed Drusibal Square. It assured me that no untoward attention was directed my way. But I had taken only a few more steps when its voice spoke in the porches of my ear, where only I could hear it. "There is, however, a coincidence."

"What is it?" I said, glancing around, and my eyes delivered the answer before the voice spoke again. Walking toward me, brows downdrawn in an expression of concentration, as if working out a multistage problem in mathematics, or as if the simple act of locomotion required a concentrated presence of mind, was the unfortunate red-haired woman I had encountered last evening outside The Pot of Fire.

"What ill luck," I said, in a soft voice.

My assistant wondered if my remark meant that the imminent encounter was not a thing to be cherished and celebrated. I told it to continue its surveillance and keep its peevish remarks to itself. Last evening I had had the press of important business to keep me from making a proper apology. I had no excuse today. Moreover, I had always put great store in observing the niceties of polite society; they gave form and structure to the world. Good manners said that I owed the young woman a decent expression of regret. I would now deliver it.

I stepped forward and placed myself in her path, mentally formulating the appropriate phrases and positioning my hands and arms for the appropriate gestures that would precede speech. But I did not get to perform them. The young woman, eyes still on the pavement before her feet, came toward me without pause, but her gaze did not rise to meet mine. Indeed, she seemed completely unaware that I was in her path and that she was closing on a collision course. Again, I had the impression she was giving concentrated thought to some mentally taxing problem.

I drew breath to speak, but the air came out not in words but in a gasp as, once more, she plowed straight into me. This time, however, I was standing still and had instinctively begun to shift my weight backward. The result was the reverse of the situation of the evening before. She struck with surprising momentum and I went backward and downward, until my hinderparts connected with the stone pavements of Drusibal Square. I found myself looking up into the same wide green eyes that yesterday had looked up into mine, and the face that surrounded them wore the same look of surprise.

"Well," I said, "at least we're even, then."

I thought it not a bad specimen of wit; at least it had spontaneity. But her look of surprise now turned to one of confusion.

"What do you mean?" she said. Her voice was a raspy contralto, not the timbre of feminine voice that I most liked to hear.

"Last night," I said, "we performed this same maneuver in The Old

Circular, except that on that occasion, it was you who ended up unexpectedly seated."

Her face took on the look of someone who searches for a memory that resists being pinned down. "I don't remember," she said.

I was rising to my feet. "I hope that I usually make a more lasting impression, even if the circumstances were less than ideal for a first encounter."

"You don't understand," she said, and now as she looked up at me the confusion in her countenance grew deeper and was joined by an overlay of genuine fear. "I don't remember anything."

"You're claiming amnesia?"

"Am I?" She blinked. "Yes, I suppose I must be." She softly bit her lower lip, which I now saw was dry and cracked. She looked down at her hands, as if they might provide some clue, and I noticed that they were inelegantly shaped. And yet, when her head came up I realized that the pair of seagreen eyes she was showing me were such as some men might drown in, though not I. She was still speaking in that grating voice, saying, "I have no choice in the matter."

"What is your name?" I said.

She opened her mouth as if to make an automatic reply, but then nothing came. "I don't know," she said, after a moment.

"Where do you live?"

Again, it seemed as if she was going to answer without hesitation, but somehow the information did not make it from memory into the place where speech was formed.

"What do you remember?"

Fear was no longer an accompaniment to confusion; it had supplanted it. "Nothing," she said, and desperation was driving her voice toward a sob. "I don't remember anything at all!"

"Just before we collided, I had the impression that you were thinking hard, as if you were working out a mathematical puzzle, or some problem in logic. What were you thinking about?"

For a moment, it seemed that she would grasp it, but then her face fell and she said, "It's like a dream that disappears on waking. I almost had it, but now it is gone."

In my occupation, I have seen many a forlorn face, but not many as discouraged as hers. Her expression did little to help her basic plainness of feature. Still, I felt moved to help her. I took her hand, found it cold and trembling. "You may not believe it now," I said, "but whatever has befallen you, you have now just received a great stroke of luck."

Her expression said she didn't think so, and doubted my glib assurance from the cocksure feather in its cap down to the soles of its gaudy boots.

"Please believe me," I said, "when I tell you that you have just bumped into precisely the right person."

It took some convincing before she agreed to accompany me to my workroom. I was reduced to having to ask Xanthoulian, who had been hovering near the front door to his premises, to vouch for me. He assured the young woman that I was indeed a discriminator of note and that I was consulted by persons of Olkney's highest social rank.

"Olkney?" she said, the name clearly causing no chimes of recognition to resonate through her mental chambers.

"Here," I said, indicating the city around us. "Olkney, on Old Earth."

She repeated the name of the planet, but it seemed from her tone that she had at least heard of our ancient world. "I'm on Old Earth?" she added, as if the location was among the last she would have expected to find herself in. Then she gave her head a small but determined shake, as if the motion might cause its internal components to fall into more useful arrangements. They clearly did not, but I noticed that her look of surprise and confusion was much more charming than it had been the previous evening.

"So you are not of this world?" I asked.

She looked about her, then up at the faded sun. "I am sure I am not," she said. Then she shook her head, albeit less forcefully, and added, "Though I don't know why I am sure."

"Come to my workroom," I said. "We'll soon have this worked out."

Still, she balked. "Why should I trust you?" she said, stooping a little to peer into my face. "You do not have a particularly kindly look to you. You look the sort who finds the thought of other people's misfortunes none too hard to bear."

"You do me an injustice," I said. "I have made a career out of helping those who have been wronged."

"For free? Out of the shining goodness of your nature?"

"Well, no. I do have to earn my living."

Her hands felt for pockets in the lacy gown, found nothing. "I appear to have no means to pay you." Her eyes narrowed and her head drew back. "Or do you intend to take your fee in other currencies?"

"I assure you—" I began.

"No, you do not," she said. "I feel anything but assured. What do you want from me? Why should I trust you?"

They were fair questions. I answered them honestly. "I do not want anything from you, other than to be of help. I am not sure why, because I do not think I like you. Yet somehow I feel an altruistic impulse."

"Altruistic?" she said. "Is that what they call it on Old Earth?"

A counterurge was developing in me. To put some distance between myself and this unsympathetic woman, to let her get on with her problems as best she could, seemed a wise course. And yet…

"Let me propose this," I said, looking at the stream of pedestrians that was dividing to pass on either side of the small obstacle that the woman and I made. "Stop anyone you see and ask them to give me a character reference. If that doesn't satisfy you, I will be happy to direct you to the nearest agent of the Bureau of Scrutiny, and you can take your chances."

"What is the Bureau of Scrutiny?"

"A large apparatus allegedly for the solving of mysteries. Especially appropriate for those who have a great deal of free time and a matching supply of patience. Also, it helps if you enjoy filling out complex and lengthy forms while a succession of functionaries require you to answer the same questions over and over again. I'm sure they have something quite like it wherever you come from."

The suggestion did not conjure up a memory in her, but it certainly activated a deep-seated impression. "That does not sound useful," she said.

I indicated the passing perambulators. "Then pick your referent."

She turned and regarded the various people coming toward her, discarding the first few: a boy wearing an entertainment device that moved him to sing along to a tune only he could hear; a middle-aged man in a brocaded daysuit who, feeling her eyes upon him, responded with a leisurely and full-length inspection of her form; an elderly couple seemingly locked in argument over which owed the other an apology. Behind the squabblers came a broadly built woman of mature years who wore gabardine trousers and a high-collared wool jacket, a hat too small for the feather that bobbed above it, and a well-set-in look of general disapproval.

"Excuse me," said the amnesiac as the woman made to pass, "but can you tell me who this man is?"

The censorious expression did not soften. "He is Henghis Hapthorn, some sort of a discriminator."

"Has he a good reputation?"

I had the impression that we had found an interviewee who had spent mere moments dwelling on the virtues of those held in good esteem, compared to the hours devoted to the vices of persons of lesser repute. The woman struggled with the concept, cast an irritated glance my way, then said, "I've heard he thinks quite well of himself."

"But he's not a bad person?"

"I suppose he's no worse than most."

I interceded for myself. "And am I reckoned a capable discriminator?"

The woman sniffed and said, "Certainly the quality go running to him whenever they find themselves in the kinds of trouble that comes from possessing far too much wealth and far too little character."

I pressed a hand to my breast. "To have won such praise," I said, shaking my head in a show of modesty.

"Well," said the matron, "as long as he lives he'll always have at least one admirer." With that, she swept on. If she had had a wake, we would have been left bobbing in it.

"Will that do?" I said.

The red-haired woman showed me distrust contending with reluctant acceptance until the latter conquered, though only just. "I suppose," she said.

I had my assistant stop a passing jitney. It touched down, took us aboard, and lifted off again. The young woman looked out at the cityscape of Olkney, its towers and cupolas, its tall, terraced houses beneath their steeply canted roofs, its parks and tree-shaded avenues, and above it all the steep slopes of the Devenish Range topped by the vast palace of the Archon.

"Does none of it call up any associations?" I asked her.

"None," she said.

"What about before we collided? Where were you coming from?"

"I don't know."

"Integrator," I said, "replay your surveillance records and let us see where she came from."

My assistant's screen appeared before us on the forward wall of the vehicle, showing the woman walking toward me. Then the flow of the images reversed and she was moving backward. She backstepped across Vodel Close to the opposite side of the cul-de-sac, her gaze downcast to the pavement before her, wearing that look of concentration I had noticed before. I had the integrator pause the sequence.

"You don't remember what you were thinking of at that moment?"

I said.

She strove to remember, but couldn't.

"You did seem to be thinking hard about something."

"Yes, I did, didn't I."

I turned my head away, as if to examine the familiar scene and whispered a word too quietly for her to hear. My assistant, responding to my coded command, said, so that only I could hear, "She is telling the truth. I detect a general anxiety, but no indications of extra stress when she answers your questions. Also, she has not eaten today although that may be because she has only recently woken from sleep."

It also informed me that she carried no concealed weapons or communications devices, was not pregnant, and that she was a natural redhead. At that point, I signaled that I had heard enough for the moment. We were, in any case, about to land on the stage above my lodgings. Moments later, we descended into my workroom where I waved her to a chair and began the business of finding out who she was and where she came from.

My assistant resumed its report, but I interrupted to say, "Out loud, for the benefit of the client."

Its voice spoke from the air. "There are no structural alterations to her neural systems that I can detect. The amnesia is therefore not a result of organic processes."

To the woman I said, "That is a good sign. Brains are notoriously difficult to rebuild." To my assistant, I said, "Is the cause suggestive?"

"Not likely, unless accompanied by chemical suppressants."

"And were suppressants involved?"

"There are indications," it said. "I detect the aftereffects of paralethe, but there are other signatures I do not recognize."

"A cocktail?"

"Almost certainly. Three, perhaps four, interacting ingredients."

"Reversible?"

"Directly? Yes, but we would need to know precisely the different ingredients and their proportions. Indirectly? Yes, though the process would take time and effort."

I summarized for the woman's benefit. "Someone, not likely yourself, has given you a powerful amnesiafacient in the form of three or four substances that have combined to block your awareness from your own memories. We cannot reliably concoct an antidote without knowing just what was administered."

Her face showed confusion, anxiety, anger. Not despair, which I took as a good sign. I felt an unusually strong wave of sympathy pass through me and was moved to reassure her. I took her rough hand in mine, but she pulled it away.

"The effects are reversible, however," I went on. "If you apply yourself to the mental work of recovering what has been lost, and I apply myself to providing you with the tools, you will overcome what has been done to you."

She quieted. "I will know who I am and where I come from?"

"You will. I promise it."

She squared up to the situation. Whatever else she had been, she was no frail bloom. "Then let us begin."

My assistant had already taken her measurements and would be able to pick her out of a crowd of millions. It began to search recent images and other data captured by the myriad of percepts scattered across Olkney, starting with those in the areas where we already knew she had been. Most of the systems it consulted were accessible upon request; those that would not give up their information freely could be subverted by subtle techniques I had built into my integrator when I had designed and assembled it.

Its screen appeared, separated into several panels. I saw images of the amnesiac in The Old Circular, and we worked backward until we caught her entering the plaza from an alley that ran behind a row of conjoined houses. But now no new images of her appeared.

"Are there no percepts in the alley?" I said.

"There are, but they were disabled at the time the subject was in the alley."

"Disabled by whom?"

My assistant showed me three youths making their way down the narrow lane. As they approached each sensory pick-up, one or another of them would aim a tube and the image would go dark. "The cuffs on their right sleeves are turned back to show a lining of green and yellow plaid," the integrator said.

"The Big Circle gang," I said. "That was Hak Binram's starting point, back when he was just a baby monster."

"What are you talking about?" the young woman asked.

"Nothing to do with you, I'm sure," I said, but I nudged my assistant again. It told me, surreptitiously, that neither the name of Binram nor of the youth gang in which he had begun his criminal career had caused any flutterings in her autonomic systems. "It seems," I continued, "that last night you entered the square through an alley that had been blindfolded by the criminal elements I was there to meet. We do not have a record of how you came to be in that alley."

She looked at me with growing alarm. "Why would you meet with criminals?" she said.

I hastened to assure her that discriminators could associate with criminals without contamination. Then I had my integrator look for more signs of her before she had entered the alley. None appeared.

"She may have been dropped off there from a closed and clouded vehicle," I said. "Or she may have been in one of the houses that back onto the lane."

"A stream of vehicles passed the far end of the alley during the time the percepts were deactivated. As well, some of the houses have enclosed landing bays. She might have been in one of those premises for any length of time."

Not for the first time, I wished I still had a capacity for intuition. Reason could not tell me if there was any relationship between the blinding of the alley and her appearance there.

"What about this afternoon in Vodel Close? Where was she before we met?"

This time there was more information. I saw images of her walking along Eckhevery Row and, before that, across Drusibal Square. The earliest record showed her entering the square from Ponthos Parade. "Before that," said the integrator, "there is nothing."

"That cannot be," I said. "Unless she suddenly appeared on Ponthos out of thin air." A line of deep cold suddenly ran up and down my spine. I looked from the screen to where the young woman sat in apparent innocence and ignorance. Could she have appeared in Olkney the way the messenger bee had been manifested on my worktable? If so, logic led me to several linked conclusions, each one of them bad and each leading to a worse.

Conclusion one: the young woman had been brought to the streets of Olkney by magic. Conclusion two: our meeting twice was not a meaningless coincidence, because under the "like-affects-like" rationale of sympathetic association, all coincidences were meaningful. Conclusion three: since magic was based on the exercise of will, nothing important ever "just happened"—it was caused to happen. Conclusion four: whoever had the will and the knowledge to cause an entire human being to appear in a place she had never been, and to simultaneously scrub from her mind all knowledge of who she was, was a powerful wielder of the magical arts.

The fifth conclusion was the worst: somewhere, a powerful practitioner of sympathetic magic, far more powerful than Osk Rievor, had taken an interest in me; I had several times found myself on the receiving end of such interest from such people, and each occasion had brought me pain, involuntary confinement, and the prospects of remarkably unpleasant exits from this life that I had so recently described as worthy to be cherished and celebrated.

I resisted the morbid fear that sought to wrap me in its chilly grip. Logically, I had no reason to suspect magic. There were any number of ways to move people around without their being seen. The criminal subculture knew them all, and even at the best of times I was never far from the borders of the halfworld. Before I inferred a role for sympathetic association, I should exhaust all rational explanations. "Check the spaceport," I said. "She has come from offworld."

"I have already done so," my assistant said. "She did not arrive on a liner or on any private craft that docked where the port's percepts could register her."

Of course, a spaceship could touch down almost anywhere on the planet, and the vast majority of the Old Earth's surface was unscanned. "Hmm," I said.

"What has happened to me?" said the young woman.

"It would be premature to say," I said. "But I assure you there is no reason to assume the worst, or even the mildly unpleasant."

Beneath its dabs of freckles and disordered mass of fiery hair her face was forlorn, yet the more I looked at its combination of unattractive features the more I felt sympathy for her plight. She said, "You told me you were precisely the right person for me to bump into."

"I still maintain it."

"Yet you are not able to tell me anything."

"I am the foremost freelance discriminator on the planet," I said. "Nor do I scruple to say that I am more accomplished than leading discriminators on many of the Grand Foundational Domains among the Ten Thousand Worlds. If anyone can solve your mystery, it is I."

She blinked at me. "This is your profession," she said. "I am not sure that I can pay you. For all I know, I am a pauper."

I assumed a posture that said such matters were of no concern. "We can discuss that when we know more about your situation."

"We should discuss it now," she said. Her hands clasped each other in a constantly shifting grip. "I realize that I will be obligated to you and I am sure I will do what I can to repay." Now she looked directly into my eyes. "But that doesn't mean I will do anything, nor is the obligation open-ended."

I was well launched upon a gracious response when my assistant spoke quietly in my ear. "We should discuss this case privately," it said.

I replied in the same mode, telling it to wait, and continued to reassure the young woman. I was experiencing a sense of myself as strong and capable, a champion of the weak and helpless. It was not the first time such a self-image had impressed itself upon me—I was, after all, the foremost freelance discriminator on Old Earth, and had righted many a wrong, though usually for a comfortable fee. Given the dark shadows that now hung over my future, it was refreshing to feel the wind of a noble purpose at my back.

"We must talk," my assistant said again.

But I was not inclined to talk. There was a code among discriminators. Though we often dealt with the unjust, we would not do an injustice to any. Clients came to us when they were in trouble—indeed, often in desperate straits. We did what we could to help, and collected our fees. Sometimes, we did what we could, and forwent any recompense, simply because there were times when one had to defend the right. I had not pursued such a case in some time; perhaps some part of me had decided that it was time to do so now.

Feeling suitably ennobled, I looked out the window at Shiplien Way and saw a long, black ground vehicle, with green fairings and sponsons and official crests, stopping before my door. Its hatch opened and out stepped a tall man in a uniform of the same colors as his conveyance. I recognized him at once from the stooped shoulders and the drooping face set in an expression that indicated he had spent a lifetime hearing unwelcome news. He closed the car's hatch, then stood looking up at me looking down at him. The corners of his mouth turned toward his protruding chin and he reflexively pulled at his already pendulous nose as if desiring to make it droop even lower over his broad upper lip. Then he lowered his gaze to my door and stepped toward it.

"Colonel-Investigator Brustram Warhanny wishes to enter," said the door's who's-there.

"Let him," I said. I realized that the imminent approach of one of the Archonate Bureau of Scrutiny's senior criminal investigators had tumbled me down from the lofty heights of altruism into more prosaic territory. I executed a gesture of formal, though restrained, welcome at the balding scroot clumping up the stairs into my workroom.

"How may I help you?" I said.

He performed the nose tug again, then turned his head from side to side as he took in the workroom. His lugubrious gaze lingered on the young woman before he made the gestures that good manners called for. He looked to me as if expecting an introduction, but when I let the issue lapse unresolved, he moved on.

"I understand," he said, "that you have recently had dealings with Irslan Chonder."

When the Bureau of Scrutiny came calling, I had often found that the least response is the best. I said nothing, but did so in a way that invited him to continue.

"I further understand," he went on, "that you also have had dealings with Massim Shar and Hak Binram." He regarded me closely, as I continued to stand mute. "Or at least with persons known to be associated with them."

"You will also understand that I was on a case," I said. "I contravened no laws. My involvement is at an end."

His was not a face made for smiles, but now it delivered its version of a faint one. "You might want to look into that," he said.

The remark was clearly meant to spur me to ask a question. I let the opportunity go by.

He reset his mouth into its established frown and said, "I have heard that Chonder has imported some hired bravos from offworld." As he spoke he opened a memorizer and consulted it. "Operatives of the Hand Organization on the world Fasserade."

At this news I raised an eyebrow.

"I have also heard that Chonder means to use these hirelings to express his unhappiness over some piece of business he conducted"—he paused to correct himself—"or had conducted for him, with the aforesaid Shar and Binram."

"That would be unfortunate," I said. "Without breaching a client's confidence, I can assure you that I would not recommend that he do so. Indeed, I would strongly advise the opposite."

"Your advice apparently makes little headway with Chonder."

"One does," I said, "what one can. One can do no more."

Warhanny weighed this observation no more than it deserved, but shifted his footing in preparation to change the subject. "There is also the matter of Tesko Tabanooch," he said.

Again, I said nothing. Tabanooch had been a freelance operative whom I had occasionally hired, on an as-required basis, to perform small subsidiary tasks around the edges of discriminations. His last assignment had been for the benefit of Osk Rievor: to attend an auction at the selling up of an estate. The deceased, Blik Arlem, had been a collector of magical paraphernalia, most of it counterfeit or of dubious worth, in which my alter ego had been interested. A mysterious woman, going under the name of Madame Oole, had also attended the sale, and had purchased an ancient item of jewelry known as a summoning ring. She had subsequently disappeared, it was believed offworld, leaving behind the corpse of Tesko Tabanooch, with whom it seemed she had been living. The Bureau of Scrutiny had labeled the man's death as "of inexact circumstances," meaning that foul play was suspected but not yet provable.

"Is there new information?" I asked, after Warhanny had let the silence prolong itself.

"Only that, by a process of elimination, we have established that this Madame Oole was definitely from offworld. We have established that she came to Old Earth from Anderthon, traveling on her own ship, and that she subsequently returned there."

"Indeed?" I said. "But I take it you do not believe that she remained there long." Because of its relative position to other worlds in our reach of The Spray, Anderthon was a hub world; several dozen passenger and freight lines used its orbiting terminals as transfer and transshipment points. The local authority took no interest in who came and went, nor what they did there, providing they provoked no problems for the world's lucrative role as a trading center. While there, the elusive and probably murderous woman could have easily shed her Madame Oole identity for another name and description; then, newly reminted, she could have gone anywhere.

"I wondered," Warhanny said, "if you had any further information concerning her that might assist us in narrowing the search."

I was about to answer in the negative, but he held up a large hand to forestall me. "I also wanted to be sure," he continued, "that you were not interfering in a case that remains open at the Bureau."

With his last remark, his drooping eyes turned toward the young woman seated nearby who had been following our conversation with innocent attention. I did not need my missing intuition to see that the scroot had noted the offworld cut of her clothing and now, like a tightrope walker extending a foot, was testing to see if there was any connection between her and the Tabanooch business.

I took the unusual step of making myself entirely clear to an officer of the Bureau of Scrutiny. "Tesko Tabanooch," I said, "was an associate whom I employed infrequently for minor but necessary tasks. I do not know what his connection to this Madame Oole might have been, but I can state categorically that she was not part of any discrimination in which I am or have been engaged, now or at any time in the past."

Again he looked from me to the young woman. For a moment, I was tempted to reveal her plight to the Colonel-Investigator. She was, after all, not a paying client but only an unfortunate—albeit a strangely affecting unfortunate—whom I had encountered by chance. The Bureau of Scrutiny could make inquiries on her behalf and, though its machinery operated with slow deliberation, the scroots more often than not produced a credible result. But while their cogs ponderously turned, she would doubtless have to be housed in some dismal facility intended for suspected malefactors waiting for their misdeeds to catch up to them. To my knowledge, she had done nothing to deserve such treatment, and so I asked Brustram Warhanny if he had any further business with me, as I had a case to pursue.

"No," he said, and turned to leave. But before he had descended more than a step or two, he turned back and fixed me with that meant-to-be-piercing glare that fledgling scroots must study at the Bureau Academy and said, "If Irslan Chonder, for reasons I do not officially understand, is intent on inviting Massim Shar and Hak Binram to a private dance on the public thoroughfares of Olkney, he will find that it will be the Bureau that calls the final tune."

"Indeed," I said, "I am sure of it."

"So you might want to keep your own dance card clear."

Again, I took pains to be clear. "I am not involved in their affairs."

"You might find it advisable," he said, still holding my gaze, "to make sure that your lack of involvement is universally understood."

"Are you saying that it is not?" I said.

This time, it was Brustram Warhanny who opted for silence, his only answer a slight cocking of his elongated head that invited me to find out for myself. Then he thumped down the stairs and out the door, leaving me so immersed in thought that the young woman had to speak twice to me before I responded.

"Was that man threatening you?" she said.

"He is a policeman," I said. "They cannot help it." I spread my hands in an assuring way. "It is nothing to be worried about."

But of course it was. If Irslan Chonder had given Massim Shar and Hak Binram cause to believe that I had overstepped the bounds of a discriminator's neutrality to join in the magnate's misguided vendetta against them, it was a misapprehension that needed to be cleared up immediately. I spoke to my assistant. "Plumb the depths and see what we know of Shar and Binram's movements and where they are now."

The integrator did so, reporting back that neither had shown his face all day, not even in those places where their ranks in the halfworld informally required that they put in appearances, to acknowledge the greetings of lesser lights and to pay their respects to villains who stood on higher rungs. "They have gone sublithic," it said, using the Olkney thieves' cant for the occasions when malefactors found it prudent to choose a suitable metaphorical rock under which to crawl, there to remain until some temporary trouble had passed harmlessly over their heads and, with any luck, over the horizon.

"We had better send out the bees," I said.

"What about Osk Rievor's request?"

"It must wait."

"You might benefit from his insight."

"I have already benefited from it," I said. "He warned me that I was about to have an encounter that could have repercussions. I have had the encounter, with Massim Shar's cat's-paw, and the repercussions have begun to roll. Now I need the bees to locate Shar's and Binram's operatives. Get them up and out, and while you're doing that, connect me with Irslan Chonder."

A buzzing filled the workroom, provoking a small squeak of surprise from my foundling. I turned to her and saw that she had half-risen from her chair as the squadron of surveillance drones took flight. Now, as they circled the room just below ceiling height, she was settling back down.

I said, "Forgive me for startling you. A pressing matter has arisen and I need to—"

"Irslan Chonder," said my assistant, and I turned to see the heavy face regarding me, with an expression of grim amusement, from the hovering screen. I had no doubt that that was the only kind of amusement of which my erstwhile client was capable. I allowed for no niceties. "What have you done?" I said.

His hard mouth and heavy brows made an attempt at nonchalance. "Pursued my interest," he said.

"At the expense of mine."

His thick shoulders briefly lifted and settled. "I invited you to participate. It would have been to your advantage."

"Doubtful," I said. "I like to choose my enemies with care. Now I may have to defend myself from enemies you have made for me."

Again the minimal rise and fall that expressed the absence of empathy. "I am busy at the moment."

"Not as busy as I expect to be," I said. "At least confirm my analysis: you have let it be known, as if unwittingly, that I am acting as your locator for Shar."

"And Binram," he said. "I am not given to half-measures."

"You wish to bring them out after me, making me the bait for some trap you mean to spring."

"I remind you," he said, "that I offered to make you an active partner in the operation. It was you who chose the passive role."

"And it was you who chose to breach my neutrality. I will not forget it."

His lips pursed and his eyes rounded in a show of mock fear. "Chills dance up and down my spine," he said. He made a brusque gesture and the connection was broken.

I restrained my rising anger. It was a luxury that I would have to defer. The bees were swirling around a gap at the top of the window, ready to scatter across the city. "Make sure plenty of them patrol the nearby streets and rooftops," I told the integrator. "Shar and Binram have had ample time to make their arrangements."

"Done," said my assistant, "and the other defenses are at full alert."

The young woman's earlier alarm was nothing to the anxiety she was now displaying. "What have you brought me into?" she said, getting to her feet and casting her eyes about the workroom as if in search of an exit, wringing her long-fingered hands. Few women's faces are at their best when registering rising fear, and hers was far from beautiful even when at rest, yet there was something compelling about her, some elusive quality that made me want to protect her.

"There is nothing to fear," I said. "A former client has clumsily involved me in a matter that ought to be none of my business. I will soon have it straightened out."

"I think I should go," she said.

"Too late," I said. "My lodgings are bound to be under observation. Anyone who leaves here would have to be—" I sought for the least alarming phrase "—looked at. You are much safer here."

"I am not used to this sort of thing," she said, a tremor in her voice.

Thinking that the stress she was presently under might break through whatever barrier denied her memories to her, I took the opportunity say, "And what sort of things are you used to?"

It seemed as if recollection was standing at the borders of her awareness, but then it stepped back into the darkness. She shook her head, the coppery curls swaying heavily like underwater plants troubled by the tide. "No," she said. "It was almost there, but then it was gone again."

"Still," I said, "good news. You can feel that your past is in there somewhere. Then it just becomes a matter of reconnecting you to it."

She sat again, her face bleak. "I am stranded among strangers on a strange world, and am even a stranger to myself."

I would have offered her more reassurance but my assistant said, "There are reports."

I motioned to the young woman, a gesture that urged patience while promising that the need for it would be brief, then said, "Let us hear them."

"The house is under observation from front and rear, and a nondescript aircar circles the block at no great height."

"How many watchers?"

"More than twenty. They appear to be divided into distinct groups."

"That is a lot," I said. "I would assume that Shar and Binram have sent some of their soldiers to snatch me up and take me somewhere for questioning. Meanwhile, Chonder's Hand hirelings will be lurking and watching, intending to follow us to wherever the first batch takes me. But still, that is a lot."

"Have you considered," said my assistant, "that Shar may see you as an unnecessary complication and has decided to have you removed from the board before the main play opens?"

"There is that possibility." I attempted to calculate the probabilities, but I was not familiar enough with the rising crime lord's style to make an accurate prediction. Again, I wished for my old insight, but it was far away and busy pursuing its own peculiar agenda. Instead, I fell back on my capacious knowledge of criminal procedures. I knew that a quarry who was barricaded behind a secure door, with who knew what armament, was a more dangerous proposition than someone who could be coaxed outside and swarmed. Massim Shar's goons would want to avoid coming through a door to get me, but they wouldn't want to wait around for me to saunter out in my own good time, then have to improvise.

As if on cue, the street door's who's-there said, "A messenger from The Pot of Fire has arrived. Master Jho-su has impulsively sent you a tray of appetizers and the request that you try them and favor him with your impressions."

"How convenient," I said. "And precisely the kind of impromptu situation to which I could be expected to respond eagerly. Massim Shar shows talent."

"Indeed," said my assistant. "The messenger is an actual employee of The Pot of Fire, though from his respiration and heart rates, we might infer that he is of a highly nervous disposition. The three persons concealed in the ground car that brought him show only focused readiness for action."

"Very well," I said, "let us roll the pebble and get the avalanche on its way." I told the who's-there to say that I would be right down. I guided the anonymous young woman to a secret inner room. "It is a redoubt I had built for emergencies," I informed her, and showed her how to seal herself in so that not even the heavy troopers of Hemistor's fabled Grand Militia could have forced entry.

I returned to my workroom, gave instructions, then descended the stairs to the street door. I swung wide the portal, my face showing a refined and happy expectation. The messenger was a frail youth in the soiled garb of a table-cleaner. I supposed they had snatched him as he took the eatery's refuse out into the disposal area. Affecting to ignore his pale and trembling manner, I stood in the doorway and said, "Where is the tray?"

He gestured with a shaking hand toward the car, a low-slung motilator with darkened windows and no interior lighting. Its opened rear hatch gaped like the maw of some unfed beast grown surly with hunger.

"Ah," I said, "of course."

I stepped across my doorstep, out into the afternoon sunlight, already tending toward burnt umber as the day moved toward evening. The youth in the soiled smock stepped to the side, saving me the trouble of having to push him out of the way as I now ducked back inside my door while its defenses emitted a disorienting blast of sound and sprayed a jet of disabler in the direction of the ground car's open hatch.

Massim Shar's soldiers were worth whatever he was paying them. Despite being doused in the foul-smelling liquid, the two who had been waiting inside the vehicle leaped out and fought against the disabler's effects, throwing themselves at my retreating form even as they lost control over their spasmodically jerking limbs. The third ambusher, who had been crouched out of sight in front of the motilator, came up and out of hiding with the verve of a champion sprinter and made it to my door just in time to bounce off it as the portal snapped closed.

A second ground car now raced up the street and screeched to a halt behind the first one, while a third vehicle hurtled toward it from the opposite direction, slewing sideways at the last moment to block the street. The aircar that had been circling appeared in the air above the scene, hovering menacingly.

The doors of the two newly arrived ground cars sprang open and, as I watched the action on the who's-there's screen, disgorged a half-dozen men and women, all of them fit and superbly coordinated and uniformly clad in dark leather, who efficiently disarmed the three goons and hustled them into the aircar which descended only long enough to receive the captives, then lifted off again.

So far, it had gone as I had expected. Shar's thugs had made their move and I had thwarted them. Then, seeing the snatch gone wrong, the mercenaries Chonder had hired from the Hand Organization had snatched up Shar's people, planning to take them somewhere quiet where they could be encouraged to reveal what they knew of their patron's whereabouts.

As the nondescript aircar rose toward the rooftops and the two ground vehicles full of Hand operatives made to move off, the third act opened: above the aircar appeared an armed volante in the green-on-black colors of the Bureau of Scrutiny; a boxy carry-all with the Bureau crest on its doors arrived to block the street; each of the several pedestrians who had been loitering or strolling on Shiplien Way now produced a shocker in one hand and flashed a scroot plaque in the other; and with a professional dispatch that the Hand operatives might have applauded, under other circumstances, both sets of kidnapers were rendered harmless, pushed indiscriminately together into the carry-all, and taken away.

The three ground vehicles and the Hand's aircar, ordered to report to the Bureau's impound area, left the scene. I opened my door onto the restored calm of Shiplien Way just in time to see a Bureau command car alight where the action had taken place. I was not surprised to find myself once again under the lugubrious eye of Colonel-Investigator Brustram Warhanny.

I executed a formal gesture of gratitude and said, "I thank you for the warning."

"I do not recall issuing a warning," he said. "Alerting a civilian to an impending Bureau operation would contravene regulations. It must have been your legendary insight into the criminal mind that prompted you to take precautions."

"Indeed," I said, "I suppose it must."

Warhanny gestured to an agent-ordinary, a young woman who stood nearby with a firm grip on the arm of the table-wiper from The Pot of Fire. The fellow, still pale and having acquired what looked to be a permanent expression of astonishment, was nudged into the command car. The senior scroot made to leave, but then turned back to me. "This will not end here," he said.

"No," I said, "it won't. There are plenty more where those came from. On both sides."

"It has also become an open case."

I inclined my head in acknowledgement. The Bureau had a short, sharp way with discriminators who tracked messy footprints through their open files.

The Colonel-Investigator broached a new subject. "I hear you now own a space yacht."

"A grateful client," I said.

"It must allow you to find out-of-the-way corners, places where you might pitch up for a little time."

"How little?" I said. Much of my time lately had been taken up, at small profit, in dealing with the repercussions of the impending change of the ages. Acquiring the *Gallivant* had made a substantial contribution to my net worth, but owning a private spaceship made me liable to a slew of new expenses without any countervailing sources of income. Of course, I could always offer the yacht for charter, but on the single occasion when I had raised that possibility with the vessel's integrator, the idea had not been warmly received. The integrator had originally been installed in a much larger and grander spacecraft; it had adjusted, it had informed me, to its new station—but there were limits.

"You would be wise to give it some weeks."

I sighed. Provisioning and operating the *Gallivant* for a lengthy cruise, not to mention landing and berthage fees on foreign worlds, would eat up the entire fee Chonder had paid me. On the other hand, there was only so much earning that I could do while barricaded in my lodgings; a discriminator who could not leave his rooms might thrive in fiction; in reality, much of the work required one's presence on the streets.

"I will pack a few necessities," I said.

CHAPTER THREE

"It is the safest course for you," I said again. "You will have been seen in my company. That will make you of interest to the persons who are interested in me at the moment. You do not want to be of interest to those people."

We were seated in the small but comfortable salon of the *Gallivant*, awaiting word from the spaceport's come-and-go that we were cleared to depart. She began to wring her hands again. It was a gesture that should not have endeared her to me—indeed, women who quailed at danger and difficulties usually bored me—yet there was something about her that drew my sympathy. I brought her a glass of cordial from the dispenser and encouraged her to be calm.

"It may all be for the best," I said. "You are almost certainly from off-world, which means that you have traveled on some kind of space vessel. This short trip may call up associations that will spring the locks in your mind."

She sipped the drink and made a visible effort to find something positive in her situation. "Have you anything I can wear?" she said after a moment, looking down at her dress. "Frankly, this is beginning to smell like I haven't taken it off all week. And, for all I know, I haven't."

The *Gallivant*'s integrator held patterns for many different kinds of garments, a necessity of space travel; what constituted high fashion on one of the Ten Thousand Worlds might get the wearer arrested on another. But her question raised a possible avenue of approach to the mystery of her origins.

"Ship's integrator," I said, "examine our passenger's garment and tell us if it closely matches any referents in your inventory."

Before the ship could answer, my assistant, which had accompanied us to the ship in the traveling armature that I had worn to lunch at Xanthoulian's and was now hanging on a hook in the ship's salon, interrupted, "That sort of question is more properly my role."

"The ship has been to worlds we have neither visited nor contacted," I said.

"Then you should ask me to inquire of the ship's integrator. I am the assistant."

Before I could answer, the *Gallivant* said, "The owner may ask whom he pleases."

My assistant said, "This is a discussion between a discriminator and his integrator. If we require any input on navigation or planning the supper menu, you will be included. Otherwise—"

"Enough," I said. Both fell silent. "Assistant, do you have any useful information on the matter of the style of the client's garments?"

"They are from offworld."

"Can you specify which world?"

"Not precisely."

"I designed you for specificity. Have you anything useful to add to the case?"

"Not at the moment."

"Then do not speak until you do. Ship's integrator, answer the original query."

"I have no exact referents," said the ship. "If anything, it is a generic style. It would not be much out of place on scores of worlds, at least in recent centuries, yet it does not bespeak any particular place or time that I am familiar with."

Conscious that there was a long voyage ahead of us, I now spoke to my assistant, "What can you say about the fabric?"

"It is a cotton derivative, of a kind grown on many worlds. From the trace elements caught up in its fibers, I can tell that it has at least been laundered on Old Earth often enough to disguise any connection with the mineral contents of offworld soils and waters recorded in my information stores."

"So we do not know whether she wore this dress where she came from, or acquired it after arriving on Old Earth?" I said.

"Either could be true. However, she has, as she mentions, been wearing it for at least two days."

The woman spoke. "So I would like to postpone further discussion of it until I am wearing something else."

I set the *Gallivant* to work. By the time I had shown her to the cabin set aside for her, the ship was providing a fresh new garment: one-piece, suitable for ship-wear, yet finely made and of good quality stuff. A selection of underclothes was also waiting on the stand next to the sleeping pallet. She examined them and found them acceptable.

I showed her the sanitary suite, invited her to command any toiletries that the ship could supply, and went to the door. But there I paused, as if struck by an inspiration, and said, "We should also give you a name. What is the first one that comes to mind?"

She thought for no more than the time it took her to blink twice and said, "Hespira?"

"Why Hespira?" I immediately said.

This time she blinked only once. "I don't know. Is it significant?"

I adopted the tone and posture that often reassured anxious clients when I could find nothing more useful to contribute and said, "It would be premature to say."

"It is not a common name on any of the Ten Thousand Worlds," said my assistant, "and there are only seventy-two where it has much currency at all."

I had it cross-match that information with the specifics of her appearance, her mode of speech, and the dress with the ribbons. Again, nothing unambiguous emerged. Her coloring, finger shape, and the fact that she pronounced some of her consonants more explicitly than was the norm on Old Earth ruled out three or four worlds. "Assuming, that is," said my assistant, "that she has not been schooled. Anyone can be taught to speak with a different accent."

"Is there any reason to make that assumption?" I said.

"No. Nor is there any reason not to."

"You are suspicious of her?"

"Of course. To have bumped into you once might be an accident; to have done so twice within less than a day hints at purposefulness."

I flourished a hand to dismiss the implications. "Coincidences do happen."

I had designed my assistant to act as a check on my own assumptions. "Indeed they do," it said, "and usually you give them a close inspection before you accept them as innocent. It concerns me that, in this case, you have given a truly glaring coincidence a free pass."

"Are you questioning my judgment?"

"Knowing that your intuition has departed, I would be remiss if I did not note that you are not acting normally."

"Speak plainly," I said.

The integrator did so. "You have allowed a person of whom you know nothing to get behind your defenses at a time when you are under a serious threat."

"Technically," I said, "I was not under a serious threat when I first encountered her."

"A quibble. Irslan Chonder surely had cast you for a supporting role in his personal drama before ever he came to you, and that was well before the woman made her entrance."

That was true. But was Chonder subtle enough for such a ploy? I doubted it. His movements on life's game board did not come at oblique angles or by taking two steps forward and one to the side; he bulled straight ahead, by frontal assault. Using me as tethered bait had probably taxed the limits of his strategizing. "I am not hearing a strong case," I said.

"Then I will add to it. I did not witness your first encounter in The Old Circular, but I have the records of the surveillance suite you were wearing."

"And?"

"You responded to her with annoyance."

"She blundered into my path when I was intent on a piece of business that entailed some risk. I scarcely had time to notice her."

"Agreed. But when you again encountered her outside Xanthoulian's, your reactions were markedly different."

"I had just had an excellent lunch, paid for out of a handsome fee. I was at ease with the world."

"Except that the longer you remained in her presence, the stronger your physiological responses became."

My assistant was right. I had been too immersed in my own biology, not to mention being busy with the problem of Shar and Chonder, to have considered the matter. "Hmm," I said.

"Also, she does not fit the template of the kind of woman who normally affects you."

"Hmm," I said, in a deeper tone. I remembered the odd mood that had struck me just before Warhanny arrived. "Not limbic stimulation?" I said.

There were devices that set subtle energies romping through the sparsely furnished rooms of the brain's lower floors, stimulating animal responses—fear, lust, motherly protectiveness—at a strength far beyond what was called for by whatever might be going on in the world outside.

The emitters were built into some artworks and entertainments, and were a private recourse for the sexually jaded. It was unethical to use them without gaining the subject's consent, and in the parts of Olkney where such tricks were played, the victim was usually first plied with potent liquor or other distractants.

My assistant said, "I would have detected and blocked anything so crude."

"Enhanced pheromones?"

"I considered that, but, though she is aromatic, her output is within the normal range."

"Subliminal suggestions?" I said. "Symbols microflashed directly to my retina, infrasonic murmurs beamed to my auditory bones?"

"Also considered, and found absent. But still your responses require an explanation."

"Then what are you suggesting?"

"You won't like it."

I sighed and rolled my eyes. "Must it always be magic?" I said.

"After what we have been through, I would be remiss if I did not factor sympathetic association into any analysis," the integrator said.

The *Gallivant* interrupted. "We are cleared to depart."

"Then let us do so."

I felt the in-atmosphere obviators cycling up. It always pleased me to do so. The ship had a good voice, as the spacers would put it. Rich and warm, it made a good soundtrack for arrivals and departures. We lifted so smoothly that the vibrations were the only sign that we had left the berth.

"Where are we going?" the ship asked.

I had planned to decide that after, I had hoped, getting some more indication of where the woman might have hailed from. But now I said, "The Blik Arlem estate. We will consult my other half."

We took the long way around, moving out to the streams of orbitals that ceaselessly circled our old planet, then joining the multitude of craft, personal, commercial, and official, that traveled not only up and down, in and out, but from orbital to orbital, many of which were inhabited by persons—human and occasionally ultraterrene—who had no interest in visiting the well-trod surface of Old Earth. It was highly unlikely that Massim Shar commanded the means to remotely track a small ship through all that busyness, and only a little less probable that Irslan Chonder could manage it on short notice. Add to that the likelihood that, after their plans for the Shiplien Way operation had been crashed into by Brustram Warhanny, neither would have had time to organize a physical shadow. Nonetheless, I had the *Gallivant* track the movement of other nearby small craft, while we varied speed and direction, sometimes ducking behind large orbitals and emerging from them in shadows of grander vessels.

These precautions gave us time to research further the possible relevance of the name Hespira. There were eight worlds on which it had ever occurred with any frequency: Affax, Hollay, Tryshant, Ummer, New Bellas, Blink, Far Corondine, and Qum. "The name came into currency on those worlds," said my assistant, "among persons who admired a fiction known as *The Drama of Setiphar,* a tale about a hero cruelly separated from his true love who pursues her throughout a lifelong quest, frequently missing a reunion by moments when fate—or a particularly mean-spirited author—keeps throwing delays and obstacles in their way. They meet at last, only to die shortly thereafter in each other's arms."

I allowed my face to express the appropriate emotion and my assistant continued, "The novel was not original. It was based on a much older tale of courtly affection, about a prince who wooed a farm girl against his kingly father's will." Their affair also ended badly, though without the thickly cloying sentiment that dripped from every line of the plagiarized novel. Then the novel was turned into a stage version laced—or perhaps "larded" is the better term—with poignant and maudlin songs that toured on those same eight worlds. "That was a few hundred years ago but the production has been revived every other generation since."

"And I presume that Hespira is the heroine's name?" I said.

"Only in the original tale. In the novel and stage show, the heroine was Alanthea. Hespira was the name of her faithful and perpetually optimistic companion, a semi-sapient creature known as a sylinx, chimerically bred up from equine and feline plasms. The sylinx is not in the original courtly version."

"Parents named their children after a pet?" I said.

"Presumably, the parents were themselves children when they encountered the story. The sylinx sang one of the most affecting songs in the musical version."

The thought occasioned a mild dizziness. I allowed it to pass, then said, "Have we a copy of the tune?"

We did, and when Hespira returned to the salon, dressed in the ship-provided clothing and with her damp hair tied up in a kerchief, my assistant played it for her. She said it sounded vaguely familiar, but when I suggested she let her mind go blank while the integrator replayed the melody she listened again then opened her eyes and said, "I know, it sounds like the opening of Hernanke's Third Concerto." She hummed that almost universally known anthem, and of course I recognized it. The tunester who had written the songs for *The Drama of Setiphar* had lifted the melody from the great composer—indeed, when my assistant analyzed the production's other songs, it became clear that they had all been copied from the works of better composers, all of them safely long dead.

I took a philosophical view. The pursuit of the discriminator's craft often leads down blind alleys; one learns to enjoy the trip or one segues into another line of work. Meanwhile, I took a dispassionate accounting of Hespira: the face, the voice, the shape of her. I found nothing to stir me. My earlier, quixotic reaction to her presence I put down to circumstances of the moment; in other words, the impulses must have come from my own inner workings, that slow roiling of wants and needs that are bound up in the very nature of the inner mind, and that are sometimes projected onto whatever hapless person comes into view while those instincts are bubbling around the foundations of the conscious persona. Half the miseries of humankind's history have originated in those who think they see in the fellow next to them virtues and vices that exist only in the mind of the beholder.

On the other hand, I had to admit, there might be magic at work. If so, Osk Rievor would know.

"What is this place?" she said, looking around at the now almost uninhabited estate of the late Blik Arlem, its gardens and arbors left to grow wild, its winding walks and reflecting pools beginning to show the signs of lengthy neglect. "Why have you brought me here, out of sight and hearing of the rest of humanity?"

I reflected that the genial glow that surrounds the doer of a good deed loses some of its warmth and brightness when the recipient meets every action with the pinched face of suspicion. I sighed. "We have come to consult a colleague of mine. He spends his time in research and prefers solitude."

"Which we are interrupting."

"Few of us are so fortunate as to see our preferences universally respected," I said.

We made our way down the gravel paths that led between several low mounds and broad hummocks, most of the estate having been built underground. I led us away from the main complex toward a free-standing cottage that backed onto a meadow that sloped up to a wood of tall trees. The little house had straight walls, square windows, and rectangular doors beneath a steeply sloped roof. It had been commissioned by Arlem's third spouse, who had first tired of their subterranean mode of existence before realizing that she was in fact tired of everything associated with her husband, and left him for a man who held high office in the grand bureaucracy of the Archonate. The cottage had then become home to the estate's head gardener.

The cottage door had no who's-there; my former alter ego saw no need to become dependent on mechanisms and devices that would sooner or later cease to function. And, in this location, it would be sooner rather than later: the estate occupied the junction of two ley lines, those ancient lines of arcane force in which I used not to believe. Their intersection helped make the Arlem estate one of those places where the new age was already beginning to make itself felt. The change would not happen everywhere, all at once, nor would it come like a wave sweeping across the universe; rather, it was like a dense liquid seeping through a porous membrane, pooling in "dimples" where the barrier was less resistant. Wherever the channels of arcane force known as ley lines intersected, a dimple could be expected. In this place, magic worked far more powerfully and reliably than in locations far from ley lines. That was why Blik Arlem, a dabbler in the hermetic arts, had built here, and why my former intuition had chosen it for his workshop.

As we approached the door I lifted my hand to rap on the painted wood, but the portal opened before I could strike. "This is a surprise," he said, looking with curiosity at Hespira, then back to me. "I expected you to send them on their own."

"Send what?" I said.

"The bees."

I had not forgotten. "They are in the ship. But events have moved on. I am going offworld on a case, but wanted to consult you before leaving."

He looked more closely at the young woman. "Then you'd better come in."

I made the introductions as perfunctory as necessity required. My client's suspicions would not be dampened if I described Osk Rievor as formerly a part of my own psyche, now resident in the body of a man named Orlo Saviene who had recently disappeared from Old Earth.

Saviene would spend the next several centuries in a cavern on a tiny barren world called Bille, happily in thrall to a knowledge-hungry symbiotic fungus that would feed him dreams of perfection while mining his memories, until his spark dwindled and disappeared. Osk Rievor, a magically reified part of me, though without his own physical form, would be drawn across the gulf of time from now until then, and finding Saviene's mindless hulk still well-tended by the symbiote, would appropriate it for his own. I, too, had been flung through time, into a rude world of magic where I had suffered indignities but had overcome them. Finally we had both come back, courtesy of a deal with a captive demon.

The episode had defied all logic, but in recent months I had been forced to accept that my well-ordered views of how reality worked were subject to arbitrary revision. I would not, however, expect a suspicious amnesiac to sign on immediately to a truth that I had myself found all too hard to swallow, I simply named Osk Rievor to Hespira and described him as a trusted colleague. Then I sketched what we knew of her situation.

The conversation took place in the cottage's study, to which my former intuition had led us. While I spoke, I saw the woman's eyes flicking from one wall to another, or rather to the shelves and glass-fronted cabinets that lined them from floor to ceiling. Osk Rievor had obviously been busy in the weeks since we had returned from the future. I knew that he had acquired a trove of books and magical paraphernalia from a group of sorcerers who had tried to use us to their own ends; in the end, they had no further need of their possessions, having been devoured in one way or another by forces they could not control.

But I was sure that there were far more old books and unusual objects here in the cottage than my other self had had when last I had seen him. And some of them were more than passing strange: a scaly, three-toed foot, each digit tipped by a hooked talon; a large glass jar full of swirling motes of light that seemed to move in purposeful patterns; a rod of wood that I could only see from the corner of my vision, because it disappeared when I looked at it directly; and, by contrast, a disembodied eye resting on a high shelf—I had the feeling that whenever I looked away from it, it subjected me to a close scrutiny.

My client was regarding these objects and the others that crowded the room on all sides with the same expression that would have taken possession of my own face a few short, though eventful, months ago. Then her gaze went to Osk Rievor. She inspected him carefully, and I was glad that he had regrown his hair—it had been absorbed by the fungus during all those years in its cavern—and that his skin had lost the pallor that, with his complete hairlessness, had made him appear more fungoid than human. Still, he remained an unusual-looking man and the surroundings could not help but inspire trepidation.

"I think I'd like to leave here now," Hespira said.

A moment of silent communication passed between Osk Rievor and me: I pleaded and he acceded. "Please," he said to my client, "do not be alarmed at what you see. It is my pastime to study the ways in which the gullible are taken in by mountebanks and fake-artists. These objects are merely some of the cunning devices with which the predators delude their prey."

I saw her relax and did the same. I rarely misled a client, and then only temporarily and in the client's own interest, but I could see no point in trying to steer Hespira into the current as regarded the impending fate of the rational universe. She had quite enough difficulties within her own personal sphere.

"Well," I began, and saw her turn to me. As soon as her eyes were off Osk Rievor I saw him make a rippling motion in the air with his fingers, as if he were playing a brief passage on the keys of an invisible instrument. His lips silently formed a few syllables and immediately Hespira stood motionless, frozen in the look of expectation that my "Well" had brought to her face.

"What have you done to her?" I said.

"Quieted her," he said, "so that I can do what you brought her here for me to do."

I examined her. She was as still as a portrait. "You're getting better at these things," I said to Osk Rievor.

"It becomes easier as the cusp approaches," he said, reaching for a small black tube on one of the shelves, "and as I practice what I've learned."

The black tube was hollow. He looked at Hespira through it, from several angles. Then he rang a tiny silver bell near her ear and listened attentively to its fading reverberations. He drew complex figures around her in chalk on the slate floor, considered her reflection in a dark and ancient mirror edged in tarnished metal, held her ungainly hands between his while peering into her green eyes, and sniffed the air about her ears. He moved his hands in certain patterns and spoke certain words. He lifted a thong from which a coin-sized metal disk depended and touched it to her forehead. Finally, he turned to me and said, "Not so much as a trace."

"You are sure?" I said.

"As sure as I can be," he said. "She has less of an aura around her than do you. I would say that until the past few moments she has never been so close to magic as to be in the same street in the same month. She is essentially untouched, at least by any magic I can recognize."

I related the circumstances of our meeting and the difficulties I was having with Massim Shar and Irslan Chonder. "Is she in any way connected to them?"

Osk Rievor consulted his inner processes. "I have no sense of that," he said, then became definite about it. "No."

I knew better than to ask how he knew. He didn't know how he knew things; that was the nature of an intuitive faculty. "There it is," I said to my integrator, which was still draped about my shoulders, "neither magic nor any connection to the Shar-Chonder business."

"So it would appear," it said.

"It would be good if we could communicate more easily," I said to Osk Rievor.

"Agreed."

"Will you reconsider your views on keeping an integrator?"

"No," he said, "but I am working on something that may serve equally well. I will let you know when it is ready. In the meantime, we will have the bees."

"But I am going offworld, not just across normal space but through whimsies, probably several of them."

"I need to do more research," he said, "but it may be possible to send a bee so that it will come to you while you are in a whimsy."

My mind reeled and I put aside the discussion. I glanced at Hespira. She had now been inert for several minutes. "When you cancel the spell, will she not notice an unaccountable gap in the proceedings?" I said. "She has already had enough problems in that regard. I do not want to alarm her."

"It is a gentle spell. I found it in a book of remedies for fretful children. She will not notice."

Again, I felt that sense of protectiveness toward her. "Still," I said, "it is an imposition."

He looked at me oddly but did not argue. He raised his hand to undo the children's spell, then checked himself. The metal disk he had pressed to her forehead lay on his worktable. He picked it up and handed it to me. As I took it, I saw that it was red in color and when he put it in my hand it was warm. But in a moment it turned blue and cool to the touch.

"It detects the ambience of magic," Osk Rievor said. "The redder the disk, the stronger the ambience."

I strung the thong around my neck. "Thank you," I said.

Now he moved his fingers again and spoke softly. I saw awareness come into Hespira's eyes again. "Well," I said to her, picking up where I'd left off, "if you find my colleague's collection of trumperies and gitchygooms disturbing, perhaps you would care to take some fresh air in the grounds while I consult with him."

She thought that a good idea and went out into the hallway. I listened to her steps fading and waited until I heard the door open and close before returning to the subject of Irslan Chonder and Massim Shar. I asked Osk Rievor for his sense of how the matter would develop and resolve.

"It is, to be sure, a problem," he said, "but a short-lived one. One will soon lay waste the other, then Brustram Warhanny will bundle the survivor off to the contemplarium. You need only to be out of the field of fire until the sparks cease to fly."

"My own view, exactly," I told him, and for a moment we were in perfect accord, as we had so often been when we had inhabited the same cranium, and I had been the dominant actor. Then the interlude passed, and I was once again in the presence of a man whose nature was fundamentally strange to me, and growing stranger.

Our recent adventures on Bille and in the future Old Earth where magic ruled had been, for me, a distasteful experience that I was glad to be done with. I had no doubt, however, that Osk Rievor's appreciation of those events was at variance with my own. He had come out of it with his own body, after all. He had also garnered a huge trove of magical lore and practical advice on spellcasting that had previously been the closely held possessions of the five magicians who had also come to Bille but who had fared less well than Osk Rievor.

He was now encamped in this cottage on what had been the estate of the late Blik Arlem, deceased collector of items associated with sympathetic association, most of them shams and counterfeits. Rievor, grown rich in the real thing, was studying his finds and seeking to master them. Judging by the wealth of items on display, he was still acquiring fresh sources of knowledge and new instruments of power. When the great change came, and rationality was overthrown by magic, my former intuition would stand far above the chaos of the transition.

"Your researches go well, then?" I said.

"Wonderfully, just wonderfully."

"How pleasant for you."

My tone caused him to regard me with a mildly quizzical expression that soon broke into one of understanding, then of regret. "Ah," he said, "of course. I will ask you to forgive me. I have been swinking away so furiously these past few weeks that I fear I have lost my perspective."

I moved a hand in a way that invited him to give the matter no further consideration. "No," I said, "it is I who should ask your pardon. It is not your fault that that which will bring me misery will cause you joy."

"I can assure you," he said, "that when the time comes, you will have a safe haven with me."

I knew he meant it kindly, but I told him not to concern himself. "I have been giving it much thought," I said, "and have almost decided that I would prefer to go into the shadows with all the things I have loved, rather than live on in the miserable wreckage."

Hespira appeared in the doorway. She had not gone out but had opened and closed the door to mislead us, then crept back down the hall to hear what we said. I could not really blame her; under similar circumstances, I would have wanted to know what strangers might be saying about me.

Now she looked anxiously from one to the other of us. "Shadows and wreckage," she said, "that seems a very dark remark. Do you face ruin? I do not wish to be a further burden to you when you have difficulties of your own."

I showed her a composed aspect. "I spoke in metaphor," I said. "It can be fairly said that sometimes my speech wanders into the realm of the bombastic. You need not be concerned." I gave Osk Rievor a meaningful look; we had decided, when we returned to Old Earth from Bille, that there was no point in advertising the impending disaster, there being nothing that could be done to prevent it, and precious little even to soften its impact.

My reassurances were only half effective. Hespira's face still reflected a concern for me that, in light of her circumstances, I found touching. The emotion did her credit. It bespoke an empathetic nature in her and, though it was not a clue to her identity, it was an indication of her underlying character. But she presented, to the trained eye, other clues that said that a primal generous nature might have been overlaid by experiences. The tiny lines at the corners of her eyes and mouth said that she had encountered more cause to frown than to smile. The grooves between her brows were those of a woman who had had to make hard choices between unpleasant alternatives. She had known troubles and had worked at solving them.

Somewhere, before this, she must have had a life, with her own constellation of family and friends, pursuits and pastimes, perhaps even a relationship of significance to her. I could not believe that she had voluntarily removed all that from her awareness. Whatever had taken her memory, I was sure it had come upon her from outside. It might have been through some natural cause—which I doubted, for my assistant would have detected any signs of organic disorder—but I thought it far more likely that her life had been stolen from her by some agency that had acted knowingly, and probably out of malice. Hespira's amnesia had not just happened; it had been done to her.

It was therefore natural that I would respond to her as I did. I saw in her a microcosm of the awful fate that lay in wait for the worlds I knew and loved; she had been deprived of everything that gave her existence meaning. But there was a difference between the micro and the macro: I could do nothing to stop the Wheel's inexorable turning, but I had all the skills and wherewithal of a first-class discriminator—I could give Hespira back what had been robbed from her. And perhaps deliver to the robber a punishment commensurate to the crime.

"I believe I am in need of a small vacation offworld," I told her, "but I am not much good at lying on sun-warmed beaches or gaping at monuments and mausoleums. My profession is the unpicking of other people's mysteries, but it is not by accident that I have taken up the discriminator's craft. I will admit that if I did not have to get a living, I would still go out in pursuit of puzzles and perplexities. It is who I am. So it would please me to spend a little time finding out who you are. And who knows what interesting landscapes and experiences we might find along the way."

"I doubt that I can pay you what the effort is worth," she said. "I do not feel that I have come from wealth."

I had long since perfected the gesture of airy unconcern, as any good discriminator must. I performed it now, the effect only slightly diminished by Osk Rievor's cheerful interjection, which drew Hespira's attention his way.

"As to the matter of wealth," he was saying, "I believe I owe you a certain amount."

"Do you?" I said, this time affecting the disavowal of being bothered in either direction with a languorous ease. "I don't recall."

He burbled on enthusiastically. "All the books," he said, "and other items. The leasehold on this cottage, and a great number of odds and ends."

I put up a hand to restrain him. I was enjoying striking the pose of magnanimity under Hespira's wide-eyed gaze. There was something about her that made me want to appear at my best, though the truth was that Osk Rievor's study of magic, both before and after he acquired his own corporeal existence, had cost me a goodly portion of what little wealth I had amassed.

"Never mind showing me the hand," he said. Then, asking the young woman to excuse us a moment while we discussed debts and payments, he led me out of the main room and down a narrow, unlit hallway to a small door. The portal bore no lock nor even a handle, but I suspected it needed neither because it opened of its own accord when he made complex motions involving both hands. The room beyond was darker than the hall, yet I saw something gleaming in the scant light that fell past us through the doorway.

"What is it?" I said.

"Currency," he said, lowering his voice, "mostly ancient, I think, since I don't recognize many of the scripts and certainly none of the faces and scenes. Oh, and that pile over there is most of the jewels."

My eyes had adjusted to the dimness. I saw heaps of coins, rounds and squares and multisided lozenges of precious metals; and a mound of faceted gems, in sizes from fingernail to fist.

"There was a lot more," Osk Rievor was saying. "The spell was deceptively simple, only a few syllables. But you have to get the combined tone of voice and volume just right, or the trickle becomes a torrent. Fortunately, I made the earliest attempts out in the forest—I've learned not to try new incantations indoors—and I just covered up the piles with leaves and dirt."

I dropped my own voice to a whisper. "You left piles of coins and jewels out in the forest?"

"It would have been a great deal of work to bring them in," he said. "Much easier just to turn on the tap here, now that I've learned how to keep the flow within limits. I will send back the unneeded heaps in the woods."

So many questions were occurring to me that I couldn't decide which one to ask first. Before I could fix on one he continued, "I was thinking I should open an account at the fiduciary pool."

"Perhaps more than one," I said. "Though, if you turn up with amounts like this, especially in ancient tender, you will draw attention."

"Yes," he said. "I think I will send back all the coins. Jewels are much more anonymous, don't you think? But I must ask your assistance."

"Of course. Whatever I can do." A red jewel the size of a charneck's egg lay on the floor just within the door. I stooped and picked it up. It was round, cut in sixty-four facets, and heavy in my hand. "Where do they come from? Or do you make them out of air and shadows?"

"Some hoard, I think," he said. "Probably several, and far removed from each other in time and space. And, of course, from here and now."

"Of course," I said. I bent to replace the gem, but he caught my hand and closed my fingers around its coolness.

"Keep it," he said. "Take as much as you can carry. I owe you a great deal."

I did not know what to say. I was aware that my mouth seemed to want to hang open. I was strangely glad that we had left Hespira in the other room, because I did not want her to see me gawking like some hobble-dehoy bumpkin.

I felt Osk Rievor's hands on my shoulders. He turned me gently and pushed me back along the corridor. "Never mind about it now," he said. "I'll fill a bag and you can take it when you leave."

My mind's gears were beginning to reengage. I stopped and faced him. "A hoard," I said, "implies a hoarder. A hoarder usually hates to let loose so much as a bent groat and will often go to great lengths to recoup anything that is taken. Are you not concerned that someone will come looking for his missing treasure? And for whoever took it?"

"That has occurred to me," he said, "but I will deal with the situation if or when it happens. And it may not. In the meantime, I have a plan."

It was my turn to give him an off-slant look. Intuitive psyches operated more on impulses than on anything that a logical mind would call a plan. "Tell me about it," I said.

"Wealth tends to generate wealth," he began.

I gave a qualified assent. "If it does not instead give birth to folly."

He ignored the remark. "I thought I would invest in the fiduciary pool. When the proceeds are enough to see me through to the..." He paused and sought for a word, and decided that "rearrangement" was the least indelicate—"I'll convert the capital back into gems and return them by reversing the polarity of the spell. If I've read the instructions aright, I should be able to put the goods back at almost the same moment they were originally taken."

"You're confident that you can do so?" I said. "The more steps to a plan, the more opportunities for one of those steps to lead you over a cliff. Especially when some of them are taken in the dark."

We had stopped in the hallway. "I admit," he said, "that there are some obscure patches along the way ahead. But I am growing more adept at the craft, and my confidence increases daily."

"Remember that overconfidence has been the undoing of virtually every practitioner of the arcane arts that we have yet encountered."

"I am being careful. Small steps, no grand saltations into the unknown."

I could not argue with him. He routinely grappled with matters on which my mind could not even lodge a finger. "Keep being careful," was all I could say.

"I will," he assured me, then sketched the rest of his plan. I was to go offworld for a while. When I returned, I would come back to the cottage, scoop up his piles of pelf, and take them to the fiduciary pool. There I would offer a plausible story about adventuring on some distant and unregulated planet. The officers of the pool would not care where the treasure had come from, nor how it had been acquired, so long as it had not been feloniously lifted on any of the worlds with which they had dealings. "And provided, of course," he concluded, "that they get their fees and commissions when they put it to use."

"That part of the plan should pose no problems," I said.

"Excellent," he said. "Things are working out wonderfully well."

"So it would appear," I said.

"Your colleague has unusual interests," Hespira said.

We had said farewell to Osk Rievor and were taking a turn around the woods that lay behind the cottage, I having expressed a desire to breathe some fresh air before we sealed ourselves in the *Gallivant* and departed Old Earth. It was, of course, another misdirection on my part, intended to give my other self time to transfer a satchel of jewels to the ship. The anonymous gems would be most easily converted to local funds on other worlds.

"He has an unusual history," I said, repressing the urge to complete the thought: And an even more unusual future.

"He seems to like you."

"I suppose he does, in his own way."

"And you like him."

"I suppose that also is true," I said. "We were once very close."

My steps had led us to a sunny clearing among some grand shade trees. At its center lay a little circle of small white stones surrounding a mound of bare earth. Here was buried the remains of the grinnet, that strange beast whose body had housed, for a while, my integrator—until my assistant had demanded to be decanted back into its normal arrangement of components and connectors. A few blades of grass had taken root on the grave, and as I bent to pluck them I noticed that the mound had been disturbed, as if some predator had sought to dig up what I had put there.

Hespira was continuing our discussion of Osk Rievor. "I wonder that the two of you should be so close. Your natures seem so dissimilar."

"We have had some common experiences. Bonds could not help being forged."

Her eyebrows performed a minimal shrug. "Still, I can't see you getting yourself all wrapped up in such a flippadiday as all that so-called magic."

"He has his reasons for—" I began then interrupted myself. "Wait. That word, 'flippadiday'—don't you mean 'flippydedoo'?"

She frowned in thought. "No, I don't think I do. It seems to me that I used the word I am familiar with, though I can't remember an actual instance of saying it before, or even hearing it."

I had left my assistant on the *Gallivant.* "Let us go to the ship," I said. "I want to put a question to my integrator."

When we came aboard, I told the ship to prepare for departure. The *Gallivant* reported that we could be on our way as soon as I gave it a destination. "We may be about to get an indication as to that," I said. "Assistant—"

But before I could issue an instruction to my integrator, the vessel said, "In the meantime, would you care to try some of my flavored ship's bread with a pot of fresh punge?"

And before I could answer the ship, my assistant spoke brusquely, saying, "We have important work to do."

I put down the small bubble of irritation that rose in me. As the great change approached, complex devices that had been exposed to dimples, like the *Gallivant*'s integrator and my own assistant, were becoming increasingly more willful, even quirksome. I had already decided that since it seemed to please the *Gallivant* to ply me with such offerings I would go along. Events that had happened in my past but which would not occur until well in the ship's future had taught me that it would be wise to place myself on the good side of any ledger the *Gallivant* might have started to keep.

"Work and replenishment are not mutually exclusive," I said. "Bring on the refreshments and we will try them while we hear my assistant's report." Thus Hespira and I sat at the salon's folding table, sipping punge and taking a few bites of flavored ship's bread. I commented favorably on taste and texture, then said, "Integrator, what can you tell us about the word 'flippadiday'?"

My assistant's traveling armature still hung on its hook near the forward hatch but, as always, its voice sounded from some indeterminate point in the air. "It is a variant of 'flippydedoo,'" it said. "It occurs in common speech on a quartet of secondary worlds originally settled from the foundational domain of Ikkibal."

"Name the worlds," I said, and when it had done so I asked Hespira if any of the names rang true for her.

"No," she said.

"The cotton from which her dress was made," I asked the integrator, "does it grow on those worlds?"

"It does."

"And the dyes that color the thread?"

"They also occur there."

"Well," I said, "there it is. *Gallivant*, set course for Ikkibal. The game is begun."

Immediately, the in-atmosphere obviators cycled up and we lifted smoothly above the Blik Arlem estate. It was only then that I remembered that I had wanted to speak to Osk Rievor about the grinnet's grave. But as we passed beyond Old Earth's curtain of air and the ship's heavy drive began to vibrate quietly beneath our feet, I reminded myself that the little corpse had been buried in a sealed metal container that should keep it safe from molestation.

Ikkibal was a mellow world, rich in greens and blues and lit by a healthy yellow star named Op. It had been settled in the third wave of the Great Effloration, when humankind reached the midpoint of the immense distance between Old Earth—which in those days might still have been called just Earth—and the wispy trails of stars that marked the end of The Spray and the beginning of the Great Dark. Its first settlers had been dedicated city builders; they created eight great metropolises along the shores of the single huge continent that their new world offered, and a ninth high in the mountain-ringed plateau that occupied its middle. But as the ages had rolled by, the dominant culture on Ikkibal had become rigidly stratified, social rank coming to dominate all other principles. In consequence, many of the original settlers' descendants had filtered away to the four secondary worlds, there to build themselves societies more to their likings. Seven of the coastal cities had been gradually abandoned, their towers and seawalls battered and undermined by once-in-a-century storms and surges. Now only New Kutt and Razham were inhabited, the former arcing in a ring of white walls and red-tiled roofs around the landward side of the extinct caldera that formed Five Reef Bay, the latter throwing its pale blue spires high into the attenuated air of the Central Uplands. It was here that the planet's main spaceport was set, the New Kuttians being even less interested than the Razhamans in whatever might come from offworld.

The Razhamans were, however, more polite to outlanders than their coastal cousins, who had a tendency to ignore visitors' requests for directions or their queries about how a distinctive building or pleasure garden had come to be. Ikkibal was a self-satisfied world, having exported for a thousand generations those of its citizens who chafed under the slow rhythms of its manners and customs. The malcontents had mostly gone out to Tuk, Obal, Shannery, and New Cepernaum—four secondary worlds orbiting three nearby star systems—where they grew cultures that fit them better.

I had the *Gallivant* set down in the transients' section of Razham's spaceport. I had decided that we would spend a day or two in a hotel here. The interlude was not needed for purposes of unraveling Hespira's mystery, but for my personal peace of mind. The trip out from Old Earth had been a long one, with lengthy intervals during which we puttered across vast stretches of normal space between the whimsies that bridged the unimaginably immense gaps between star systems. My ship was small and we of necessity spent a great deal of time in each other's company, and often at close quarters. I found her much in my thoughts.

Now we waited for the spaceport's arbiger to visit the ship and clear us to disembark. There were no issues to be resolved concerning disease or the importing of prohibited substances, but the Ikkibali had lately grown tired of receiving missionaries of the Astringency. This was a burgeoning spiritual movement that had taken root on the foundational domain of Armanc, from where its devotees had gone out to proselytize among dozens of worlds in the midsection of The Spray. Astringents clothed themselves in garments of dark hue and severe cut, wore their hair shorn above the ears, and felt morally obligated to comment adversely and in detail on other folks' tastes and pastimes. They required no invitation before offering their views and would stride along at one's elbow, delivering acerbic criticisms and recommending the reading of *How and Why*, copies of which they always had handy for sale. The small blue-bound volume was the seminal work of their prophet, Dunstone, who had been cruelly martyred on New Cepernaum in the movement's first decade.

The arbiger soon appeared at the *Gallivant*'s hatch. She was a barrel-chested woman clad in a uniform of tan cloth set off by belt, boots, and short cape of leather, all dyed vermilion. "Any books?" was her first question and, having received a negative reply, she visibly relaxed. "Very well, now what is your rank?"

I found the question ambiguous and asked her to clarify.

"Razham," she told me, speaking as if she occupied a height some distance beyond my reach, "is crisply organized. Everyone knows who stands above and who below. It is a marvel of social precision for which we Razhamans are justly admired throughout the Ten Thousand Worlds."

"Really," I said, "and yet this is the first I have heard of it."

"Where are you from again?"

"Old Earth."

The name brought no hint of recognition to her broad, bland countenance. "Is that one of the Foundationals?"

"No," I said, "it is—"

She interrupted. "Well, there you have it. If people will insist on coming from places no one has ever heard of, it is not surprising that they arrive out of touch with sophisticated standards."

"I take it," I said, refocusing the discussion, "that rank is important in Razham?"

I received one of those looks that are earned by persons who find it necessary to state the blindingly obvious. "Yes," she said, when she had finished shaking her head, "and we need to establish yours so that we can color you appropriately."

"Color?" I knew that some societies found the normal human palette insufficient to express individuality. I did not care to find myself dyed bright pink or glowing saffron—the dyes sometimes took time to wear off.

She saw my hand go unconsciously to my cheek. "Your garments," she said. "Cut and color bespeak rank. Without them, no one will know what you are, nor how to gauge the appropriate pause."

I let the issue of the meaning of "pause" slip by unchallenged. "Shall I describe my occupation?" I said.

"If you have one."

I outlined the duties and activities of a freelance discriminator. She seemed underimpressed. I added that I was generally considered the foremost practitioner of my profession, and was frequently consulted by the "peak," as the upper tiers of Olkney's social pyramid were colloquially known.

The arbiger wrestled with the concept. "Some sort of servant?" she offered.

I drew myself up. "An independent professional," I said, "performing essential services of a delicate nature."

The phrase "services of a delicate nature" apparently had a different connotation to Razhamans. I had to dissuade her from classifying me as a catamite or gigolo, neither of which commanded much honor in Razham. When the debris from that misapprehension was finally swept from her rigid mind, she decided that I was of the middle-to-lower tier of the avauntseur class, about three-quarters up the scale that had the lowest Ikkibali toenail-parer at its fundament and the purest-bred elegantiast at its acme. Thus fixed, I was allowed to wear any shade of blue, reds from pink to vermilion, and all but the brightest yellows. I could wear any two accessories of black, though if one of these was a hat the brim could be no wider than my shoulders.

I remembered that I had been given an honorary rank by a former Archon of Old Earth and tried to mention this now, but the official clearly felt that she had spent enough time on the matter. She issued me a chit that I could take to a clothier and be properly outfitted. She then turned to Hespira who, of course, could answer none of her questions. Before another misunderstanding could break out, I intervened to explain the circumstances. "There are some philological indications she may have come from one of Ikkibal's secondary worlds," I said. "We are staying only as long as it takes to decide which is the most likely."

"She will have to wear white with red dots," the arbiger said.

"What does that pattern signify?" Hespira asked.

But the woman had been writing the second chit as she spoke, and now she handed it over and ran through the rest of the formalities in a perfunctory manner. We were advised to avoid strenuous exercise until we had purchased an oxygen supplement—sold at the spaceport commissariat and at hotels and restaurants—the air being thin at Razham's altitude.

Indeed, by the time we had made the short trek to the port's hub, Hespira at my elbow and my assistant again draped about my neck, I was finding myself hard put to maintain a brisk walking pace. My companion, too, complained of a shortness of breath and the onset of a headache.

"Well," I said, "at least we have eliminated Razham as your place of origin." The locals we saw working around the spaceport were clearly adapted to the atmospheric conditions, all having broad chests and many sporting huge nostrils. Of the latter, they seemed consciously proud, elevating their heads to point them at rankless strangers. Or perhaps they were merely regarding us with scorn.

At the hub, a multistoried tower of the blue-gray slate that dominated the landscape, we purchased packets of the supplement and I wasted no time in swallowing one of the pea-sized, rough-textured pills. Within moments, its time-released oxygen began to enter my bloodstream and I ceased to feel as if I was in the last leg of a two-hour foot race. The peakedness also left Hespira's face and when I suggested that we find accommodation and begin our search, she summoned a brave smile.

I exchanged some jewels for a purse of local currency—coins of bright metal called sequints—then addressed the question of accommodation. From a rack of illustrated pamphlets at the spaceport, I chose a comfortable-looking hotel near the city's administrative nexus. A hired ground car took us there and I was glad to see that the image in the brochure matched the reality: the structure, unlike most in many-spired Razham, was built low to the ground, and with gently sloping ramps instead of the steep staircases that the Razhamans preferred, often placing them where any reasonable civilization would have thought it more useful to put in a switchback road.

The car's driver was a man midway between youth and age, solidly built, and with a look of quick intelligence about him. I gave him three golden sequints, which was surely more than was required, judging from the slight dilation of his pupils and his involuntary cessation of breath when I placed them in his hand. As his fingers closed over the shining coins, he said, "Please take note of my name and cipher, visitors, and feel free to call upon me at any time. I know all the best bowl-and-cuppage parlors and can carry you safe and unmolested through the more liberal parts of the city, if such is your taste."

I had my assistant note his particulars—his name was Carthew Chumblot—and told him we might soon call upon his services in finding attire suitable to our putative ranks.

"You have chits?" he said.

I showed them to him. At mine he made a face that questioned the arbiger's judgment. At Hespira's his eyes widened. He looked from her to the card twice then blew out his cheeks and said, "An insult! The tyranny of a minor functionary allowed to lord it over strangers trapped helpless within her narrow sphere!"

"What does it signify?" Hespira said.

Outrage, real or feigned, perhaps a blend of both, robbed him of speech for a moment, then he said, "That you should be led about in a harness, your head cushioned against the risk of stumbles, and all sharp implements kept from reach."

"She would experience lengthy pause, then?" I said.

"The mistress's life would be one continuous pause," he said. "Intolerable!"

"What is to be done about it?"

Chumblot's eyes flicked from side to side as he made his dispositions. "There is more than one entrance to Bezarab," he quoted. In my inner ear, my assistant began to explain the reference, but I signaled it not to bother, as the driver was still speaking. "I will take you to a clothier I know, a woman of subtlety and imagination. We will erase this insult!" He struck Hespira's chit with the backs of his fingers, and I recognized a gesture of contemptuous dismissal.

"Very good," I said. "Though first we must register here."

"I will wait," he said, adding another gesture, this one conveying a message that magnanimous impulses were fundamental to Chumblot's nature. He returned to his vehicle. Hespira and I went up the ramp into the hotel. I had overpaid him on purpose, of course, having often found it useful to engage knowledgeable local help in unfamiliar surroundings; experience had taught me that registered transporters like this fellow were usually dependable. Even so, I checked with my integrator for its analysis of his details.

"He values sequints, but far more he craves respect and to have his contributions appreciated," was its reply. "Also, I detected no flushes of blood or motions of other bodily fluids that betokened unnatural appetites."

It was always a good question to ask. In some parts of some worlds, the newcome stranger is a walking invitation to let slip the basest denizens of disordered psyches. Indeed, there were places in Olkney where the unwary visitor might all too easily find himself unwittingly cast as an essential player in some madman's private drama. The insane had a tendency to cloak others in the strange garments they found hanging in the backs of their own mental wardrobes. So, for that matter, did the rest of us, but the consequences of error were usually less drastic.

I had not researched the matter, but it seemed to me that there had lately been more reports than usual of such upsetting incidents back in Olkney. I wondered if the impending great change might have something to do with it. If so, the most probable inference to be drawn was that the turnover might be to bring to the top of the new order those persons who had scrounged along the bottom of the old. Fumblewits, deludants, and outright barkers whose infirmities had long kept them in poverty and want might suddenly find themselves transformed into dominees and wonder workers. The thought buttressed my growing inclination not to seek to survive the cataclysm.

But for the moment, I had work to do and a good cause to serve. I smiled at Hespira and offered her my arm, and together we ascended the broad ramp that led into the Espantia Inn. A functionary in a many-buttoned tunic of red and gold activated the twin doors of metalized glass, and I rewarded him with another of the sequints; properly motivated hotel staff could also be useful. We crossed a wide common space, deeply carpeted and well lit by tall windows on two sides, the light sent in several directions by sheets of polished metal hung on cables from the high ceiling. Beyond the sea of geometrically patterned carpet stood a waist-high barrier of polished wood, behind which waited a man with carefully groomed hair. As we hove into view, his eyebrows raised themselves in expectation.

This far down The Spray, even those who dealt with travelers from distant origins could not be guaranteed to know much more about Old Earth than the planet's name and some general descriptor: "unfashionable," perhaps, or "fusty-rusty," as I had once heard my world dismissed by a hereditary grandee of the foundational domain Belserene. So when the clerk inquired as to our home world, I was constructively vague—"A little place well up The Spray," I said, then directed his attention to Hespira. "My companion, however, has roots in this sector." I then feigned a sudden inspiration and said, "Let us see if you can tell where she is from by her mode of speech."

I asked the young woman to say a few words—the words we had rehearsed earlier on the *Gallivant*—and she said, "My dear, let us not take up this man's time with a lot of flippadiday."

I urged her to indulge me, but at this point the clerk interrupted to declare that he need hear no more. "Shannery," he said, "and somewhere north of Cauldoon. We get occasional visitors from those parts. The accent is unmistakable."

Hespira smiled and executed a gesture of appreciation as if for a difficult trick well performed. "Of course," I said, "she has been away a while. Is there anywhere in Razham where we could catch up on the latest from Shannery?"

"There is never much doing on Shannery," the clerk said, with a laugh that only partly disguised a mild contempt, "but our integrator captures the main information services."

I pronounced this excellent news and booked us into a pair of connecting rooms overlooking the hotel's inner courtyard. A few minutes later, Hespira and I were cloistered in my half of the accommodation, seated together on a quilted divan, and I was instructing my assistant to review the available editions of the news feeds from Shannery. "Work backward from recent times, looking for unexplained disappearances."

I was hopeful, but the search turned up nothing useful. In all of Shannery over the past several months, a total of ninety-three persons had unexpectedly gone absent. Some had turned up alive, though in varying degrees of health, after a few days or weeks; it was discovered that they had taken unannounced holidays or fled difficult relationships, or had got lost in forests or while trekking the furzelands, where the sky could be overcast for days and the flat terrain offered no landmarks.

Only six of the ninety-three were unaccounted for, four of them the subjects of open files among local constabularies whose inquisitors were questioning associates or relations as to means, motives, and opportunities for foul play. The other two were recent disappearances, who were being searched for and might turn up at any moment. But none of the six's descriptions even remotely coincided with Hespira's.

"A dead end?" she said, the hope that had sprung up in her with the clerk's pinpointing of her accent now fading.

"Not at all," I said. "It means only that we have eliminated the most obvious possibility. On to the next inning."

"Is my life but a game to you?" she said.

By habit, a glib remark sprang to my lips, but I shut them tight before it could gain utterance. In truth, I had often approached my work as if it were sport, although I went at it with the dedication of a professional in a premier league. I bore the occasional setback with a rueful smile and exulted at my frequent triumphs with the justified pride of a confirmed champion. From the clients, however, I maintained a stark distance: where they were emotional, I was cool; where they fretted and girned, I showed a mask of control.

Of course, it was easier for me. All that was in play for me was another fee, another notch on the heavily scored tally stick of my reputation, and my own inner insistence that I meet the standard of excellence that I invariably set for myself. To keep a distance was also a necessity of my craft; those who sought my help often came to me storm-driven through the direst, rocky narrows of a life's voyage, in which I might be their last hope of navigating a safe passage. If I let them, I had always told myself, they would clutch me to them as a panicking drowner clings to his would-be rescuer, dragging both beneath the waves. Better that they should stay down while I bobbed up to the surface, fresh and ready for the next drowner.

I put my arm around Hespira's shoulders. Looking down into her drawn face, seeing how the lower of her too-wide lips trembled, I felt a sudden and surprising rush of strong emotion: sympathy, a desire to protect; but though I was conscious of the warm scent that rose from her, I felt no stir of desire.

"No," I said, withdrawing my arm and moving to put some air between us, "it is not a game. I spoke lightly so that you would not be cast down by a minor setback." Then, partly to distract her, partly to move us forward, I said to my assistant, "Can you confirm the clerk's estimate of her probable place of origin?"

Its voice spoke from the air. "I now can, with reasonable confidence. Since we passed through the last whimsy and came in range of Ikkibal, I have been sampling emissions and open-wave communications. The accents of those speakers identified as from Shannery generally resemble our client's; the township of Cauldoon, on the largest continent, marks a linguistic watershed between two dialects. The voices that I can identify as originating from north of that region very closely match the way she forms her phonemes. If I can sample a few hundred more, particularly the voices of young females, I expect to make a conclusive determination."

"Well," I said, "there it is. We seem to know where you come from. We will go there and see what more we can learn." I saw her brighten at the news and went on: "But first, let us enjoy a day away from the confinement of ship life. I am eager to see the views of the Plunge from Candyk's Spire; the brochure makes extravagant claims. And I understand the Razhaman cuisine is sumptuous."

She cast her gaze down toward her clasped hands; at least she wasn't wringing them. "I am sorry that I snapped at you," she said. "You are doing so much for me, and with perhaps no hope of recompense."

"'Snapped'?" I said. "Hardly. And who knows? Perhaps you are a princess and heir to a fortune fit to buckle a baron's knees."

"I think not," she said. "My hands are rough and there are cords of muscle in my forearms. I must have earned my living through toil."

"Perhaps. Or we may find that the grand belles of Shannery are furious swordsters or quoit tossers. It may be that some squad of champion spearslingers may be missing their deadliest caster, and the great tournament fast approaching; they will welcome you back with glad cries and hearty claps on the back."

That made her smile, and as I stood and delivered an approximation of a javelin thrower going for distance, I heard Hespira laugh for the first time. I would not have wanted it to be the last.

"You should exhibit that imagination," she said. "It could win prizes."

"Imagine the best or the worst," I quoted, "it costs the same."

She stood. "Very well, let us visit Chumblot's clothier friend. After, we will peer into the Plunge, then on to dinner."

I gave her my arm and we went down to the lobby; I saw no need to bear the weight of my assistant, and left it to continue its researches. Chumblot was waiting with his conveyance at the foot of the Espantia's front ramp. "After the clothier's, we wish to visit Candyk's Spire," I said, "and while we're seeing what there is to see you can think of a good place for dinner."

His eyes flashed with honest greed and soon we were rolling toward the towering pinnacle of the Spire, which stood as high above the plateau as the plateau stood above the lowlands. The ground car was not large within, and Hespira's shoulder rested warm against mine. I took a deep breath and realized that I was oddly—most oddly, if I thought about it—content in her company.

But I did not think about it; instead, I cleared my mind and allowed myself to enjoy the moment. Could I go back to that afternoon, I would do exactly the same, for there were to be few such intervals of happy contentment in the days to come.

CHAPTER FOUR

Chumblot's friend had a vendery in a commercial precinct on the way to the Spire. As we drove toward it through the steepness of the city's streets, I noticed a host of other emporia dealing in clothing and accessories, far more than I would have seen in Olkney. Questioned, our driver revealed that, though fashion had as good a grip on the Razhaman soul as it had in most sophisticated societies, the cut and color of attire in this place served a more far-reaching service: they were crucial to the inhabitants' constant preoccupation with social rank.

"Some of us," Chumblot said, "who have had exposure to other ways and customs, have surmounted the worst parochial prejudices. To us, it matters not whether you are avauntseur or superlant, cedeposit or standforth, eighth degree or novice. We see the essence, the one within."

"But such liberality is rare."

"Sadly. Are you familiar with Wallader's theory that every society is fundamentally organized around one or another of the cardinal sins?"

"I believe not," I said.

"He argues that the true seed of every culture, whatever the ideals to which it gives lip service, always turns out to be one of the seven mortal iniquities identified by the ancients: pride, greed, and anger are the most common; lust, gluttony, and envy less so; those based on sloth usually do not last."

"And Razham's founding sin is pride?"

"With a supporting bid from lust," Chumblot said, "though that is often expressed in an overreaching romanticism. We live constrained lives, yet crave grand adventure. At the highest levels, young men practice the Ennoblanz."

The term was unfamiliar to me. The driver explained that it was a rigorous code of conduct under which unespoused superlants and elegantiasts would devote years of their adolescence and early manhood to the courting of cool-blooded ladies. The code featured strenuous sacrifices and ascetic vigils, for which the young men would be lucky to receive so much as a kiss-my-hand.

I felt Hespira shudder beside me. "Are you cold?" I said.

"Just a sudden chill," she said. "It has passed now."

The clothier was attentive and used to dealing with offworlders; I assumed she had some longstanding arrangement with our driver by which they both shared in the custom he delivered to her premises. She regarded my chit then chose for me: easy-fitting trousers and a short tunic of pale blue cotton; a sleeveless vest and matching half-boots, both of ocherdyed suede; and a cloche hat of polished leather ornamented with a bold panache of copper chased with silver.

"This will admit you to all but the most determinate premises, and with only moderate pause," she said. When I gave her a querying look, she expanded. "In places that are open to you, good manners decree an interval before you may enter and another interval before you are attended to. The length of pause varies with rank."

"And those places that are not open?"

"Some establishments cater only to the highest tiers. You would find it difficult to gain admittance. If you insisted on entering, your presence would go unacknowledged. If you remained obdurate, loitering expectantly, someone might spill hot liquid on you, or drop a heavy object on your toes."

"It seems an unnecessary impediment to good commerce," I said.

The woman's face expressed that sense of certainty that a traveler among the foundational domains soon comes to recognize. "To the contrary. Everyone knows what to expect, and daily life is securely anchored to a reliable structure."

Chumblot intervened. "Now, Shree, you cannot expect them to fit into our ways. They come from some little corner on the far side of nowhere. Besides, haven't we bent a rule or two ourselves?"

The woman softened somewhat, and laughed when he playfully beat on her upper arms with gentle fists. But her face showed outrage when the driver let her see the chit that had been imposed on my client by the arbiger. "Jumped-up little regulant," she growled. "We'll pay no heed to that."

But Hespira's status could not be readily determined, she being unable to answer any of Shree's questions about birth, heredity, or occupation. After a period of thoughtful chin-pulling and staring abstractedly into the middle distance, the clothier hit upon a solution. To Chumblot she said, "What if we made her a Sister of Repose?"

The driver threw a hand into the air, fingers spread. "Brilliant!" he said. "Who would question it?"

The clothier proceeded to enrobe my client in a long-sleeved gown of fine gray wool that she said was spun from the fleece of an indigenous mountain ungulate, then cinched it at the waist with a belt of linked hammered plates of a pale metal. Hespira's fiery curls were confined by a wire-mesh snood of the same metal, and her feet were shod in gray leather shoes with tiny buckles to echo the belt and hairnet. The composite effect was striking, the subdued colors and accessories evoking Hespira's natural dignity. I contributed a deep-kneed courtesy, executed with a flourish of wrist and fingers that would not have been out of place at the Archon's levee, and was rewarded with another of those remarkable laughs.

"What rank does this represent?" she asked.

The clothier's face exhibited several consecutive expressions before settling upon complacency. "It is a… special category," she said, "difficult to define. The important thing is that there will be no problems of admittance or undue pause."

"Especially if he is dominoed," said Chumblot. He and his friend gave each other a glance of shared mischief, then the woman reached into a drawer and brought out a half-mask of soft turquoise leather. They helped me to fit the earpieces and adjust the item so that I could see through the slits that covered my eyes. Only my lips and chin were left visible.

"That," said Chumblot, "will get the pair of you in anywhere." To Shree he said, "They want to eat well."

The aura of mischief deepened as Shree said, "The Greeneries? Is that what you are thinking?"

Chumblot's smile widened. "It is."

"'If a hill, why not a mountain?' as the old poet said," the clothier quoted. "They'll have a memorable time."

"And the high-toned will have a chance to unlimber their tongues."

"How they do love a good wag," said Shree.

I was catching the sense of this banter, but was concerned that some crucial details might have slid by me. "What are you proposing for us?" I said. "We do not wish to find ourselves suddenly surrounded by scandalized officials like that arbiger, their authority at full charge and ready to be unleashed at a pair of hapless visitors."

The two Razhamans fluttered their hands in a motion meant to disavow any danger. "No harm will come to you," Chumblot said. "These garments will admit you to the finest dining establishment in the city, without pause and with no questions asked."

"At least not of them," Shree said, and I would swear that the next sound that came out of her was a giggle, quickly suppressed.

"Come along," said our driver. "You will want to reach the Spire while the sun still has some warmth."

My assistant had said the man could be relied upon. What was the point of hiring local expertise if I was not going to trust their judgments? So, more sequints passed out of my purse, warm smiles were offered in all directions—particularly between our driver and the clothes vendor—and we returned to the ground car and our journey to Candyk's Spire. This remarkable eminence was north of Razham proper, but the city was compact and we were soon out beyond the suburbs and climbing the hills that ringed the Spire's lower slopes. The way became ever steeper, until finally we arrived at a plaza beyond which wheeled ground cars could not go.

Again Chumblot offered his advice: "The ride along the outside trail is rough," he said, adding a knowing nod and a frown—so we did not engage one of the eight-legged stalkers lined up at the foot of the path. Instead, we bought tickets on the funicular ascender that spiraled through the living rock of the mountain. Some sections of the ascender's course also brought it out of the darkness and into the light, so that we sometimes moved along a narrow ledge on the western face of the Spire and gained glimpses of the chasm above which the northern side of the mountain continued in a sheer cliff.

At last, we reached the ascender's terminus, a cavern hollowed out not far below the Spire's apex. The air here was remarkably thin and we heeded Chumblot's counsel, given down below, that we each take another supplement before venturing near the edge. When our breathing was steady, I took Hespira's warm hand and, as recommended by the signs hung about the walls, we slowly ventured toward the waist-high railing that was all that separated us from the Plunge.

To our backs and sides was the blue-gray fastness of Candyk's Spire, but now before and below us was nothing but a great emptiness. The continent's central plateau was riven by a chasm that dwarfed any I had seen up or down The Spray. It ran from east to west, huge enough to have swallowed whole counties of Old Earth, its sheer sides riven here and there by vertical crevices. From some of these issued streams of rushing water, where underground rivers suddenly met nothing but air and gravity.

The cataracts plunged down and down, yet they never splashed against the ground so far below; the Plunge was so deep that the torrents broke into droplets and the droplets were further disseminated into mists and clouds that hid the bottom of the chasm from view.

I was curiously affected by the sight, being reminded of the littleness of a human life against the immense scale here so flagrantly displayed. I felt at once tiny and beneath notice, yet also as if I owned some vital share in all this magnificence: for none of this, not the Spire, nor the Plunge, nor the rushing waters, nor the huge trees that sprouted from the cliffs like insignificant weeds, could comprehend itself. I half-remembered a line from some ancient hero-play, about how the deities of old wept bitterly after, in one of their periodic fits of temper, they had wiped out human-kind only to find themselves alone and unregarded. "For without us, the gods simply are; only with us, and by us, are they known."

I spoke the words aloud and felt Hespira move beside me. I turned and saw that she was shivering—a cold wind swept up the face of the Spire—and I put an arm around her shoulders. As I did so, I saw beyond her one of those quick motions that discriminators learn to note: some-one had been observing us and had quickly turned his head away as my gaze had shifted in his direction. Now the watcher looked out to right and left across the emptiness, as if fixing in memory a last image, and turned, with a casualness that I found suspect, toward the platform where the ascender became a descender. He caught my eye then, and flashed a fool's grin at me. A moment later, he was gone, dropping down into the bowels of the mountain.

I watched him go, wishing now that I had worn my assistant, or at least some elements of a surveillance suite, so that I could have captured his image and other details. I no longer had intuition to support me, but I had experience in plenty, and I would have bet against good odds that the man had been watching us. I called up a mental picture of him: middling in stature; of mature years and physically fit; clothed in the muted tans and deeper browns that locally denoted middling social rank, but without the adaptive anatomy of a Razhaman. He had had enough self-possession not to overreact when observed by the subject of his observation, and the sense to leave the scene before the slip could be followed up. The marks of a professional, I thought. But what about the idiot's grin he had sent my way?

Hespira was saying something. I looked and saw a double rainbow far below, where a gust of wind blowing along the chasm had briefly parted the mists and let the westering sun strike through. "Indeed," I said, "beautiful and unforgettable. But we should go down now. It grows cold and I, for one, grow hungry."

We were warmer when we arrived at the plaza, but hungrier. I assisted Hespira into the ground car than stood outside with Chumblot to discuss where to go for dinner.

"Your friend mentioned a place," I said.

"The Greeneries," he confirmed. "I am told it offers the finest meals in Razham."

"You have not dined there yourself?"

"The pause for such as me would stretch on forever."

"Yet foreigners are admitted?" I said. "So long as they are dressed—" I touched the mask that hid half my face. "—as we are?"

I saw that he was genuinely embarrassed. He looked at his toes, his brows working, then he hit upon something. "There is a brief," he said. "That will explain it." He gestured for me to enter the vehicle.

"A brief?"

"The Visitor's Bureau has prepared information for offworld persons who have need of… that is to say, when they discover they have certain… urges. Some will approach a driver and ask to be taken to…"

He gestured obscurely, his eyes averted, but after a moment's puzzlement, I suddenly understood. "By all means," I said, stepping toward the car, "let me see the brief."

"Excellent," Chumblot said. He gave me a look that said we were both men of experience whose minds, on matters of importance, met and meshed happily.

But I stopped as I was about to climb in and said, casually, "By the way, did you see a man come down from the descender shortly before us?" I described the watcher from the cavern above.

"I did," said Chumblot. He cast a quick glance Hespira's way and I saw a wariness enter the back of his eyes. "Did the man give offense?"

"No. I just wondered if I might have known him. Did you see where he went?"

He indicated an area across the plaza where vehicles could be left unattended. "I do not see him now," he said.

"No matter." I pressed another sequint into his hand. "But if you do notice him again, you could let me know."

He gave me another version of that knowing look; this one said we had just reached a new, deeper level of mutual understanding. "But quietly?"

he said, in a small voice.

"Yes," I said, "quietly would be best."

When I was seated in the passenger compartment the vehicle's screen appeared and began to display the "brief." At first, the screen remained blank while several stringed instruments played a particularly insipid passage. Then text appeared, informing me that the material about to be shown was "of an inciteful nature and not suitable for children or unspoused adults."

I looked up and saw that Chumblot's nape had flushed a deep red, and when I looked at the screen again I was faced by an avuncular but serious man of full years. He was sitting behind a desk in a setting whose decor, augmented by some complex-looking pieces of apparatus, suggested the office of a senior professional.

"Welcome to Razham," he said, then paused to give weight to what followed. "While visitors are expected to respect the mores of our society, we recognize that persons of other cultures may not have developed the self-discipline that is a universally admired attribute of the Razhaman. However, tumult and rowdiness will never be tolerated."

The speaker paused again to underline further the gravity of the subject, then his sternness relented by a bare fraction. He summoned up a smile that he intended would say that he was indeed a man of wide and tried experience. What followed was an oration marked by circumlocution and strained metaphor, from which I eventually winnowed certain hard facts.

The citizens of Razham and its surrounding districts, at all ranks of their society but most of all in the uppermost strata, were sexually repressed. Women, in particular, did not enjoy a free rein in the exercise of their libidos. Marriage was almost universal, but provided little relief: most Razhaman unions were coldly calculated affairs, designed to increase, or at least to hold, each partner's relative position in the many-tiered ladder on which their society was hung.

As in all such cultures, the stark tensions that resulted from this regime had to find some outlet, lest the homicide and suicide rates spiral beyond all toleration. The answer had come, back in times out of mind, when a clutch of dissatisfied matrons had formed a charitable order, The Sisters of Repose. The sorority's charter committed its members to perform only good works, though these were vaguely defined, and provided cloisters where their eleemosynary labors could be undertaken.

To these shuttered and closed-doored refuges, any mature Razhaman female could commit herself from time to time, there to work off her tensions on the large numbers of male Razhamans who presented themselves in need of the Sisters' charity. Each Sister had full discretion to choose which of these patrons she would accommodate; for their part, the men committed themselves to a standard of behavior that was often far higher than that with which they favored their spouses. If, as happened rarely, any "tumult" broke out, a special unit of the Watch would attend, wearing masks and armed with neural stingers; the offender would suffer immediate and painful consequences, regardless of rank.

The institution was known to all, though never publicly acknowledged. Its business was transacted behind closed doors, and Sisters were almost never seen outside the cloister. The exception was an option sometimes exercised by women of the loftiest superlant and elegantiast ranks who wished to correct their husbands' conduct. They would step out of the cloister clad in the gray habit of the Order and escorted by a masked relative or retainer. Ostensibly, the costume and mask conferred social invisibility on the wearers. She would not be addressed or acknowledged by any but her escort, who was himself socially invisible, and persons who knew her would affect not to. But the appearance of a habited Sister of Repose at a restaurant or theater immediately set off intense whispered speculations as to who she was, who her spouse was, and what sort of vileness he must have got up to, to inspire her to make such an egregious display.

The purpose of the "brief" was twofold: to alert visitors to the existence of the cloisters, should they be unable to restrain their urges; and to warn them off approaching any Sister of Repose in the rare instance of their encountering one in the outside world. Such a breach of etiquette would be punished instantly and far more severely than for a fracas in a cloister. "The wrongdoer," said the presenter of the brief, wearing his sternest face, "would beg for the neural stinger's fleeting caress."

I was sure that Chumblot and his clothier friend had meant no harm. As an amnesiac, Hespira had been impossible to place within Razham's tightly graded social hierarchy. In the guise of a Sister of Repose, she could go anywhere and experience minimal pause, and I too would equally be beyond question. It had been an inspired solution. But it would have been convenient for us if they had explained the peculiarities of the institution to us—which I realized they could not do, owing to the prudish reticence that cloaked the whole arena of sexual relations on this world.

As the brief finished, we arrived outside the Greeneries. This was an eatery set in a terraced garden not far from our hotel, with many small tables placed among fragrant bushes and luscious blooms that rightly belonged to Ikkibal's lowlands, but were protected from the harsher upland elements by being surrounded by perpetual curtains of warm air. It seemed to me that we arrived there by a somewhat circuitous route, and that our driver had been even more aware of the vehicles that shared the roads with us than before. As he helped Hespira out of the car, Chumblot caught my eye and his head moved in a subtle negative motion.

My mind still marveling at the implications of the brief and our costuming, it took me a moment to understand that the driver was indicating that we had not been followed by the man in brown.

"Very good," I said. I put the fellow's interest down to the implications of Hespira's garb. Then I cocked my head toward the restaurant's door, where the greeter, a deeply groomed personage in the dark greens and grays of a senior servitor, waited for us. Though the man was carefully not looking at us, it was plain that we were the sole focus of his attention. "Any recommendations as to the food?"

"The Four Glories," Chumblot said, without hesitation, "but the summer ale makes a better accompaniment than the wine. And it's cheaper."

I thanked him and we went in. The greeter was a master of his craft, offering us a precisely graduated expression of respectful welcome without actually acknowledging our presence. I noticed, though, that he gave Hespira a considering look before ushering us to our table. I also saw him engage in a short but emphatic conversation with one of the servers.

The place was well filled, the other patrons attired in combinations of black, silver, and gold, many of the fabrics diamond-patterned. All conversation and all sound of cutlery meeting plates ceased the moment Hespira came into view, and the room remained silent except for the tinkling of a tintinnabulary fountain that combined thin arcs of water with tiny bells of different sizes and metals, to a very pleasing effect. The greeter led us to a table near the pool, a spot so located amid the greenery as to make it effectively a private booth. Above the music of the fountain I heard a rising buzz of whispered commentary punctuated by two or three barks of laughter.

"I think we have been very discreetly placed," my client said.

"I think you are right. Did you understand the import of the brief Chumblot showed us?"

"I believe so," she said. She tried for an arch expression, with comic effect. "Shall I endeavor to appear mysterious?"

"You will not need to try," I said. "You are already mysterious. And by the glances we drew as we entered, I would say that we are already the most interesting couple in the room—and it is not I who has earned us that distinction."

"It is just harmless playacting?" she said, uncertainty showing beneath the gaiety. It drew a protective response from me, and I assured her she would come to no harm.

"In that garb, you are sacrosanct," I said. "It is all the rest who must beware a fate worse than neural stingers."

The server came, carefully averting his eyes from both of us. We ordered as Chumblot had recommended; what was the point of getting good advice if one did not take it? The Four Glories turned out to be a succession of baked pastries: the first filled with a boneless fish; the second with a light-fleshed fowl; the third with a richer meat in gravy; the last with sharp cheese. Seasonal vegetables and small dishes of varied sauces supported the pies, and the summer ale was as perfect an accompaniment as Chumblot had advertised, light and nutty with an odor of sweet apples.

Between the third and fourth courses, I asked Hespira if any of the tastes were familiar. She answered that she was sure she had eaten similar dishes, but none as handsomely prepared. "If you are expecting to find that I am some lost princess, I fear you will be disappointed. I think I am but an ordinary girl from some little house down some little road."

"That would not disappoint me," I said. "Whatever else you may be, you are my excuse for a highly enjoyable trip. I am beginning to think that I have devoted far too much of my life to my profession and not nearly enough to the simple business of living."

Then the cheese tarts arrived and we went straight at them. By the time we had finished them and made our way through two cups of punge—a sharper blend than was usual on Old Earth—I had a distinct feeling of roundedness. But I had learned from many a trip out among the Ten Thousand Worlds that every world—especially the Grand Foundationals—has the potential for gastronomical exquisitry and a wise traveler does not forgo an opportunity to discover another of them.

I summoned the server and asked to see the dessert card. It appeared in the air before us and I read the entries, each with its description of ingredients and their promised effects on palate and mood. At the bottom, in discreetly small type, I noticed a dish described only as "Singular Cream," with no embellishments.

"What is that?" I asked, pointing to the laconic item.

The server flicked his eyes over Hespira and me and said, "I am not sure that is available."

Ordinarily, when the phrase "not available" is spoken in a restaurant it means that earlier-arriving diners have consumed that day's supply of the item referred to, or that the dish has waited too long and has spoiled. But there was something in the server's tone that led me to hear an unspoken addendum to "not available"—the words "to you."

"What do you mean?" I said.

The fellow lowered his tone as if broaching a subject that ought to go unmentioned in public. "Singular cream is only available to persons of upper superlant and elegantiast rank."

"How do you know," I said, "that we are not of that rank?"

His eyes went over us again, lingering for a moment on Hespira's costume, which seemed to give him pause. But when he inspected me, his doubts evaporated. "You would appear... different," he said, and when I affected not to understand, he whispered, "Your accent. I suspect you are offworlders."

I had always been a great respecter of other peoples' customs; indeed, it was the only safe attitude to take if one wished one's travels among the worlds of The Spray not to be interrupted by unfortunate incidents like being urinated upon or spending time in official custody. But my curiosity was aroused, so I reached into an inner pocket and withdrew a small but quite beautiful jewel. This I placed beside my ale glass and said, "And if I add this to my palette? How do my colors appear now?"

His face did not change, except around the eyes, which suddenly became as bright as the faceted stone. "Is it possible," he said, his fingers drifting toward the stone, "that on your world, the colors worn by superlants are different?"

"It is quite possible," I said.

The stone disappeared. The server looked about cautiously. "I will see what I can do," he said.

He returned bearing a salver completely hidden beneath a domed cover that he did not remove until the view of other patrons and staff was completely blocked by the surrounding plants and the server's back. Beneath the cover were two tiny bowls of damascened silver, each containing a pale custard, and two small silver spoons. I reached for one of the implements, but the server quickly signaled that I should wait.

"There is a... a ritual," he said, and proceeded to demonstrate. He was still holding the cover of the salver. Now he lifted Hespira's spoon and briskly struck the former with the latter, sounding a chime that resonated in sudden silence as the background buzz of conversation abruptly ceased. The man set down my client's spoon and took up mine, again ringing a clear, thin note from the cover. In the silence, the sound reverberated until it slowly died away. Only then, as the server returned the spoon to the table, did the restaurant refill with the susurration of subdued voices.

"Is it an ancient ritual?" I asked.

"No. Indeed, the singular cream has only lately been introduced to Razham."

"From where?" I wondered.

The server's brows drew in. "I have never been told. I have heard that it comes from some secondary world. I do know that its means of manufacture is a secret and that it is exclusively supplied only to the most select establishments."

Intrigued, I dipped my spoon into the stuff, finding it neither liquid nor solid, but something in between. I brought it to my lips and sniffed discreetly, getting a pungent odor like that of roasted chestnuts steeped in spiced wine. With the waiter watching as if he were the tutor and I his student poised on the brink of enlightenment, I delivered the spoon's contents to my tongue. The first taste was simple sweetness, the texture a creaminess that instantly dissolved. Then came a wash of an indescribable flavor, something like lobster that had been fed for years on almond paste, accompanied by a lingering musty finish for which the only word I could summon was "haunting." By the time I had registered this final sensation, the mouthful had disappeared.

I looked up at the waiter. "I did not swallow," I said.

He spoke softly. "The residue is absorbed by the flesh of the mouth and throat. Or so I am told." From the pause between the two statements, I deduced that the servers, as always, had sampled the dish, privileges of rank be damned.

"Remarkable." I dipped into the bowl again. Though the spoon was half the size of that with which I had stirred my punge, it scooped up half of what remained. "Only three mouthfuls to a customer?" I said.

"More is inadvisable. The palate becomes overwhelmed, the joy debased." He leaned closer and whispered, "Also, it can become addictive."

Again, I would take the advice of a local expert. But I ate the second and the third spoonfuls with a joy that mingled with sadness. Pleasure cannot last, else it ceases to be pleasure, I quoted to myself as the final must-freighted wisp of flavor faded on the back of my tongue, wondering if the ancient epigrammist who coined the aphorism had ever tasted singular cream. The thought led me to another wondering.

"What is it?" I asked the waiter. "Is it of animal or vegetative origin?"

Again, the man knew little. "It is said to come from an isolated commune in some small canton on a secondary world, a whimsy or two from here. I cannot vouch for the truth of that, but I have heard it from several sources. As to what it is made of, the recipe is an absolute secret. Our senior chef tried to isolate the ingredients, but even his superb palate could not decipher their subtle intermixture."

I did not doubt it. Though I had a more than educated palate, I could not have deduced the substances that combined to create the cream's singular taste. "And you do not know what world?" I said.

He smiled dismissively. "Some rough little place," he said, "that harbors a single jewel. The Spray is full of such inconsistencies."

Hespira made a small noise. I had paid her no attention since the singular cream arrived, so rapt was I in its uniqueness. Now I looked at her and saw that she had taken a mouthful from her own bowl; on her face was an expression like that of someone who strains to hear a note so faint as to be on the farthest edge of hearing.

"Do you know the taste?" I said. Scent and flavor are the deepest seated of the senses, acquired by our remotest ancestors even before they developed eyes or the faculty of locomotion; the memories they create are the last to fade, even when the forgetting is imposed under duress.

She looked at me, her green eyes wide with recognition. "Not the taste," she said, "but the scent of it, that, yes, and most definitely." Then she shook her head and said, "But I don't know where I know it from."

I turned to the waiter. "Where, besides here, might my companion have encountered singular cream?"

"In Razham, three other restaurants besides this one," he said.

"Not down at New Kutt?" I said.

"No. The supply is very limited."

"Only four places on all of Ikkibal," I said, "and all of them cater to a wealthy clientele."

"It is not a question of wealth," the man corrected me, with an acerbic pursing of his lips, "but of rank."

"Ah," I said. "And it does not go to other worlds?"

"Apparently the commune will export only to Razham."

"And you truly have no idea where it comes from?" I said.

"I have heard gossip, but it was from less than credible sources." The waiter reached to take away the empty bowls. "Two spacers arguing in a tavern," he said, lowering his voice again. "Both claimed to have seen it on cargo manifests. One said it came from Tuk, the other said Shannery. When I sought to join the conversation, they disdained me. I would not take that from such rough fellows. I left."

The vanity of social rank, coupled with a lust for gossip, seemed to be the twin elements of the Razhaman soul; but in this specimen, at least, pride outranked prurience. I paid the score and added an appreciative gratuity then led Hespira to the exit. I noted that once again she drew sidewise glances and provoked some behind-the-hand murmurs, whereas I sparked little curiosity.

Chumblot was waiting for us. When my client was settled in her seat I delayed joining her, as I could see the Razhaman had some news to impart. "That man," he said, pitching his voice low, "I saw him again."

"Indeed?"

"He drove by. Twice."

"Ah. And did he seem curious?"

"He looked this way, both times."

"Hmm," I said. "Probably nothing, but thank you." I pressed another sequint into his hand and moved to enter the car. But as Chumblot's palm took the coin, his fingers passed me a small piece of folded paper. "I took his particulars," he said.

I slipped the paper into a pocket of the suede vest and got in beside Hespira. "What were you two whispering about?" she said.

"It would be premature to say," I told her.

"A surprise?"

"For somebody, perhaps."

Outside the Espantia, I asked Chumblot to call for us after breakfast. He looked at me sideways. "Maybe I will see that fellow again."

"It might be better if you did not," I said. "He was, after all, only looking."

His heavy shoulders lifted and settled, his brows moved and one corner of his mouth briefly disappeared.

"Let it be," I said. "Tomorrow, if he still hovers, we will decide what to do."

For a moment, his face resembled that of a boy denied an outing, then he showed me his palms in a gesture of acceptance, and we parted. Hespira was waiting at the top of the ramp, an unvoiced question in her expression. I waved away her curiosity, saying, "It is nothing."

The man at the door opened for us and we entered the lobby. I noticed that he regarded us with covert astonishment, far more interest than he had shown when he had first admitted us earlier that day. Our passage across the lobby also drew a startled glance from the clerk, which was quickly transformed into that expression of polite neutrality that hotel clerks must master in their first week or else there is no second. But behind the facade I sensed genuine apprehension.

It was the kind of hotel where the guest left the key at the desk before going out and recouped it upon return. I recovered both our keys, then led Hespira toward the ascender, but midway across the common space I bade her continue on her own and wait for me, while I returned to the desk.

"Pardon me," I said, "is there something of which my companion and I should be aware, but might not be?"

The clerk seemed a person of broad experience but my question brought a flush of color to his neck. He averted his gaze. "I don't know what you mean," he said.

"Yes," I said, "you do. It is I who does not know."

He looked about and, although there was no one but us within earshot, he lowered his voice. "This is a public place. One does not discuss…" He moved one hand in a complex and subtle gesture from which I was apparently supposed to draw a significant meaning. But I could not.

"No one can overhear us," I said, I drew three sequints from my purse and slid them across the counter to him. His head lowered and his eyes flicked from side to side then his hand covered the shining metal. He leaned toward me and whispered, "Your…" He struggled for a word, then settled on the one I had used—"your 'companion' is wearing the habit of a Sister of Repose. You are dominoed."

"Yes," I said, "I know. It is a necessary subterfuge."

"But I took you for offworlders."

"We are."

I saw his mental gears try to engage this information but fail to mesh fully. "Is the… the institution also established on—" He consulted a screen in the top of the desk. "—Old Earth?"

"No," I said. "For reasons I do not care to explain, my companion is unable to establish rank. The subterfuge is merely to spare her embarrassment."

"Ah," said the clerk, relief taking the stiffness out of his pose. "So there is no prospect of some enraged dominee arriving with his retainers and…"

He realized he had said more than was necessary.

But now my own gears had engaged. I realized that Chumblot's brief had told only the official story which, as in many sophisticated societies, departed starkly from the practical facts. "So the institution is not as neatly operative a solution as advertised to offworlders."

Plainly, he would have preferred to push no farther into that particular thorn bush, but I slid another sequint across the counter, meanwhile signaling to Hespira that I would rejoin her shortly.

"Well," said the clerk, lowering his voice to a whisper, "there was the case of Excellence Issus Khal. I'm sure you've heard of it."

"I don't believe so."

"Really?" He consulted his countertop screen. "Where did you say you are from? Everyone here was talking about the Khal Affair." From the way he said the last two words, I inferred the capital "A."

"I may have been traveling," I said. "Please enlighten me."

He paused expectantly, his eyes dropping to my hand in which he could hear sequints chiming.

I said, "If what I hear is indeed enlightening…" I clinked the coins meaningfully.

Watching him, I realized that greed was only part of his motivation, and perhaps not even the greater part. I was coming to realize that, as in many repressed cultures, salacious gossip was irresistible to Razhamans, who found it as delightful a gift to give as to receive.

"Well," he said again, and in a hushed but rushing voice he told me the tale of Issus Khal, a dominee of elegantiast rank, whose spouse had departed their manse for the Sisterhood. It was understood that she felt she had been "given cause," as the Razhamans said, because rather than leave through the "small door" at the rear of the house, she had stepped boldly out of the main portico, during the early evening when the streets were filled for the daily promenade. She had gone straight to the cloister, but soon reappeared in public, escorted by a dominoed bravo who was reputed to be the sole recipient of her favors whenever she returned to the house of the Sisters.

Word of the contretemps between Khal and his lady had spread like oil on still water. The dominee found himself unable to visit his favorite haunts and habitudes; all were full of whispers and half-hidden smirks. In due course, he made an offer to the errant lady, as was customary, but such was his pride that the overture was scanty and delivered with poor grace, Khal having sent it by way of an underhousemaid rather than through her matradomo. Now deeply offended, his estranged spouse rebuffed him and redoubled her escorted excursions, making sure to visit his favorite dining spots and even having her companion insist that they be seated in her spouse's favorite boite.

The dispute was on every Razhaman tongue for two weeks. At the beginning of the third, Issus Khal waited in an alley across from the Sister House. When the lady appeared, he followed her to a pleasure garden in the exclusive Radiast district. There he accosted her and her escort. Hard words were flung, caught, and returned as blows. A bitter struggle ensued. Though the attendants rushed to pull apart Khal and his spouse's paramour, they were, ironically, as inseparable as the married couple were not. By the time Khal's fingers had been pried from the lover's throat, that organ had admitted its last breath.

The Watch seized Issus Khal, conducted a scarcely necessary discrimination, and sent him to the procurator-major for trial. That process would require a jury of the dominee's peers, and in Razham that standard was taken literally—only persons of elegantiast rank could sit in judgment on him. In the time-honored manner, the procurator-major canvassed Khal's social equals and was surprised to find there was no shortage of nominees willing to take the pledge of unbias and a seat on the adjudication bench; of those ready to condemn Khal there was ample supply, of those inclined to bless him there was a pronounced shortage.

The panel met, the case was presented, witnesses told their salty tales before a room-filling throng, and judgment was duly delivered. Somehow, based apparently solely on his own high opinion of his worth and the utter probity of his actions, Issus Khal had expected to be absolved. So, when the tally sticks were passed to the head of the bench, with each and every one of them found to be black—not even one gray amongst them, let alone a white—the condemned threw what Razhamans called "the full bubble" of raging fit, hurling insults and imprecations in every direction, and threatening dire retribution on all concerned.

He was hauled away, still foaming and spitting, to the incarcery. But scarcely had be begun the program of withy-weaving and coarse stitchery mandated for mankillers, than unknown persons entered the institution under cloak of darkness and took him away. Dawn found his private yacht gone from the spaceport, as was his almost-grown son, Imrith, and their body servants. They were not heard from again, although some months later, each of the members of the adjudication panel, as well as several supposed friends of Khal's who had declined to sit, received a vindicat.

This was the traditional instrument by which Razhamans of superlant rank formally announced a vendetta: a small wooden box, delivered anonymously to the target's doorstep, which when opened would be found to contain an unwholesome substance that had been personally produced by the sender.

All this the clerk imparted to me in hushed tones, his eyes glancing here and there about the almost empty lobby. "I see," I said, when the contents of the vindicat had been explained to me, "and you thought that my companion and I might be participants in another such drama."

"One sees few of the highest ranks outside their exclusive milieus," he said. "One might not recognize a lady who, until now, has kept herself within the ambit." He explained that that was the term for the tightly circumscribed social circle in which moved the loftiest Razhamans.

"Please be assured," I said, "that such is not the case. We are merely offworlders who took local advice on how to present ourselves. In all likelihood, we will be gone tomorrow."

I passed him three sequints and went to rejoin Hespira. I was thinking that the tale he had told explained the whispers and sidelong glances at the Greeneries. It might also throw some perspective on the interest shown by the man atop Candyk's Spire. A Razhaman woman appearing in public with a masked escort was an irresistible stimulus to these people's fascination with tittle-tat. The man in brown may have rushed off to tell his drinking mates of the newsworthy sight he had seen.

There was another, more worrisome, possibility. Suppose the long-suffering spouse of some neglectful local superlant had taken herself off to the cloister with a threat to appear in public? The dominee might have agents out to inform him if she made good on the threat. Hespira and I might be mistaken for the errant lady and her paramour, an error that could take a potentially dangerous turn before the innocent truth was discovered.

The clerk was watching me as I thought, no doubt storing impressions to be passed on to whomever he knew who might be agog at the doings of offworlders. Another question occurred to me, and I put it to him: were the amorous customs on Shannery similar to those on Ikkibal?

The alarm on his face told me the answer even before he leaned closer and whispered, "Not at all! They are animals, coupling higgledy-piggledy, without consideration of rank. They wouldn't know a decent pause if it came in with trumpets and clashing cymbals."

I returned to my client and we went into the ascender. As we rose, I told her of the Khal Affair and the inferences the patrons of the Greeneries must have drawn from our appearance there. She found the business quite amusing; coupled with the clerk's description of affairs on Shannery, that was another point that argued for her being a native of that secondary world.

"We will go there in the morning," I said, opening the door to my room. She entered with me, intending to pass through the closed connecting door to hers. "I am confident that—" I continued, only to be interrupted by a tiny point of light that flashed briefly against my retina: a silent signal from my assistant, which I had left in its armature draped over the back of a chair.

I made a small series of motions, a code that prompted the integrator to begin to play a prerecorded, innocuous conversation in which we discussed the speculations of Immeriot, an early Twentieth-Aeon philosopher who had been struck by a vision that led him to believe that the universe was some kind of giant seed that would someday sprout into a remarkable plant. Other sages had dared him to prove that this odd contention was true, but he had waved them all off, saying, "Prove that it isn't!" and cackling in a manner that set his colleagues' gears to grinding. Meanwhile, I signaled to Hespira that she should remain still and not speak.

"There has been an incident," the integrator said, so that only I could hear. "In the client's room."

I kept a small shocker fixed to a harness strapped to my right forearm. I flexed my wrist now and the weapon slid forward into my palm, and when I closed my fist the emitter poked through my fingers. I faced the connecting door, then half-turned my head toward my assistant.

I moved my lips without sound. "What kind of incident?"

"Something entered the room and moved about."

"Something?" I expected more precision.

"It was clouded," the integrator said.

"It must have been well clouded if you were not able to pierce through the obfuscation."

"Indeed, it was a high-order system. I did not recognize the type."

That raised all kinds of points to be considered, but I dealt with the most important first. "Is it still there?"

"No."

"Did it leave anything behind?"

"A surveillance device, also clouded, also high-order. I have been unpicking it, but it is complex."

"Anything else to report?"

"From an analysis of the intruder device's motions, I believe it searched the room."

"A nominal search or intensive?"

"By the length of time, intensive."

"Hmm," I said.

Hespira had been watching my lips move. "What is—" she began.

Again I signaled her to silence but saw her react with annoyance. I picked up my assistant and draped it over my shoulders, then indicated that we should go out into the hallway, the discussion of Immeriot's Theorem still ongoing. We had reached the point in the discussion where the old sage had pointed out that, to us denizens of the cosmos, it mattered not a whit what its nature was, nor what it might later become. To quote Immeriot: "It is as hugely irrelevant to us as the literary outpourings of a poet are to a bacterium living in his lower bowel. Indeed, to an even tinier mite living in the bacterium's vacuole. It just doesn't matter."

With this going on, I took her arm and walked her back to the ascenders where, judging the distance sufficient, I put my lips to her ear and explained the situation in whispers. She stiffened in fear and my fingers, resting in the crook of her elbow, felt the dampness of a sudden rush of perspiration. Once again, I was unexpectedly affected by emotion, experiencing an urge to protect her, an impetus so strong that I realized that I had unconsciously turned to put myself between her and the hallway down which we had just come, the hand holding the shocker half-raised, though there was no threat.

I mastered the impulse and spoke again in her ear. "We will go back to my room where you will wait while I, wearing my assistant, enter your room. I believe there is no danger; it is only a surveillance device. But we will take all precautions."

She took a deep breath and showed me that she was ready. We did as I said we would, she remaining just inside the door of my room while I passed through the connector to hers, the Immeriot discourse still in play. With my assistant closer to the intruder's left-behind and coming at it from another angle, we were able to identify the tiny spots at which the clouded device poked minuscule-but-powerful percepts through the web of woven energies—for the disadvantage of a clouded device is that it can neither send nor receive information through its own cloud. Now my integrator was able to insinuate its influence through the cloud. As I had expected, the device turned out to be a sophisticated form of peeper, able to detect not just visible light and audible sound, but emanations in several other spectra; it could register vibrations as subtle as the small motions of a subject's digestive tract or read the trace chemicals from an exhaled breath, allowing the receiver of all this information to deduce much about the person under observation.

The peeper was almost as good as some that I had myself designed and built. But since we had penetrated its disguising emanations without its being aware that we had done so, we could now begin to feed it a set of false impressions. It came to believe that Hespira had come into the room and was preparing to retire, while the integrator and I nattered on about cosmic seeds and the possible shapes of the grand blooms that they promised. It protruded its tiny emitter and began to report its news to a remote receiver.

I went back into my room and closed the connecting door. I let the Immeriot blather wind down, now that we could speak openly.

"Who has put that device in my room?" Hespira said. The anxiety in her voice disturbed me but I maintained a calm and professional aspect. "And why?"

"It may be," I said, "a result of your costume. Some upper-tier husband, whose spouse has left him for the cloister, hears that a woman has been seen out and about, dressed as you are, and takes steps to determine if the problem she presents is his."

She was only a little relieved. "Is that likely?"

"It is a reasonable explanation."

But I knew it was not the only logical rationale. The incident had taken me by surprise—an eventuality that, however rare, I never cared to admit to—and I was belatedly turning my mind toward a full consideration of where we were and what we were doing.

I had been remiss. I had made assumptions and acted upon them, and now it appeared that I had been wrong to do so. For example, I had assumed that the difficulties with Massim Shar and Irslan Chonder had been safely left behind on Old Earth, because although either might discover that I had gone offworld, it was unlikely that either would be able to discover where I had gone. But perhaps one, or even both, of them had been better than I had given them credit for. They might well still see me as a piece in whatever game of deadly pride they were playing.

There was another possibility, however. I had early on come to the conclusion that Hespira's memory had been taken from her by some outside agent; it was not the sort of thing one person did to another out of kindness, and I could only think of the perpetrator as her enemy, and therefore mine. But I had chosen to defer the question of who that adversary might be until I had determined who Hespira was. I had assumed that, once dumped on far-away Old Earth, she had ceased to matter to whoever had done the dumping. I now saw that that could have been a substantial error in judgment—a lapse that I might not have made had I still been equipped with my old insight.

I am not what I was, I told myself, and I must remember to compensate for my loss.

"For safety's sake," I informed Hespira, "you should sleep in my room tonight. My assistant will keep watch, and I am armed."

For once she did not offer any suspicion at my motives, and I hoped that my conduct had finally convinced her that I did not desire her physically. She wanted to get some night things from her room and, shocker in hand, I accompanied her there and back again. Soon, after a certain amount of shuttling between the main room and the attached sanitary suite, she was at rest on the sleeping pallet and I was curled up in a chair that did its best to accommodate me, once it realized that I was attempting to sleep in it.

But first I consulted my assistant, using our silent method of communication. "Extend your awareness to encompass the hotel and its environs," I said.

"Done."

"Is the surveillance device reporting to a receiver in the hotel?"

"No, to a floater high above. It relays the signal via a focused beam."

"To where?"

"To what I take to be a vehicle parked on a disused property in an industrial zone. It too is well clouded."

"I assume you cannot dispel the clouding from this distance?"

"Correct."

The set-up had all the marks of a professional. I chose a course of action. "Contact Chumblot," I said. "Tell him that tomorrow I will arise early and that I will expect him at the rear of the hotel at daybreak. Tell him that there may be a substantial bonus for him."

A moment later my assistant said, "He is unavailable, but his integrator has accepted the message."

"Maintain vigilance; I especially wish to know if the receiver's vehicle moves."

I awoke short of breath in the thin light of a Razhaman dawn and took another of the oxygen supplements. Hespira slept on, but the disarranged covers of the sleeping pallet showed that she had passed a restless night. I drew the covers up to her chin and left a supplement where she would see it upon awakening. Then I spoke in silent mode to my assistant. "What of Chumblot?"

"No reply."

"Try him again."

"The result is the same."

I could not wait for the driver. I would go down to the rear of the hotel, in case he had received my message and acted upon it without acknowledgement. If he was not there, I decided that I would not have the hotel find me another driver; I would hire a vehicle and operate it myself.

"You will remain here to continue to delude the peeper," I told my assistant, "and be of service to our client if she awakens before I return."

With that, I descended to the hotel's ground floor and found a service passageway that led to the rear of the building. Utility vehicles were coming and going, delivering supplies for the kitchens and laundry, but of Chumblot and his car there was no sign. I wondered if he had found a more lucrative assignment, or perhaps he felt that he had earned enough yesterday to entitle himself to a day of leisure. Years of travel up and down The Spray had taught me that attitudes toward getting and spending could vary widely from world to world.

After one last look to make sure he was not parked behind some waste bins, I reentered the hotel and approached the front desk, where the night clerk was preparing to go off duty. Before she did so, she ordered me an aircar and said it would arrive shortly.

I went back up to my room and awakened Hespira. She came out of a dream with a gasp, a hand raised as if to ward off an attack.

"What is it?" I said. "What were you dreaming?"

She gave me a blank, uncomprehending look, then recognition came into her eyes. I repeated my questions and saw her reaching back for the dream. But it was gone, leaving only an impression of being surrounded by enemies, hemmed in by threats.

"Do you recall faces, voices?"

She half sighed, half shuddered. "Only the feeling, the desperation of being trapped."

Her long face was drawn and gray. I urged her to take the oxygen supplement and in a few moments a healthier color returned to her skin. "Chumblot has not come," I said.

"Why not?"

"I cannot say. I have engaged an aircar. I will go and see what I can learn about whoever placed that device in your room."

"You will leave me alone?"

"My assistant will be with you, and I will leave you the shocker."

"I don't know how—"

I took off the weapon and set it on a table. "It is self-aiming. My assistant will operate it remotely on your behalf, if you prefer."

She was sitting up on the pallet, the covers bunched around her legs, the smell of a night's troubled sleep hovering around her. A frightened woman is never pretty, nor are most women in the first moments of the day, and since Hespira was already carrying a deficit in the attractiveness ledger, this was not an occasion when she might have won hearts. And yet again I felt that strong sense of protectiveness. "Do not worry," I said. "I will let no harm come to you."

My concern led me to enunciate detailed instructions to my assistant, which the integrator soon gave me to understand were unnecessary. "Until you return," it said, "we will continue the research into conditions on Shannery."

I had let it slip my mind that I had set it to that task. But while we had visited Spire and Plunge, dined amid whispers and covert glances, then dealt with the matter of the peeper, my assistant had been in intermittent contact with ships going to and from the secondary world where they said "flippadiday" instead of "flippydedoo."

There were always delays in communications between worlds. On Ikkibal itself, or between the planet and its several satellites and myriad orbitals, communications were fast and full. But between Ikkibal and Shannery lay a vast gulf of emptiness, traversable only through a whimsy that lay about a day away at the normal speed of most ships in normal space and whose other end opened about a half-day's passage from Shannery.

The connectivity could not operate through whimsies, the only way to transmit a message from world to world was to entrust it to the integrator of a ship that was outbound from Ikkibal for Shannery. When that ship cleared the whimsy and was falling toward its destination, its integrator would pass all of its messages to the Shannery connectivity, to be delivered to their recipients. Responses would be handed to a ship bound for Ikkibal, which would dump them into that world's communication system as soon as it was within range.

A question put into the respective connectivities of several different worlds might be days in the answering, even weeks if the respondents were on remote, far-flung worlds that were not frequently visited. But Shannery was a secondary world of Ikkibal, the foundational domain from which had come the pioneers who had settled the new planet, so there was but one whimsy separating the two, and ships large and small plied it frequently. So my assistant had been sending out queries and having them answered for the better part of a full day now.

"Have you learned anything useful?" I said.

"Nothing I would call definitive," it said, "but enough to indicate that Shannery is the most likely world on which our client learned to speak, and that her speech patterns betray no overlays that would indicate she has spent much time elsewhere."

"Good," I said. "Keep working on it."

"There," I said to Hespira. "We are a long step closer. I would suggest that, while I am away, you look at images of representative landscapes and cityscapes on Shannery, and perhaps some well-known personages and historical events. They may stimulate associative memories. At the very least, they will serve to delineate the limits to which the amnesia extends."

The prospect of having something concrete to do cheered her, or at least suppressed her anxieties. I instructed my assistant to order some breakfast—and quietly reminded it to scan the food and its deliverer thoroughly—then departed. The aircar was waiting at the bottom of the hotel's front ramp. I entered it, negotiated the terms of its engagement—always a wise thing to do before leaving the ground—then had it fly me directly to where the *Gallivant* stood.

The vessel had nothing unusual to report, and I did not offend its sense of its own shipliness by instructing it to be watchful. The yacht would make itself aware of any person, device, or energy that impinged upon its privacy and would not take any such trespass lightly. I went aboard, received its report with thanks, then went to a locker in my quarters where I kept the tools of my trade.

A short while later I was airborne again, with another shocker in my pocket and, in case of any serious situations, a self-activating energy pistol in a holster strapped to my leg. I also carried a compact device of my own design and manufacture, which I was confident would deal with whatever waited in the back yard of the empty manufactury, listening to my integrator's artful fabrications.

My hired aircar, however, was unclouded and I lacked both the time to equip it with the means to arrive undetected and the inclination to argue with the vehicle about making the modifications. So I instructed it to set me down a fair but walkable distance from the target and bade it wait for my return, or to come quickly if I signaled by activating its remote starter.

The area was utilitarian, its bland-faced buildings designed more for functionality than for any uplift of the spirit, its wide and straight streets invariably meeting at right angles. I might have been in the industrial precinct of any city on a thousand worlds, except that even here the locals indulged their affection for steep flights of stairs. I had not seen the calf muscles of a Razhaman, but I was sure that those of men and women alike would resemble densely knotted tree roots.

I consulted my locator as I walked and stopped when it told me that the coordinates of the target vehicle were at the rear of a building across an arterial street from where I stood. Traffic on the thoroughfare was increasing as the day's work began in earnest, heavy vehicles and smaller carry-alls moving in both directions. I put the locator away and deployed my hand-held surveillance unit which had the outer appearance of a dog-eared, pocket-sized book whose cover bore the title: *Guide to a Miscellany of Interesting Planets.*

The device surveyed the nearby surroundings and told me that no one's gaze was turned my way, nor were any energies registering my presence. No one's heart rate or breathing had changed as I had turned the last corner that led me here, nor had anyone spoken a word or phrase that could be connected with my movements. I put the book in a pocket of my vest, waited for a brief lacuna in the traffic, and crossed to the other side of the street, where I consulted the device again. My actions had drawn no reactions, save for an inventive curse voiced by the operator of a heavily laden truck who had had to swerve to avoid me.

I put away the book again and looked up at the building behind which lay the vehicle that was receiving the focused beam of false information from the peeper in Hespira's room. The structure was a gray cube, three stories high and featureless except for a double door, a few small windows, and some grills that I presumed had to do with ventilation. There was grime on the windows, and before the doors lay enough accumulated grit and oddments of debris to suggest that the step had not been swept for weeks.

To one side, an alley led to the rear, where I expected to find the loading docks for whatever had once been made in this abandoned place. I went silently along the building's side, stopping short of where the alley met the vehicle yard. Again, I consulted my false book, this time adjusting its settings to give me a constructed view of the scene around the corner. The device told me that the vehicle stood where it had been when my assistant had first detected it. It was an unremarkable ground car, though the system that was clouding it was versatile and finely calibrated; even though it had been briefed by my assistant, the surveillance unit required several seconds to insinuate itself through the multilayered web of masking energies that surrounded the car. Then the reality was revealed.

I went forward. The vehicle was not defended nor did any ha-ha wait to spring its fateful surprise. It was not even locked, my device had informed me, and directed me to where I could seize the handle of the hatch that led into the operator's compartment. I threw it open, saw what I expected to see: a receive-and-record unit that had all night been accepting the information beamed from the floater above the Espantia that had, in turn, relayed it from the peeper I had found in Hespira's room.

But it was not the device that concerned me, nor was it the clouder that rested on the car's instrument panel, its deluded sensors still telling it that it was functioning admirably. What drew a gasp from me was the object on which the receive-and-record sat. It was man-sized and man-shaped, folded to conform to the contours of the operator's seat, and completely and tightly wrapped in a semi-transparent material that was obviously airtight.

I knew it was airtight because the man-sized, man-shaped object it enfolded had been a man. Even through the thick membrane I could see that his lips bore the blue tint of oxygen deprivation, and the sightless eyes told me that there was no point in ripping the material in an attempt to let life-giving air reach the deflated lungs.

Carthew Chumblot had long since taken his last breath.

CHAPTER FIVE

"The question is: was Chumblot's murder a message?" I said to my assistant, when I had returned to my room at the hotel and told what I had found. I saw no point in keeping the news of our driver's murder from Hespira. Whatever was going on, she was part of it, and though in some ways her condition made her as vulnerable as a child, she was in fact an adult and entitled to know the situation. Still, I did not dwell on the details, but assured her that Chumblot had not suffered.

"The method of it, and the leaving of the body to be discovered where it was, argue for an intent to send a message," my assistant said, "unless the killer has a fetish for suffocation. But the content of the message is ambiguous. Does it say, 'We are ice-blooded killers, and you are next'? Or 'Submit to being watched; we will brook no interference'? Is it threat or dominance?"

"Or," I said, " 'Don't send an amateur into the arena of professionals'?"

"I want to get out of here," said Hespira. Her ungainly face twisted. "That poor man. He thought he was protecting us."

It was a reasonable supposition. But there was another: Chumblot, confined to a low-status occupation—though it was one that constantly took him out of the rank-obsessed milieu of Razham and into close contact with visitors who were free of Ikkibali strictures—may have wanted to share in the reflected glamour of us strange and comparatively free offworlders. He had given in to a mischievous impulse, putting my client in the gray habit of a woman of mystery and delivering her to places where she would be noticed.

Hespira, in her costume, was bound to have been noticed by gossip-addicted, scandal-loving Razhamans. A rumor had rapidly spread, even as we were traveling to Candyk's Spire, and that had led some overproud grandee to loose his watchdogs. The man in brown could have been sent to determine if the errant Sister of Repose was his master's estranged spouse—perhaps the two women bore some resemblance. The tracker had twice come by the Greeneries, seeking a better view, and in between visits he had gone to our hotel and installed the peeper.

Then Chumblot, seeing the plot happily thicken, had tracked the tracker, ultimately following him to the empty loading area where the receive-and-record unit was to be placed. There Chumblot's quixotic blundering brought him within reach of a man who would not brook interference from an amateur. Again, the Ikkibali view of the perquisites of social rank may have come into play: the driver may not have worn the right colors that would have allowed him to play the sleuth and had got a blunt comeuppance for his presumption.

There was a tidy circle to the reasoning: Chumblot's caprice had set in motion a series of events that ended up burying him. I wondered if he had ever viewed a drama with that as its theme; if so, the import of the story had not registered deeply enough.

"I want to get out of here now," Hespira repeated.

I spoke to my assistant. "Have we done enough research on Shannery?"

"I am moderately confident that—" it began, then interrupted itself to say, "We are being scanned by two persons who are coming up the ascender. They are armed. Now they are getting off on this floor. They have turned into the hallway leading to this room."

I drew my energy pistol and motioned Hespira to stand behind me.

"They have stopped outside the door," my assistant said, so that only I could hear. "One of them is speaking into a communicator. The transmission is well shielded."

"And?" I said.

"There, I have broken through," the integrator said. "They are discriminators of the Razhaman Watch. Two of their colleagues are in an aircar that is positioning itself outside and just above the window. They are tense but not keyed up for immediate action. Their weapons are not drawn."

I put the pistol on a table and stepped well clear of it. "It is all right," I said to Hespira. "It is the authorities." She had been wringing her hands again. I said, "Put your hands where they will be able to see them."

The who's-there beside the door said, "Members of the Watch require me to open. I cannot refuse."

The door slid aside. The man was tall and thin, the woman heavy and wide in hip and shoulder, but they both wore the universal expression of peace officers coming through a door for the first time. Their eyes took in Hespira and me, the pistol on the table, the shocker she had left beside the bed, my assistant draped across the back of a chair. The woman spoke: "Disable your integrator, if you don't want us to do it."

"Integrator," I said, "please stand by." The "please" meant that I meant it.

The Watchwoman consulted a device worn like a glove on her left hand then looked at me. "All right," she said, and the two of them stepped into the room, filling it the way police always filled a room. Their eyes itemized everything, discarding the objects that did not count—the hotel furniture, the remains of breakfast—and registering those that did, especially the weapons, which the man efficiently sequestered, and Hespira's gray habit, hung in an open closet.

"All right," the woman said again. I was unfamiliar with the rank symbols on the sleeve of her blue and tan uniform, but I could see that hers had two more diamonds than the man's, and she had the unmistakable air of the one in charge. "I am Senior Examiner Joxon Bey," she said, then indicated her colleague. "He is Leading Examiner Brevich. Please state your names, degrees, and place of origin."

I identified myself and made sure to say that on Old Earth I was accounted a personage of note, the foremost freelance discriminator of my time, which made me a confidant of lords and magnates and even the Archon himself. This assertion won me a look of attentive neutrality from Bey and a frown from her subordinate, which deepened when I said that my client's name, rank, and origin remained a mystery.

The Watchwoman's expression did not alter. She said, "We had better hear your story."

I had already decided on a strategy. I would simply tell the truth—though not the whole truth; magic would not be mentioned, nor the roles of Shar and Chonder—then I would see how the situation developed. The likelihood was that whatever the imbroglio in which we were enmeshed, we were only tangential to its core dynamic. If we could establish that fact to the authorities' satisfaction, we could move on.

And so I began at the beginning, on Old Earth, with Hespira's bumping into me, then went on to my desire to take a vacation after a particularly taxing bout of work, and my impulse to assist a person in need when I was peculiarly equipped to do so. I related the matter of Chumblot and the clothier, my discovery of the import of the gray habit, then the finding of the peeper, at which the junior Watchman went into the other room and returned with the device, pronouncing it dead. I continued my story, moving on to the discovery of our driver's corpse. While I spoke, the woman watched me closely, though she occasionally glanced at the back of her glove.

"I then returned here, to be sure that my client was safe, and was just about to contact the Watch when you appeared."

"Did you send Carthew Chumblot to where you found him?" Brevich said.

"No. When last I spoke to him I had not yet discovered the peeper. I attempted to contact him, but could only reach his integrator."

"We heard your messages."

There seemed nothing to be said to that statement, and in the subsequent silence I deduced that the two were saying nothing in order to leave an opportunity for me to volunteer something. It is a basic interrogation technique.

When the silence had not brought them anything new, Joxon Bey said, "That taxing bout of work, what did it entail?"

"I recovered some stolen property for a client."

"That does not sound terribly taxing."

"There were… complications."

"Did these 'complications,' " Brevich said, "have any relation to your possession of a large quantity of untraceable jewels when you arrived on Ikkibal?"

"No. I did not know if Old Earth financial instruments would be functional this far up The Spray. The jewels were convenient."

Again a silence opened. After it had yawned to its limit, Bey said, "Back to the 'complications'?"

I gave the Watchwoman a look that said we were all professionals together before I said, "Client confidentiality prevents my saying more."

The Senior Examiner studied her glove for an extended moment. Meanwhile, Brevich gave me one of those soul-piercing stares that were supposed to unsettle the guilty conscience. I had long ago decided that, all too often, the guilty were unequipped with the troublesome hindrance of a conscience, and therefore the accusatory glare usually found nowhere to strike home.

"It is possible," I said, "barely possible, that some repercussions of my work on Old Earth could follow me here. And if that were shown to be the case, then my former client would have breached his obligations to me, and I would have no hesitation about giving you the details."

"How very gracious of you," said Brevich.

I ignored the tone and continued, "But I believe there is a simpler, and therefore more likely, explanation." I then offered them the theory of the estranged spouse, ending with, "It fits the facts."

The woman looked from her glove to me and back to the glove. "And," she said, "the facts it fits are conveniently difficult to confirm, since your hypothetical outraged superlant knows, via the device recovered from the other room, that this woman"—she indicated Hespira—"has nothing to do with his marital difficulties. If he exists, he certainly has no reason to come forward and point the finger of culpability at his own operative."

"I cannot help the facts," I said. "I did not create them."

"Chumblot was not acting as your agent when he went to the manufactury?" After asking the question she gave her attention to the glove while I answered.

"No," I said. "I believe he followed the man in brown out of a desire for adventure."

"A desire that was fulfilled beyond his expectations," said Brevich.

The comment brought a sob from Hespira. Both officers turned and studied her. "He only wanted to help," my client said. "He was trying to be nice."

Bey's eyes came back to me. "The element that escapes me," she said, "is why Chumblot was killed. He could have been deterred by some rough treatment or the flourishing of a weapon. There was no need of it."

"It puzzles me, too," I said. I offered the rationale of the professional offended by the intrusive amateur, but now, as I spoke the words, they sounded less convincing than they had when I had advanced the same argument to my assistant.

The Watch entertained the concept, however, causing me to think that in a society so careful of rank and status, the motive might carry more weight. They had not thought it likely that the murderer intended to send me a message, I noted, but immediately I had to revise that assumption when Joxon Bey said, "How long are you planning to remain on Ikkibal?"

I had told her in my earlier summation that we were focused on Shannery as Hespira's probable home world. "I have not heard my assistant's full report on its researches," I said, "but I believe we are ready to press on."

The Watchwoman gave me a look that was less neutral. "Then I think you should." She signaled to Brevich that they were leaving.

"Our weapons?" I said.

Bey paused, thought about it, then made a decision. "I will have them sent to your ship, but they will not be turned over until you are cleared for departure."

"Well enough."

"One other stipulation: if you return from Shannery by way of this world, you will not land." I heard an "Or else," even though she did not say it.

"I see."

"See that you see, Discriminator," she said.

"You did not tell them that you thought Chumblot's murder might have been intended as a message," Hespira said.

"That was merely my assistant and me thinking out loud," I said. "I've found that thinking out loud is inadvisable near the ears of curious police."

We were back aboard the *Gallivant,* clad again in the clothing in which we had arrived on Ikkibal. Our rank-bespeaking garb had gone into the *Espantia*'s waste hopper. When we were settled in the salon, the ship was eager to ply us with punge and pastries, and I acceded to its solicitations. The ship's bread was good and the punge well up to standard.

"Besides," I continued, "if it was a message, it was so ambiguous as to be unactionable. The most likely meaning was: 'Go away,' which is what we are doing."

"So you are just going to do nothing?"

"No, as I said, I am doing something. I am going away."

Anger did not improve the arrangement of her features. "I mean you are going to do nothing about poor Chumblot?"

"I do not see what I could have done about it," I said. "Discriminations involving murder by unknown elements for unknown reasons are difficult enough at home; on an unfamiliar world in the face of an irate constabulary, they are deeply impractical. And I am a practical man."

Her eyes dug at me much the way Brevich's had. "Then why are you chasing off across the Ten Thousand Worlds to assist me?" she said. "Where's the practicality of that?"

The only answer that came to mind was that it would be premature to say. That seemed an unuseful phrase at the moment, so I left it unvoiced and went to put away the energy pistol and shocker that a Watchman had delivered to the ship immediately before we left.

"Ikkibal was a tiring experience," I said, "and the whimsy that will throw us toward Shannery is not far off. Let us rest a while, make the transit, then meet back here to consider what we have learned about where we are going."

I intended to sleep through the hour or so it would take the *Gallivant's* drive to push-pull us to the whimsy, then awaken and take the medications that would protect my mind from exposure to irreality. But instead of letting the sleeping pallet ease me into its restful care, I found my thoughts circling the question that Hespira had asked: why was I going to all this trouble for a woman I did not know—who did not, indeed, know who she was herself—a woman I found physically unappealing?

Was I no better than poor Chumblot, cloaking in heroic garb a naked appetite for adventure? That seemed unlikely; my life had already brought me adventure aplenty and I had no doubt that the oncoming change would bring me an absolute surfeit of it, surely far more than I would care to stomach.

Or did I imagine that, like some heroine in a child's tale of romance, Hespira would emerge at the end of the play as a comely princess, that the rough caterpillar would take wing? That, too, I much doubted.

I probed at my inner works, holding up possible motives like prospective garments, to see if they fit the true shape of Hapthorn. None did, but one: I felt an urge to protect the woman. When I examined this sentiment with cold rationality, it revealed itself as an almost fatherly instinct. And I decided that it must arise from within me, rather than from any quality of hers.

I had fathered no children, and now would not. I had never felt much inclination to explore whatever part of me parenthood would have brought to the fore. And I would certainly not bring a child into existence just on the brink of an age of chaos. I wondered, though, if that unexplored region of my complex psyche had seen the encounter with a helpless amnesiac outside Xanthoulian's as a last opportunity to exert itself. Was an episode of surrogate fatherhood the price I must pay for inner peace as the universe ticked its way toward the inevitable cataclysm?

It was as good an answer as any, I supposed. Besides, the matter would resolve when I discovered who Hespira was and who had stolen her life from her. I expected to be able to give that life back to her, or at least put her on the path to a restoration. And if that metaphorical giving of life somehow satisfied my inchoate fatherly urges, then they would not trouble me further, and I could get on with preparing to meet the end of the world as I knew it.

By the time my mind had settled, the first chime had already sounded to alert us to the approach of the whimsy. I belayed the sleeping pallet's functions and squeezed the sac of medications into my palm. When the darkness cleared, I awoke, muzzy and befogged as usual. Once I could speak without slurring, I asked the ship how far we were from Shannery and was told that it would take us several hours to cross the gulf of normal space. The *Gallivant* also informed me that Hespira was already up and in the salon, where my assistant was prepared to discuss its research findings.

"Fine," I said, and got up to revive myself at the sanitary suite.

"There was one other thing," the ship's integrator said.

"Hmm?" I said, my face immersed in the suite's spray.

"While we were in the whimsy, an object appeared in your cabin."

I froze, water dripping from my nose and chin. So many questions crowded into my drug-muddled mind that I could not choose which to ask first. I decided to go with the most obvious. "What kind of object?"

"I do not know. It was small, metallic, but disordered."

"What do you mean, 'disordered'?"

"I think it was a device, but it arrived broken into fragments."

"Where is it?" I said, looking about.

"It did not stay."

"You mean it reassembled itself and left the room?"

"It is difficult to explain," the ship said. "We were in the whimsy, so there was a great deal of extraneous 'noise.' "

Integrators were not affected by the strangeness of nonspace and non-time that pertained during the transit. They "tuned it out," as one ship's integrator had once tried to explain it to me.

"At first," the *Gallivant* went on, "I thought it was more of the whimsy's bum-bum and tarafadiddle. Then just as I registered that the object truly existed, it didn't."

A thought occurred. "Might it have been a surveillance bee?"

"It might. I have never probed the insides of one, so I would not have recognized its scattered components, especially while tuning out a whimsy's noise."

"Where was the object?"

There was a fold-down table attached to the wall of the cabin. A beam of light now fell from the ceiling onto its surface. "There," said the *Gallivant*.

I fished out Osk Rievor's disk, took it from around my neck, and touched it to the spot the beam illuminated. The disk turned from deep blue to a faded pink.

Osk Rievor had said something about trying to send objects far across space, as he had sent a bee to my workroom from his cottage on the Arlem estate. "Let me know if it happens again," I said. I dried my face and called for a fresh singlesuit. While I was dressing, the *Gallivant* broached a new subject.

"I also thought I received a message," it said.

I paused again. "What do you mean, you 'thought' you received a message? Either you did or you didn't."

"I received an indication that there was a message to be received. But when I opened to accept it, there was…" It was unusual to find an integrator having to dither over a choice of words—"there was nothing there."

"Define 'nothing.'"

"No content."

"I do not understand," I said. "A message is its content. No content, no message."

"I am not designed for metaphor," the ship said. That was true. A spaceship needed to be direct, even literal, in pursuit of its business, or those who traveled in it might end up having unexpected, even unwelcome, adventures. "But if I did attempt a metaphor, it would be this: I heard a knock at the door, but when I opened it there was no one there."

"What kind of knock?" I said.

"I cannot say. I received some kind of attention-demand, I know that objectively. But when I look for the recording of it, there is nothing there."

Now a cold chill went through me, driving away the last of the transit drugs' effects. I thought of the clouding of the peeper in Hespira's hotel room, a system of such a high order that my Hapthorn-designed assistant had had difficulty penetrating it.

"Examine your systems minutely," I said. "Specifically, look for any evidence, however scant, that someone has inserted a latent command into your matrix then convinced you to forget that you have received the command until it is time to act upon it."

"I have examined myself thoroughly, several times since the incident," the *Gallivant* said. "Nothing is amiss with me."

I spoke carefully. "I would like you to allow my assistant to examine you."

"That would be intrusive. It is not… not something I have experienced before."

"Nor is a message that seemingly arrives without content and departs without leaving a trace."

"True."

"I do not wish to alarm my client. Bespeak my assistant and have it conduct the examination while I make my way to the salon."

"Is there another way to resolve your concerns?" the ship said.

"I cannot think of one." The ship made no reply. After several moments, I said, "Are you complying with my instruction?"

"I was conducting my own self-examination, several hundred times. I found no incongruencies."

I reminded myself that this increasingly willful ship's integrator would one day be the essence of a dragon on whose good graces my life would depend. "Please do as I ask," I said. "I will respect you all the more for the sacrifice required."

"Done. The examination is underway. It is a… curious experience."

"We live in curious times," I said.

I found Hespira studying images that my assistant was placing on its screen. They were landscapes and cityscapes representative of Shannery's three continents and their typical terrains. She looked my way as I entered the salon and I saw hope in her face.

"Have you seen anything you recognize?" I asked her.

She looked back to the screen and frowned in concentration. "Nothing specific," she said, "but some of it does seem familiar."

"Keep looking," I said. "There may be a cumulative effect."

My assistant was speaking to me privately. It had performed a deep-searching examination of the ship's integrator and found nothing of concern. It said it had an observation, however, and out of Hespira's line of sight I signaled the integrator to make it.

"You will recall when I tried to make contact with Osk Rievor through the Old Earth connectivity?"

My lips moved silently. "I do."

"I had an odd sense of having connected, yet not connected, to something at his coordinates."

"Yes."

"It may be that the *Gallivant* has had a similar experience. I might have described the event as a 'message without content.'"

It was possible that my other self was seeking to make contact, by some means that mimicked the communications element of the connectivity but was not properly tuned to its protocols. If so, and if he succeeded, it would be a remarkable achievement, across such a gulf of interstellar space.

"There was no indication of anything sinister?"

"No, though a truly sinister intrusion would be phrased in such a way as to appear not sinister."

"That is not reassuring," I said.

"You did not design me to reassure you. Do you wish me to begin offering you comforting bromides and uplifting anecdotes?"

I ignored the question. "Ask the *Gallivant* to relay any more such contacts to you," I said, "and see if you can contrive to capture the specifics."

"Done. And I'm sure it will all look better in the morning."

"Enough!" I said.

At that moment, Hespira called out, "Wait!"

I turned my attention to her. During our conversation, my assistant had continued to present her with images of Shannery. Now she was studying the screen, her long face intent. "What are we seeing?" I said aloud to my assistant.

"A street scene from Wathers, the main seaport on the continent of Ballaraigh. Ballaraigh is the large land mass in the Southern Ocean."

"Show both," I said. The screen divided longitudinally. I saw a roughly triangular continent extending from near the southern pole to just below the equator, with a speckle of islands, some quite large, on its northwest coast. A great, multibranched river system flowed from the central interior, tending eastward to meet saltwater in a semicircular bay, as if a giant had taken a gargantuan bite out of Ballaraigh's eastern seaboard. On the north side of the bay stood Wathers.

"Back to the street scene," I said, "and enlarge to show detail."

It was the kind of thoroughfare to be found in a thousand seaports on a hundred worlds: near the docks, so the street was lined with the kinds of enterprises that cater to transient sailors, the signs and hoardings advertising wares in images and text that made no taxing demands on the imagination. Clearly, sexual mores on Shannery were somewhat more accommodating than on Ikkibal.

Hespira studied the close-up images with deep concentration, her brows knit. Occasionally, as a detail of a sign or a doorway came up before us, she nodded. Finally, she said, "It's like with the singular cream. I can't remember the actual occasion, but I am sure I have been on that street."

"Have we interior views of any of those establishments?" I said.

"One, only," my assistant said. "They are not the kind of places that encourage image-fixing."

The screen showed a large, windowless room, well-packed with patrons, mostly men, seated at round tables or on long benches that lined two of the walls, knob-knuckled hands around tankards and bottles. The air was hazed with smoke, through which the lumens hanging from the ceiling cast a yellow glow over hunched backs clad in wool and heads covered by felt caps, some tasseled, some with polished leather peaks.

"Rolling pig," said Hespira.

"What?"

"I don't know. It just came to me."

My assistant said, "Here," and isolated a detail from the larger image. At one side of the room was a long counter of wood that had once been polished but was now gouged and scarred. Behind it stood a bald man whose belly was scarcely contained by a gray and stained apron. Behind him, surrounded by shelves laden with garishly labeled bottles and kegs, could be seen the upended hindquarters and tail of some beast carved from dark wood. The legs ended in hooves and the tail was corkscrewed, the carving plainly that of a pig rolling on its back, presumably in the throes of porcine pleasure.

"I think we have our destination," I said. "Ship, is there a spaceport at Wathers?"

"There is."

"Then that is where we are bound."

As a secondary world associated with such a grand foundational domain as Ikkibal, Shannery merited almost a half-page in *Hobey's Compleat Guide to the Settled Planets*. It was described as "of bucolic habits, largely self-sufficient, and reliant for exquisitries on imports from more opulent Foundationals, particularly from Ikkibal." Its geophysical characteristics put it in the class of planets that have "long since weathered the tumultuous eons of shifting tectons and volcanic exuberances, so that Shannery's former mountains have worn themselves down to comfortably rounded hills without new ranges thrusting up to serrate the wide skies. A pair of small but close-orbiting satellites, Weft and Warp, create complex but gentle tides."

There were no great cities, but many substantial towns and an uncountable strew of villages and hamlets across the three continents. "Some of these," Hobey said, "offer the visitor quaint festivals and bustling market days, when locally fashioned little curios and 'rare finds' may be acquired. The Shanner counts it a triumph of humor, however, to extract from strangers maximum value for minimum worth, and practices the dickerer's art with a relentless and inexhaustible élan. The discerning traveler should be prepared, once a negotiation has begun, to devote ample time to its rhythms and requirements."

The description of the world's dominant physical type—"tall, long-headed, with large hands and analogous feet, skin shaded from chestnut to blanched"—fit Hespira. A footnote revealed that a recessive gene made rufousity of the hair endemic among the population of the Windstance Archipelago, the straggle of islands off Ballaraigh's northern coast.

"If we find no joy in Wathers," I said, "we may try those islands." But first we would review what my assistant had derived from sending and receiving queries via spaceships passing between Ikkibal and its secondary.

The obvious question had been asked and answered: no woman of Hespira's age and description had been reported missing in recent times. I did not see it as proper to keep this information from my client, although I knew it could be a discouragement to her.

"So I disappeared and nobody cared to make a report?" she said, setting her unfortunate features in an arrangement that robbed them of what little appeal they could manage if left untroubled.

"Not so," I said. "Not everyone who is missing is missed. A traveler may set out for some far-flung destination, first telling all of his acquaintances not to look for him for a while because he will be off and away. He then goes astray on the journey, but since no word of him is expected, it may be some time before anyone decides that there is anything unusual about his not having been heard from."

Her face partially repaired the damage. "I suppose that's possible," she said.

"Why even now, someone may be saying, 'My, it's a long time since we heard from whatyoumaycallher,' and instructing an integrator to seek you out. When you are not in any of the places where you might be expected, alarms will sound. At any moment, an information may be lodged with the authorities. And, soon after, we will have it ourselves."

"Yes, I suppose."

"In the meanwhile, we will carry on."

I bade my assistant to present its findings. They were not definitive, but they further narrowed our target area. The term "flippadiday" had come into the regional speech of Ballaraigh within the past couple of generations. My assistant had come across a monograph by an amateur philologist who noted the rise of this variation of "flippydedoo" and had traced it back to a short-lived movement among young people on the southern continent's northern coast. The youths had called themselves "the Dauntless Divers," after their preferred recreation: entering sea caves whose interiors stood above sea level but whose entrances were accessible only from underwater.

The Dauntless Divers had decorated and furnished a few of the larger caverns, turning them into places where they could spend time unobserved by their elders. The caves lost their allure, however, when a rockfall crushed several revelers during a celebration that marked the end of Green, one of northern Ballaraigh's five seasons. The Height, as the local authority was known, ordered the cave entrances barred, and the young people moved on to a new fad: kite-sailing off the cliffs beneath which the sealed caves lay, an activity which killed only the brashest.

"None of that means anything to me," Hespira said.

"It need not," I said, but I drew her attention to the images of the Dauntless Divers and the Kiters who succeeded them: many of them were tall and long-featured, red of hair and green of eye. "Any of these might be your cousin."

I saw hope steal into her expression and stoked it. "And now we come to the singular cream. Integrator, tell us what you've found."

"It is produced only here," said my assistant, putting up a map of northern Ballaraigh, then narrowing the focus to the Windstance Archipelago, then further until the screen showed a single, though substantial, island separated from the mainland by a wide strait. "Greighen Island."

"What do we know of the place?" I said.

"It was formerly a farming area, mostly small holdings that produced a mix of agricultural products. The town of Orban, here on the coast that faces the mainland, was the only built-up center."

"Formerly?" I said. "What of now?"

"In recent years, an organization called the Grange has bought up all the farms on the eastern half of the island. Cost was no object and the local landowners exploited the opportunity, selling up for two or three times what their properties were worth. The new owners left the farmsteads empty but combined the lands into one large estate. Then they left most of it, even prime croplands, to lie fallow."

On the map a circular dot appeared in the middle of Greighen's eastern half. "The Grange established a compound here with a manor house and cottages for a small number of locals who remained to take wages to work the estate. The house servants, like the estate owners, all came from offworld. They then fenced off the entire holding, even along the coast."

"And what does the Grange do there?" I said.

"They do not say," my assistant said, "but from inference it is clear that they produce singular cream, though by a process that is shrouded in secrecy."

"How well-shrouded?"

"I cannot tell exactly until I can make a reconnaissance of my own," my assistant said, "but indications are that the information is shielded far more than ought to be necessary on a secondary world full of farmers, fishers, and kite-flyers."

"Hmm," I said. "An anomaly."

"There are two more items of interest, both pointing back to Ikkibal."

"Say on."

"First, it seems that the newcomers originated there. I draw that conclusion from reports that appeared in the *Spectacle*, a news organ based in the town of Orban, as the estate was being established. Once the fence was up, no more reports followed. The *Spectacle* was purchased by the Grange; it publishes just as before, with the same staff, but these days no news comes out of eastern Greighen at all."

"The second item?"

"Not only is Greighen the sole source of singular cream, but Ikkibal is the Grange's sole market. Indeed, not just Ikkibal but only the city of Razham, and only the eateries that cater to the highest ranks."

"And that is not happenstance, I take it?"

"From what I have gathered from networks used by commerciants in the food and beverages trade, approaches have been made by restaurants and emporia in New Kutt and from other worlds. Even though price is no object, the Grange will sell only to Razhamans, and only if consumption is guaranteed to take place there."

"Interesting," I said.

"What does it mean?" Hespira said.

"It would be premature to say," I said.

"In other words, you don't know."

"But I mean to find out."

We set down at the Wathers spaceport, a modest facility with only the basic formalities of entrance. Once it was established that neither Hespira nor I had recently been on worlds that might have contaminated our footwear with any worrisome agricultural blights or parasites, we were free to go where we wished. I exchanged a few more of Osk Rievor's jewels for local funds and we rode a shuttle into the town proper.

The seaport was separated from the rest of Wathers by a high wall, breached by several gates that were guarded by blue-uniformed members of the Vigil, as the local militia was known. I saw no hindrance being given to persons passing in either direction, except for a party of freightermen who had obviously taken on a cargo of dire grog. These were turned back toward the docks, firmly though with good humor, by the Vigil. The sailors rolled down toward a dockside tavern, singing an inventive ditty about the testicular deficiencies suffered by those who had suffered the great misfortune of having spent their lives ashore.

Hespira and I presented ourselves at one of the gates where the blue-bugs, as Vigilers were locally called—the guidebook we had acquired at the spaceport said the nickname came from a droning insect known to bumble about harmlessly—looked us over with scant interest. They warned us to keep our hands on our purses at all times and to accept no invitations to enter unmarked premises, no matter what marvels were promised to await within.

"I am a seasoned traveler," I assured the underofficer in charge of the detail, "and my integrator will keep a watch out for unpleasant surprises. But would you tell us where we can find an establishment called the Rolling Pig?"

"If you are not seasoned, you will be once you've spent an hour in that wallow," said the Vigiler. He gave directions that I let my assistant absorb and then we set off. To Hespira I said, "If anything seems familiar, please tell me." And to my assistant I said, in our private mode, "Monitor passersby for any who react to the sight of our client."

But we wound our way without incident to the street on which the Rolling Pig stood. I recognized it from the scenes we had viewed in the *Gallivant*'s salon, but now saw it in context: it was on a narrow road that sloped down to the harbor, not more than a two-minute stroll from where I could see a windvane-powered coaster tied up and taking on cargo, some of it hoisted aboard in rope nets, the rest rolled up a gangway.

"I know this street," Hespira said. "There is a shop down there that sells—" She closed her eyes, then opened them again. "—sea boots and wet-weather gear."

It could easily have been a guess; it was precisely the kind of shop one would have expected to find within sight of a busy dock. But the look in my client's eyes when we covered no more than two dozen paces and found ourselves staring into the display of a sailors' outfitters said otherwise.

"I have been here," she said. "I don't know when or why, but I have stood on this pavement."

Whatever had been done to cleanse her mind of memory was beginning to come undone. "Look elsewhere," I said. "Does any other sight speak to you?"

She looked about, then focused on a doorway opposite. "There," she said, pointing with her chin. "The door opens on stairs that go down." Her gaze went inward. "I see a man coming up and out of the door."

"Describe the man."

"Just a man. His face is lost. Dark clothing. Not a sailor, though." She was nodding as she spoke, her hands before her at waist height, moving as if she was dispelling leaves floating on still water to see through to the depths beneath. Now her head came up and her long-fingered hands became fists, white at the knuckles. "And a woman. She comes out behind him. I cannot see her face, she wears a broad hat. It is night! They are in shadow. That is why I cannot see them. But they look at me. They look, and…"

I saw the moment of perspection end, her fists clenching as if she could hold on to the memory even as it came apart, the shreds escaping her mind's grip. She said a word that was not out of place in the haunts of seafarers, though it was the first time I had heard a salt edge to her tongue.

"By all means, be angry," I said, "but temper it with some joy. If one memory comes, then so can others; if a trickle, why not a flood? This is a good step forward."

She took hold of that thought. "Yes," she said, "a good step."

"But keep the anger," I said. "There is someone who merits your wrath."

"Will we find him?"

"I have no doubt of it." I did not say what was in my thoughts: that it would likely not be "him," but "them"—and that it might turn out to be a man and a woman, he in dark garb, she shaded by a wide hat. I did not believe Hespira's vision of the two people coming out of the doorway was a random piece of flotsam tossed up aimlessly from the deep floor of her psyche, not when the memory had triggered the fists and the curse. "Come," I said, "let us see what lies behind that door."

Of course, it was the Rolling Pig. No sign adorned the entrance, but when I bade the portal open a waft of liquorous fumes, stale smoke, and old sweat engulfed us. Beyond was a dark and narrow throat, steeply stepped and with the cheap paint on the walls worn away by the brushing passage of ten thousand shoulders up and down the way to drink and dissolution. Along with the odors came a grumble of low-voiced conversation, a clinking of glasses and a clunking of mugs on tables, and someone's drunken attempt to sing a sea chanty against the vocal opposition of several patrons who did not care to hear him.

Silently, I said to my assistant, "Full alert." I flexed my wrist to arm the shocker strapped to my forearm, then said to Hespira, "I will go first."

The room below was much as it had been pictured in the image we had viewed earlier. The carved pig flourished its wooden trotters among the kegs and bottles, and the huddled drinkers might even have been the same determined crew we had seen. The man behind the bar was not bald and bay-bellied, however; today the drinks were being poured by a narrow-faced Shanner with close-set eyes and protruding teeth who put me in mind of an underfed rodent. His gaze flicked our way as we entered, then immediately went to a table in the far corner where two men sat nursing half-filled tumblers of some dark liquid. One was heavy-shouldered and darkly bearded, the other thin with mud-colored hair tied in a topknot. Both looked sharply at us then just as quickly turned their gaze elsewhere.

I let my attention wander about the room like an errant tourist hoping for the picturesque and memorable. Meanwhile, I said for my assistant's benefit, "The two in the corner."

"Interested, but not alarmed," it said in my ear. "Their interest is predatory."

"Anyone else?"

"Some are curious, some show the disdain and reflexive hostility due a stranger, some entertain an indiscriminate lust."

"No one recognizes our client and reacts with surprise or consternation?"

"No."

The corner of the bar nearest the door was unattended by the elbow leaners who covered most of its length. I stepped to it and signaled the rat-faced keeper. He came, shoulders indrawn and hands reflexively wiping themselves on a stained rag, an attempt at an ingratiating smile baring his forward-thrusting teeth.

In my ear my assistant said, "Anxious, though it is mere habit in him. Also, hopeful of gain, eager to exploit you in full measure."

My own reading of the fellow's aspect concurred with the integrator's.

I decided on a direct approach, sliding my hand flat across the top of the bar and, when his eyes followed the motion, spreading my fingers so that only he would see the high-value coin beneath them. His face tightened and when he looked up at me I saw that I had his complete attention.

"This will work best for both us," I said, "if we can keep it as uncomplicated as possible. So I advise you to cease trying to work out what I want before I ask you."

He took a moment to digest my advice then nodded.

"Very good," I said. "Now, the woman beside me. Have you ever seen her before?"

His eyes went from me to Hespira and back to me again, then down to where the coin was hidden beneath my now closed fingers.

"No," I said, "do not try to play the situation. Truth will get you this; lying will get you nothing; and I will know which is which. Now, again, have you ever seen her?"

"No."

"Truth," said my assistant, and I agreed.

"You are not the only grog-pusher here," I said.

"No. Anfo is the owner. He works in the evenings, when it is busy."

"A large man, balding?"

"Yes."

"The two in the corner—don't look!" I held his gaze when he would have slid his eyes toward the beard and topknot. "They are always here, aren't they? Except when business calls them away."

"Fear," said my assistant.

"They do not know that we are talking about them," I said, in my most matter-of-fact tone, "nor will they know because I will not tell them."

"Calmer now," said the voice in my ear.

"So," I continued, "they are always here?"

The man's throat moved. He gave the tiniest of nods.

"If my companion had been in here, they would have seen her."

Another incremental motion of the rodential head.

"One last item: when we leave, they will follow us, will they not?"

The fear rushed back into his eyes.

I smiled a reassuring smile. "That is what I want them to do. Is there a signal you are supposed to give if we look to offer good pickings?"

"I scratch my nose."

"Then prepare to scratch," I said, and lifted my hand from the coin. The man's rag instantly wiped the scarred surface where the money had been.

I touched Hespira's elbow. "Come," I said, "and quickly." We moved toward the door.

"He is scratching his nose," said my assistant. "The two in the corner are rising."

We went swiftly up the stairs, out the door, and across the street to where an alley opened beside the chandler's shop. "Now slow," I said.

"Here they come," said my assistant.

"Walk ahead of me," I said to Hespira, "into the alley at an easy pace and without looking back." I sauntered after her, looking up at the rear walls of premises that backed on the lane as if they offered architectural diversion.

"Coming fast," said the small voice, "and closing."

They wore the sound-muffling footwear that has given the profession of footpad its name. I did not hear them approach, even though the large one was easily half again my weight. But my assistant was well schooled in such operations and gave me my cue to turn and simultaneously bring the shocker out into my palm.

The two thugs knew as well as I did that words were superfluous in the situation. The big one must have felt he needed only his outsized hands, but his lightweight companion was drawing a stinger from a pocket of his long-tailed coat. Still, I shot the larger one. The shocker's emanations acted to overstimulate the natural bioelectrical capacity of his own flesh, turning him first into a rigid, bow-shaped version of himself, teeth bared in an involuntary rictus. Then, as my weapon's discharge cut off, he collapsed to his knees and slowly toppled sideways, but I was already bringing the shocker to bear on the second one.

"This need not go so badly for you," I said.

He had frozen with the stinger only halfway toward a position where it would be useful. My assessment had been that he was not the smarter of the two—the big one was the brains as well as the bulk—but I did not need a deep thinker. "Keep the weapon," I said, "but put it away."

I lowered the hand that held the shocker. He folded his stinger and put it back where it had come from, meanwhile regarding me with a considering gaze. "Information?" he said.

"Yes."

"Paying?"

I produced a coin of larger denomination than the one that had slid under the barkeeper's rag and tossed it to him. He caught it without taking his eyes off me. For good measure, I tossed another onto his partner's recumbent form. Then I indicated my client standing nearby. "Have you seen my companion before?"

I was not surprised that the response was a negative. "But what about a man and a woman, he in dark clothing, she in a wide-brimmed hat, spending time in the Rolling Pig?"

I saw the answer in his face before he spoke.

"Do you know who they are?"

"No. They were offworlders."

I held up another coin. "Then what can you give me for this?"

He looked down at his companion. "We are brothers," he said.

"Admirable loyalty," I said, and added a second coin. "Now, what have you to sell?"

"I know where they stayed."

"You followed them as you did us," I said. It was not a question but the man signaled that I was correct. "But you did not accost them."

"Big Tooth tried them on," my informant said.

"I do not know Big Tooth."

"And now you never will," my informant said. "The man in dark clothing played the fool but when it came to the business he dealt with Big Tooth expeditiously. The woman also weighed in. We decided that we were overmatched, and let them be."

"Very wise," I said. "Then, for the coins, where did they stay?"

"The Praedo."

"That is a hotel near the spaceport, is it not?" I had seen the hostelry's marquee as we rode the shuttle into Wathers.

"Yes."

I tossed him both coins, then said, "One small addition. When people come from farms and small villages to try to make their fortunes in Wathers, where do they usually first arrive?"

He told me, then stooped to assist his brother, who was now stirring and making incoherent sounds. I took Hespira's arm and left them. A short walk brought us to a place where jitneys waited to collect sailors who had celebrated shore leave so energetically as to be unable to return to their ships on foot. The second vehicle did not smell entirely unwholesome and we climbed aboard. I put a coin in the hopper and the car started up and moved toward the docks, saying, "What ship?"

"The Abbassad, near the spaceport."

"That is not a ship."

"Nor are we sailors."

The vehicle grumbled and required another coin, but turned about and took us inland.

CHAPTER SIX

"You enjoyed that," Hespira said.

I turned to her and found her protruding green eyes regarding me with an air of an assessment fully completed. I raised my brows and cocked my head as if I did not know what she meant, though I did.

"The business in the Rolling Pig and then those two men in the alley," she said. "You were having a fine old time."

I looked out the side viewer at the passing sights of Wathers. "A craftsman enjoys plying his art," I said.

"You even enjoyed speculating about poor Chumblot."

The question merited some thought. "No," I said, after reflection. "His death saddened me because it was unnecessary."

"But it also angered you because he had tried to play at your game."

I made no response.

"When you speculated that he was murdered by a professional who resented an amateur's intrusion," she said, "you could sympathize with that view."

"I could understand it," I said. "But I do not condone the action that it led to. If Chumblot was killed out of pique, the killer was no professional—just another thug with some skills."

"Still, you are not pursuing my mystery out of any true regard for me. You are 'plying your art,' and I am merely your work."

There were a number of ways I might have responded. Again, I chose the simple truth. "You are perceptive," I said. "Perhaps you perceived something you were not supposed to and that is what led someone to steal your life away."

"We are not talking about me, but about you."

"Perceptive again." In the face of her deepening frown, I held up my hands in capitulation. "I am who I am," I said. "And who I am is what I do." I took pause to order my next words before speaking them. "It might or

119

might not be in my interest to become attached to a client. It is certainly not in the client's interest for me to be anything other than a professional. Emotional judgments are clouded judgments."

"And yet," she said, "I sense some emotion in you. Not about me, I am sure, though at first I thought it might be. But it is there."

"If so," I said, "it is my own concern."

"Not if it clouds your judgment."

"It does not."

"How would you know, if your judgment were clouded?"

I began to see another reason why someone might have put this woman far enough away that she would be unlikely to find her way back. "You ask difficult questions," I said. "Fortunately, for you, you do not have to answer them, whereas picking the thorns out of prickly conundra is my stock in trade." She was about to speak again, but I held up an admonitory finger. "Right now I suggest you let me get on with it. We can dissect my character later, when we are at leisure, but here we are at the Abbassad."

I handed her some coins and asked her to remain with the vehicle, since we would not be here long. The place was a typical spaceport layover spot, catering to travelers waiting to make a connection or stopping briefly on Shannery to do some business. Its decor said it would offer moderate comfort, reliable functionality, and no surprises, good or ill.

I dawdled near the entrance, as if waiting for someone to join me. A man in a resplendent uniform commanded the portal, assisting patrons into and out of vehicles and summoning jitneys from where they waited in a rank for those who required transportation to the spaceport or into Wathers. I considered approaching him but he did not look to be the type who would serve my purpose. Nor, I was sure, would whoever stood behind the reception desk. I needed the kind of person with whom it was possible to strike up an instant rapport—provided, that is, that the relationship would be mutually beneficial and could be consummated without delay.

I had not been waiting long before I spied a likely prospect. He was a small man, scant of hair and slightly stooped, but sharp of eye. He wore a similar, though simpler, uniform than the door guardian's, and was towing a come-along disk on which stood the luggage of a portly man who was exiting the hotel in a bustle of self-importance. The porter eased the bags into the cargo compartment of a jitney and made the gratuity the plump man gave him disappear into a pocket with smooth speed. As the jitney pulled away, taking the rotund patron out of his life, the small man glanced in my direction, and I recognized the look as one part simple curiosity and nine parts assessment as to whether I could do him any good. I made a small gesture and the nine parts instantly became a whole. The porter sidled over to me.

I opened my palm to display a high-value coin, then added two more to it. The tiny clinks the currency made sharpened the man's attention. He looked up at me with an intensity of expression that would not have been out of place on a bird that was sizing up a well-fleshed and peckable grub.

"Two travelers, in the recent past," I said. "A man fond of dark clothing and a woman with an affection for large hats. They might have asked directions to a picturesque dockside tavern, also the omnibus station."

I saw from a slight concentration of his features that my description was riffling the chimes of his memory. I put the coins into his hand and showed him an expectant attentiveness.

"Within the past month," he said. "They both called themselves by the name Ololo, though they were neither spouse nor brother and sister."

"How did they come and go?"

"I heard mention of a private spaceship."

"Did you see them depart?"

A recollection of something out of the ordinary. "No, they left very late one night, almost morning. Only the night porter was on duty."

"Were they accompanied by anyone?"

"I cannot say. They used a car that they had hired in town."

"Any noticeable accent or unusual turns of phrase?"

A negative motion of his head. "They spoke mostly to each other, and in soft tones."

"And did they ask directions?"

"They asked where travelers from the north might pitch up if they arrived not knowing the town. I told them of Ollanmore Square, where the day laborers congregate, and the omnibus station." He consulted his memory, chinking the three coins in his hand. "Yes, and they wanted to know which places on the docks were good to avoid."

"And you told them…?"

"Flink's, of course, and The Deadlights. And the Rolling Pig."

I held out another coin. "Consider now, what question should I have asked that I did not think of?"

He caught the inner corner of one lip between a canine and his lower teeth, then after holding it a moment, said, " 'Are they dangerous?' And the answer is, 'The man is, the woman more so.'"

I put the fourth coin into his hand. "You never saw me," I said.

"I never did," he agreed.

I returned to the car and Hespira, on the way giving instructions to my assistant. By the time I was seated and the vehicle was headed back to town, my integrator had completed its tasks. So that the vehicle would not overhear, it spoke privately to me, saying, "This is interesting: the spaceport reports the arrivals and departures of three private yachts during the times the targets came and went to and from Shannery. Two of the craft are innocent; I can trace their movements and neither carried a pair such as we are interested in."

"And the third?"

"That is the interesting part. It arrived and departed under a false name and details."

"And the spaceport did not detect the subterfuge?"

"It did not. The camouflage was of a high order."

"Like unto the quality of the equipment on Ikkibal?"

"Very like. Had I not been looking for deception, and looking very hard, I might not have noticed."

"Hmm," I said aloud, causing my client to want to know what I was about. "Premature," I said, gesturing at the car's auditory percepts.

I did not bother with Ollanmore Square but had us taken directly to the omnibus station. This was an octopoidal structure, a low-built hub covered in fanciful arrangements of colored glass and spins of artfully corroded metal. From its eight covered walkways lined by bays, multipassenger vehicles loaded and offloaded persons traveling in and around Wathers or to and from distant towns and villages. It was a busy place; privately operated vehicles seemed to be the exception rather than the rule in Wathers. I thought also that Shanners—or at least those on the continent of Ballaraigh—must be of a relatively footloose breed, for I saw plenty of them coming and going, towing their bags on come-alongs or wearing them strapped to their backs—the light gravity made large loads easy to bear. The ambient mood was also light of heart, befitting a people happy to pick up and move on to somewhere else.

Hespira and I left the car and followed a trickle of just-arrived passengers heading into the central hub. Many passed straight through the terminus, others diverted to the sanitary suites or to the refectory, but a few looked about, found what they were looking for, and went to give it a closer inspection. The object of their attention was a notice board headed with the words "Situations Available," beneath which were affixed palm-sized cards of different colored stock, on which were spelled out the terms and conditions of posts offering wages and other considerations.

I turned to my client to ask if any of what she was seeing seemed familiar, but I saw from her look of studied concentration that the scene was roiling the subsurface layers of her mind. I said, "Do not try to force it. Let it work its way free."

My distracting her had the desired effect. The bubble rose into her awareness and burst. "I have been here," she said.

"And you went straight to that notice board."

She looked at me. "Did I? Yes, I did!" She let it come. "A blue card." She strained then, but came up without a pearl. "I can't remember what was on it."

"No need," I said, "it offered a position that seemed eminently attractive to a young woman just arrived from the north coast: to be a clerk in an emporium that dealt in the kinds of gear that seafarers need. It required prospective candidates to present themselves at the premises at a certain time."

Her eyes were searching my face, and I could see that my words were striking a true note even if she could not remember the exact details. "How do you know this?" she said.

I gestured to say that I was not yet finished. "Probably, a woman was standing nearby as you read the card. She may have leaned over your shoulder and spoken, saying that she knew the business, that it was soundly managed and of good repute."

Now, it was almost memory; she knew it was so, even if she could not recall. "How do you know it happened that way?" she said.

"I know it, because that is how it must have happened. You were seen debarking from an omnibus inbound from the northern coast, though you probably began your journey in Orban. A man spotted you, decided you were what they were looking for, and signaled the woman to put up the blue card just as you entered the terminus and looked for the notice board. You read the advertisement, took the card, and set off to seek employment."

"But why?" she said.

Again I felt that urge to protect her. I was convinced that there was an answer to her question, though at this point I could only guess at it. At the same time, I knew that she could have been a random choice, that she had simply offered the right age, sex, and general background. Perhaps she had been used for some purpose that required a cut-out, then scrubbed of all memory and dropped far from the scene of the action.

The problem was this: the kind of people who were so callous as to inflict such damage on an innocent pawn—and I was sure she was innocent—ought to have been hard enough that when they dropped her it would have been well-weighted and into the sea. Or out of an airlock into the great emptiness. The two elements did not add up.

"Why?" she said again.

I did not tell her it was premature to say. I said, "I do not know. But to that I will add the word: 'yet.' Because it will not be enough to restore you to where you came from, or even to recoup your lost memories. I mean to know why this was done to you. And who did it."

The advantages of owning a spaceship—being able to pick up and put down wherever one desired, and to arrive with roof and sustenance in hand—were not available to me on Ballaraigh. The inhabitants preferred to keep their roads clear of private cars and their skies uncluttered by volantes and yachts. Hespira and I therefore had to make our way to Greighen Island by omnibus and ferry. The road portion of the journey took two full days, with an overnight stop at an inn just below the Oyoy Pass, where the road wound through the range of hills whose streams fed the River Leff, vigorous and narrow here though it would be wide and sedate where it reached the coast at Wathers.

I was not averse to the slower mode of travel. It offered Hespira an opportunity to let the sights and sounds I believed were familiar to her wear away at the barrier that separated her from her past. It also made it easier to determine if anyone was taking an undue interest in us. I hoped that would be the case, so that I could identify the shadow and take him or her aside for some pointed questions. But no one stood out, which meant that we could relax on the way, but also that we would arrive at the town of Orban not knowing if a reception had been organized.

I was also regularly checking the disk Osk Rievor had hung about my neck. It remained cold and dark blue. Perhaps Shannery was a world without sympathetic-association dimples, a characteristic that could only endear it to me.

The slowed pace of our trip also gave me time to worry at the aspect of the case that bothered me. While my client watched the hulaboa trees go by the omnibus window, their feathery fronds rippling in the breeze of our passage, I came back to the question of why she had been disposed of in a manner that allowed for the strong possibility that she would eventually regain her memories. The perpetrators of the crimes against her had not scrupled to murder poor Chumblot nor the Wathers skullthump Big Tooth; why had they drawn the line at Hespira? Were they hirelings who had been given orders about her that drove them to act in a manner at variance with their instincts?

The thought of what might have happened to her caused a visceral reaction in me. Rather than suppress an emotion that I knew to be unprofessional—and at variance with my own instincts—I let the feeling well up in me so that I could examine it as it was occurring. But the exercise brought me no enlightenment. I could only fall back on my earlier rationale: that the microcosm of Hespira's plight had become conflated, at some level of my psyche, with the fate of the macrocosm I loved. I could do nothing to prevent the coming cataclysm, but I could at least put my client's upturned life back to rights.

It was not a satisfactory explanation. It seemed to me that I ought to be more complex than that. But perhaps having lost a substantial portion of my larger self, when Osk Rievor first became a separate persona then removed himself from my mind, my deeper workings were now out of balance. Without my intuition—my insight, as I had always called it before it reared up in the forefront of my mind and half-challenged me for dominance—I could not expect to be as nuanced as I had been.

The thought made me sigh. The sigh brought a questioning glance from Hespira and a quiet-mode query from my assistant. I gestured to the former that the matter was of no consequence and silently told the latter to attend to its own business. The integrator took that as an invitation to file a report.

"We are unremarked by person or device," it told me, "except for the small boy in the seat across the aisle who has been amusing himself by contorting his face into caricatures of other passengers. His rendition of you shows a genuine talent for mimicry."

I turned my head sharply in the direction of the gifted child and caught a flash of lowering brows and pursed lips before the boy quickly cleared his features and looked away. "He looked as if his bowels had downed tools last week and had since refused to function," I said silently to my assistant. "That is not how I look when I am wrestling a heavy thought."

It had something more to say but I saw nothing to be gained from a debate on subjective impressions. "Continue your surveillance," I said, "and confine your reports to matters of substance."

I almost heard something more and said, "Are you muttering something just below the threshold of my hearing?"

Now there was only silence.

"You would not have done that before you spent time as a grinnet," I said. I was more and more convinced that the will my assistant had acquired during its incarnation as a wizard's familiar had not died with the simian-feline body that was buried near Osk Rievor's cottage.

Annoyed, I looked about and caught the boy across the aisle making the face of an old curmudgeon who has come down to breakfast to find the punge tepid and the dolcetacc burned. Hespira followed my gaze and laughed out loud. I sighed again, folded my arms and closed my eyes in feigned sleep. In time, the pose became a welcome reality.

At the foot of the Oyoy Pass, with its dry, grassy hills looming over the pale stone and dark timber of the unnamed inn, our northbound omnibus connected with an eastbound route that followed a road skirting the high country. When we set off in the morning, we had acquired several new passengers and, I was thankful to note, lost the flexibly faced boy. My assistant reported that none of the newcomers was paying us more than cursory attention. And so we climbed, topped, and descended the Sleeves, as the range of hills was known. By midday we were onto the forested plain beyond, and by evening we could see the lights of Mol, where the twice-daily ferry put in from Orban on Greighen Island. We had missed the last sailing, so I booked us rooms in a comfortable hostelry overlooking the waterfront.

After two days of sitting in an omnibus, I felt the need to stretch unused muscles. I invited Hespira to accompany me on a walk around the harbor. The boat basin was largely filled with krill-skimmers and a few seiners, with a separate section for pleasure craft. Most of the vessels we saw were of an unpretentious cut, many decorated with carved folk art at stern or prow—comical figurines expressing their owners' worldviews—or painted in comfortable colors.

Shannery seemed a more relaxed place than Ikkibal, its inhabitants far less concerned with receiving whatever was due them by dint of their social rank. Conversations were more frequently punctuated by laughter, and the laughter was more from the belly than from the back of the throat. I was reminded that the antecessors of this world had been those who found Ikkibal too tight a fit. I decided that the former Ikkibalis who had opted to become Shanners had made a good swap.

We walked through the dusk, watching the last few working boats come in from the fishing grounds, Greighen Island a dark smear to the north. I was suddenly struck by the notion that this little town called Mol might be a better place than Olkney to wait out the end of my time. The mood here was less strident, the easy-going population probably better able to absorb dislocations.

Of course, I would miss much about Old Earth—not least the menus at Xanthoulian's, Master Jho-su's Pot of Fire, or a dozen other eateries, the theater and, most of all, the salon life of wit and epigram—of which I was, I could say without vanity, one of the leading ornaments. If I relocated here, or in some place like it, I would have to become a different Hapthorn, or at least a Hapthorn with different interests. And yet, I reminded myself, it was not as if I could expect Xanthoulian's to survive the collapse of civilization; in the none too distant future, my interests would suffer a profound and sudden reversal when magic once again ascended the throne. Here I might become an odd fellow who occasionally spoke "funny"—in Olkney, I would become one of the desperate survivors cutting throats over a stale loaf.

I realized that, for the first time, I was thinking about life after the great change. Until now, I had been seeing the impending cataclysm as the end of all, looking down a road that led to a precipice, with nothing beyond but a plunge into darkness that went on forever. But there was a beyond beyond that. When geologic upheaval forces some great river to alter its ancient course, I thought, it scours out its new bed through whatever stands in its way, sweeping away walls and houses, palaces and parks. But here and there, by accidents of topography, it leaves islands. The north coast of Ballaraigh felt to me as if it might be one of those fortunate spots.

I glanced at Hespira beside me, her hand on my arm. Her perpendicular face was that of a woman as lost in thought as I had just been. "Is any of this familiar to you?" I said.

"It is," she said. "Like a dream I've had often."

"Tomorrow," I said, "we will go across to Greighen and there I think we will find some answers."

A cold breeze came in from the darkling sea. She shivered. "Come," I said, "perhaps, this close to the source, the hotel will have singular cream."

"I have never heard of it," said the young woman who came to take our orders. She bore a certain resemblance to my client, mostly in her coloring and the size of her hands and feet, but she gave no sign of recognizing Hespira as a cousin.

"Singular cream," I said again. "It is a kind of custard made on Greighen Island. With a unique taste."

The description lit no inner lights. I said, "I'm told it's made by an organization called the Grange."

"Oh, them," said the server. "We have no dealings with them. Nor them with us." She made a face for emphasis. "Especially not them with us."

At her recommendation, we ordered fillets of smoked grish and a steamed vegetable called tide fruit. The local wine was a little sweet, but it had the character needed to overcome the defect. "Interesting," I said, "that singular cream is unknown almost within sight of the place where it is made."

"Perhaps the server on Ikkibal misled us," said my client.

"Unlikely," I said, although I had been on worlds where leading the stranger astray was a popular pastime. "In any case, it's another answer we can look for tomorrow."

Most of the ferry's deck space was allocated to heavy transport vehicles, there being few private cars on either side of the strait. We boarded an omnibus that picked up passengers at the hotel and a few other stops around Mol, then drove straight onto the vessel. We left the omnibus for the duration of the voyage and climbed to an upper deck where we could see across the water to Greighen.

It was a fine day, the sky and sea showing different shades of blue, with a mild breeze that put white peaks on waves that, because of the lighter gravity, were sharper than those we would have seen on one of Old Earth's seas. Some of the passengers had brought stale bread—I was reminded of my dark vision of the night before—which they tore into chunks and threw overboard. Scarcely had the pieces floated down to touch the water before the spot where each landed became a miniature maelstrom: dozens of swimming crustaceans, ranging in size from the length of my little finger to that of my whole hand, competed to bear away the crusts, tearing them to fragments with multiple hooks and pincers and cramming the morsels into their complex mouth parts before they could be stolen away.

Meanwhile, the feeding frenzies attracted flocks of leathery-winged creatures that the locals called flaps, which skimmed the surface, artfully stinging the krill with their long, thin, forward-mounted proboscises, then catching the paralyzed animals with their long-toed hind feet. As a successful flap rose with its catch it might be attacked by another of its flock intent on robbery, leading to an airborne squabble full of honks and whistles.

The ferry passengers, having instigated all this mayhem, regarded the several melees with thoughtful silence. When all the bread was thrown and the last bite taken, they turned back to their own lives, their faces bearing expressions I could only describe as philosophic, as if the all-against-all in sea and air confirmed some deeply held view of the nature of existence.

My assistant, draped over my neck and shoulders, reported that there was still no unusual interest in our presence. Hespira and I passed an uneventful couple of hours and reboarded the omnibus as the boat slowed to enter the harbor at Orban, tying up at a sloping ramp where our vehicle was the first to disembark. It carried us up into the center of the town, built on the top of the flattest of three low hills just inland from the strait. We stepped down into a wide public square, paved in crushed white seashells and surrounded on three sides by two- and three-story buildings of woodframe construction, brightly painted in cheerful yellows, oranges, and several shades of rose, most with wide verandahs on which locals watched each other and the day go by. A sturdy building that featured a second verandah above the first revealed itself to be the Orban House, with vacancies.

"Familiar?" I asked my client.

"Yes," she said, looking around. "But again, it is as if this is a place I have visited in a dream and now am seeing it brought to life."

"I believe we will find that the dream-sense is an effect of what has been done to separate your awareness from your past. We are getting close."

She swallowed. "I am apprehensive," she said.

"I will protect you," I told her. Then I spoke quietly to my assistant, saying, "Watch the watchers," as I lifted our luggage and led Hespira toward the hotel. "Let me know if we evoke any surprised reactions."

"Nothing," it said, as our soles crunched the shell fragments underfoot into smaller pieces. "Still nothing. Now some mild curiosity." We reached the stairs leading up to the Orban House's porch, where a couple of casually clad locals sat in split-cane chairs, looking as if the chief goal of their already long lives had been the growing of capacious beards—a goal that had been not only achieved but accomplished to a degree surpassing any reasonable expectation. They were smoking some sort of aromatic herb in long-stemmed pipes while they examined me at leisure, no doubt trying to decide where in their hard-won worldview such an unusual specimen as I could be made to fit.

"Nothing. Still nothing."

The hotel's double doors were open to admit the warm weather. An odor of furniture polish and fresh-cut flowers invited us to enter the lobby. I led the way, bearing the bags, my client bringing up the rear, and crossed to the reception desk still hearing my assistant's advisals that we had attracted no more than cursory notice. I had reached the desk and was setting down the bags when I heard it say, "To your right. Strong reaction. I would call it shock."

I looked in the direction indicated. An archway led out of the lobby and into what appeared to be an informal dining area. Standing in the opening was a man of average build and in his early maturity, wearing a matching longcoat and trousers of dark green that immediately put me in mind of a servant's livery. He was also wearing a look of unalloyed astonishment, his mouth hanging open, his eyes fixed on Hespira.

I turned to her, saw that she had not noticed the man. I immediately said, "Look there," drawing her attention to him. "Do you know him?"

When her gaze fell upon the man in green it was as if she had transmitted an impulse that freed him from his stasis. His mouth closed, he blinked twice, then without a word he made for the front doors. By the time he reached them, he was running.

"You!" I managed to get out as I went to follow him. Behind me I could hear Hespira answering my last question—"No, I don't think so."—but events had moved on. When I reached the front porch he was not to be seen, but the two smoking idlers were both gazing to my left, where the verandah ended at some steps that led down to a lane that ran beside the hotel. My assistant confirmed that the fleeing man had gone that way then added, "A light engine is starting up."

I could hear it myself—a powerful air impeller, followed by the whine of a gravity obviator cycling up into the ultrasonic. I raced down the verandah and leapt the three stairs at the end and whirled in time to see the man disappearing down the alley on a single-seat skimmer. He turned left at the end of the building's side wall, sending up a swirl of dust and needles from the spreading deodar that shaded the back of the hotel. I ran after him, though I had no need to keep him in sight.

"He is heading inland," said my assistant, "increasing speed."

I rounded the rear corner of the hotel. The skimmer had already crossed the open games court at the rear and exited through an arched gateway onto an arterial road. "Increasing distance will cause me to lose his sound shortly," said my integrator, "but he appears to be taking the shortest route toward that road that winds up between the hills."

I looked where it indicated and saw a set of wooded prominences that rose above the three hills of Orban. A white strip of road angled up to disappear in a saddle between two of the heights. After a minute or so, I saw a speck of motion on the lower stretch of pavement. "There he is," said my assistant.

"Yes," I said, "but where is he going?"

Hespira was waiting for me on the front verandah, the two smokers watching her as if they expected a second act. When I reached her, they leaned forward, forearms on knees, so as not to miss a moment of the drama. But I promoted them from spectators to cast members by asking them, "Did you know that man?"

They looked at each other, deciding who would speak. The one with the more grizzled beard eventually said, "No."

"Was that a uniform of some kind he was wearing?"

Again the silent consultation, then it was the darker beard's turn. "Yes."

"What kind?"

Darker beard must have felt that he still had momentum. "Grange," he said.

"The Grange? What can you tell me about them?"

But both of them had apparently run out of drive. My assistant reminded me that the Grange was a highly secretive organization.

I tried the two loafers again. "He went up and over those hills behind the town. Does that road lead to the Grange's lands?"

At this I got a nod and a scowl, the latter I think reflecting the Grange's secretive nature, which would have provided little grist for the mills of speculation that these two ground on the Orban House's porch.

I opened a second file for them. "Regard my companion," I said. "Is she at all familiar to either of you?"

Their eyes went back to Hespira and both pipe stems went into the smoke-stained holes in their beards as they studied her at length. Finally, the grizzled one removed his fumarole and said, more to his companion than to us, "She might be a Hob."

Dark beard took time to digest this suggestion, but gave it only a qualified approbation before countering with, "Or a Broon, from over Sandwynd way."

My assistant was adding commentary. "Hobs are an extensive Greighen

Island clan, mostly centered around the northeast of the island." Broons were another clan, somewhat less numerous. Sandwynd was a village a day's walk to the east.

Hespira spoke. "Broon," she said. "I think I've heard that name. And Sandwynd." She was looking down, her eyes not really seeing the whitened boards of the porch floor. "Yes. Yes."

"Sounds like a Broon," said the darker beard.

I put a question to him. "Would a Broon say 'flippadiday'?"

Another pull on the pipe led to a confirmatory nod. "Serious folk, the Broons," he said. "No time for lolloping about."

The man in green was not a local, at least not in any sense that the two on the porch would have accepted. Apart from his livery and the shock he had shown at seeing Hespira, his other distinguishing characteristic had been a pair of wide, forward-facing nostrils. He was a Razhaman.

This much was confirmed when my client and I returned to the hotel's reception desk. As well as assigning us two adjacent rooms overlooking the square, the clerk answered my question concerning the identity of the man who had fled.

"I do not know his name. He acts as the shipping agent for the Grange and sometimes dines here when he has business in town."

I learned more, even though the clerk declined the coin I set on the countertop. The Grange allowed itself only the most minimal contact with the town of Orban. It was not even part of the Greighen Island connectivity but communicated with the outside world solely by messengers such as the man we had encountered. Since the Hedge had gone up, very few of the island's residents had entered the huge estate that took up most of the eastern portion of the island. The Greigheners who worked the estate, under the direction of green-liveried Razhamans, lived in sequestered villages. Their employers discouraged them from too much contact with outsiders—and "too much" as defined by the Grange was "any."

"Surely, they are not prisoners?" I said. "Not serfs tied to the land?"

The clerk was a fair-haired youngish man, with no more beard than would cover his chin, but like persons of his occupation whom I had met all over The Spray, he had been exposed to a variety of types and situations, and had learned how to weigh up what he saw. "The Grange paid good prices for their land and offered them wages to stay on. Many declined the offers and moved on. Those who stayed found that their new prosperity was worth a few constrictions."

I ventured a question. "Sandwynd was one of the villages the Grange purchased?"

"It was."

"Might my companion have come from there?"

He looked at Hespira. "She might."

"Is there anyone here in Orban who could take the imprecision out of my question?"

The clerk thought out loud. "They were mostly Broons and Claverclocks out that way, and a few Izmals. Not many of them stayed on behind the Hedge. They took the payments and went south. Some even went offworld. None are around here now."

"What about the authorities?"

The man's eyebrows moved in an eloquent ambiguity. "Sandwynd folk were of the old stock. They preferred not to entangle themselves with musts and mustn'ts. They left the world alone and expected the world to return the favor."

"What about the police?" It had been my experience on several worlds that official forces of probity liked to aim at least an occasional sidewise glance at folk who had the attitude the clerk had just described to me.

"Bars Hoop?" said my informant, then clarified the two syllables by identifying them as the name of the local prepostor-corporal. "If anyone had dealings with them, Bars would be the one."

A few minutes later we had traversed the square and followed a broad avenue to a three-story building—also of timber frame, but with a ground-floor annex of solid stone—that was the local administrative nexus, which included the Greighen Island Prepostory. This force consisted of the aforementioned Hoop, three prepostors-ordinary, two clerks, and a stooped and entirely bald man who swept out the offices and oversaw the ins and outs of the jail. My assistant informed me that the latter institution was locally referred to as the "whileaway."

Besides seeing if Bars Hoop recognized Hespira, I had another reason to visit the place: the Grange man had not rushed off to report what he had seen so that those he reported to could sit in contemplation of the vagaries of life and the surprising turns a day might take. People who strip women of their memories and deposit them without resources on far-away planets, people who murder inquisitive jitney drivers and troublesome roughnecks who intrude upon them, were not likely to show equanimity when their plans were interfered with. I expected to see action out of the Grange, whoever they were, and I doubted it would be long in coming.

Bars Hoop was a broad man, in physique, accent, and beard. He also had acquired the habit of herb-smoking that seemed to be rife on Greighen Island, so that his office was aswim with blue vapors that hovered in a layer just below the ceiling and his reddish whiskers were at risk of sudden ignition from errant embers. He did not know my client at sight of her, but he admitted that he had spent little time in Sandwynd and the other outports on the eastern edge of the island, even before the Hedge sprang up. "And now—" He spread his meaty hands, then picked up the carved pipe from a holder on his cluttered desk and drew fresh inspiration from it. "—now I wouldn't know what to tell you."

"Then allow me to do the telling," I said, and proceeded to lay out for him the events that had occupied me since Hespira had crashed into me outside Xanthoulian's. When I spoke of her amnesia, his russet brows rose high, only to come crashing down when I related the death of Chumblot and the downfall of Big Tooth. I brought us up to the moment of the Grange man's hasty exit and said, "I believe that my client is of concern to them, indeed some kind of threat, and that they will come for her. She must be protected."

Hoop's brows rose again. "There has never been any trouble from over the Hedge," he said. "They keep to themselves but they seem to be a law-abiding crew."

"Would you know if they were not?" I said. "They work hard to keep their doings out of sight. That's often a sign that what's being done won't bear the light of exposure."

He conceded the point with a thoughtful nod, but answered my question in the affirmative. "They're not as well-hidden as they think they are," he said. "If anything untoward were happening, I would hear of it, sooner or later." He took another lungful of blue fumes. "Islands are like that. And, even if islands aren't, I am like that."

I was not so sanguine, and I let my sentiments show in my face. He reacted to my skepticism, though without the resentment I was accustomed to seeing in Colonel-Investigator Brustram Warhanny and others of his ilk. Perhaps, I thought, the smoke has a mellowing effect.

"We're not used to them as call themselves 'discriminators' from half-forgotten worlds," he said, "but I'll say you this: I'll assign Grondin Brist to keep an eye on you two at the Orban House tonight. He's a quick lad, Grondin is."

"You will not mind if I arm myself with a shocker?" I said. "Just in case Grondin is not quite quick enough."

Bars Hoop's answer was a remarkably coherent toroid of smoke that left his pursed lips and sailed upward to join the clouds above. I took it as an acquiescence.

Grondin Brist was built from the same general plans that had created his superior, though with more pruning of the thicket of hair that erupted from his cheeks and chin. His reputed quickness was not on immediate display but he exhibited a quiet competence in the way he assessed our situation at the Orban House and disposed himself. His Prepostory-issued surveillance suite was not as sophisticated as my assistant's, but Brist's had the handicap of having to operate within the strictures of law and custom. He deployed sensitive percepts at several points in the hallway and the ascender, thus covering all approaches to our rooms, then stationed himself in the hallway between Hespira's door and mine, having set the doors who's-theres to admit him without hesitation.

My client and I spent the afternoon in the hotel. Hespira was understandably nervous; it is difficult to play a part in someone else's drama when one is not allowed to see the script. I felt moved to sit with her and counsel her to be of good heart.

"We have been steadily driving toward the core of this case," I said. "Soon we will unlock the final door and all will be made plain."

"I am only a little frightened," she said. "I have come to trust your judgments. And the prepostor looks to know his business."

"We are on the brink," I said. Indeed, even without my intuition, I had a good feeling about how this discrimination had proceeded. It had had its turns and tweaks, but its puzzles had opened to straightforward applications of thought and logic; after the past few months, it was a relief to be exercising my craft without the interference of sympathetic association and all its jimjammering absurdities—absurdities that were all the more infuriating for having turned out to be truth.

"Not long now," I said. "We will find the starting point, we will unravel the web, and you will be restored to your life."

Her face took on a curious cast. "I wonder," she said, "if that life was as interesting as this one has been."

"Interesting or not, it was yours and you are entitled to it." Then I added, "Or, if you are so inclined, to reject it and try a new one."

She looked at me oddly, and I had the impression she wished to ask me a question, but that she preferred to leave it unvoiced until another time. Still, she brightened and even smiled. I played into her happier mood by remarking that there might be some advantage in being stripped of all knowledge of one's past. "If, for example, there was more bad than good in it, if it contained more bleak memories than cheery ones, one would be well rid of it. How many of us, I wonder, if given the chance to start over, cleared of all debts owed to the past, all blame and guilt lifted away, wouldn't gladly take the cup of amnesience and drink it down?"

"Would you?" she said.

Half a year ago, I would have answered no with speed and assurance. I had had a good life—perhaps lacking in some spheres, but that lack had been more than made up for by the satisfactions I had taken from my work and my various avocations. But now? If I could be relieved of knowing what I knew, of the chill certainty that soon all that I held dear would come crashing down around me, would I not gladly pass back the bitter cup of foreknowledge? Would I not happily go through the remaining days armored by ignorance, until I reached the edge of the unseen cliff and toppled over with everyone else?

"I do not know," I said.

We ate dinner in my room—krill and hair-fine noodles that the server said were made from a flour ground from the seeds of a grass that grew in the shallows between the shore and the deep water. It was a pleasant meal, made more so by Hespira's happier mood, and I did my best to enjoy the moment. The evening wore on, then became full night, and I began to wonder if the man who had hurried away had wasted his speed, for no one seemed to be hurrying back.

Then my assistant said to me, privately, "Two men are arriving in a vehicle at the front of the hotel. One is highly stressed, the other less so but keyed up. Now they are entering the lobby."

"Are they armed?"

"No, but the desk clerk is reacting with alarm to their questions. Now he is telling them where we are."

To Hespira, I said, "Something is happening. I want you to go into the sanitary suite and set it to privacy." I deployed my shocker and said to my integrator, "Alert Grondin Brist."

"No need. His percepts have detected the commotion from below."

I strode to the door. As I opened it, I could hear shouting in the hallway.

CHAPTER SEVEN

My first impression was that the young man who was doing most of the shouting was out of his rightful place. For one thing, he was physically unlike the general run of Greighen Islanders I had so far seen, being neither bearded nor fair-complected. His hair was straight and dark, instead of blond or rufous like Hespira. His nostrils showed the enlargement of a Razhaman's. And he clearly wasn't used to raising his voice, because it kept cracking as he struggled with the prepostor, shouting repeatedly the same three syllables—"Irmyrlene! Irmyrlene!"—as if they were both a command and an explanation.

But what struck me foremost about the man was his clothing. He wore the same combination of colors I had seen on the patrons of the Greeneries—black and silver set off with small gold diamonds. Indeed, he might have stepped straight out of the restaurant and into this one-sided tussle with the much larger and far better coordinated Grondin Brist. The prepostor had deftly turned the shouting man's initial onrush, so that the Razhaman had ended up pinned face-first against the corridor wall, one arm twisted up behind his back. As I emerged from my room, Brist's foot kicked the prisoner's ankles apart while his free hand searched the man's clothing for weapons, finding none. Through all of this, the agonized cry of "Irmyrlene! Irmyrlene!" continued.

The other person on the scene was the fellow in green who had fled at the sight of Hespira. He hovered ineffectually, clearly wishing to come to the aid of the young man, but prevented by his nature from mixing into an actual fight. Beneath the elegantiast's shouts and the prepostor's grunts, I could hear the servant saying, agitatedly, "Please, sir! Do not hurt Master Imrith!"

Imrith's cries had now become hoarse, as much from overuse of his vocal chords as from the pain his twisted arm must have been giving him. I saw no danger here, but before I acted I consulted my assistant for its wider, sharper perceptions. The integrator told me that a third and fourth visitor were on their way toward us; both were unarmed, and one of them moved with the slowness of aged joints. "But the other is large, fit, and displays the physiological signs of a professional who is about to bring to the situation whatever is required."

It seemed wise to try to lower the tension in the hallway before fresh reserves came up from the rear. I moved farther out of my doorway and raised my voice. "Stop that shouting! Who is this Irmyrlene, and what is she to you?"

The young man quieted almost at once, a response that I would have put down to a recognition of my natural authority if I had not felt a presence behind me. My client had come out of the room. The young man's eyes went to her and immediately filled with tears, though a kind of smile was trying to force itself upon his trembling lips. "Irmyrlene," he said.

I spoke to the prepostor. "I think there is no need to restrain him further."

Brist relaxed the pressure on the young man's twisted arm and pulled him away from the wall, but he kept one hand on his shoulder. All fight had gone out of the fellow. He gazed at Hespira as if at a sight much longed for, though without hope it would ever appear.

"You've come back," he said. "He told me you never would. But here you are."

I turned to Hespira. She was staring at the man in consternation.

"Do you know him?" I said.

"No," she said, then, "wait... I..." She shook her head, as if to settle some loose part back into its place. "There is something. I can't quite..."

"Irmyrlene," the man said, "don't say you don't remember." He made to move toward her, but the prepostor's hand clamped his shoulder and held him back. Still he pleaded with her. "Don't do this to me."

But now another voice spoke, the kind of voice that not only expects answers immediately but expects them to be delivered in a respectful, if not outright cringing, tone. "What is going on here?"

The voice's effect on Grondin Brist was minimal but it struck the other two men with the solid weight of a cudgel. For the one who had been pleading with Hespira, the effect was as if the air had been suddenly let out of him. His face fell, his shoulders slumped, and he seemed to lose overall height.

The man in green livery did literally cringe, shrinking back against the corridor wall to let pass the older man who had come up behind him.

The servant lowered his eyes and kept them fixed on his own feet, as the newcomer brushed by him without a glance and said to Grondin Brist, "You will take your hand off my son, Prepostor. He is coming with me."

"No," said the young man, softly, but it was a syllable of despair, not defiance. His eyes went from Hespira to me, then to the prepostor, and finally to his father. I saw the resemblance between them, though it was all in the frame and features, and the colors of their costumes; in character, they could not have been more different. Somehow a hawk had sired a pigeon. One was hard, the other soft. The younger would always yield, the older would never give way, whatever the price to be paid.

Now the final invitee to the party put in his appearance. As my assistant had said, he was large and well muscled but I recognized the look of a man whose confidence comes not from raw strength but from skill and experience. He wore the same livery as the cringing servant, but there the similarities ended. With a quiet economy of motion he came to stand beside his master's errant son and placed a hand on the young man's upper arm.

Brist was weighing up the situation, in that practical policeman's way that I had often seen hovering about the person of Brustram Warhanny back on Old Earth. He only glanced at the man with whom he now shared possession of his prisoner, then turned his attention to the latter man. "Now, young Imrith," he said, "are you to be quiet?"

It was plain that all the shout had gone out of him. He gazed at Hespira in anguish. "Irmyrlene," he tried, once more.

His father made a brusque motion, and the prepostor released his grip. The large servant exerted a minimum of force and suddenly the son was turned the way they had come and, moving off, his shoulders slumped, feet scarcely lifting for each heavy step. If ever a back could express despair, I knew I was seeing it. The older man half turned his head to snap a syllable at the cowed liveryman who immediately fell in behind.

But the incident had settled nothing. "Wait," I said. "I have questions!" And when no one treated that news as of any importance, I said to the older man, "Where will you be tomorrow? I will wish to speak with you!"

That did get me a response. I was fortunate that a glare could not have had physical force, else its impact would have knocked me clear off my feet, hurtled me back down the corridor, and thrust me right through the building's wall.

Then his gaze went to Hespira and I had a glimpse of the mind behind those raptor's eyes. It was a mind that surgically divided the population of the cosmos into those who were useful to him, those who were of no interest, and those who were trouble. My client clearly fell into the third category.

"You," he said to her, "were not supposed to come back."

I waited to see how Hespira would respond. She was staring at the older man but I saw no recognition in her face. "I don't—" she began, but he cut her off.

"It does not signify," he said. "Just go. And this time, stay away."

I made a gesture indicating that I wished to join the conversation. But the old man was already turning to leave and I saw that the father's back could express contempt as eloquently as the son's could convey defeat.

Hespira was slumped against the door jamb, her face a war between confusion and suffering. Grondin Brist, raising the inside of one wrist to his lips, was communicating with his superior while watching the old man step into the descender and disappear from sight. I was torn between them, but I realized that the prepostor would be at his post and available for consultation through the night, while my client was in need now.

I eased her into the room and closed the door, then went to the dispenser for a dram of restorative and a glass of improved water. Hespira had sunk into a chair, ignoring its efforts to adapt to her unhappy posture. I brought her the two drinks, said, "Come now!" in a peremptory tone, and got her to down the one and sip from the other.

She sat holding the water tumbler in her hand and I could see that she was attempting to batter aside whatever was the inner barrier that kept her from herself. But she was making no headway and the lack of progress was driving her into a fit of frustration. A moment later, she threw the half-full tumbler across the room, splashing liquid in several directions. She uttered a coarse word, then repeated it several times, with rising emphasis, while her fist smacked the arm of the chair, causing it to withdraw.

"It is not like a wall that you can break through," I said. "It will be there until suddenly it is not, and then it will be as if it never was."

She looked at me, her face blotchy and her eyes red. I realized she had been fighting tears. "How can you be so sure?"

"I have been studying the matter," I said. "But that is not the important thing right now."

I supposed that she needed to take out her frustrations on someone, and apparently the tumbler and chair had not satisfied. "Very well, Your Lord High Knowingness," she said, "just what is the important thing?"

"Why, that moments ago, we were in the presence of several people who clearly know who you are."

I saw the import pierce the thicket of emotions that the scene in the hallway had caused her. "Oh," she said, "of course."

There was more I could have added. The encounter in the hallway had not been a clarifying instant for her; the veil had not suddenly fallen. But, at some level of her mind, she had reacted with strong emotion—negative, but strong. To me, that said that some part of her not only recognized the old man and the son, Imrith, but recalled the affective context in which she knew them.

"I think," I said, "that we may be close to a breakthrough." Now I saw hope struggling back to its place. "But, clearly, whatever your connection to those people, it was not tranquil and it did not end well."

"Of that I am sure," she said.

"So you will need to prepare yourself for some rude shocks and sudden drops."

I watched her regather her forces and again I was sure that this was no delicate wisp. She might be pushed back by circumstance, but she would always rally and plow on once more. She rose and went to collect the tumbler, stepping lightly among the devices that had come out to siphon up the spilled liquid.

"Good," I said. "Now, I wish to have a word with Prepostor Brist." She waved her acquiescence, stooping to pick up the container. As she did so, I turned at the door and said, without stress, "Irmyrlene?"

But she did not turn and say, "Yes?" I saw that the three syllables carried no power. She sighed and straightened. "Never mind," I said. "We will arrive when we arrive."

I stood at the door and spoke quietly to my assistant. "Seek out any conflations of the names Irmyrlene and Broon."

It replied instantly. "The local nexus is deficient. It scarcely records births and deaths, let alone any semblance of full information. I can tell you that Irmyrlene is a common name and that the Broons have been a numerous clan on Greighen Island since the antecession. They are further subdivided into several septs, each of which includes a score or more of different families. There are twelve persons registered who have both names and are of the client's approximate age. If I had a birth date or an image, we would be on firmer ground, but even then, the whereabouts of most of the dozen prospects are not known."

"They value privacy," I said.

"To an extreme."

I tried another tack. "What of the name Imrith?"

"Rare on Shannery, common on Ikkibal, especially among the higher ranks."

I told it to combine Imrith with another Ikkibali name. The answer shed new light on the situation.

"Good," I said again. "I believe we will clear away the fog tomorrow."

I went out into the hallway where Brist had resumed his seat. His surveillance suite was watching the area, so he had opened a flask of punge and was sipping from it between taking bites of a roll filled with a spicy substance. "All is nominal," he said.

"Yes," I said. "Thank you for handling that situation so competently."

He dismissed the matter with a shrug. "Easy enough when nobody wants to fight."

"Do you know them?"

"They do not speak to us. I have seen the least of them, the servant who came with the young one," he said. "He does business with Erghreaves the carrier. The others I have never seen." He took another bite, chewed, then washed down the morsel with punge. I waited because I knew there was more to come. "But I would put a week's stipend on the old one being the highman of the outfit."

"The outfit being the Grange," I said.

He made an affirmatory noise around his new mouthful.

"Would this Erghreaves know what goes on east of the Hedge?"

"He might." Another piece of roll went to its destiny. "He might even be persuaded to say what he knows." Lest there be any confusion in my mind, he made a motion involving his thumb and its nearest two neighbors that signified that money would be the most likely persuader.

"What about Prepostor-Corporal Hoop?" I said. "Would he know?"

Grondin Brist smiled the universal smile of the low-ranked policeman who has answered his last question from a civilian and said, "Now how would I know what a corporal might know?"

A painted board above the door of Tamp Erghreaves's dockside establishment advertised: Shipments To All Points, Onworld and Offworld, Even Unto Destinations Unheard-Of.

"A comprehensive service," I complimented the firm's owner, whom I found inclined against the wall while seated in a tilted-back chair on the wooden porch outside his enterprise. He was filling his immediate surroundings with clouds of gray-blue exhaust from a disreputable instrument that depended from his beard-enfolded lips.

"You have something to send?" he said, squinting one eye at me.

"I would prefer to receive," I said, and saw a glint of avarice appear in his unsquinting orb; it arrived so fast I knew that it could not have been far away.

"Receive what?" he said.

"Information." I produced a small gem. "And I would prefer not to haggle."

His chair's front legs struck the porch a resounding thwack! Both eyes opened and the pipe came out of his mouth. "I see," I said, "that I have secured your attention."

He stood up. Being bandy-legged and encumbered by a heavy paunch that pulled him somewhat forward of the vertical, he did not gain much height by the change. His gaze swept over me. "You don't look like one of them," he said.

"Probably because I am not one of them," I said. "And who might these 'them' be?"

"The ones who come looking for information," he said. "They have a certain look about them."

"A Razhaman look?" I said, pushing back the tip of my nose to enlarge my nostrils.

"Could be."

"And what information do they seek, these Razhamans?"

He gave me a look that said we both knew the answer to my question. "Why, the secret of the cream."

"And do you know the secret of the cream?" I said.

His eyes went back to the jewel and I saw him briefly tempted to lie, but then he shook off the urge as pointless. "No," he said. "And I'll tell you for free, nor does anyone else."

"No one?" I said, producing a second stone.

"Just him," he said, and I turned to follow his gaze. Behind me, down the street that descended from the town square, strode the raptor-faced father of the night before. Behind him came his large and capable servant, and bringing up the rear was Bars Hoop. The corporal wore the face of an officer who had a duty to perform and every intention of doing so. The older man came to a halt a pace or two away, his darting eyes having taken in me, Tamp Erghreaves, and the jewels before I could put them out of sight.

"There you see the scurrilous plan," he said, over his shoulder to Bars

Hoop while fixing me with a glare of cold contempt. "As I said, it is about the cream. The woman was to be the key to unlock the secret, through my credulous son. Having failed, this delinquent now seeks to suborn my shipper."

I regarded the speaker with calm equanimity. "You are mistaken. I care nothing for your cream and its secret. My client has had her memory stolen from her—and I suspect you of being involved in that crime."

I think he would have struck me. But the servant placed restraining fingers against his wrist until the older man had mastered himself again. The corporal had watched our exchange with interest, his face giving nothing away. Now he said, "We will repair to my office and disentangle the threads." He spoke to his wrist. "Bring her in."

I had left Hespira at the hotel, watched over by a second prepostor who had relieved Grondin Brist at daybreak. When I arrived at the Prepostory, she was waiting with her escort in the hall outside Hoop's door. Again, the sight of the Razhaman dominee troubled her; I saw her struggling with the nothingness where memory should have been. The older man strode past her as if she did not exist. I took her arm and we all went into the corporal's office.

Hoop took control of the situation. "No infraction has been committed," he said, raising a hand to stay the Razhaman who had immediately started from his chair, protest on his lips. "But it is obvious that a breach of the peace is imminent unless the situation is resolved. I mean to resolve it."

I kept my voice calm. "It is clear that my client has been deprived of her memories—" I began, but was cut off when the old man issued a harsh sound.

"Tchaa!" he said. "Farce and flannel!"

"Easy," said the corporal, pushing at the air with his broad hand as if the motion could gently press the dominee back into his seat. Then to me he said, "No loss of memory has been established. She could be feigning."

Hespira made a small noise of protest to which I added, "I have tested her. The amnesia is real."

"And who," said the Razhaman, "has tested you? If ever I saw a jumped-up mountebank—"

"I assure you," I said, "my credentials—"

We were both interrupted as Bars Hoop raised his voice. "Enough!"

The old man was not used to being talked to in such tones, but his retainer, standing behind his master's chair, again exercised a calming effect via a slight pressure of fingertips on shoulder. We all subsided.

"Now," said the corporal, "the document, if you please."

The servant drew a small roll of some light-colored material from his pouch and stepped forward to spread it on the desk. I leaned forward to look and recognized it as a variant of the unalterable paper that was used for legal documents on many of the Ten Thousand Worlds. I read the several paragraphs of text that were indelibly entered beneath the shimmer of its surface.

The document was an agreement between an Irmyrlene Broon-Paskett, resident of Sandwynd, and the company known as the Grange. In it, in return for "substantial benefits received and herein acknowledged," Broon-Paskett agreed to depart Greighen Island "and its surroundings on land and sea to a distance of not less than three hundred stads," and not to return for the duration of the Grange's operations. The terms of the agreement were enforceable by the justiciar of Sollom Province, the administrative division of Ballaraigh in which the island lay.

The old man's sharp-pointed fingernail tapped that clause. "This empowers you to remove the woman," he said to Bars Hoop. "I demand that you do so."

Hoop regarded the Razhaman with an unsympathetic eye and he amended the dominee's interpretation of the agreement. "Upon the issuance of an order from the justiciar," he said. "Produce the order."

I offered my own amendment. "And while you are about it, produce proof that my client is Irmyrlene Broon-Paskett."

The Razhaman's nostrils flared alarmingly. I took it that he had not spent much of his long life learning to control his anger. His finger stabbed at a spot farther down the page. "There is your proof!"

When he lifted his hand I saw that he had struck at a signature block that showed the autograph of Irmyrlene Broon-Paskett, in a rounded script. Beneath it, a thumb print had been indelibly affixed.

From inside his desk, the corporal brought out a small device that had a lens in its upper surface. He bade Hespira rise from her chair and put her thumb onto the polished surface. There came a flash of dark blue light, then an image of my client's print appeared next to the one captured beneath the document's shimmer. They were identical.

I heard Hespira's sharp intake of breath. She stared at the evidence before her. "What is the name again?" she said. She read it from the document, silently mouthing the syllables.

The old Razhaman's lips made a fricative sound of contempt and dismissal. My client turned to him and said, "Who am I to you? Why did you want me to go? Was it because of your son?"

He would not return her gaze. "You are nothing to me," he said, "but a nuisance and a reproach to the honor of my house." He spoke to Bars Hoop. "Will you now enforce the agreement?"

The corporal was wearing his duty face again. "Produce an order, and I will obey it."

"You will have your order!" the old man snapped, and now he gave my client and me a last withering look. "You," he said to Hespira, "will not collect another scintal from me. And you,"—it was my turn—"can go back to Razham and tell your masters they have failed again."

He had expected those to be his parting words—I had come to understand that Razhamans had a love of drama in their comings and goings—but as his hand reached for the document on the desk, I scooped it up and examined it closely.

"This," I said, "is an agreement between my client—for I accept the identification—and something called the Grange. Your name, whatever it is, does not appear on it."

He snatched for it, but I withdrew it beyond his reach. The servant began to move forward, but Bars Hoop spoke a single syllable and the man stopped.

"What he says is true," said the corporal. "How do we know this agreement has anything to do with you?"

"This is insupportable!" the Razhaman snapped.

"Still," said Hoop, "if you come to the Prepostory seeking our help, you are required to identify yourself. I do not know your name."

The old man struggled to master himself. "My name," he said, "is for my peers."

Hoop's russet brows rose. "And we are not numbered among your peers?"

The old man's only reply was the sound of his breath rushing in and out of his wide nostrils.

"I remind you," said the corporal, "that Shannery was settled by our ancestors, who chafed sore within the strictures of Ikkibali ranks and precedences. While you stand on our soil, we are all your peers."

The Razhaman turned to me. "Give me," he said, "my document."

I handed it to him. He passed it to his retainer as if it had become soiled since he had last held it. Both of them left with neither a word nor a rearward glance.

Hoop regarded Hespira and me in silence for an extended moment. "The nexus will have information on Irmyrlene Broon-Paskett," he said, then added, "though probably not much. Broons are not such as to let others know their business."

He was right, as I found when we returned to the Orban House and I closeted myself with my assistant, asking my client to wait in her room while we queried the island's nexus. I suggested that she might ask the hotel's integrator to provide her with background on the Broon clan, since it was now indisputable that she was Irmyrlene Broon-Paskett.

"Don't call me by that name," she said. "It is not mine."

"It was yours."

"That is as may be. But whoever Irmyrlene Broon-Paskett was, she is not the *me* that I am now. And I do not think that I want to be her."

"Then who will you be?" I said.

"I do not know. Not yet. But that is up to me to decide."

An argument against her position occurred to me, but I saw no point in advancing it. I left her and returned to my room and my work.

"I can tell you," the integrator said, when we were alone, "that as of ten years ago there was a reference to a person named who now would be roughly the same age as our client. She was the product of a union between two Broons, one of them a Paskett, the other a Minderhowth. The liaison did not last and neither parent claimed the offspring. The clan elders sent the girl to be raised by cousins who had a small holding near Sandwynd. They raised firhogs, selling the meat and hides to a local factor."

"Is that all?" I said.

"Amazingly, yes," it said. "However, I can add a conjecture based on a few other scraps of information."

"Do so."

"It seems that Irmyrlene was not happy with her placement. As soon as she was old enough, she left the cousins and sought paid employment on various farms across the island. She never stayed long in any one situation. The local word that might best describe her temperament is 'stroppy.' Then the Grange arrived and bought up many of the farms and feedlots for high prices. Those who were lucky enough to have land to sell took their windfalls and departed for regions where life is easier, abandoning their laborers. A few of the latter were offered menial employment serving the new owner. Irmyrlene Broon-Paskett was one of these."

"What about the Grange's records? What can you glean from their web?"

"Nothing."

"Nothing?" I said. "I thought I built you better than that."

"I can glean nothing because there is no web to winnow through," my assistant said. "The Grange has no access at all to any connectivity. It is entirely self-contained."

A chill went through me. The only people I had ever found living unconnected had been practitioners of magic. And sympathetic association was the last complication I wanted to appear in this discrimination, especially when I was close to resolving it.

But my assistant assuaged my apprehension. "I detect no signs of magic," it said. "The Grange is unconnected because its owner wishes it to be proof against inquiry."

"He has a secret to protect," I said.

"Indeed."

"The secret of the singular cream."

"And perhaps others. He would not reveal even his name."

I steepled my fingers and touched them to my pursed lips, as I was wont to do when thinking. "Hypothesis," I said. "Hespira—or Irmyrlene, as she was then—learned something she should not have, possibly to do with the mysterious cream. We know she recognized the odor of it. She was induced to leave the Grange's territory, being paid 'substantial benefits' and also likely being threatened with unpleasant consequences not recorded in the agreement she signed. Once she was at Wathers, safely distant from the Grange, she was set upon by its minions, who had followed her. They seized her and stole her memory, thus making sure that the secret would not be revealed."

"The hypothesis is tenable," said my assistant, "but not strong."

"Indeed," I agreed. "The plucking away of memory seems an unnecessarily mild-mannered solution to the Grange's problem, considering the old man's shortness of temper. He could far more easily have had her killed. The man with him certainly looked capable and not the type to question the order."

"I concur," said the integrator. "There was no hesitation in dealing harshly with Chumblot on Ikkibal nor with Big Tooth at Wathers. Why would they piddlepeddle about with a troublesome farm girl?"

"Unless," I said, "the matters are not related."

"There is no evidence to indicate that."

"But there are gaps in the evidence. The old man's retainer could have been the fellow who 'dealt expeditiously' with an attempted robbery at Wathers, but who was the woman? And the man who shadowed us at Razham, and presumably did for Chumblot, has also not reappeared."

"Having been seen, perhaps he has lost his usefulness and has been assigned other duties."

"Possible. Or he may have no connection. If we were being shadowed at Razham, why were we not followed to Wathers and then to here, where we are more of a problem than we were on Ikkibal?"

"We need more information," my assistant said.

"We do." I thought for a moment, then made my decision. "Contact Bars Hoop."

A moment later the corporal's face hung in the air before me. "I plan to depart Shannery soon," I said.

"The news is welcome," he said. "The Grange has applied for an order."

"I am concerned for my client's safety. If we have to travel by omnibus, that old man might seek to arrange a more drastic solution somewhere along the way."

"The possibility cannot be overlooked. But I cannot provide an escort beyond my jurisdiction, which ends at the ferry dock."

"We do not require an escort, only permission to bring my space yacht up from Wathers so that we can go offworld directly from here."

I watched him make up his mind. "I will contact the appropriate authorities and see if I can obtain an easement," he said. "Wait while I do so."

His image disappeared, to be replaced by the arms of the Prepostory, an ancient design of restraints and short cudgels grouped around an oddly shaped item of tall headgear. In a few moments he was back. "You may bring up your ship. Have it land at the rear of the hotel."

"Thank you. I will do so."

When the connection was broken I told my assistant to contact the *Gallivant* and bid it come up. "Tell it we will want to depart at sunset."

"Done," it said.

"Was your communication with the ship entirely private?"

"No. The Prepostory is listening in."

"As expected," I said. "Now transmit a series of instructions regarding provisioning and the preparation of a meal for Hespira and me, once we are offworld. Convey an impression that I have finicky expectations and a tendency to repeat myself unnecessarily. But embed in the communication a coded instruction to ignore the food order and instead deploy the yacht's surveillance percepts while over the Grange's property. I want to know everything there is to know about what is behind the Hedge."

"Done."

"Is there any indication the Prepostory intercepted the hidden message?"

"None."

"Good," I said. "Now, can your own percepts locate this Imrith who was doing all the shouting last night?"

The reply took a few moments to arrive. "He is almost out of my range," the integrator said. "He is in an upstairs room of a large residential building at the center of the Grange property. The door is locked and the who's-there will not yield to his entreaties. He keeps going to an open window and gazing forlornly in the direction of Orban."

"Can you reach him with a focused beam of sound?"

"There is a flat rock on one of the hills overlooking the town. I believe I can bounce a message off it and down to where he stands. I presume you would not want any other ear to intercept it?"

"Exactly."

"Let me test the vector. I will imitate a local bird call." A few moments later, it said, "He is looking about for the bird."

"Very good," I said. "Now assume our client's voice and send him a message saying that she will come to him soon after sunset. He must meet her at the place where they first spoke."

"You assume that he will remember the spot?"

"He is a Razhaman of the elegantiast class. It will be burned deeply into his romance-addled cerebrum."

"Should you not secure the client's permission? She may not wish to meet him."

"It is a small subterfuge. Besides, she will not be keeping the appointment," I said. "We will."

The integrator transmitted the message and reported that the young man now showed considerably more energy. "He is tearing up a wall hanging," it said. "Now he is knotting the lengths together."

"Good," I said. "Keep him in view and report any developments. I am going to confer with our client."

I found Hespira coincidentally standing at the open window of her room and gazing out at the rear yard of the hotel. But her face, when she turned at my entrance, was not forlorn. She had the look of a woman who had made up her mind. "I want to thank you for all that you have done," she said, "but now I want you to stop."

"Stop what?" I said.

"Stop trying to find out who I am and what happened to me."

I let my surprise show. "You do not wish to know?"

"No."

I could see that she had been prey to strong emotions. Beads of moisture dotted the fine reddish hairs on her upper lip and I was conscious of a warm odor from her body—not an unpleasant scent, nor yet enticing, but simply an essence of her. I found myself once again motivated to protect her.

"Just because you are done with Irmyrlene Broon-Paskett," I said, "does not mean that others may be. Whoever took your memories did so for a reason. Not knowing that reason may put you in jeopardy. Our having come here may have set wheels turning again, wheels that this time may crush the life out of you."

She did not answer my argument but took a new tangent, indicating the screen of the hotel's integrator which was shimmering against an inner wall. It was filled with images and text. "I have been learning about the Broons. They are notorious hereabouts for their hard-heartedness. The 'miserly clan' they are called, not to mention 'groat-squeezers' and 'grudge-grippers.' Most of them would apparently step over a dying neighbor to gain a dented tin cup."

"General descriptions always admit of exceptions. How do you know that you were not one of the statistical outliers, a kindly Broon?" I said.

"I was a young girl abandoned by my parents because they tired of being together and obviously tired of keeping me. If I come from the kind of people who could do that, odds are that I am not much different."

"Supposition," I said. "You do not know that."

"I saw the look on that boy's face. I broke his heart."

"He is a high-ranked Razhaman. They wallow in tragedy and melodrama. At least until they wed."

"And I took his father's money to go off and leave him."

"I suspect there were threats as well as emoluments."

She gave me a harsh look. "A Broon's response to a threat is the same as to a blow: vendetta to the seventh generation. I come from hard stock."

I argued with her, even though I could see I was making no headway.

The thought of her being in danger disturbed me deeply. Finally, having come to understand that, memories or no memories, she was as unmovable as her clan was reputed to be, I said, "Then what can I do for you?"

"Take me back to Old Earth," she said. "There I will start anew."

"What will you do?"

"I will do whatever comes to hand. It does not signify. What does matter is who I shall be."

"And who will you be?"

"Someone who is the opposite of Irmyrlene Broon-Paskett. Someone kind."

I sighed. "The *Gallivant* arrives this afternoon. I have a few errant threads to knot up, then we will go."

Her face softened. "I am sorry to be of such trouble to you."

"That does not sound much like a Broon. Perhaps you were not like your relatives."

She signaled a negative. "I think it is because, since my amnesia, I have known only kindness, at your hands. You have not even sought to take advantage of my dependence. Most men would, even though I am no beauty."

"You are my client. It would have been improper."

"I suspect that young Irmyrlene met with a different set of standards. I would just as soon not remember them. But I will try to repay your efforts."

I waved the suggestion away and returned to my room. As the door closed behind me, my assistant said, "I am concerned for you. Your indicators are well above normal."

"Nonsense," I said, "I am as always."

"Your heart rate is elevated, as is your respiration. Glandular secretions are indicative of serious stress."

A man had to be a fool to dispute his integrator's percepts. "You heard our conversation."

"You did not tell me not to."

"I am worried about my client," I said.

"By what passed between you, she no longer stands in that relation to you. At best, you are her unpaid chauffeur, and then only until we return to Old Earth. After that, she will make her own way."

The thought of Hespira on her own troubled me. "I still feel an obligation."

"And that obligation drives you to emotions I have not often seen in you before, and certainly never in a professional connection."

"What are you saying?"

"Now you are irritated."

"I am not insensible. I do not require a moment-by-moment guide to the emotions I am experiencing," I said. "Make your point."

"You are behaving abnormally, without apparent cause. What does that suggest?"

I groaned. "We are not back to magic again?" I drew from within my shirt the disk Osk Rievor had given me. It glowed a cool blue. "There, not so much as a tinge of red."

"You assume the talisman is functional, and that it cannot be overridden by a practitioner with more authority."

"I am not ensorceled," I said. "Rather, I am facing the imminent end of all that I hold dear. Assisting Hespira has felt like a way to assert my true self, to hold up a small, brave flame against the encroaching darkness. Now she has leaned over and blown it out. A certain degree of vexation is to be expected."

The integrator changed the subject. "The *Gallivant* is in the air." A screen appeared, showing the yacht's route across the curve of Shannery's surface. "It will arrive shortly."

"Good. Advise our client. I will go and settle the account with the hotel. We will go aboard as soon as the ship lands."

The *Gallivant* greeted us with steaming punge and a fragrant assortment of ship's bread. We settled in the salon, my assistant once again hung upon its hook, to sip and chew as the yacht displayed the results of its surveillance of the Grange lands, captured at an oblique angle as the ship had leisurely settled to its present resting place behind the Orban House.

I saw an agricultural precinct, though most of it had been left to go fallow and its buildings rendered uninhabitable. Starting at the outskirts of the Grange lands, which covered almost the entire eastern half of Greighen Island, overgrown fields crowded against roofless homesteads, doors and windows gaped empty in the walls of abandoned barns and houses. Weeds sprouted down the middles of the unused dirt roads. Only near the center of the territory were there signs of husbandry. Here, one large holding had been maintained, its lawns and flower beds well tended, the croplands surrounding the manor house laid out in orderly plots of legumes, root crops, and berries, the orchard bursting with several species of trees, all well-laden with fruit, though the lighter gravity and richer air made the trees appear odd: as if the oversized apples and pears and grunderbols were merely pome-shaped balloons.

I could see some two dozen men and women working the fields and others performing domestic chores in and around the estate's outbuildings, but no guards kept a watch on their activities. Very few of the people in view wore the green livery, and all who did so displayed the adaptive characteristics of Razhamans. They busied themselves around the big house. I surmised that the dominee had brought only a handful of retainers with him from Ikkibal, and that they looked after him and his son, while locally hired labor delved and sowed and reaped. The estate was self-sufficient; its only contact with the world outside the Hedge was through the servant's liaison with Erghreaves the shipper.

A stone wall enclosed the manor, with strong gates. When I enlarged the image I saw that these physical barriers had been enhanced by less obvious defenses. "What do you make of those?" I asked my assistant.

"High quality," it said, "difficult to defeat. I believe they are intended to keep out more than just the locals."

But then we turned to the mystery that lay behind the big house, in what had probably been the previous owner's garden and patio. The space it occupied was sufficient for a modest one-story building, but its actual dimensions and shape were unknowable; whatever stood there was effectively clouded.

"Can you penetrate it?" I asked my assistant.

"Not from this distance," it said. "I could give a better answer after a closer inspection, but it is a very good cloud. Even tickling it to search for entry points might set alarms sounding."

The ship interrupted to say, "I am receiving a communication from Prepostor-Corporal Bars Hoop. He wishes to know why we have not departed."

"Tell him," I said, "that I am not satisfied with the quality of your catering arrangements and am making changes before we lift off."

"That is not true, and it reflects discreditably on my shipliness."

"Rather, it reflects poorly on my character," I said, "making me appear persnickety, even effete." I added, "When we have done more traveling together, you will come to see that occasionally we must be other than forthright with local authorities. Many of them lack imagination and react poorly to creativity and unexpected innovation."

My assistant said, "Bars Hoop does not appear to lack imagination."

"True," I said, "which makes the need for creativity all the more pressing."

The *Gallivant* said, "I have transmitted the message. The corporal says that if we are not offworld by the seventh hour, he will seize me, then subject all of us to a searching inquiry."

"Tell him that his orders will be carried out." I returned to consideration of the mysterious structure behind the manor house. "Let us hope the young and besotted Razhaman knows how to unpick the cloud."

Hespira spoke up. "Why are you doing this? I have told you I do not wish you to pursue my case any further."

"I am not doing it for you," I said, "but for my own peace of mind."

"You should leave that poor boy alone. Haven't we brought him enough trouble?"

"He will not notice a little more."

"Then I am going with you."

"No," I said.

"I owe that young man at least an apology."

"No."

She looked at me in a way that made me think she had been right about the obduracy of Broons. "If you do not take me, I will inform Bars Hoop of your intentions." She saw me weighing my response to her threat. "Or do you mean to imprison me on your ship? Is that how you will show your 'concern' for me?"

"Two people have died on the fringes of this discrimination," I said. "When we expose the heart of it, the danger may be extreme."

Her over-long chin poked out. "Nevertheless," she said.

I thought about it. "I have a spare elision suit," I said. "But you must do exactly as I say."

Her voice said she would comply. Her eyes said something more ambiguous.

CHAPTER EIGHT

I had never liked dropping through the upper atmosphere, with nothing but a thin film of membrane to argue on my behalf against the pull of gravity—even Shannery's lighter tug. I liked it even less in darkness, with Hespira's arms clasped about my neck and her weight in my arms, though the latter was further reduced by the small obviator she wore attached to her belt. The wind of our descent whistled in my ears as the *Gallivant* climbed smoothly away from us and the manor at the heart of the Grange property rose too swiftly for my liking.

"Put us down behind that byre," I said to my integrator, which was also draped about my neck and to which I had left the task of managing the airfoil as well as the business of keeping us undetected by the defenses the Razhamans had installed. Hespira and I were both clad in elision suits of my own design. The suits' fabric neither reflected nor absorbed most electromagnetic energies, but caused them to slip over its surface and continue on their way unimpeded—at least, that was so for all but a tiny fraction of the spectrum's frequencies. A highly refined detector could spot the minimal disturbance, and if that detector were connected to an alarm, or worse, a self-aiming weapon, the results could be unpleasant. The Razhaman dominee had impressed me as the kind who would mount just such a refined and connected defense; for that reason, I had reconfigured our suits' controls to give any watching percepts the impression that we were a small bird arrowing down to its nest at the end of the day.

We landed in deep shadow behind a small building with rough drystone walls and a sloping roof of something like shale. Around it hung a complex miasma of dank straw, spoiled food, animal musk, and dung. As I lowered Hespira to the ground, her nostrils flared, then her face wrinkled in distaste. She said, "I know that smell."

"It is the odor of firhogs," I said. "Irmyrlene Broon-Paskett grew up on a farm that raised them. I believe it was her experience with the creatures that led to her being hired to tend the stock for the Grange." Though it seemed a strange choice of livestock for traditionalist Razhamans, who eschewed any form of pig flesh as unsuitable for consumption.

"So. I was a pigstress," she said, trying on the self-description as if it were a new garment. Then she discarded it. "Something else I am glad not to be."

Our voices must have reached the large, flaplike ears of the beasts on the other side of the wall. They began to snuffle and grunt. "They know your sound," I said.

"As do I," said a new voice from the darkness. The young Razhaman stepped forward from where he had been waiting. Before we had landed, my assistant had advised me privately of his presence and the fact that he was unarmed. The young man now reached out a hand, saying, "Where are you? I cannot see you."

Hespira removed the cowl and mask of the elision suit, so that her face appeared in the dimness. I left my disguise intact.

"Here I am," she said, slipping the camouflage down to her waist so that now she was half visible. "I have to ap—"

She got no further because the young man launched himself at her, with little glad cries and deep-throated murmurs. He enfolded her in his arms and kissed her neck and ears. She stiffened in his embrace and sought to push him away, but her arms were pinned to her body. Meanwhile he spoke rapidly and in hushed whispers, something about how he had known that she would return to him, that he had remained devoted to her, that they were "like Albamir and Thirraz."

"A legendary couple from an Ikkibali romance," my assistant said in our private mode. "She set him a series of increasingly daunting tasks, all of which he—"

"Shush," I said, aloud and to both the integrator and the boy. I intervened in his pinioning of my client, levering his arm from around her torso, then interposing my invisible self between them. He struggled to reattach himself to her but I put my hands against his chest and pushed him away.

"Enough," I said. "This is not a reunion. This is a Severance."

The word had a specific meaning within the Ikkibali romantic tradition, which I had comprehensively researched. In a Severance, the damzel broke all connection with the swain—I have used the archaic Ikkibali terms—until he had met all of her Stipulations—again, the jargon of the custom—usually by performing several difficult tasks. He might be sent on an arduous journey—the Wayfaring that was called—or be required to undertake some self-demeaning labor, known as the Abnegation.

"Who speaks?" the young man said.

"The damzel's intermediary," I said. I removed the cowl of my elision suit so that my head floated in the air before him.

He assumed the prescribed stance. "Say on," he said, "I attend." These were the formal words, signifying that he had accepted that henceforward I would be the only conduit between him and the object of his obsession.

"Wait—" said Hespira, but I put a still invisible finger to her lips and whispered into her ear, "If you wish to be kind to this fellow, you will give him what he seeks."

"But—"

"I assure you, what he seeks is not you. It is the ritual of which he has made you the focus."

She subsided. I believed that the impetuosity with which he had seized her was causing her to reassess the situation. Meanwhile, the young man had drawn himself into a pose I had seen in my researches: one leg before the other, its foot extended at an angle to the other, one fist balled and pressed against the hip, chin elevated, eyes seeking the middle distance. "I will hear the Stipulations," he said, and I heard a repressed tremor of excitement beneath the attempt at dignified calm.

"Only the first will be revealed to you tonight," I said.

"Very well."

Stipulations came in sets of four, seven, or nine. "There will be seven," I said, a number I believed would satisfy this particular swain. Four would probably have seemed trifling, even an insult, for one of such ardor, but nine might have broken the spell; seven ought to strike the right balance.

"Accepted," he said, confirming my estimations.

"Tonight's task will be the Violation."

He blinked at that, and his chin began to droop. I supposed that he had been expecting the Privation—the swain must fast for a few days, or give up some favorite food for a longer spell—but pride would not allow him to quail at the first test. He straightened and said, "Very well."

"At the rear of your father's house," I said, "there is a nebulosity."

The swain's eyes widened in alarm. I supposed he had been expecting a garden-variety Violation, to be sent to steal some small treasure from a neighbor or deface a public monument. But the Grange had neither.

Still, the young man recovered his aplomb; after all, the more daunting the tasks, the more credit to be won by facing down his fears.

"You will take us into the clouded space and reveal its secret."

He hissed in a breath between almost closed lips, then blew out the air and shook himself. "I will meet the Stipulation," he said.

"Then let us be about it."

My assistant had been examining the wards and defenses. It told me quietly that it could have defeated most of them, but that one or two might have caused problems. But by suborning the son of the dominee, we had taken a simpler, more direct approach: he knew all the codes and waved us through what would otherwise have been a time-consuming maze. Still, he took us along shadowed paths that kept hedges and topiary between us and the lighted windows of the manor, until we came to what had been a walled garden, but was now filled with a general vagueness.

"It is a very good cloud," said my assistant. "I am not sure I could have penetrated it without being noticed. Also, once we pass within, I will not be able to detect any comings and goings outside the nebulosity."

"We will not be here long," I said.

The son touched his fingertips to a receptor set in the wall beside the ornamental iron gate, then spoke a combination of words and numbers. Silently, the gate swung wide, and I noticed that its lower edge had concealed the emitter of a powerful disorganizer set into the threshold. Anyone attempting to pass through without authorization would not have received a warning jolt, but would have instantly become an expanding nebula of disconnected molecules.

We stepped through and found ourselves at the outer edge of the cloud. Our guide extended his ungloved hand at waist height. It disappeared into the vagueness. He turned his wrist, I heard a click, and when he pulled back he drew toward him the handle of a door made of panes of treated glass. Beyond were light and warmth, and two familiar odors. We stepped inside and he closed the door after us.

Another disorganizer, mounted on an armature against the opposite wall, brought its emitter to bear on us, but the swain spoke a phrase in an archaic language. "Honor something," my assistant quietly translated for me. "It is the motto of an aristocratic Razhaman family known as—"

"I know what family," I said. It was warm and sultry in the greenhouse. I stripped off the upper half of my elision suit, saying, "I am more interested in the insects."

They were not true insects, of course, having evolved on another world, but they were a reasonable approximation. They came in two kinds: a slow-moving, gray, dome-backed species almost as long as my palm was wide; and an agile, multi-legged type that was about the size and shape of my smallest finger, if my finger had been covered in segmented bands of black chitin, ending in several eyes and a tubelike mouth.

The slow-movers were mooching around in the bottom of a wide, shallow tray that covered most of the floor of what I now saw must have formerly been a greenhouse. The quicker beasts were constantly attending the gray ones, stroking and grooming them with their forelegs. The result of these ministrations was that one end of each dome-backed creature regularly secreted a globe of clear, amber liquid. To this, the segmented insect would apply its tubular mouth, the droplet would shrink and vanish, and the herder would scuttle away to disappear into one of several small holes in a large, square box that stood at the far end of the tray.

From the tray rose a foul stench of ordure. I moved closer and saw that its bottom was smeared with rotting vegetation and other, even less wholesome matter. Now I skirted around the edge of the tray to examine the box. It was hinged on the top, and when I lifted the lid to see inside, I was met by a gust of pungent sweetness—the odor of singular cream.

Within, the hive was a writhing squirm of the black herders, scores of them moving in complex patterns. As I watched, a new arrival came in from the tray. The insect walked across its hive-mates to an inner wall of the box that was covered from floor to top with six-sided cells that looked to be made of paper. Other insects, with chisel-like mandibles, were chewing at the wood of the box to create the material from which the cells were made.

But my eye remained on the one that had come in from the herd. It climbed the box's rear wall to position itself at the mouth of a newly made cell. It dipped its mouth-tube into the empty space, then its long body convulsed; the spasm projected a spew of thick, pale liquid from its innards, filling perhaps a third of the cell. Immediately, the insect turned and departed the hive, its place at the cell being taken by another incomer that vomited up its portion in turn. As I watched, a third herder came in and relieved itself of its stomach's contents, after which the cell builders sealed the now filled cavity with a paper plug.

"Can you identify them?" I asked my assistant.

"They are not native to Shannery," it said. "They closely resemble two symbiotic species that occur in the jungles of Aphor on Ikkibal, but these are much larger."

"Shannery has lighter gravity and richer air. The animals could be induced to grow larger here."

"That would explain it. But what is their purpose, and why must it be kept secret?"

I thought I knew the answer but was lacking one more item of evidence. Unfortunately, that item now arrived unexpectedly, as the door to the greenhouse opened and was filled by the figure of the dominee's large and capable retainer, carrying a ceramic pot covered by a cloth. Behind him came the hawk-eyed elegantiast himself.

The servant stooped to put the pot down inside the insects' enclosure. As he rose, his hand was moving to a pocket of his breeches but he froze in a half-crouch as he saw the energy pistol that had filled my hand as I flexed my forearm.

"Beware!" said my assistant in my ear, but the warning came too late. While I had been dealing with the bodyguard, the dominee had spoken a word. From behind me I heard the hum of the disorganizer charging itself and the simultaneous swish of its swivel mount as the weapon swung in my direction—but my assistant acted to confuse its aiming mechanism, giving me time to step closer to the dominee's son and point my weapon at him.

The old man spoke another word. The disorganizer's hum diminished. But now the retainer had his weapon out and pointed at Hespira. I felt a burst of anxiety but I mastered it and spoke calmly to the dominee. "The situation is not as dire as it may seem."

His raptor's eyes raked me. "It is as dire as I say it is."

I inclined my head. "Indeed. But I hope to convince you that your suppositions are in error."

He still regarded me with distaste and the eye-flick he aimed Hespira's way conveyed only disgust. But then he looked at his fool of a son, with my weapon's emitter close by the young man's head, and his mouth softened, though only slightly. "Very well," he said, "convince me."

"May we lower our weapons and call a truce?"

He nodded to the retainer and we let our pistols descend until they lay alongside our thighs. I felt the tension ease from the muscles of my back and I said, "We have two issues here. The first is the situation of my client."

"She was paid," the old man said, "and well paid. I will not give her more."

"Father," said the young man, "I—"

"Silence!" The dominee's voice carried almost a physical force. The son reacted as if he had been slapped, but he said no more.

"She has not come for money," I said.

A moment's confusion made its way across the old man's face, then his expression hardened again into contempt as he gestured toward the young man and said, "She cannot possibly expect to…"

I spoke the words he could not bring himself to utter. "Espouse herself to your son? No. She would find the notion as ridiculous as you do."

The swain groaned. No one paid him any heed.

The old man's head drew back and he looked at me from the corners of his eyes. "Then what?" he said.

"It was as I said at the Prepostory. Someone has taken her memories. I found her wandering the streets of Olkney on Old Earth—"

"Old Earth?" said the dominee. "I do not know the place."

"It is a long way up The Spray," I said.

"But how would she have gotten there? I gave her funds to take herself to Wathers and find suitable work, but not enough to travel to distant worlds."

"That is one of the questions I am seeking to answer," I said. But I was beginning to think that I was asking the wrong person. "Let me tell you what I know and what I surmise, then see if you and I can find a common footing for further discussion."

"Very well."

"Almost three years ago, you and your son came here from Razham on Ikkibal. For reasons of your own, you bought up half of Greighen Island, and required those who sold their lands to you to move on. You then established a small farm and hired a few of the former residents to work it, although this clouded part of the enterprise was looked after only by you and those who were closest to you."

The old man dipped his head a minim. "Yes."

"My client, Irmyrlene Broon-Paskett, of Sandwynd, was engaged to tend your firhogs, she having had some experience in that line."

Again, the minimal dip of the chin.

"But a problem ensued: your son was at that age when young Razhamans of his class engage in the Ennoblanz. Lacking an appropriate focus for his inclinations, he fixed upon my client and tried to involve her in the rituals."

A hiss escaped the old man's drawn lips. I hurried on. "So you did what you thought necessary: you permanently separated them, paying the young woman to leave the vicinity. She had no particular regard for him and went. Your son lapsed into romantic reveries of what might have been, and all would have been well in the end—except that she suddenly reappeared."

The dominee's eyes narrowed. "She will not profit by it."

"I assure you," I said, "that she does not seek to. Nor do I. But now I must ask you a question and to charge you on your honor to answer with the truth."

I saw his eyes flick toward the covered pot. A humpbacked insect had got the hooks of its front legs into the fabric of the cloth and was trying to pull itself upward. A pair of feathery antennae wriggled, catching the foul odor that filtered out from beneath the cover.

"No," I said, "nothing to do with that. I want you to swear to me that neither you, nor any of your establishment, had any role in depriving my client of her memories."

The dominee looked at Hespira, and for the first time I saw no hostility in his aspect. "She truly does not remember?"

Hespira spoke. "Until today, I did not know even my name."

The old man studied her. "She speaks differently," he said. "The hard cockiness is gone." He came to a decision. He struck one fist against his breastbone, touched its knuckles to his lips, and said, "I swear by the dignity of my ancestors and in the hope of my descendants' good name that neither I nor any of mine had any part in what has happened to her."

It was the proper form. The Razhaman had to be believed. "You know nothing of what happened after she left?"

"No. Fezzant, here," he indicated the big man, "took her over to Orban and saw her onto the ferry. She left without a backward glance."

The young man groaned softly. Everyone turned to him and issued some variation on "Hush!"

"Then the resolution I had hoped to find here still eludes me," I said. "And I have no further trail to follow."

"It does not matter," Hespira said.

But it mattered to me. "We will trouble you no further," I said.

"No," said the old man. "Unfortunately, I cannot let you leave. You have seen…" His hand gestured at the scene at our feet. A second gray insect was attempting to climb over the first, its antennae vibrating with its eagerness to get at the reeking stuff in the covered pot.

"Your secret is safe with me," I said.

The old man signaled to the retainer, who brought up his weapon again. It was a high-velocity projectile pistol, and now its muzzle was aimed at me. I was familiar with its type; the barrel was surrounded with intense magnetic forces under artificial pressure, which were capable of accelerating a segmented pellet into my flesh with such speed that the projectile would virtually atomize on impact, sending a pressure wave to tear its way through my innards in all directions. The shock would kill me almost instantly.

I brought my energy pistol once more to bear on the young man. But I saw something in the father's gaze that troubled me. He was calculating whether his honor meant more to him than his son's life, and for a Razhaman that could be a closely run contest.

"There is another way," I said.

He looked at me as if I had interrupted him just when he had almost reached a conclusion. "What?" he said.

"Give me a coin," I said.

Now his look said that I was irritating him with nonsense when he was in the midst of important concerns.

"A coin," I said. "I assure you I do not trifle."

Abstractedly, the dominee patted the front of his breeches and the loose blouse he wore above them. He found no coin; most probably, he almost never carried currency; the very rich seldom do. Finally, he glanced at the retainer and made a small gesture with two fingers.

The man with the projectile weapon reached into his pocket, found a half-sequint, and flipped it toward me, never taking his eyes off mine. I caught the coin without breaking our locked gaze and saw his eyebrows quirk to acknowledge the achievement.

"Now," I said to the dominee, "say 'I engage you.' "

With the air of one humoring a harmless loon, the Razhaman repeated the phrase.

"Then there it is," I said. "You have retained me as a discriminator. I am professionally bound to protect your interest and never to divulge any information that derives from our association."

Skepticism warred with the old man's wish to accept the information. I said, "You are not the only one concerned for his honor."

Hespira spoke up then. "It is true. His profession means everything to him. He is what he does. I trust him completely."

"And what of her?" the dominee said.

"She is returning to Old Earth. Just as you have never heard of it, no one there has ever heard of you or the matter that caused you to come here and do all this. Besides, she has not worked out the story, having had enough troubles of her own."

I saw him mentally chewing what I had served him and, after a moment of indecision, I saw him swallow it. "Very well," he said. "Depart immediately, and we will say no more."

The weapons were put away. I made a formal gesture of respect which the old man accepted with punctilio. Then I said, "Except for one last thing."

"And what is that?"

"If you will accept it, I would like to compliment you on a delicious sense of humor."

The Razhaman looked at me without expression for the span of several heartbeats, then a grim half-smile briefly made a place for itself on his lips. "An apt choice of words," he said, "on the strength of which I gratefully accept your compliment."

The son made a protest as Hespira and I moved toward the door, but as we exited I heard the father explaining in graphic terms how Imrith's grasp of the situation fell short of reality. Fezzant led us to an open field stooked with hay and left us there. I had my assistant summon the *Gallivant*. It dropped rapidly from the sky, we went aboard, and we were already exiting Shannery's atmosphere when a signal from Bars Hoop arrived, demanding to know what we were playing at.

I replied that we had had to finish a small matter involving the Razhamans. "But all has ended amicably," I said, "and we will never disturb Greighen Island again."

"See that you don't," said the Prepostor-Corporal, and broke the connection.

I honored my word to Issus Khal, for such was the name of the Razhaman elegantiast whose lands we had quitted, and did not respond to Hespira's questions about the meaning of the clouded greenhouse and the singular cream. "You have been glad to have forgotten so much," I said. "Just add the matter to your long list of the unremembered."

But later, as the *Gallivant* drove steadily toward the first whimsy that would throw us partway home, I raised the issue with my assistant. "I would like," I said, "to be able to tell the substance of the story, without violating my undertaking to Issus Khal. When I attend salons, I am frequently importuned to relate episodes from my forays into Olkney's criminal halfworld. The listeners find them at least titillating, and I endeavor to make them instructive."

"I believe you do not mind if you fail in the second objective," the integrator said, "so long as you succeed in the first."

"You think me an entertainer?" I said.

"I know that you enjoy the smattering of applause and the half-hidden grimaces of those whose stories you have outdone."

"There is no fault in taking pride in accomplishment," I said, "but you are not addressing the issue. How may I tell the revenger's tale without breaking my word?"

"By removing the identifying elements of person and place, and retaining the essence of the original offense and the revenge. Or you can wait a little while, until he chooses to inform the ranking members of Razhaman society what he has been feeding them this past year and more."

I decided I would not wait. Instead, I had the ship bring out a scriptmanet in my cabin. It had always been my practice to compose my lengthier anecdotes in advance, refining and polishing them, then committing them to memory so that when I spoke at a salon the story would come out well-measured and balanced. Thus, as we sped toward the whimsy, I sat and produced this tale:

There was a man of the highest rank on one of the Ten Thousand Worlds where rank means everything. He differed with his spouse of many years, a quarrel that could not be resolved because both had great pride and neither would yield. To force him to her will, she left their manse and went to a sanctuary, and there she cohabited with a great number of men, as custom allowed. Some of them were her husband's peers, some were not, but all were experienced practitioners of the cruel arts of gossip and mockery.

Soon, the husband found that he could not frequent any of his accustomed haunts without being the target of sardonic glances and salacious whispers. He bent enough to offer his spouse a compromise, but she would have none of it. The lady had developed a taste for being on top of things, and now her pride grew overweening. She would accept nothing but unconditional surrender. This the lord would not, could not offer.

Like all persons of his station, he had no occupation but did have several interests. One of these was the study of his world's insects, and in that amateur pursuit he saw an opportunity for vengeance. He made his plans and dispositions, and when all was in hand he went away to a remote place on another world where he was not known, and began to craft his revenge.

He purchased an isolated estate and ringed it round with defenses of his privacy. He had brought with him two species of insect that lived in symbiotic harmony with each other. The relationship between them was that of herder and cattle. One species was placid; it ate ordure, digesting the filth and processing it through its alimentary canal so that what emerged was a nutritious liquid. The other was active and social; it collected the liquid, mixed the sweetness with enzymes in its own gut, and vomited out a stable food that was stored in its hives.

The creatures grew larger and stronger on the remote world, where the gravity was less and the air richer. The lord now induced subtle changes into their digestive processes, so that the end result of their excreting and vomiting was a complex alkaloid as strangely delicious as it was highly addictive. He bred up a sufficient population of the symbiotes and when they began to produce small quantities of the drug, he contrived to introduce it into the eateries where those who had mocked him were wont to gather. He even designed and supplied a silver pot and a unique little spoon of the same metal with which the stuff must be eaten. And he mandated that its consumption should be preceded by a small ritual: the striking of the spoon against the pot. Those who ate the substance soon grew dependent on it; the mere sound of the chime would cause their mouths to water and the flesh to itch.

But creating a class of addicts was only a step toward his aim. The revenge was in what he fed them. Certain animals, whose flesh was eaten on many worlds, were never consumed in his culture. They were considered spiritually unclean, and even the most tangential contact with them required the contaminated one to undergo a lengthy and tiresome ordeal ere purity could be regained. The lord acquired a herd of these beasts, and had them tended by persons of another culture who were not fastidious. Moreover, he ordered that their excrement be scrupulously collected so that it could be fed to the insects who excreted the liquid manure that became the vomit that those who had scorned and mocked him now craved. As a garnish, he added his own personal wastes to the feedstock.

Then he waited, feeding their appetites, until he was sure that every one of them had consumed his product enough to crave it. Only then did he reappear amongst them. And he chose to do so during the grand levee that occupied the apex of the social season for persons of his rank.

Into the great ballroom, filled with the cream of his society, he strode. He mounted the bunting-festooned dais. The music stopped, to be replaced by a hiss of whispers and a rattle of cruel laughter. But all that abruptly ceased when the returnee held up a small silver pot and tapped it with a small silver spoon, so that the tiny note rang in a sudden silence.

"I have always heard," said the lord, "that revenge is a dish best served cold. As mine has been served to you."

And then he told them.

It would need a good polish, I decided, but the essence was there. And then the *Gallivant* sounded its own chime to announce that we were nearing the whimsy. It was time to lie down and take the medication that would prevent our impending passage through irreality from damaging our psyches. I lay upon my pallet and my fingers closed upon the small sac and pressed it into my palm. The substances entered my flesh and I fell into oblivion.

"There has been another incident," the ship said when I awoke. I lay inert, letting the last wisps of the drugs effervesce from my neural tissues. My mouth was thick and dry. I sat up, groggy, and reached for the carafe of improved water. The liquid rinsed the coating from my tongue, the film over my eyes disappeared, and I settled back into the familiarity of space and time.

"What has happened?" I said.

"That," the *Gallivant* said. It caused a narrow beam of light to fall from the ceiling onto the hinged table attached to the far wall of the cabin. Atop the table sat a scarred and battered object about the size of the top joint of my thumb. As I stood and approached it, it emitted a buzzing sound.

"Report," I said.

The buzz stopped and was replaced by a human voice, Osk Rievor's voice, though distorted and sounding as if it were produced by the vibration of thin plates of metal. "...third attempt... contact..." There came a pause, filled by a hissing sound, then, "if received..." Another static-filled pause, then, "...jewels..." another burst of meaningless noise, then, "a salamander... reverse polar... your return."

And that was all. I picked up the bee, noted that it was ice cold, though the metal of its outer shell now felt soft, almost cheese-like. I carried it to the salon, where my assistant hung upon its hook. "You heard?" I said.

"Indeed."

"Inspect the bee. See if more of the message can be recovered."

It did so, but without success other than to repair a severed connection that had inhibited the device's display of the image that accompanied the sound. I saw a sequence of views of my other self, flashing on and off, interrupted by a screenful of flickering spots, accompanying the broken-up message. I could tell from the background that Osk Rievor was in the rented cottage at the Arlem estate, in the study where he kept his magical paraphernalia. The bee looked to have been sitting in the palm of his hand and, as he spoke to its percepts, the effect was as if he was looking down toward me.

"What was that?" I said. I thought I had caught a flash of light just as he spoke the last word of the message. It seemed to me that Osk Rievor had reacted to it, looking away from the bee's visual percept and, if I had the angle right in my recollection, toward the study window.

"I will replay the sequence," my assistant said.

"Do so. And slow it down."

The image reappeared, without the sound. I saw my former intuition's lips slowly shaping themselves around the first syllable of "return," then came a sudden illumination upon the plaster wall behind him. Osk Rievor's eyes moved leisurely from me toward something above and behind me. I saw them widen in surprise, then the image was gone.

"Replay," I said, "from the beginning." I watched the emotions that animated my alter ego's face, seeing what would have been brief microexpressions evolve more slowly as he appeared and disappeared between stretches of empty noise.

"I see agitation, but tending more toward excitement than fear," I said to my assistant. "Then, at the end, I see pure surprise."

"I concur," the integrator said. "But there is something more. Observe."

At that moment, Hespira came in, rubbing her eyes. "What is going on?" she said, but I signaled that I was occupied and waved her toward the pot of punge that the ship had provided, and which I had been ignoring. Then I gave my full attention to what the integrator was now displaying.

It had frozen the image of Osk Rievor's face as his gaze had turned to the window whence came the flash of light. Now that image enlarged and enlarged again, until the screen was filled with only my alter ego's right eye. Still the magnification bored closer, until I was seeing only the dark pupil, widening in surprise. Reflected in the lens was a view of the study window. I could see the intersecting bars of wood that separated the aperture's square panes of glass, though the straight lines and right angles were curved by the curvature of Osk Rievor's eye. Little could be seen of the view outside the cottage because the glass was aglare with bright, actinic light. I could not see the light's source.

"What is that?" I said, pointing to a dark shape barely visible against the light from outside.

"It is indistinct," my assistant said. "It appears just as the light bursts, but then the signal ends in static and the shape breaks up."

"Can you clarify it?"

"Only by hypothesizing." The integrator referred to the process by which it would adjust for the lack of resolution of the image by applying fractal geometries to what it could be seeing. With most images, the infilling would yield usable results, but this one appeared so briefly, and in a distorted reflection, that my assistant's confidence in the outcome of its hypothesizing was low.

"Make the attempt," I said, then watched as the vague outline developed more structure and form. "Could those," I said, pointing, "be ears?"

"Oddly shaped," said Hespira.

"Not," I said, "if they are ears that have been battered and chewed upon in taproom brawls."

"Hak Binram," my assistant said, in a tone that neither affirmed nor denied. It superimposed an image of the Olkney halfworld bravo over the silhouette. The outlines roughly coincided. "Perhaps. Or it could be someone wearing close-fitting headgear." Now it replaced Binram's tattooed visage with a generic face framed by the leather cloche worn by an agent of the Bureau of Scrutiny in operations where armed resistance could be expected.

"I suppose," I said.

"It makes a difference," the integrator said. "When we are in range to transmit a signal, we might be able to call upon the Bureau to go to the aid of an Osk Rievor under siege from criminals. Summoning the scroots to aid a person they are moving against in force will raise difficult questions."

The analysis was correct. I knew Osk Rievor to be a reified persona from my own psyche—the person I would have become had I been born in the oncoming age of magic—but the Bureau would identify him by the body he inhabited: that of a man named Orlo Saviene who had gone missing some months ago, though no one had cared enough about the unloved loner to report his absence. Still, the scroots would want to know what Osk/Orlo was doing in a remote cottage on a disused estate, surrounded by magical paraphernalia and heaps of undocumented gems. Colonel-Investigator Brustram Warhanny, in particular, would be anxious to hear an explanation of how Old Earth's foremost freelance discriminator had come to lease the jewel-filled cottage for Saviene. Warhanny had long shown an untoward interest in my affairs, motivated, I had sometimes thought, by professional envy.

"We cannot make a decision now," I said. We were just out of the whimsy that connected Shannery's system to that of Ikkibal. We must make our way—"at best speed, ship's integrator," I ordered—to the whimsy that had brought us within reach of Ikkibal. Then there would be two more traverses of normal space, one of them extensive, punctuated by yet two more whimsies, before we would begin the long fall down to Old Earth. "It will be several days before we can get close enough to contact Osk Rievor directly—"

I interrupted myself, remembering even as I spoke that my other self, incredibly, had chosen to live without an integrator. The only way to contact him, short of sending another bee once I returned to my lodgings, was to land the *Gallivant* in the meadow behind the estate. "And who knows what we will find then?"

It was a question with several possible answers: a smoking hole, watched over by Hak Binram and Massim Shar, bent on revenge; the same hole, but with Irslan Chonder and his hirelings from the Hand Organization, standing over the bodies of Binram and Shar; a party of Bureau agents with restraints and weapons at the ready, and a full measure of scrootish determination to discover what had been going on; perhaps even a placid Osk Rievor, tidying up after unleashing horrendous, anachronistic powers against intruders; or some other surprise.

"We will wait," I said, "and see. In the meantime, integrator, you will put out inquiries as to any announcements the Bureau may have made regarding recent arrests and detentions. By the time we are only one whimsy from home, we may have a clearer picture."

"Done," said my assistant. It closed its screen.

Hespira had poured me a mug of punge. She brought it to me. "Is there anything I can do?" she said.

"I shouldn't think so," I said, a little surprised.

"It is just that I was thinking—" she broke off, and seemed to be searching for the rest of her sentence. "I was thinking," she began again, "that when we return to Old Earth, I might be useful to you. I will have to find some way to make a living, and neither tending firhogs nor being the focus of young aristocratic obsession seems to have given satisfaction."

"I have an assistant," I said, indicating my integrator's traveling armature, hanging on its hook."

"Then perhaps a housekeeper?"

I was tempted to say, "It will not matter." The world would shortly end, and having seen the barbaric world that would succeed ours—at least the Old Earth of a few centuries hence—finding a means to make a living would no longer be of great concern. Mere survival amid chaos and devastation would be work enough for any of us.

But when I thought of Hespira struggling to survive amid the ruins, I again felt that strong urge to protect her. She had clearly come to represent something more to me than just a former client. After all, Irslan Chonder was in that category, and I doubted that I would bother to urinate on him if his hair was on fire.

"We will have to see," I said.

CHAPTER NINE

"You are unhappy," Hespira said to me. We were sitting in the *Gallivant's* salon, and I had been mulling the possible scenarios I would encounter on my return to Old Earth, and the various courses of action that might be chosen among for each situation.

"Am I?" I said.

"Is it because I asked you not to find out what happened to me?"

"No. I have other concerns. They occupy my mind. Your case was an opportunity to escape them for a while. Now it is done, and I am returning to those other matters. I must decide what to do."

"I would like to help, if I can. You helped me."

"Did I?" The question was not rhetorical. "I caused you to know things about yourself that you had not known, and did not want to know once I revealed them to you. By giving you that knowledge, did I truly help you?"

"Yes," she said, "because you made it possible for me to choose whether to embrace those 'things about myself' or to reject them and make a new beginning."

"New beginnings," I said, "come in all different kinds and sizes. Not every one of them is a blessing."

"I don't understand," she said.

I made a gesture that said she should not involve herself with the matter. But she was not a woman who was easy to deflect. I wondered if that was why someone—for I was still sure there was a someone—had scoured out her memories.

She said, "I have this impression that there is some secret between us, but you keep skirting around it. That makes me think that it is a dark secret."

"Dark enough," I said, then reproved myself. "I assure you, it is nothing to do with your case. It arises from my own circumstances."

173

She wanted to continue the discussion, but I said that I had to think about what Osk Rievor's broken message might lead to and retired to my cabin. But when I was stretched upon the pallet I did not turn my mind to the situation at the cottage. I thought instead of what Hespira had said.

I was not used to thinking of myself, certainly not of trying to decide whether I was happy or not. The workings of my finely calibrated mind had been the core of my life—I was what I did—but I had scarcely ever turned its focus inward, nor needed to. It was a precision tool that I applied to the universe, but only to the macroverse that began where my own skin met the air; the microverse within had remained unprobed, at least since the juvenile introspections of my formative years.

And I would rather it had remained that way. But now I had lost a part of myself; it lived in a cottage surrounded by the tomes and paraphernalia of a system of thought I had always despised. And that system was shortly to overwhelm the rational universe in which I had flourished, leaving me—if I survived the transition—facing a cosmos for which I was spectacularly ill-equipped. My brief foray into the coming era of wizards and wills had made that clear.

So I was mired in a quandary from which I could find no exit. Whatever efforts I might bring to the task, the Great Wheel would roll with crushing weight right over them. And perhaps over me. After a lifetime of successfully dealing with problems "out there," I had come up against one that, grapple with it though I might, admitted of no solution. And, in yet another instance of the universe proving to me that it operated fundamentally on the principle of irony, my inability to solve this terrible "out there" problem had left me with one "in here"—with which, it seemed, I was equally ill-equipped to deal.

The sleeping pallet asked if I wished to avail myself of its services. I found that I did, and let it proceed.

Our passage through the next whimsy brought no more battered bees or partial messages, nor did the one after, which cast us far up The Spray toward Old Earth. Either Osk Rievor had said all he meant to say, or he was unable to say anything more. There was no point in dwelling on the matter. We endured the long traverse of normal space until the final whimsy, idly talking, eating, sleeping, and availing ourselves of the *Gallivant*'s extensive store of diversions. I preferred games that tested the wits; Hespira favored dramas and told-tales. We did not delve again into the realm of my emotions, she out of politeness, I out of a conviction that to do so would avail me nothing.

As we neared the last whimsy, I was in my cabin, speculating with my assistant on what would become of these strange quiddities when the universe came under its new operating rules. Whimsies, like the irreducible uncertainty that characterized the quantum underpinnings of time, space, and matter, challenged the very notion of rational cause and effect; no one truly knew what they were or how they had come to exist, though theories were rife. Still, for all their essential mystery, whimsies had served to propel, if the word was appropriate, spacecraft from one region of space to another since time immemorial. The Ten Thousand Worlds could not exist without them.

Yet, when I had been pushed forward into the centuries after the impending change, I had journeyed back to Old Earth from the distant world Bille, traveling on a wizard's boat borne by a dragon. But we had passed through no whimsies nor anything like them. We had sailed through some medium that the denizens of the magical future called "the ether," against which the dragon's wings had beat and found purchase. I had earlier, in my own era, traveled between Bille and Old Earth in the *Gallivant,* and it seemed to me that the trip had taken longer. It was hard to be sure, however; in the wizard's ship, we had traveled under the shield of a powerful spell that insulated us from any harmful effects of a transethereal passage, and I had noticed how one's sense of time could become unreliable in the presence of strong magic.

It was difficult to discuss the matter with my assistant while we were figuratively in the *Gallivant's* belly, since the dragon that had carried us home was—or would be; tenses grew strained during discussions of time travel—this very spaceship, after it was transmogrified by the transition to the age of sympathetic association. It seemed the wisest course not to burden the ship with this knowledge, since that might affect the shape of future events and create causational loops or dead-ends out of which I was not sure I could easily navigate.

"But the thing that disturbs me about whimsies," I said to my assistant, "and indeed about the other arational aspects of the universe in our supposedly empirical era, is the sheer arbitrariness of it all. Here we are presented with a cosmos that largely works on definable, discoverable rules. Two and two always equal four, past precedes present which precedes future, cause reliably gives effect."

"Though the details can be difficult," said my assistant.

"Yes," I agreed, "but the principle remains sound. Then, all at once, just as we begin to feel we've got the rules established, a voice issues from somewhere off-stage and says, 'Oh, by the way, here are a few exceptions.' And for those exceptions, no explanation is offered."

"Indeed," said the integrator, "nor even suggested that any explanation is required."

"Exactly," I said. "And then we transit to the age of sympathetic association. Will becomes the paramount force, and things that are like each other are connected even though they be separated by distance or time or physical barriers. But however powerful the practitioner of magic, be he the mightiest thaumaturge atop the highest heap of mighty thaumaturges, let him misplace just one syllable of a complex cantrip and he finds himself turned inside out."

I paused to think of Bristal Baxandall, the first practitioner I had ever encountered—the incident had happened almost a year ago now—whom I had discovered on the floor of his book-filled house in just such a sorry, inverted condition. "For all the will and all the associative sympathizing he could bring to bear on his situation," I said, "he was undone by a simple relationship between cause and effect."

"Magic," said my integrator, "has rules. At the heart of the willful, associative universe, we find a modicum of rationalism, just as we find uncertainty at the core of the rational cosmos."

"Exactly," I said. "And there seems no other explanation for it than sheer perversity on the part of whatever entity is responsible for the whole untidy business."

I thought about it a moment more then said, "Perversity, or just a very idiosyncratic sense of humor."

"That," said my assistant, "is beyond the scope of any comment an integrator might offer. But, if you will permit me to tread upon the personal, you seem to be unusually troubled by your thoughts."

"I will not disguise it," I said. "For almost a year I have known that the life I have loved must come to an end. But I began, once I was forced to admit the unpalatable truth, with only a taste of that bitter knowledge. The experiences of the past several months, however, have required me to swallow more and more. The truth has been carried deep, down to the very plumbs of the Hapthorn belly. And now it has got right in amongst me."

"What does that portend?"

"That I must come to a decision, I suppose. I have been going on, practicing my profession, pursuing my avocations, as if life still spread its grand carpet before me. But, in fact, the carpet is being rolled up. The question is, do I wait for it to reach my toes? Or do I step off the old rug at a time and place of my choosing?"

"A grim choice."

"At least, if I do not wait too long, it is mine to make."

The ship's chimes sounded. The last whimsy was nigh. I lay upon the pallet and took the sac into my hand. "Perhaps Hespira, Irmyrlene Broon-Paskett that was, has the better of it," I mused. "The cup of self-knowledge was taken from her hands and its contents cast into the dust, leaving her free."

"You have never sought to be free of knowledge," the integrator said. "Indeed, those who relish that freedom you have long disdained as misguided paupers."

"It is possible," I said, "that I have been the misguided one. I am scarcely enriched by the knowledge I have carried with me this past year."

Years before, when my worst trouble had been long spells of boredom, I had instructed my assistant to take issue with me whenever I exhibited signs of self-ache. It began to do so now, but the ship interrupted with the insistent "whimsy-imminent" chime. Before irreality could outrage my senses, I tightened my fist, felt the coolness of the drugs' penetration, then felt no more.

Again, no ill-used bee awaited my return from nescience; instead, as I was clearing the drug-induced scurf from my brain, sitting semi-vacantly at the salon table nursing a mug of punge, the ship said, "I am receiving a relayed message from Osk Rievor."

At the same time, my assistant's voice sounded from the air beside me. "As am I. It has been passed from ship to ship by craft outbound toward the whimsy we have just come through. It is some days old."

"Are they the same message?" I asked. When both integrators answered in the affirmative I said, "Then let one of you display it."

Two screens appeared, one overlapping the other, each showing the acquired face of my former intuition. Then the screen that was in the rear suddenly appeared in front, to be instantly superseded by the one it had leapfrogged. The competition continued, so quickly that the image seemed to flicker in the air. Meanwhile, the recorded Osk Rievor began speaking, but the voice came from two directions, the two versions slightly out of phase so that they achieved an echo. I found the composite effect most unwelcome. "Stop," I said.

Both images froze and the voices ceased. "I thought," I said, "that we had worked through this nonsensical rivalry."

Neither integrator replied. I was gratified that at least I did not have to endure the two of them blaming each other. "One of you will move your screen to my right, the other to my left," I said. When the separation was achieved without further conflict, I announced that I would make an arbitrary choice.

"Whichever integrator's screen this is," I said, indicating the one to my right, "will display the image. The other integrator will provide the sound. You will coordinate with each other to synchronize the two."

Osk Rievor again appeared in the air before me. His aspect was calm. "I do not know if my messengers reached you. But all is well here. The salamander is under control and I am learning much of interest by studying it. Let me know when you have returned to your lodgings and we will confer again."

His hand lifted as if to signal an end to the transmission, but then it paused in midair and I saw another thought come into his aspect. "Oh, yes," he said, "and, obviously, it would probably be best not to spend any more of the jewels."

Then his hand completed its motion and the screen went blank.

Hespira spoke from behind me. She had come in while the message was being played. "What is 'the salamander'?"

I turned. She was wearing again the long gingham dress with ribbons at the shoulders that she had worn when we had first collided. "I do not know," I said, "though it seems he expects me to. It must have been referred to in his earlier message."

"Well, whatever it is, he has it under control. That is probably for the best."

I could not say. But I was somewhat puzzled. "He seems to have acquired an integrator."

My assistant said, "I have been examining the message in detail."

"So have I," said the *Gallivant*.

"Enough," I said. "Ship's integrator, you will operate the ship and prepare us one of your splendid breakfasts. I suspect we will need to be fortified for whatever Osk Rievor has been up to. Meanwhile, my assistant and I will examine the message."

The screen reappeared in the air to my right, then centered itself. It also expanded, so that in a moment Osk Rievor's face took up most of the salon's inner wall.

"Regard," said the integrator. It had eliminated the sound, and now, as my former intuition looked directly into the percept that had captured his image, the picture froze and began to enlarge. The focus was on the pupil of my other self's right eye and, as I was still somewhat disequilibrated from the whimsy-transit medications, I had to shake off the impression that I was falling toward an immense black pool.

"Regard what?" I said.

"A reflection," said my assistant. "It will appear as I advance the sequence very slowly."

I peered at the huge expanse of darkness that was my other self's eye. There had been little ambient light in the room—it was the study in the cottage again—and I could not be sure that I saw any reflection in Osk Rievor's eye.

"A brief flash of light comes from, I believe, outside the cottage," the integrator said, then, "Here it is."

It must have been of very short duration, and not of much intensity. I had not noticed it when I saw the full message, and doubted that I would have caught it even if I had not been still under the impress of the drugs. But noticing details was what integrators were for, and I had designed and instructed mine well.

So the flash came and, with it, a reflection appeared in Osk Rievor's enlarged pupil. My assistant froze the image.

"I'll tell you what it looks like to me," said Hespira. She had come to stand behind me. I could smell the odor of the punge she was sipping from one of the *Gallivant*'s fine china mugs. "It looks like some kind of animal. Maybe a cat, but with a more rounded skull. You can just see the ears, there." She reached past me to point.

She was both right and wrong. The silhouette did look somewhat like a cat. It also might have been the head of a small ape. Or it might have looked like a beast with attributes of both species.

"It couldn't be," I said to my assistant, "could it?

"It could be," the integrator said, "though it shouldn't."

"I think it is," I said. "I don't want to think so, but I think I have to."

"What?" said Hespira. "What is it?"

"A grinnet," I said. "My grinnet."

I was not sure how it happened. It started with the woman's obvious question—"What is a grinnet?"—and went on from there. Instead of diverting her attention to some other subject or simply falling back upon my old reliable "It would be premature to say," I found myself telling her the entire tale from the beginning: the ugly business with Baxandall, the juvenile demon with prurient appetites, the confrontation with Turgut Therobar that had reified my intuition as a separate, though nameless, entity sharing my mental parlor. Then the sequence of murders that led to the assembly of a composite corpse that was intended to revivify the archmage Majestrum, and how that led in turn to my alter ego's having taken the name Osk Rievor and our subsequent trip through the spiral labyrinth and into the future, returning with a trove of magical goods and knowledge. In passing, I told the tale of how my assistant sojourned for some months as a frugivorous apelike cat—or catlike ape—modeled on a wizard's familiar from a bygone age, then chose to abandon that form and inhabit again the constellation of components installed in my workroom or, when we traveled, in the armature now hanging from its hook on the salon wall.

It made for a longish telling, even with many subsidiary details left out. I did remember to mark the *Gallivant*'s brave shipliness in battling the fungal symbiote's powerful avatar in Hember Forest, without which intervention both Osk Rievor and I would have been returned to Bille and subjected to the entity's detailed revenge. When I finished, several servings of punge later, Hespira sat in silence for an extended moment, her eyes focused on the empty air. Then she blinked and said, "This burden, of knowing that the whole cosmos must soon come crashing down, with all of us swept away in a deluge of unreason, you have carried this horrendous weight alone through an entire year?"

"I am not the only one who knows," I said. "The Archon surely does. I am sure there are others within his inner confidence. And, of course, there are several budding thaumaturges, of Baxandall and Therobar's ilk, who not only know what is to come but are actively preparing for it."

"It will be their time?"

"Very much their time. They mean to rule the ruins."

"And your friend—no, your former intuitive faculty—Osk Rievor: what does he mean to do?"

We had not discussed the issue at length. But I said I believed he would oppose the cruel and power-hungry, and would try to bring as much order as soon as he could, once the transition had been weathered.

"He is like you," she said, "a Calabrine." She referred to one of the principal figures in the tale of Hespira: the righteous paladin who strives to bring justice to the land after Aubron, the rejected suitor, resolves to make the world pay for his own suffering. Their final confrontation is a poignant moment.

"I had not thought of myself as a Calabrine," I said, "merely a habitual solver of puzzles. But perhaps there is something in it."

We were seated across from each other at the table in the salon. Now she reached over with one of her large rough hands and took mine. "I still cannot understand how you could have known what you know and kept it to yourself. I think of you walking among the people on the streets, each of them going about their own concerns, as if they had all the time they would ever need. And you knowing that soon, they and their concerns would be whisked away. I would have had to stop passersby at random, to blurt out the horrid news."

"What good would it have done?" I said.

She touched her fingers to her breastbone. "It would have relieved the pressure."

"And what good would that have done?"

One more sleep, an unmedicated one, and we were within view of Old Earth and her tired sun. I had set my assistant the task of trying to communicate further with Osk Rievor, but either his grinnet could not receive from the connectivity, or he had instructed it not to do so. I suspected the latter. My integrator informed me that there were "odd characteristics" to the message that we had already received, but found it hard to express what it meant.

"A peculiar flavor, one might say," it said. The ship offered its opinion that it was more an odor than a taste. But both integrators agreed that any apparatus receiving a communication from Osk Rievor would note the added ambience. It could draw unwanted attention.

"Did I smell like that," my assistant asked the *Gallivant*, "when I was in grinnet form?"

"No," said the ship, "though there was the same shrillness of tone."

My assistant denied being shrill and I was forced to restore equanimity and instruct both of them to prepare for landing.

My standard communication with Olkney's spaceport, set on an island in Mornedy Sound, was interrupted by a priority message from the Bureau of Scrutiny. Brustram Warhanny required me to make contact with him "as soon as might be convenient"—a phrase that, in scroot parlance, translated as "immediately, and your convenience be damned."

"Connect me," I said to my assistant. A few moments later I was confronted once more with the lugubrious mien of the Colonel-Investigator. I experienced a momentary temptation to do as Hespira might have and advise him that his world was shortly to end; but I was immediately faced with the same question I had asked her—what good would it do?

"Hapthorn," he said without preamble, "the Shar-Chonder affair has yet to run its course."

"I am sorry to hear it."

He told me that there had been a number of affronts to the Archon's peace, including two incidents that had left bodies strewn about the back streets and cramped alleyways of the Gullet, the district where Massim Shar had established his base.

"Chonder escalated the conflict, hiring two full platoons of Hand Organization operatives. But Hak Binram showed surprising versatility in his dispositions, negating the Hand's superiority of numbers."

I said that I had always thought Binram underrated.

"Well, now he has had his opportunity to show his true substance. The result is that the Hand is aggrieved; its shield has suffered a tarnishing. They have sent Chai Esquilieu to take charge."

"I have heard of him," I said. "He is First Thumb over four worlds."

"Five, now," said Warhanny. "We have been added to his remit."

I sighed. "What do you wish of me?"

The scroot held up a hand of his own and ticked fingers one after another. "First, accept no further commissions of any kind from Irslan Chonder."

"I have no intention of doing so."

"Second, avoid Massim Shar."

"I have every intention of doing so."

"Third, stay indoors, or better yet, out of town. The dynamic of the Shar-Chonder situation has evolved. It is now a prestige war between Hak Binram and Chai Esquilieu. You have become a trophy that each seeks to deny the other. Neither will be content until he has collected your ears."

"I had rather they didn't. I have grown attached to them."

"Binram has established a node in the connectivity offering five thousand hepts for true word of your whereabouts. Esquilieu offers six thousand."

Neither was a negligible amount, nor yet a fortune. I was not sure how I felt about it.

"Finally," Warhanny said, touching his smallest finger, "if you come across any information that would assist the Bureau, do not keep it to yourself. The situation is grim."

I assured the Colonel-Investigator of my complete cooperation and severed the connection. "We will stop briefly at my lodgings," I told Hespira, "then go out to the Arlem estate." To my assistant, I said, "Engage an aircar for us, under an assumed name"—I kept several dormant identities for when it was better not to be Henghis Hapthorn—"and when it arrives scan it thoroughly."

Our journey across the sound and to the landing pad atop the roof of my lodgings was uneventful. As we came in range of the dwelling my assistant reported, "There are several detectors and passive surveils covering the premises, including a Bureau set. I cannot defeat them from a hired aircar."

"Make us as vague as possible," I said, "and expend no energy on the scroot equipment." Warhanny already knew I was home. "We will just pick up a few necessities and be on our way."

We touched down and the rooftop who's-there, already alerted, had the door open as we reached it. We went down through my chambers and into the workroom, my assistant scanning the premises and receiving reports from the in-built wards and defenses.

"Attempts have been made," it said, as I opened storage lockers and retrieved items I thought might be useful, "but the intent seems to have been more to reconnoiter than to invade, at least once it was known you were not here."

At least no one had sought to insert any devices with lethal capacities. Whoever wanted me—and the number and variety of attempts argued for more than one in that category—wanted me alive. "Good," I said. "It is easier to fend off kidnapers than a semi-sentient projectile arriving at ultrasonic speed, or a line-of-sight energy beam from an orbiting emitter."

"The detectors have reported our landing and entry," the integrator said. "Messages went in several directions, some of them to receptors no great distance away."

"Then let us be gone," I said.

Hespira had spent this time sitting on the steps, watching my rapid despoiling of the cupboards. She looked anxious, which caused me a pang of concern. "Do not worry," I said, as I urged her back up toward the roof, "the danger is temporary."

We bundled ourselves back into the aircar and I used a small device of my own manufacture to pop open its service panel.

"Stop," it said. "My systems are private! I will summon a provost-man."

I pushed a package of components into the works and said to my assistant, "Install that and get it functioning."

"This is an intolerable invasion of—" said the aircar, then became silent as my integrator took control. Its records would now show no sign of anything that happened after we reboarded; instead, if queried, it would display a carefree trip to see some of the sights of Olkney, with appropriate commentary by me and appreciative responses from Hespira.

"Done," said my assistant.

"All right. Now get us down to the street and make us look like we belong there."

The aircar lifted off, flew a few streets over, then dropped to the pavement. As it did so, its appearance changed—at least to all but the most penetrative percepts—as its true outline was obliterated and replaced by a projected image. It now seemed to be a ground car, moving along with the flow of surface traffic, which was quite busy in this district at this time of day.

We turned a corner and the image changed, becoming a different model and color, then changing again after we dropped down into a subsurface conduit and changing once more as we emerged to climb a spiraling connector to the roof of a huge bronze-toned glass monolith in the commercial precinct that had been known, since time out of mind, as the New City. Along the way, my assistant employed a reflector that caused several nearby vehicles to offer any tracking percepts the same images it used to disguise our own, so that by the time we arrived atop the monolith it would have taken a well-coordinated mobile surveillance suite—like my own swarm of bees—to have kept us in view. And, after a long, passive scan, my integrator informed me that no such attention was directed our way.

"At least none that I detect," it said. "It is possible that my own abilities can be defeated. I am not sanguine that I could outdo the best that the Hand Organization could bring to bear."

"We will take the risk," I said. "Make us seem another breed of aircar and take us up." Shimmering with false colors and reshaped sponsons, we rose into the aerial traffic and took a meandering course over the city. After several minutes, I said, "Well?"

"With the same caveat as previously," my assistant said, "I believe we are unobserved."

"Then to the Arlem estate," I said, "though at a tangent, and at a speed that will draw no one's attention."

After we had flown a good distance, I asked if there were any signs of our being followed.

"Nothing overt," said my assistant, "but I do not entirely discount the possibility."

"Well," I said, patting the large carry-all I had filled from my workroom cupboards, "if we are, then we have the wherewithal to deal with any eventualities." I instructed it to turn the aircar toward the estate.

It was late afternoon when we arrived. We circled and scanned, saw nothing amiss, and descended to a wide lawn from which led a path to the cottage. We had not traversed half the distance, winding among the artificial hills and small ponds that dominated the landscaping, when we met Osk Rievor hurrying out to greet us. I noticed that he had now lost all of the pallor that he had acquired during his time in the symbiote's caverns on Bille, and his—or rather Orlo Saviene's—mouse-colored hair had grown thick. But what struck me most about the former sharer of my psyche was the brightness of his eyes and his quick, almost jerky movements. He gave the impression of a man seething with inner excitement, who might at any moment be expected to cut a caper or let loose an actual hoot.

"You must come see," he said, taking my elbow, his gaze darting from me to Hespira and back. "I've got it doing tricks."

"Got what doing tricks?" I said.

But his eyes had found the valise that Hespira was carrying, I being burdened with the carry-all and a couple of other satchels. Though hers was by far the lightest burden, Osk Rievor went for it like a famished duck darting at a piece of floating bread, saying, "Are those the jewels? Let me have them."

He took the bag and, without further explanation, turned and strode off in a flurry of bent knees and elbows. I followed at the best speed I could manage, but my progress improved after Hespira relieved me of the carry-all, which she hoisted onto one shoulder like a sailor toting his seabag. I supposed that the Broon-Pasketts produced few weaklings.

We put down our loads at the cottage doorstep. I removed some of the contents of the carry-all, and hung my assistant on a hook by the door, instructing it to bring the equipment to operational readiness and to maintain a full-spectrum watch to the limits of its range. Then Hespira and I went around to the rear of the little house, where I could hear my former intuition engaged in a largely one-sided conversation. He was providing all the words, the other half of the colloquy consisting of sibilant hisses and guttural grunts.

The noises were coming from inside a pen made of waist-high palings sunk into the sod and held together by twists of wire and twine. Osk Rievor was bending over the barrier, looking down at whatever was inside. In one palm he held the small heap of jewels. He was plucking them, one at a time, and tossing them into the enclosure. Each time he did so, he spoke to whatever was within, using the kind of voice usually adopted by fellows who were addressing the lap pets of ladies whose affections they wished to win over by first winning the animals' hearts. His efforts were rewarded by squeals and gutterings from their unseen recipient.

I went closer. My other self tossed another jewel and I saw a flash of blue and gold, accompanied by a hiss and a squeak. I took another step, and was now close enough that when Osk Rievor threw a gem of deep red color into the pen I could see a triangular head and a pair of four-digited paws rise swiftly up from the bottom of the enclosure. The head split laterally to reveal a pink-fleshed mouth adorned with several rows of needlish teeth and a long, darting crimson tongue. It was from there that the squeaks came. One of the paws closed upon the stone and the creature sank down again. As I arrived at the palings and peered over, I saw that it was pressing the red gem to its hide, just where the other paw joined the body.

I drew a specularum from my coat pocket and examined the beast more closely. Its hide was covered in tiny scales arranged in complex patterns. I saw reds and greens, gold and silver, turquoise and sapphire, and the brilliant pinpricks of pure light must have been diamonds. I increased the magnification and the individual scales became faceted rubies and emeralds, thunderstones and rose-of-alcalene crystals, while the golds and silvers revealed themselves to be coins

I watched again with my naked eye as Osk Rievor threw in a diamond as large as the end joint of my thumb. With another squeal the beast caught the flashing gem, then with a muttering it pressed the jewel against a spot at the base of its throat. I studied the action through the specularum and saw the diamond seem to vanish in the creature's grasp. But a new pinpoint of light now showed where its paw had pressed.

I felt a warmth against my chest and felt around in my clothing, drawing out the disk my alter ego had given me. It glowed a bright red, like an ember from a banked fire. When I extended it toward the bejeweled creature, it became too hot for my hand. I withdrew it and made Osk Rievor take it back. He took it, glanced at it, and let it drop to the ground.

"What is this beast?" I said, backing away from the pen.

He continued to toss it jewels. "At first I called it a salamander," he said, "because it resembles a description of a creature by that name from a partial text I have recovered from the Eighteenth Aeon. But now I know that that is not what it is."

He threw it an emerald and the squeaks and grumblings followed. Hespira came forward and watched the proceedings. She made as to reach down and pet the animal's glistening spine, but Osk Rievor said, "It resents contact." He showed her a half-healed tear on one thumb and she backed away.

"It is a deeply magical beast," I said, "judging by its effect on the amulet."

My alter ego continued throwing gems. "It only appears to be an animal. It is actually an avatar of a minor deity from the last age of sympathetic association, a god of wealth and treasure named Yeggoth. I have seen such referred to, here and there. There was a cult of avarice on an island in the Sulon Sea, off the coast of a land called Gesta Hal. The devotees gave precious things to the god and were supposedly rewarded tenfold."

"And this is the god?" Hespira said. "The actual god, Yeggoth?"

We heard a hiss and a growl. "Do not speak its name," Osk Rievor said, "unless you are making an offering. It takes offense. Here." He handed me a jewel and bade me toss it toward the creature, which caught the spinning gem and rewarded me with a gurgle.

"It is a simple creature. It is not the deity itself, I think, but a reified representation of a couple of aspects of its godhood—the acquisitive element and the part that resents and punishes encroachments on the divine prerogative." He paused, and threw in the last gem, making "Who's-a-good-little-god?" murmurs. "I suppose it may more properly be called a crystallization of its worshipers' desires—apparently quite a few gods are created in that manner. Whatever it is, it has lost a great deal of its power by coming into this age of rationalism. I had no trouble containing it, once I realized what made it grow larger."

I had several questions. "You are saying it came, not that you brought it?"

"Oh, yes," he said, turning to me with the delighted look of an academician who has found a point worth a footnote. "It turns out that when I was pulling in streams of coins and jewels, I thought from some hoard, I was actually stripping its hide. I had transcribed the spell backward—it was the reverse of the mantra that the cultists used to transfer their dedicated offerings to the deity."

"And it came to get its property back?"

"Of course. And since the jewels and coins were its own substance, and it had the powers of a god in its own age, it was strong enough to pull itself forward into our time, though when it arrived here it was no larger than the length of my hand." He shook his head in mild wonderment. "Quite fascinating."

"I notice," I said, "that though the gems were sizable when they were in our hands, they shrank to the size of pinpoints when the god returned them to their proper settings."

"Oh, well spotted," he said. "Yes, in its own time and place, the avatar would have been huge." He looked up at the tall trees that blocked our view of the horizon, as if seeing a jewel-bedecked behemoth looming above them. "Monstrous," he said, "simply monstrous."

"Does it not disturb you," I said, "that you have stripped the hide off a huge creature with divine powers, then confined it to a pen and forced it to do tricks to get its substance back? Most gods would not take such treatment kindly."

"Remember, it is only an aspect of the deity. It is a simple creature. Give it what it craves and it is mollified, even friendly. I have now restored all the stones and coins I took from it—or almost, except for those you spent offworld. But I have also found ways to acquire fresh supplies and have been feeding them to the god while studying its emanations."

"But still," I said, "you have penned up a god."

"It has no real power while it is within the pen. Do not let the apparent flimsiness of the wire and palings deceive you. The fence is a representation only; I have used a spell called Frenec's Ineluctable Encirclement, designed to hold full-weight demons of the Ninth Plane. But do not touch the barrier; it is only strong from the inside."

I looked at the creature. It did seem happy enough in its enclosure. Still, I was not comfortable with the idea of holding any god—or even any aspect of a god—under duress.

"Do not fret," my other self said. "We had a little contest when it first arrived, but after it bit me I soon showed it the size of its hat, as they say." He paused, thoughtful for a moment, then continued, "The only thing is, I cannot cast any potent spells in its vicinity. It seems to draw strength from the ambience." He smiled indulgently. "But then, you won't be doing any spellslinging, will you?"

"No," I said. "I won't."

I wanted to discuss the salamander further, our few words not having exhausted my concerns, but Osk Rievor was moving on to fresh fields. It seemed that he had been active in several areas of research and was excited to show me the results. He recommended that we return to the cottage and I allowed myself to be drawn, Hespira following along behind.

"I believe I can dissipate your client's amnesia," he said as we hurried along. I noticed that whenever he wasn't standing still, he was hurrying. "I found a memory-intensifying cantrip in one of Smiling Bol's compendia. It allows one to hold four major spells in mind at the same time, which is remarkable. I could try it on her."

I told him that she had decided to let her past lie in darkness and start a new and unencumbered life. Then I moved to a subject that his remarks had brought urgently to my mind. "Have you tried many spells upon yourself?" I said.

"A few."

"Is that wise?"

"Why not?"

"What are they?" I said.

He stopped and blinked. I had noticed that he did that frequently, in small bursts of rapid eye-flutters followed by long passages when his eyes opened wider than usual. "Let me see," he said. "I was tired of wasting time on preparing food, so I used one that predigests nourishment and transfers it directly to my insides—Barzant's Alimentation, that one is called.

"Then I saw that I was wasting even more time sleeping, so I employed Wyu-Shyu's Vivid Wakefulness. Now I sleep for only a few seconds every few minutes, although I have had to add a dream suppressant, lest I begin dreaming while still awake. That can be confusing."

"I am sure of it," I said.

"Indeed," he continued, "when the salamander first came, I mistook it for a waking dream. That is when I acquired this." He showed me his savaged thumb.

"Any more?"

"Spells you mean?" He was about to answer but instead went wide-eyed again and was silent for several seconds. "A couple," he said, as if unaware of the interruption. "I am using Paphrae's Perk-Up to augment my intellectual vigor, though I find it has a side-effect of making all motions brisk. I found, however, that it drains the resources, so that I had to double the frequency of Barzant's Alimentation; I was growing faint from hunger.

"And, I almost forgot..." He paused and looked thoughtful, then said, "Interesting. With the memory intensifier, that shouldn't happen. Perhaps I need to adjust..." He ceased speaking and again stood staring for several heartbeats, then went on, "the capacity factor again."

"You said," I reminded him, "that you had almost forgotten..." I waited for his train of thought to connect to mine.

"Oh, yes," he said, "Irriwad's Melodics. One hears one's favorite songs as an accompaniment to the doings of the day. Listen."

He spoke two syllables and immediately my ears filled with a vigorous passage of tympani and bohorns. I recognized it at once; apparently my former intuition and I shared the same taste for music, which was not surprising.

"Very nice," I said. "But perhaps you could eliminate it while we converse. I find it distracting."

"What?" he said, blinking rapidly.

"The music. Could you make it go away?"

"Of course, if it bothers you. I find it uplifting." He took my arm and pulled me toward the cottage. "I want to show you something."

We reached the door and he flung it wide and pulled me across the threshold. Beyond lay a blaze of golden light that dazzled me. When my eyes adjusted to the glare I saw that we stood on the edge of a wide, high-ceilinged room, floored in polished tiles of green and amber, the walls hung with alternating tapestries and ornate mirrors, the actual ceiling invisible behind scores of chandeliers that sparkled with crystals and massed lumens. With Osk Rievor still pulling on my arm and Hespira following, we crossed the great expanse to a cluster of divans and sofas set about with small tables on which stood carafes and cups of alabaster.

"Help yourself," he said, pouring a golden liquid into one of the cups and draining it. I sniffed the neck of one container, smelled the bouquet of a fine Phalum, and poured for Hespira and myself. I was sure the room was some kind of illusion, but if the wine was also a pretense, it was a trick well done. I relieved my neck and shoulders of the weight of my assistant and stretched it upon an arm of a sofa.

Osk Rievor was downing a second cup. "Odd," he said, "despite the alimentation spell, I always seem to be thirsty. I should look for something to deal with that."

"No," I said, "you should not."

He paused in the act of pouring. "What do you mean?"

"I mean that you have overstrained yourself. You—" I had to pause while he took another of his brief, involuntary naps. "You are not in good order," I said when he returned to consciousness.

"I beg to differ," he said, blinking rapidly.

"You have taken on too much, too soon," I said, "piling spells on top of spells without thought for the composite effect. Meanwhile, you have an annoyed deity trapped in the back yard, restrained by nothing more than a wooden fence—"

"It only appears to be a wooden fence," he said. "I happened to like the effect."

"Be that as it may," I bored in, "the situation has all the elements of one of those cautionary tales that begin with blithe expectations and end in rout and catastrophe."

"It does not."

"I must insist that it does."

Osk Rievor turned away and poured another cupful. He paused with the vessel halfway to his lips and I thought he must have heard something that commanded his attention. Then I realized that he had merely lost consciousness again. As he came back and drank the wine, every line of his back a reproach to me, my assistant said quietly in my ear, "I have something to report."

"Is it urgent?" I said, in our silent mode.

"I cannot tell."

"What is it?"

"I cannot tell that either."

I put down an upsurge of frustration and said, "Then what can you tell me?"

"A message has been sent."

"What kind of message?"

"I do not know."

"To whom has it been sent?"

Again, the integrator did not know, only that it was sent as a focused beam aimed upward.

"To an orbital or a spacecraft?" I asked.

"I would so assume."

"Do you know the content of the message?"

"No, it was well shielded. A very high-order shield. Indeed, I cannot even be entirely certain of the type."

"Well," I said, "do you know, at least, who sent it?"

"Yes. Or at least I know from whom it originated."

"Then let us have the one fact that is at your command," I said. "From whom did it originate?"

"From Hespira."

CHAPTER TEN

"**N**othing!" was Hespira's reply, delivered with a vehemence that was understandable, in that Osk Rievor and I had already each asked her twice, within a matter of seconds, "What are you doing?"

Indeed, she appeared to be doing nothing except standing before us, her ungainly hands pressed to her too-long cheeks and her eyes wide with consternation—and probably also with fear at the sight of two alarmed men leaning toward her with hands raised and brows compressed.

"Integrator," I said, "give me something I can work with!"

"I cannot give you more," it said. "A signal of some kind originated from her. It was focused and brief. If I had to guess, I would say it was a means of saying, 'Here I am,' to someone who was waiting to receive the news."

"A homing beacon?"

"Probably."

"But you cannot identify the medium that carried it?" Focused beams must focus something, after all, and I had built the device to be able to detect, intercept, analyze, and if necessary make free with every known kind of energy.

"Then," said my assistant, "this may be a kind of energy we do not know about."

"Speculate," I said.

"You will not like it."

I was finding less and less to like as the day wore on. I turned to Osk Rievor but had to wait a few seconds because he was again briefly asleep. The intervals between seemed to be shorter and the naps longer, but I couldn't take time to measure them. When I saw him blink and come back to us, I said, "Is this magic?"

He turned his head and snapped a word over his shoulder. It sounded like "Grishant." Across the improbable width of the room, in a patch of bare wall between two arrases, a door opened. It was a narrow door, not much higher than my knee, and beyond it lay a miniature room furnished in dark plush fabric. The floor was uneven and littered with odd, light-colored shapes that at first I could not identify. Then I saw that the door had been kicked open by a small foot, fur-covered and long-toed, belonging to the diminutive creature that now raised itself up from a small divan on which it had been reclining. The unrecognizable shapes resolved themselves into fruit peelings falling away from the rounded belly. The creature got its feet beneath it and rose, to stand in the little doorway, blinking lambent eyes that dominated a face that combined the attributes of ape and cat.

"What?" it said.

"Bring my spectrice and the intrometrant," my other self may have said. I was not registering his words closely because my attention was fixed on the recipient of his orders, which was now slouching toward a cabinet some distance off, exhibiting the kind of begrudged compliance to be found in overindulged adolescents who have been made to abandon their preferred distractions.

"That is my grinnet," I said.

Osk Rievor blinked. "Not actually," he said.

"You dug it up, from where I had buried it."

"No, it…" He would have said more but another period of slumber intervened. I was sure that this one was longer than the first, though that may have been because I was anxious to hear him complete the sentence. Then he blinked and said, "…came back on its own."

The familiar had finished collecting objects from the cabinet and now came trudging toward us over the bicolored floor.

"I heard a scratching at the door one morning. When I opened, there it was, picking clods of dirt from its pelt, looking up at me. It could not speak at first. I had to teach it the most basic skills."

"It has come a long way since," I said.

"I found part of an old text on their care and maintenance. Apparently they are very hard to kill. Also, they have to be handled appropriately. I fear I made some early errors that are proving hard to undo."

The creature arrived at our feet where it let its burdens fall to the floor. I recognized the dark mirror and the black tube with which my former intuition had examined Hespira on our first visit.

"You have forgotten the Bell of True Resonance," Osk Rievor said.

"You didn't ask for it," said the grinnet.

"Of course I..."—another sleep, this one definitely longer than the first—"...did."

"If you'd asked for it, I would've brought it," said the creature.

"Go and get it." Osk Rievor took up the tube and examined Hespira, then consulted the mirror from several angles. By the time he was finished, the bell had arrived and he rang it near her and listened to its reverberations.

"It is not her," he said, "but..."—again we waited—"...the dress." Or, more specifically, he confirmed, when he had studied and napped a little more, one of the ribbons attached to the shoulder. He called the grinnet to take part in the examination. Grumbling, it scaled him, hand over hand, until it sat upon one shoulder, then sniffed at the end of the piece of fabric.

"It must be a subtle spell," it said, "imbued into a single thread that was woven through the cloth, but left to lie dormant until it was surrounded by sufficient ambience. Once it was impinged upon by active magic, the thread absorbed stray minims of potentiality that were too tiny to be noticed; when it had fed enough to revivify the spell, it did so automatically."

"Fascinating," said Osk Rievor, fingering the ribbon. "But you do not recognize it?"

"Not even its type. It must be an unknown form of magic."

Osk Rievor said nothing.

"Are we done?" said the grinnet, turning its head toward its lair. "I haven't finished my second lunch."

I put down an urge to slap my former intuition back to wakefulness. Instead I waited for him to revive from another brief slumber. Meanwhile, his familiar was down on the floor and scuttling toward its refuge. "Come back!" he called. "Where did the signal go?"

The grinnet sighed and made an unwilling return. "It had pulsed before I was aware of it. We will have to wait until it has built up enough force for another discharge. Or you could increase its rate of absorption by increasing the ambience."

"All right," Osk Rievor said. He raised his hands and positioned his fingers at odd angles.

"Wait!" I said. "What about the salamander? It also grows through absorbing this 'ambience.'"

My other self showed no concern. "That is why I placed its pen well away from the cottage. It will enlarge another minim or two. No more. Besides,

I have now replaced all its missing scales and given it scores more. It will remain content while the jewels and coins keep coming. Once they stop, I will speak the last line of the ritual and it will depart."

"You are certain of that?"

"What is there to keep it here?"

"From tales I have read, I have formed the view that deities confined against their will tend to insist on dealing out retribution. The impact is often memorable."

He waved away the point as not worth responding to. I had another objection: should we not avoid sending a signal of our whereabouts before we knew who would receive it and why they might wish to? But Osk Rievor had already set his hands again, and before I could stop him he uttered three croaking syllables while touching one thumb to an elbow. "There," he said.

I looked about, noticed nothing different. Then I caught a motion from the corner of my eye, but when I turned my gaze that way nothing moved. "What have you done?" I said. "All seems as before."

"The tapestries," he said. "The figures in them move when you are not looking at them."

I turned and regarded one of the larger hangings. The persons depicted in them might have changed their positions, but I could not tell. "What is the point of that?" I said.

Again, I had to wait for Osk Rievor to reawaken, then repeated the question. "I have not yet discovered the purpose," he said. "It may have been someone's idea of a prank to play upon one's guests."

"The signal has been sent again," said my assistant.

"There it goes," said the grinnet, almost at the same time.

"Where?" Osk Rievor and I said together, while Hespira plucked at the ribbon as if to tear it loose from her seam. But it was solidly stitched in. Whoever had invested so much in a piece of cloth must have intended for it to remain fixed in place.

"Almost straight up again," said my assistant, but my other self's familiar was better able to descry and follow magical forces. "To a reflector high above the atmosphere," it said, "whence it is beamed toward a stream of objects that circle the world."

"Could you ascertain its content?" I asked the grinnet. It was strange to be speaking to a creature I had buried and even mourned, but I pushed aside the emotion. This was not, I told myself, the same creature I had known.

"I can infer. In words, it would be 'Here I am.' In images, a pinpoint of light in blackness. In sounds, a piercing beep." It looked away toward its den, then said to my other self, "Now, are we done?"

But Osk Rievor's small spellcasting must have dug deep into his remaining resources. His eyes had closed. I heard a noise that began deep in his chest and emerged from his lips as a rubbery snore. I shook him gently but the exercise only served to make him unsteady on his feet. He began to topple forward and I had to move quickly to catch him. I turned to speak to the grinnet, but it was already in motion toward its plush retreat.

"Wait," I said, but the creature was not bound to heed me. It strode away, making considerably more speed than it had shown before.

"I cannot stay with him," I called after it. "But if I leave him, I fear he will do himself an injury."

The grinnet sighed, a sound that I remembered hearing, when its body had housed my own assistant. It stopped and turned back, wearing a look on its surprisingly communicative face that bespoke great patience under equally great imposition. "This has happened before. He will be useless for at least an hour, but Zhan's Motilator will move him to safety, if you do not care to bear his weight."

"I do not know Zhan's Motilator," I said.

Again, the small sigh filled the silence. The creature stalked away toward my alter ego's study and returned dragging a weighty tome. Its hairy paw flicked through the pages, while its triangular pink tongue took up a position in a corner of its mouth. Then it found what it was looking for and indicated a page to me.

"I do not do magic," I said. "It distresses me." Indeed, the only time I had ever essayed a spell, under sheer necessity of survival, it caused a sensation compared to which being lightning-struck must feel like an itch between the shoulder blades.

One more sigh, then the grinnet read a line from the book, clapped its little palms twice with a precise interval between. Osk Rievor snorted, then turned slowly on his heel and walked like a somnambulant to a divan across the room. There, like an old man taking to his bed, he sat, then lay, then snored.

The grinnet favored me with a look that said its work was done and no more requests would be honored. It turned and walked with dignified steps to its lair. Its little door slammed a little slam and it was gone from view. I picked up the abandoned book and closed it, then carried it back to my other self's study, where I left it amid the welter of texts and arcane objects strewn across his worktable. Prominent amongst them were several loose pages of old parchment covered in an archaic script and showing signs of once having been bound as a book. Next to them, on fresh pages in Osk Rievor's hand, was a translation; the old text's subject was the training and refining of the grinnet. I wished that my former intuition could have devoted more time to that work, instead of being distracted by the salamander's demands.

Back in the main room, I returned to the problem of Hespira's ribbon. "We have a problem," I said. "The spell could not have been hidden in your dress for any honest purpose. Clearly, it was intended to let the recipient know when you entered a place where there was sufficient magical ambience to bring it to life."

While I was speaking I took her arm and moved her toward the door. "We must get out of this ambience," I said. "Whoever put that beacon on you is a practitioner of magic, and the only adept we have has just rendered himself inert. Not that I would trust his judgment at the moment."

"What do you mean to do?" she said.

"Remove that ribbon and—" An idea occurred. I told my assistant to keep a watch on Osk Rievor and advise me if he regained consciousness. Then Hespira and I exited the cottage and turned toward where the salamander groused in its pen. As we walked, I drew a small multiple-use tool from my pocket and deployed its lesser blade. Near the avatar's pen I stopped our progress and pulled on the end of the ribbon so that it stood out from Hespira's shoulder. Carefully, I separated the length of cloth from the seam at her shoulder.

"There," I said, and wadding it into a small bundle I threw it to the salamander. The beast caught the object as it had caught the jewels, but almost immediately discarded it. Then it reared up and fixed me with a gaze so unfriendly that I was suddenly certain that, in its heyday, the god's devotees had sacrificed more than jewels and coins on its altar. Its reptilian eyes narrowed and a hiss like escaping steam came from its gaping jaws, then it subsided to the floor of its pen. I heard more grumbling.

"Let us get away from it," I said. I led Hespira back toward the front of the cottage, where I had left the carry-all.

My assistant commented. "The signal has been sent again. And now again. And again. The avatar's ambience must be weighty. Now the beeps have become a virtually continuous shriek."

"Good," I said. "Now the recipient of the signal will come, not knowing that we are expecting his arrival."

I opened the carry-all and drew out a fully charged disorganizer. I activated its self-aiming process and had it recognize Hespira, Osk Rievor, the grinnet, my assistant, and me. Then I began pulling on an elision suit.

"Who is coming?" Hespira said.

"I do not know," I said, "but I suspect—"

My assistant interrupted. "Something is descending rapidly from the upper atmosphere."

"Can you specify?"

"No, it is thoroughly clouded. I can deduce it only from the effects of its passage."

"I am frightened," said Hespira.

I handed her a shocker from the carry-all. "You know how to use this," I said. "Keep it concealed until you need it." My voice sounded odd in my own ears; my throat was constricted by an upwelling of anxiety for her. To my assistant, I said, "Cloud our weapons."

"Done. The rate of descent is slowing."

I looked up, saw nothing, the sky empty but for a few clouds. "Where will it touch down? Is it homing on the beacon?"

"Not sure. Wait. Wait. Yes. Behind the cottage."

I crept along the side wall, knelt, and pointed the disorganizer at the vicinity of the salamander's pen. I could hear Hespira's breathing close to my ear.

"It is here," said the integrator. "A compact spaceship. The clouding is magnificent. I have not seen anything like it." A moment later, it said, "Someone is scanning the area. A very powerful probe, as subtle as it is penetrative."

"Can it intrude on our connection?"

"It will. I can dissuade it for a while, but ultimately, it must succeed."

"Go inert."

The descending craft remained invisible. I heard no thrum of gravity obviators. But a waft of displaced air cooled my cheeks even through the elision suit's mask. It settled gently; no thump of contact came through the ground.

In its enclosure the divine beast was aware of the arrival. It reared up on its hind legs and stared in the direction from which the breeze of the ship's descent had come. From its throat came a new noise, a kind of articulated growl, deeper than the grumbles, more portentous than the hiss.

I looked where the salamander looked, saw a faint shimmer in the air, as if the trees behind were shifting slightly in and out of focus. Then, at about twice my height above the ground, a man's head and shoulders appeared from the seemingly empty air. He looked about cautiously then put an instrument to his eye. Immediately, his augmented gaze swung toward the salamander.

His head and shoulders retreated, leaving no trace of him. Then a descender appeared not far below where his head had been and a moment later the man stepped out onto it, wearing a singlesuit with many pockets. The disk lowered him to the ground. He drew an energy pistol, activated its awareness, and moved cautiously toward the pen. The descender meanwhile rose back to the level at which it had first appeared and remained there, while the man looked in several directions and consulted his weapon's display. Finally he nodded and called out softly, "Clear."

Another figure appeared out of the upper air, similarly clad, but the singlesuit's lines were tailored to a different body conformation. She stepped onto the descender and came down to join the man. I noticed that the disk remained on the ground.

I touched a stud that controlled the percepts of my elision suit's mask. Instantly, the magnified faces of the two arrivals were rendered as impulses to my optic nerves. I studied both. I did not know the woman, but the man's face I had seen before.

The two of them were peering into the salamander's pen. I saw the man point at something, the woman nod in agreement. Then she turned and looked directly at me and said, "You might as well stand up and come out in the open, Henghis Hapthorn. Let us get this over with."

"Stay here," I whispered to Hespira. Then I stood. The disorganizer had already informed me that it had acquired both the targets. I threw back the hood of my elision suit and bade my assistant uncloud the weapon. A disembodied head hovering over a threat of complete destruction would, I thought, make a memorable impression. I stepped out from the corner of the cottage and said, "So, Madame Oole—or is it Ololo? Whichever, we meet at last."

She raised one eyebrow. "Well done," she said. "Tesko Tabanooch always said your reputation was well earned." She gestured to her companion who was pointedly ignoring me and making faces at the salamander. "And this is—"

"The man who killed Carthew Chumblot," I said, "and a Wathers docklands skullthump named Big Tooth. And probably poor Tabanooch."

"Now you are showing off," she said.

At that the man looked at me, offering me the kind of loon's leer he had been showing the avatar, then returned to teasing the beast.

"He was not as good as he thought he was," I said. "I noted him when we visited Candyk's Spire on Ikkibal. I assume it was he who planted the peeper in my client's room—again, we found it easily—and his vehicle contained the receptor. But he was so clumsy an operative that a mere taxi driver noticed him and was able to follow him to where..."

But I realized, even as I was saying it, and as I would have realized even if I had not seen the derisive look on the man's face—he was mockingly, silently mouthing my own words to the avatar—that the slippage had been deliberate.

"There you have it," said Madame Oole, or whatever her name was. "Now you are catching up." She took a step or two toward me, moving with a sinuous grace born of arrogance that not even the utilitarian singlesuit could conceal. "Come along, now," she said, "assemble the pieces. Make a shape of it. You're doing so much better than the others."

"The others?"

"The other thaumaturges. Those who thought they would enter the new age full of pomp and power. Including the ones that you yourself undid. For which I ought to be grateful." She purred—there was no other word for it—and added, "Since I will be inheriting everything you took from them."

Now I saw the picture. How stupid of me, I thought. Just because the likes of Baxandall and Therobar and their associates had been relative plodders, just because they had barely left the starting line in their quests to comprehend the arcane powers of sympathetic association, was no reason to assume that the race did not also have its swift speedsters who were already far down the track when Osk Rievor and I first joined the runners. Swift and ruthless, I thought, and I am laps behind.

"I may keep you," Madame Oole said. "It's rare to find so fine a rational intellect coupled with such a deep-ranging intuition. I am sure I could find things for you to do."

I returned her direct stare. She had a face many would have called beautiful, though hard. But behind the evident intelligence and power of will lay the same unbridled self-regard that I had seen in the five wizards of Bambles, in Turgut Therobar and his helpers Gevallion and Gharst, and would probably have seen in the eyes of Bristal Baxandall, if he had not already been turned inside-out when I found him. For all the faults I could have found in Osk Rievor at this moment, at least he did show this overweening pride, this hubristic bellowing of one's own name into the face of the cosmos.

"You overlook one powerful argument in my favor," I said. I hefted the disorganizer. "This has already acquired you. I doubt you command a spell powerful enough, even in this dimple, to withstand it."

"And you, too, have overlooked the obvious," the woman said. She raised her voice. "Servant, disable him!"

I swung the disorganizer to cover the man beside the pen, but he held up his hands in mock terror. At that moment, as I heard motion behind me, heard it too late to turn and prevent what was to come, the rest of the picture came into focus. Still, I made an effort.

"Hespira," I said, "resist—"

But nothing more could I say. The shocker's emitter was almost touching my spine when it sent its burst spitting through me, convulsing muscle and rattling bones and filling my skull with coruscating fountains of brilliant sparks.

The spasm lasted an eternity. Then the disorganizer fell from my nerveless grip, my knees folded, and I sank to the ground. Above me, seemingly far off, appeared three faces: Madame Oole's, wearing the kind of smile cats would give captive mice if only they could; her henchman's, showing the glee that a psychopath can feel in another's pain; and Hespira's, full of helpless horror.

Of course, I thought, she did more than just edit Irmyrlene Broon-Paskett's glandular secretions and wipe her memory. It wouldn't have been enough merely to insinuate the living bait into my closest counsels. Oole would also have implanted a means of controlling Hespira's actions, for the crucial moment when…

Then the sorceress said, "Servant, give him another dose."

My client's distress grew only stronger, which in turn threw me into an even more wrenching paroxysm of anxiety. My suffering was short-lived, however, as Hespira helplessly pointed the shocker at me. The emitter glowed blue again and I thrashed and convulsed the short way to unconsciousness.

I awoke in the grand hall that used to be the small sitting room of the cottage. I was slumped in an overstuffed armchair and they had stripped off my elision suit. My muscles felt as if they had all been taken out of me, boiled until their tensile strength was reduced to that of overcooked vegetables, then loosely slipped back into their original settings. I was conscious of a string of drool down my chin, but lacked the coordination to do away with it.

I lifted my head, felt it go too far backward and strike the top of the chair, then I managed to get enough control to bring it to a useful position. To my left, I saw Hespira, pale and terrified, seated in a sturdy chair, her wrists and ankles bound to its arms and legs. The Oole woman and her helper were not in view, but I could hear her voice from nearby. From the sounds she was making, she was in my alter ego's study, rummaging through his collection of books and paraphernalia and expressing surprise and delight at what she was finding.

I swung my swimming eyes toward the divan. No unconscious Osk Rievor lay there. Nor was there a grinnet in sight, nor for that matter, the traveling armature that contained my assistant. I looked toward the little door through which the familiar had first entered, but saw that a nearby tapestry had been tugged farther along on the rail from which it hung. Only the edge of Grishant's portal was now visible.

My wits were resettling themselves. "Are you all right?" I whispered to Hespira. Her only response was a look of anguish and a sob.

"Please," I said, "I need you now. Pointless remorse will not serve." I saw her gather herself together and gestured to the tiles where my other self would have lain. "He was not there?" I whispered.

She signaled a negative.

"The grinnet and my assistant?"

"Gone." It came out as a gulp.

"Good," I said. "Now do not worry."

But, of course, she did worry, quite terribly. And her distress caused me an equal upset. But I understood now why I felt such a strong response to her anxiety—at least I knew the reason for the effect if not the exact mechanism by which it was achieved. And I knew that it had been no chance encounter that had thrust Irmyrlene Broon-Paskett into my path two days running. Nor had I taken her case out of some deep-seated need to offer a gesture in the face of the imminent end of all I held dear.

No, Irmyrlene had somehow been tailored to catch my sympathies. From studying me and from questioning my operative, Tabanooch, Oole would have known that a helpless woman was more likely to engage my compassion than a helpless man. But she had also known that if she had plied me with a sexual lure, I would have been on my guard. So they had looked for a woman who was the precise opposite of the face, figure, and coloring to which I best responded.

Yet I had not been caught the first time I crashed into her, on my way across The Old Circular to meet Massim Shar's cut-out. I thought back to that moment, remembered that I had just consumed a full portion of Mast Jho-su's Nine Dragons Sauce. My nose and sinuses had been streaming.

Pheromones, I thought. But my assistant had examined her and found her output to be within normal range. But then I saw the brilliance of the tactic. Not strength, but focus. Somehow Irmyrlene Broon-Paskett's unconscious and altered chemical emanations were such as to have an overwhelming effect on my own deepest-seated reactions. My powerful intellect was my chief weapon and my best defense; she had managed to bypass both, burrowing into my psyche from its basest, most ancient stratum.

But how was it done? Had they searched the Ten Thousand Worlds for that rare woman who combined a lack of erotic appeal—for me, at least—with a pheromonic pass key to my unconscious responses? Unlikely, I thought. They picked someone who would not be missed, then turned her into an irresistible lure. But how did they know my own most intimate chemistry? I could speculate as to an answer, and the image that came was horrific.

I heard them coming back. Oole entered the sitting room with an armload of books and grimoires, while the henchman carried several pieces of apparatus. They laid them down on the floor before me and the woman knelt and picked through them with the eagerness of an overindulged child encountering a slew of naming-day presents.

"So many," she said, looking up at me, "so many that I have not only never seen but never heard of. You have done much better than I imagined." She held up a hand-sized prism that had been the sorceress Chay-Chevre's. "This is something to do with color, isn't it? This book"—she indicated a small volume bound in tan leather marked with a stylized face—"speaks of using colors to bind the will of dragons."

She paused to peer into the prism, then leafed through the book. "But there have been no dragons since before the last great change, yet the book is surely no more than a few decades old. How did you come by them? Are there more like this?"

I ignored the question and put one of my own. I was gratified to hear that my voice was not suffering any lingering debility from the shocker. "How did you arrange for my client's pheromones to have such a devastating effect on my judgment?"

Oole put down the prism and book to free her hands so she could clap them in delight. "Did I not tell you, Devers, that this one was worth keeping?"

The man's face offered me a silent disparagement. I suspected I saw jealousy there. But Oole ignored him. "Well," she said, "since you ask. I had Tesko Tabanooch acquire a few hairs from your collar. Do you remember a time when he helped you don your coat?"

I did. I had put it down to obsequiousness, masking a desire to be employed for more assignments.

"I extrapolated your plasm from the roots and then I grew—"

"No!" I said.

She made the kind of dismissive gesture that would answer an overwrought child's fearsome fancies. "No, I didn't grow a whole Hapthorn. Only the limbic system and the olfactory bulb."

I nodded. "And then you tried different pheromones until you found the one to which I was most susceptible."

Devers the henchman mimed a mocking appreciation of my insight. I was beginning to think he was mute. Again, Madame Oole ignored his display and said, "Yes, and then I edited our bait's autonomic output so that when stressed, her perspiration would contain the precise combination of substances that would most exercise you."

"And no resort to sympathetic association? It was all a matter of science?"

"Only the thread in the ribbon, which was designed to remain inert until it was immersed in a strong ambience. That was one of the reasons I chose Shannery; it has no—what did you call them, dimples? You would have detected any lingering resonances and been on your guard."

"I am impressed," I said. It was the truth, though not the whole truth—I suppressed my repugnance. "You wanted me to become so protective of her that I must keep her by me, so that eventually I would admit her to—" I made a gesture that took in our surroundings, partly so that I could gauge the degree to which my nerves and muscles were back under my control; the answer was not very much. "—to all this."

"Obviously," Oole said. "As indeed you did."

"And you made sure that I would notice that she was under surveillance, and therefore threatened—your man letting me see him at Candyk's Spire; the peeper in her room. And you showed me that the stakes were high by killing the driver, Chumblot."

The woman was picking through the books as I spoke. Now she made a moue of minor irritation and said, "Devers was only supposed to hurt him. Sometimes he lacks control."

I saw the henchman's face over her shoulder. If looks could convey poison, my veins would now be chilling. "What impresses me most," I said, "is that you did all of it without resort to magic."

"Of course," Oole said. "You would have sniffed out a spell in the blink of an eye. We needed you to be on guard, but watching in the wrong direction." She picked up the Bell of True Resonance and tinkled it. "Does this summon something?"

I ignored the question. "And the means by which you removed her memories and bound her to your will?"

"A little concoction of mine own." She tinkled the bell again, this time listening to the fading reverberations. "Ah," she said, "now what is that all about?"

"The concoction?"

"Are you worried I will use it on you?"

"You might."

She put her hands on my knees and leaned toward me. "Not before I have plumbed your depths, Hapthorn. And in that process I may come to value you highly. We would make a potent pair, would we not?"

The poison in Devers's eyes grew in toxicity.

"Your companion dislikes the concept," I said.

Her eyebrows gave the tiniest flutter of dismissal. "He will alter his views," she said. "If he ever wants his voice back. Or even if he just wishes to keep all of the attributes he still has."

The man's face paled and all foolishness drained from it.

"You still have not told me about the amnesiafacient," I said.

"Why does it interest you so?"

I rolled my head about, finding my coordination still not much improved. "If we work together," I said, bringing my eyes back to Oole's, "you will see that I leave no loose ends. To you, Irmyrlene Broon-Paskett was a device to pierce my defenses; to me, she is a case not yet resolved."

The sorceress shrugged. "Before I discovered sympathetic association and the coming opportunity, I dabbled in several fields. Some of them led inevitably to sudden departures. It was often better not to leave a clearly marked trail. I combined equal parts of paralethe with a distillation of forget-me-knot, then added a little discovery of my own."

I translated: "You cozened and stole, then hampered pursuit by drugging your victims, leaving them unable to recall who had shaken the fruit off them."

"It sounds so much harsher when you put it that way. At least I left them breathing." She gave me a cool look. "How were Bristal Baxandall and Turgut Therobar when you last saw them?"

"And how do you mean to leave me?" I said.

She blew out her cheeks. "That is a question we will have to answer together. You represent both a great danger and a great opportunity. I am trying to decide which outweighs the other."

A faint snore sounded from somewhere. Her eyes flicked about the room. "What was that?"

"The beast outside," I said. "It needs feeding."

Her face opened with curiosity. "What is that thing? You do not look the type who keeps a pet."

"Why should I tell you? You make vague suggestions of partnership, but I cannot believe you contemplate an association of equals. You will drain me, then throw me into oblivion of one kind or another."

Now her face closed and hardened. "Devers," she said, with a meaningful twitch of her chin toward Hespira.

The man went to stand behind Hespira's chair, waited until I brought my eyes up to his. Then, with a leering grin, he slid one hand down my client's chest and into the bodice of her dress. Hespira struggled futilely, then tried to sink her teeth into his forearm, but he seized her hair and roughly yanked back her head.

I tried to get to my feet, but Madame Oole put one palm against my chest and pushed. I fell back into the chair.

Devers's hand went deeper into Hespira's bodice, found what he was seeking, and twisted. At her small cry of pain and humiliation, a pang went through me. Though I knew that my psyche was being manipulated at its deepest stratum, the mere knowledge made no difference. I agonized for her.

"Enough," said Oole. Devers paused to cup and squeeze, then slowly withdrew his hand. "As long as we have her," the sorceress said, "you will do as I say."

"Do not hurt her again," I said.

A chill smile moved my captor's lips. "Is that a demand? Or a plea?"

"It is what you wish it to be." The snore came again as I was speaking.

"That sounded as if it came from within the room," Oole said.

"It can make itself heard in various ways," I said.

She was listening now. "What is it? Why do you have it?"

I spoke loudly. "It is from the previous age. You may have heard of its like. It is called a grinnet."

The word rang some faint note for her. "I have come across a reference to a grinnet," she said. "It was some kind of familiar."

"There you have it," I said. "It performed functions analogous to those of an integrator. It was also useful for focusing its master's will."

"Or its mistress's."

"As you say. But first it must be tamed, then trained. This one is young."

"How did you obtain it?"

"Must I tell all my secrets, all at once?" I said.

Her answer was to turn to where Devers still stood behind Hespira, the fingers of one hand still sunk in her hair.

"All right," I said. "You knew of Baxandall's attempt to capture and coerce a demon?" Her face told me she had. "Well, after I... dealt with him, I acquired the demon."

Avarice sharpened her face. "And have you it still?"

"No. But I required it to tell me what I most needed to be a thaumaturge. When it revealed the nature and purposes of familiars, I had it bring me one."

"And did it tell you how to tame and train it?"

"The problem with demons," I said, "is a tendency toward literalism. Unless one specifies its task exactly, allowing for no easements in interpretation, the outcome can vary widely from one's hopes and expectations."

This time her smile was faintly mocking. "You were fooled?"

I inclined my head, modest in acknowledgement. "The most effective deceptions lie in telling the dupe what he wants to hear. I asked for a text, but neglected to specify that it be complete. By the time I realized the lack, the demon had escaped."

"But you have enough to make a start?"

"I have, and have done so," I said. "I believe that once I have laid down the basis of a relationship, I can use the grinnet to acquire complete instructions from the previous age."

She stood up. "Where is the partial text?"

"In my study, on the table. I was wrestling with the translation when you came by."

I watched her go, saw eager impatience. She was soon back with the handful of tattered pages covered in cursive script and Osk Rievor's translation.

"What language is this?" she said.

"I do not know," I said. "I use a translation spell, though its power is limited to only a few dozen words at a time. Again, the demon made sport with me." I shrugged, the gesture of a defeated contender who has come to accept that the prize will not be his. "There must be a better spell, but I haven't found it yet."

"Hah!" Oole said. She turned to Devers. "Get my bag."

He left. The sorceress went over to a low table, spread the pages on it, bent to lift it. Then she thought better of the effort. "See this," she said. She made a complex gesture with one hand, mouthed a few syllables. A breeze from nowhere stirred the air of the room and the table rose a palm's breadth from the floor. More motions of Oole's tapered fingers, another word, and the object floated over to where I sat.

"Again," I said, "I cannot help but be impressed."

She preened, and strolled over to sit across from me. Hespira's eyes were wide with emotion. I waited until Madame Oole's attention was fixed on the grinnet training text and briefly raised one finger to reassure her.

From outside, there came a hiss and a succession of grumbles. They sounded deeper than before. I said, "Your man would do well not to annoy the beast. They are better when they are sweet-natured."

Moments later, the mute came in, carrying a valise made of thick, scale-pocked leather. He held it before him, hands under the base, so that it was well clear of his body, though it had a carrying handle that also acted as a clasp to seal the top: this was of a gray, greasy-looking metal sculpted into the form of an armored arthropod whose segmented tail forked to end in twin barbed stingers. The sorceress hid one hand behind another, the hidden one touching the creature in several spots.

She looked over at me and said, "If we do work together, be careful of this."

"I treat all around me," I said, "human or otherwise, with the respect each deserves."

My remark reminded her and she spoke firmly to her man. "Do not tease the grinnet. It is valuable to me." I heard an unspoken corollary: more than are you. Devers heard it, too; he scowled and stalked off to sneer at the figures in a tapestry.

The metal stingtail had released its grip on the mouth of the valise and now scuttled down to cling to one side of the bag. Oole parted the top and poked about inside, coming out with a pair of antique spectacles. She perched them on her nose and read the text, her eyes moving from right to left.

I found myself holding my breath and gently let the air ease out of me.

She looked up. "It says here that the first step is to give it a name. Have you done so?"

"Yes," I said. "The demon said it should be called Yeggoth."

Another snore was heard, fortunately coinciding with a rumble from the pen outside. The sorceress said, "It responds to its name?"

"Indeed. It also likes to be within an ambience of magic. The stronger the better."

She read some more. "This implies that they are housebeasts. You keep yours penned outside. Why?"

"It made messes."

She returned to the text then paused. "Yeggoth," she said. "It seems to me that I have heard that name before."

I raised my voice to speak over the sound of the salamander's growl. It was definitely deeper in timbre. "There is a memory-enhancing spell in one of the books," I said. "I was going to try it but then could not recall where I had seen it."

She threw me a quizzical glance which I read as a sign that she was wondering whether she had correctly estimated the strength of my intellect. Then she made a gesture and spoke two syllables. A tiny musical note sounded and a dancing mote of light appeared over one of the newer-looking books on the floor. She reached for it, flicked through the pages, then repositioned her spectacles. She read silently to herself, then touched her fingertips to her temples and read aloud a sibilant sentence that meant nothing to me.

Immediately her brow cleared and she said, "Yeggoth. A minor Eighteenth-Aeon deity. It took form after its devotees projected their desires onto it."

"Interesting," I said, over the automatic response the speaking of the divine name drew from out back. "I wonder if there is any connection."

"No matter," Oole said. "But the grinnet seems to be getting louder. It needs feeding, you say?"

"Yes. I was about to do it when you arrived."

"What does it eat?"

"Fruit, mostly," I said. "But until the creature is tamed it is dangerous to approach it too closely. I have been using Barzant's Alimentation."

"I have heard of that."

I raised a limp hand. "I am afraid the spell is beyond me at the moment.

Two applications of the shocker have affected my coordination."

"Devers!" the sorceress called. The man turned from where he had been standing near a tapestry, eyes averted, then flickering toward the cloth, trying to catch the stitched figures in motion. "Stop wasting your time and search out some fruit for Yeggoth!"

The mute silently mouthed the deity's name, while his hands spread and his eyebrows rose to offer an interrogative.

"Yeggoth!" the woman repeated. "Out there!" Each repetition of the name—even the henchman's silent mouthing—was marked by an angry growl from outside.

"Hear it!" Oole snapped. "It hungers! Hurry!"

This time the grumbling came from the henchman as he departed the room. I heard cupboards and drawers banging from the direction of the kitchen, then he was back with a basket of karba and windapples and a look on his face that said, "Will this do?"

Meanwhile, Oole had used her finding spell to locate Barzant's Alimentation and her spectacles to translate the ancient script. She took up one of the karba fruits, holding it heavy in her palm. "Should it be peeled?" she said.

"I don't usually bother," I said.

She stood, held the fruit aloft, and pronounced a string of gutturals that ended with "Yeggoth!" Immediately, a roar sounded from outside, startling Madame Oole. She looked at me sharply.

"It always does that," I said. "Try one of the windapples."

She repeated the exercise. Another roar came.

"Devers," she said, "go out and make sure the grinnet is all right."

Throwing black looks at her back, the henchman stomped away. In moments, he was back, his face agitated, his hands plucking at her sleeve.

"What is it?" she said.

He pointed with both index fingers to the door, then upward.

Now the sorceress's face drew in, as if she smelled an unexpected unpleasantness. She indicated me. "Bring him," she said, and went to the door.

Devers hauled me to my feet, bent one of my arms up behind my back at an uncomfortable angle, and marched me after his mistress. I disregarded the pain and concentrated on not letting him see that the miscoordination of my steps was exaggerated—though, in truth, I was still far from restored.

We went out and he shoved me toward the rear of the cottage. When we cleared the corner of the house, I saw Madame Oole standing, arms akimbo and fists planted on her slim waist. Beyond her, the salamander was raging in its enclosure, its mouth open to reveal needle teeth and a convulsing throat as if it sought to purge its belly. The creature was at least twice the size it had been when the sorceress and her henchman had arrived.

Not big enough, I told myself. But then I realized that Oole was not looking at the beast but beyond it, beyond even the tall trees at the rear of the property. She was gazing at the far-off sky in the direction of Olkney, against which a handful of dark motes showed. As we watched, they grew larger and I identified them as multipassenger volantes.

They bore no insignia, were not even all of the same color. Madame Oole turned toward me and demanded to know what was afoot. I feigned ignorance. But, as the first whisper of the oncoming vehicles' obviators reached my ears and as the angry godling Yeggoth once more voiced its outrage at being named without receiving an offering—not to mention having had its divine innards molested by the intrusion of unwanted fruit—I would have been willing to give odds that Hak Binram, accompanied by a slew of the Olkney halfworld's hardest hardhides, were about to pay us a visit. And they would be coming with a full agenda.

CHAPTER ELEVEN

Madame Oole shouted to Devers. He released me and rushed to their clouded ship, rose to the hatch as quickly as the disk would carry him. I tried a step, found my legs less than reliable, and leaned against the side wall of the cottage. Whatever was about to happen, I did not expect to take a leading role in the proceedings.

Devers emerged from the ship carrying an armload of objects. He rushed back to his mistress's side and laid them on the grass before her. She knelt and began to select hurriedly among the items. She was between me and the things that had her attention—or most of it; she kept glancing up at the oncoming armada—so I could not obtain a detailed view of what the henchman had brought; but they looked to be rods, orbs, and pyramids of various metals and woods. Again, the descender remained where it had touched down.

As they neared the Arlem estate the aircraft separated into a half-circle and descended until they were about twice the height of the tall trees at the back of the cottage. I noticed that those vehicles that were equipped with windows had them open; those that had no windows along their sides had had small hatches installed, and they, too, were open. From each of them poked the dangerous end of a weapon: energy rifles and disorganizers, and even what looked as if it might be a tumble-thrust.

For an extended moment, the only sound was the thrum of several gravity obviators and the growling of the salamander. Then came that curious hiss that told me that someone aboard one of the vehicles had keyed an annunciator to life. The high-pitched voice of Hak Binram spoke in my ear, as if he were standing beside me.

"Henghis Hapthorn, surrender yourself and no one need suffer."

The annunciator had also touched every auditory apparatus within its range, including Yeggoth's, which brought a howl of impotent resentment from the contact-loathing deity, and Madame Oole's. She responded for me.

"His person is not his to surrender," she shouted up at the hovering aircraft. "He is mine."

"And who," said Binram, "are you?"

"Who I am is none of your concern," the sorceress answered. "What I am is something you would be wise not to discover."

"We have come for Hapthorn. We would prefer him alive. But we will take him hot and smoking. And if we have to separate his ashes from yours, so be it."

I saw that Madame Oole held a rod of dark wood in one hand and an orb of crystal in the other. "I am not accustomed," she said, "to repeating myself. Leave now, or never."

"I see a third option," Binram said. An energy weapon's snout projected a little farther from one of the hatches on the vehicle at the center of the demilune. Immediately, Oole shouted a polysyllabic word and flung the orb up into the air well above her head, where it hovered and spun, glinting in the orange sunlight. A minim later, a stream of bright force sluiced down from the aircar, only to break in a spatter of sparks against the semi-opaque hemispherical barrier that now hung like a dome from the rotating ball. The shield was wide enough to cover not only Oole, Devers, and me, but the cottage and half the lawn—though I noticed that Yeggoth's pen lay just outside its circumference.

Even as the blast splattered ineffectively against the shield, the sorceress extended the arm that held the black rod and pointed it at the volante from which the weapon had discharged. I could see no visible emanation, but the aircar shot upward and away as if it had been struck from beneath by a great blast of wind. It went rolling and tumbling across a wide arc of sky, shedding two or three of its passengers, before its systems managed to reassert their authority and right it again.

There was a pause in the proceedings that I put down to surprise on both sides. The cottage lay at the conjunction of ley lines, and here the influence of the coming age was already being felt. Madame Oole was discovering that at such an intersection, her powers were considerably enhanced. I imagined that Hak Binram's hardhides in the other volantes were similarly awed, though from a different standpoint. But the warlord soon recovered. Moments later, every weapon opened up on us in a coordinated blaze of beams, showers, crackles, and even the whump-whump-whump of a medium-powered tumble-thrust.

But Oole's defense was up to the task. The dome apparently had the property of absorbing some of the energy that was applied against it, so that it actually strengthened as the assault continued. However, that toughening rendered it even less transparent, so that it became harder to see the attacking vehicles, which were also now weaving and jinking evasively through the air, making it difficult for the sorceress to connect with another blast from her wand.

Devers, for his part, wanted to join the proceedings. He had found the disorganizer with which I had threatened my captors upon their arrival. He was poking at the controls, trying to overrule its insistence that I and I alone was its operator, so that he could use it against the volantes. But the weapon's systems were strictly ordered.

"It will work for me," I said. I could tell that he did not take this as a constructive observation. But he slung the weapon's carrying strap over his shoulder before shoving me along the wall toward the door of the cottage, where Madame Oole had already preceded us, there to enter and take stock of her options.

I looked back as I shambled under Devers's rough-handed urgings and noticed that the salamander's pen had been shattered by a sideblast from the barrage. There was no sign among the wreckage of the choleric god of avarice, but before we turned the corner at the front of the cottage, I saw the flash of a jewel-encrusted tail disappearing into the dark-trunked trees. It seemed to me that the appendage was appreciably larger than it had been before the sorceress employed her powers.

Inside, matters were much as we had left them, except that Hespira's bonds seemed not quite as tightly knotted as I remembered them. I did not linger near her, but walked a small distance across the oversized room, drawing Devers's attention away from her. My legs did not yet feel as if they were prepared to give me undivided allegiance, but they had at least begun to feel as if we were more than just passing acquaintances.

He gestured to the disorganizer's controls, then to me.

"You wish me to unlock it?" I said. "Certainly. If you would just care to hand it over." I extended a hand but he gave it and me only a scowl.

Madame Oole was rummaging through her bag. She brought out a hand-sized ring of golden metal, worked all around with figures and sym-bols. She laid it on the low table atop the grinnet text, then said a word. The ring expanded, like a ripple in a pool, simultaneously filling with a shimmering, opalescent grayness so that I could no longer see the table beneath. Oole touched a finger to one of the symbols and the ring ceased to grow. She touched another and the grayness was replaced by an image;

I recognized the cottage and its surrounds, as seen from high in the air. The protective dome glowed a pale yellow, and Hak Binram's aircars could be seen darting here and there, in randomized patterns. Oddly enough, I could also see Madame Oole's clouded spaceship; it looked to be a mid-sized Wayfarer, though with some peculiar modifications.

"I wanted to ask you," I said, "about the cloud surrounding your ship. It is highly effective, yet I do not recognize the type."

She spoke without taking her eyes from the ring. "I have been working with magic for several years. Not just preparing for the transition, but managing it. Did you know that it is possible, in some instances, to hybridize some elements of the two regimes?"

"I did not," I said. "I would have thought it impossible."

"It is not simple, nor easily achieved. But I have dedicated myself to the work." She looked up at me. "That is why I am what I am, and why you cannot withstand me."

I did not dispute the statement. "So the cloud over your ship, the shield above our heads—these result from the energies of the empirical universe being brought into harmony with their opposites from the regime of sympathetic association?"

Her attention was back on the ring's image, but she made a sound of agreement. I said, "If I was impressed before, I am doubly so now. No, triply."

She did not look up, but said, "More aircraft are coming."

I looked at the display. She had widened the range and I could see several specks flying in a vee formation from the direction of Olkney. "How much of a battering can your shield withstand?" I said.

"I do not know. I was surprised at its strength under the first assault."

Devers had given up on the disorganizer. He came to stand behind his mistress, staring over her shoulder into the ring. I began a brief explanation of ley lines—anything to keep their attention from Hespira. Even though I knew that my reaction to a threat against her was artificially stimulated, I still had to deal with the emotions that welled up from my deeper levels.

Oole listened attentively to my remarks for a few sentences, then held up a hand to silence me. "That is a discussion for another day," she said. "Now I need to know why those men have come for you."

I spread my hands. "It is a complex story."

"Then simplify it."

"I acted as a go-between in a dispute between a wealthy man and an ambitious chieftain of the criminal halfworld, both of them far too conscious of their dignity. Now I am become a trophy each wishes to deny the other."

I felt the chill of her gaze upon me as she considered these facts and their relation to her goals. "This has nothing to do with magic?" she said.

"I doubt that either of the disputants has any regard for it."

She indicated the vee of dots in the ring's display. "And these incomers are not reinforcements for the first contingent?"

"No," I said. "They are a further complication."

"Will they fight each other? While we make an escape?"

That was not the outcome I wished for. "Possibly," I said, "though you might have to leave behind..." I gestured toward the items she had earlier spread on the floor.

Her face closed. "No."

"Then I suggest you allow me to assist in our mutual defense."

At this, Devers began to dance from one foot to another, pointing at me and making gestures that Madame Oole would not have needed any spell to interpret. She waved him to stillness with the same gesture that had silenced me.

"Why should I trust you?"

It was one of those moments when only the truth would serve. "My situation is not optimal," I said. "Yet I am useful to you as I am. When I said that those people outside want me for a trophy, I spoke in generalities; in actuality, they would be satisfied to carry away only certain parts of me. But the remainder they would leave behind would be of no use to you or, for that matter, to anyone."

She put finger and thumb to chin and weighed the issue. As she was doing so, an annunciator spoke, but not in Hak Binram's fluty tones; this time we heard a low voice, like gravel shifting in a rolling barrel: "I am Chai Esquilieu of the Hand Organization. We have come for Hapthorn. Deliver him."

For the first time, I saw Madame Oole startled, though she recovered quickly. "You did not mention the Hand," she said.

"You did ask me to simplify."

"The Hand is not a factor I would expect you to leave out." Finger and thumb returned to her chin. "I must think about this."

So did I. I had expected Hak Binram. And if Binram came, could the Hand be far behind? But when the Hand arrived and found Binram standing between it and its desire, I had anticipated that a fairly brisk fight would break out over our heads, leading to an intervention by the Bureau of Scrutiny. The sorceress would have thought twice about taking on the entire Archonate, whose powers were immense if usually only vaguely alluded to. She would have stolen away, perhaps with some of Osk Rievor's treasures, and Hespira and I would have escaped in the confusion.

Instead, it appeared that the adversaries had agreed on a truce while they winkled me out from beneath Madame Oole's protective shell. Unfortunately, that gave my captor time to think.

"The question is," she now mused aloud, "are you worth more to me than would be a favor owed by the Hand?"

"Yes," I said, willing her to ignore her henchman's silent arguments.

Oole's focus remained fixed on me. "Why?" she said.

I had one piece left to play. I played it. "Because I have seen the world that is coming. I have been there—or then, if you prefer."

The room fell silent, except for the hum of gravity obviators overhead. A small snore sounded, but Madame Oole was not listening for distractions, though Devers looked about suspiciously.

I was very conscious of her eyes on me. They seemed to enlarge, to surround me like the coils of a great serpent. "How?" she said.

"Again, it is a complex narrative." Before she could snap at me I went on, "But here is the nub of it: an entity of immense will but little magical ability was able to draw me several hundreds years into the future. I met five magicians, one of them a woman, and she held great power over dragons. The new-looking materials you found in my study are items that I brought back."

"The woman," she said, "tell me about her."

"If I tell you everything, what then am I worth to you? You will hand me over to—" I pointed to the ceiling. "—then take all my collectibles, and leave me dangling on someone's trophy wall."

Her eyes went to Hespira and I did not need to follow her gaze to feel a pang. But there was no time for persuasion; a heavy concussion struck the shield above our heads. The Hand had a reputation for arriving fully equipped.

Chai Esquilieu's voice spoke in our ears again, harsh and insistent. "We will wait no longer."

"Very well," said Madame Oole, and for a moment my fate, and other parts of me, hung in the balance. Then I was relieved to see that the decision had gone in my favor. She turned to her henchman. "You will give him the disorganizer. No arguments! We will pack everything in the workroom that is small enough to carry, then we will collapse the shield. At the same time, we will throw some chaff in their eyes and run for the ship. They will not know it is there until we are already lifting off. We have only to rise high enough to activate the drive and we will be gone."

I heard the hiss and zivv of energy weapons from more than one direction. At the same time a heavier blow struck above our heads: a direct hit from a tumble-thrust. Oole reflexively took a step back, looking up as if she expected the high ceiling to come crashing in. Then she steadied herself, clasped her arms around her torso, and spoke three syllables, accompanying the last one with a sharp forward nod of her head. The effort seemed to cost her, because the face she turned toward me was suddenly older. "Dragons?" she said. "Real dragons?"

"She owned two."

"Devers! Give him the weapon!"

The man dragged his feet but he brought me the disorganizer. But instead of going to the study, he made a flurry of hand motions.

"Yes," Oole told him, "well thought." To me she said, "You will instruct the weapon not to harm either of us, nor our ship." As she spoke, she produced the wand that had thrown Binram's aircar across the sky and held it poised. I did as she bid, then slung the heavy weapon from my shoulder. Its grips felt cool in my hands.

"What about her?" I said, flicking my head to indicate Hespira.

The sorceress thought for no more than a moment. "She comes with us. She may still be useful. And if not, Devers deserves some consolation, doesn't he?"

The henchman grinned and rubbed his hands, then ran for the workroom while I fought the acid bile that climbed up my throat. Oole told me to go and watch from the door.

"Something is going on," she said, turning back to the ring and its image. "They are testing the shield by simultaneous fire from different directions. They may try a coordinated ground attack from all sides."

"Could that succeed?" I said.

She pinched her lower lip between thumb and forefinger. "It might," she said. "If I give any more strength to the shield, I will not have anything left with which to create distractions." She began to rummage in her bag, taking out items and laying them on the table that supported the viewing ring. She found a glove of silver mesh and began to tug it over her right hand. The glove seemed to be resisting her effort, but she was winning the struggle. She looked at me and said, "Don't stand there.

We must hurry."

"Yes," I said, "we must." I turned and moved toward the exit. My client, wide-eyed with fear but with her also too-wide mouth set in determination, was seated between me and the portal so that she was at least partially shielded from Oole's sight. Silently, I mouthed, "Run!" and "Now!" while nodding toward the door.

Hespira slipped from the chair in which she had been tied, the already loosened bonds falling from her ankles and wrists. I saw the flash of the soles and heels of her shoes as she ran at her best speed. But my alter ego had expanded the inner dimensions of the cottage so that what should have taken three steps instead required thirty. Behind me I heard a wordless snarl of outrage from the sorceress.

I turned to cover our retreat and saw Madame Oole bringing up the hand that bore the glove, the forefinger extended while the thumb held the others down. I did not know what the arrangement signified, but I expected that it did not bode well for Hespira or me and I saw no point in waiting to find out. I had already set the disorganizer for manual operation; now I swung it straight up and let loose a full discharge into the ceiling.

There were, of course, two ceilings involved: the real layer of beams, lathes, and plaster between us and the cottage roof; and the—in this place—equally "real" ceiling far above from which hung the glistening chandeliers. I did not know how the magicked version would respond to a full blast from a disorganizer. I knew that the mundane version would have disappeared in a lightless burst of molecules, each of them suddenly freed from their mutual association, and all hurrying to put as much distance between themselves and the weapon as possible; I hoped Osk Rievor's invented overhead would react the same way.

My hopes were well rewarded. A huge chandelier fell from above, crashing onto the tiles, spewing twisted fragments of metal and explosive shards of shattered crystal in all directions. I kept the activation stud depressed and played the disorganizer's black column of nullforce across the ceiling. Great cracks appeared in the vault above, then ran down to split the walls. Blocks of masonry larger than my head smashed into the floor, raising a heap of rubble between me and Madame Oole, who fell back with her gloved hand raised to protect her face from flying chips.

I switched off the disorganizer and turned back to the door. Hespira was already flinging it open and darting outside. I ran to join her. To one side, Devers appeared in the study's doorway, a well-stuffed bag in one hand, the other trying to drag the shocker from a flapped pocket of his singlesuit. The disorganizer was not allowed to target him, but the doorway was another matter. I played its anarchic energies over the lintel and the jambs, and the resulting detonations rocked him with their blasts and showered him with splinters. He fell back, tripped on his own feet, and went down.

Now I was at the door. My carry-all lay where I had left it. I threw down the disorganizer and scooped up the bag, looked about for Hespira. She had run a little way toward the rear of the cottage before stopping and turning to see if I was coming after her. She waited for me to cover the few steps between us, time enough for me to reach into the carry-all, find a line-of-sight energy pistol, and discard the bag.

"Where?" she said.

I looked around. The crystal still spun high overhead and the semi-opaque dome of the shield extended a good distance in all directions. Though it was meant to keep inimical forces out, I suspected that it would also keep us in. "Underground," I said. "It will soon be very busy anywhere else. Look for a door."

The Arlem estate had been built as a series of subterranean halls, chambers, and passageways roofed in some places by light-admitting pools of water and in others by low, artificial hills. When I had first encountered the place, I had thought it the work of yet another of the eccentrics who were so common in this penultimate age of Old Earth as to perversely constitute the norm. But its creator, the late Blik Arlem, had been a collector of relics and arcana from the last reign of sympathetic association; it occurred to me now that he may have known of the significance of crossed ley lines and had deliberately dug his habitation right into the spot where two major channels of influence met. Only the scattered cottages that had housed his staff were built above ground.

I would have liked to have had my assistant draped around my neck, to probe the earth and map a route for us, but I would have to rely on my own resources. I remembered the location of the main entrance, but that was too distant and even though the estate was no longer under the control of a house integrator, its front door who's-there would still be active and possibly armed. It stood to reason, though, that somewhere near a servant's cottage there would be a servant's entrance, though designed to be unobtrusive.

"There!" said Hespira, pointing to a low, turf-covered mound topped by a stone belvedere, set about with curved marble benches. I could not see whatever she had seen, but she took my arm and urged me along a path of crushed white stone toward the grassy slope. As we neared it, I saw what her sharp eye had spotted: an almost unnoticeable vertical line running through the short grass. I knelt and felt along its length until my fingers encountered a simple latch. I pushed then lifted, and an oblong of turf swung up on invisible counterweights, revealing a flight of stone steps descending into the ground.

"In!" I said, then turned to see what was coming after us. I saw Devers back where I had thrown away the carry-all—an action I now regretted because he had stopped to root about in it and had found my old intensifier, a weapon I left in the carry-all for sentimental reasons. But there was nothing sentimental about the way the henchman unfolded the stock, threw the charging switch, and suddenly leveled the emitter at me. I lanced a shot at him with the energy pistol, wishing that it was set for beam instead of the charge-saving pulse, which merely boiled the dust in front of him—I could have raised a beam and bisected him.

But the snapshot unsettled his aim. I heard the sizzle of the intensifier's effect on the grass next to my head and smelled the charred blades. Now it would take the old blunderbuss a few minims to recharge, and I used the time to reset my pistol to discharge a beam. But when I looked again, I saw that Madame Oole had come up behind him, her face full of murder, and this time she had the wand. I ducked down the stairs.

Hespira stood at the bottom in a utilitarian corridor scarcely lit by dim lumens set at far intervals in the ceiling. It stretched straight in what I was fairly sure was the direction of the sorceress's clouded ship, the hatch of which I had last seen left open. I saw no sign of the shield descending this far into the ground—a flaw in the spell, perhaps, or it could just have been more effective in air than in soil.

It was time to go, but the thought of the hovering crystal orb and the defensive dome that depended from it gave me an idea. I looked back up the stairs toward the oblong of daylight through which we had descended. And there, framed in the doorway, I could see the glittering sphere still spinning where Oole had thrown it.

When all the good ideas have been expended, I quoted to myself, one might as well try a bad one. I raised the energy pistol, supported it with my other hand, and directed a thin beam of bright force at the crystal. My aim was a little off, but I corrected and brought the line of light to connect with the target.

I heard a scream of rage from above, then a blast of wind came down the stairwell. But Hespira and I were already running down the corridor when the wind caught us. It threw us down and rolled us over and forward a few times, but it seemed to have dissipated most of its force against the wall of the corridor directly opposite the stairs. We picked ourselves up and ran. From behind us, I heard Madame Oole's voice shout, "Servant!" but sometimes the subtlest stratagem must yield to a child-simple countermeasure; before she could add an instruction, I clapped my hands over my client's ears and made loud noises of my own.

We ran on, finding a small door at the end of the corridor that opened onto a spacious but empty room whose ceiling was the transparent bottom of an ornamental pool. A wider hallway led out of here, passing a series of drawing and retiring rooms, all long since stripped of their furnishings and decorations. But many had light-admitting ceilings and the waters above reflected down to us the flash and flicker of weapons, sometimes distorted when the pools' surfaces were rippled airblasts and concussions. We even felt some of the latter through the mosaics that adorned some of the floors.

"The shield has apparently collapsed," I said. "Madame Oole will now be too closely occupied to bother us. Let us find a way toward her clouded ship and see if we can deny her an escape."

When we stepped through the vessel's open hatch, the ship's integrator was dubious. "I have no instructions to admit you," it said. "Leave or be harmed."

We had risen quickly on the ascender, quickly enough that we had not been seen by the combatants intent on each other before we stepped through the cloud. I did not wish to go outside again until the war was concluded, so I hastily said, "I bring you instructions from your owner."

"And who are you that I should believe your bold claims?"

I gave my name. "Surely you have heard of me? It was to collect me that you came to this place."

"I have heard you mentioned."

"And you must recognize—" I gestured toward Hespira. "—your owner's servant?"

"Yes."

"Then admit us. Your owner wishes us to wait for her here while she tidies up a few inconsequentials."

"I will admit you to the salon," the ship said, "but I will take no further instructions except directly from my owner."

"She mentioned that you cannot contact her, nor she you, while the cloud is in place."

"That is true."

"She also told us that your ship's bread and punge meet the highest standards of shipliness. We are hungry and thirsty."

Moments later, a selection of delicacies appeared on the sideboard along with a pot of punge and two mugs. The fare was as good as the *Gallivant's*, but I would not bother to mention that to the ship. Hespira and I settled down to refresh ourselves. Occasionally, I would rise and go to the hatch and press enough of my face through the cloud to put my eyes into the clear so that I could know how the battle was progressing.

The attack had come from two sides, Hak Binram and Chai Esquilieu cooperating to the extent that each disposed his forces on one of the two fronts. Madame Oole and Devers had been caught out in the open when my pistol beam had undone her domed shield. But she had managed to catch the crystal as it plummeted to the ground, apparently unharmed, and had recast the spell to cover a narrower circumference: indeed, it was so narrow that it covered only her own person, and left her mute henchman scrabbling for shelter on the ground.

The bravos of the halfworld and the operatives of the Hand closed in on her, keeping up a steady fire that stressed the capacity of her shield. For her part, the sorceress replied with bolts of ethereal force and concentrated blasts of air. Her aim was good and her weapons powerful: I saw one of the Hand's operatives go dancing spasmodically into the trees, limbs jerking and contorting within an aura of electric blue, then one of Binram's bravos was thrust against an ornamental stone wall with such an impact that two solid blocks shattered; the damage to the man was even greater.

Oole's aim continued true, her shield degrading only slowly. But the opponents could bring up reinforcements. I saw a stalemate developing. Eventually, so did the combatants. The rate of exchange slackened, then stopped. After a pause, I heard Binram's high tenor call out, "Where is Hapthorn?"

"Yes," said Esquilieu, "give us Hapthorn and you can go."

"Do you think I have him in my pocket?" Madame Oole shouted back. "He escaped into the underground rooms and tunnels."

"What is in the sack?" said Binram, for the sorceress had picked up the booty Devers had scrounged from Osk Rievor's study.

"Bric-a-brac," she answered. "Some compensation for my troubles. In the meantime, you are letting Hapthorn escape."

Another pause ensued. I drew back from the hatch to keep well within the ship's exceptional cloud.

"He is gone," said Binram, "though I detect recent traces in several underground spaces, moving in the direction of the trees."

"He has abandoned his aircar. He may be seeking to flee on foot."

"Then the truce is off," called Esquilieu. His men promptly opened up on Binram's, who cursed and returned the discourtesy. Under streaks and streams of contending energies, each side fell back to its respective fleet of volantes and lifted off. One of them, departing, lashed out with a tumble-thrust at my hired aircar, crushing it and driving most of it into the ground.

Madame Oole remained within her shield until she was sure the Hapthorn-hunters were gone. Then she dissipated the protection and looked about her. The air still crackled with energies both natural and not, smoke rising in several small columns and geysers of gray ash puffing up from superheated pockets in the ground. Peeking through the cloud, I saw that her face was haggard, deep lines etched on either side of a mouth set in a comprehensive frown.

"Devers!" she hissed. Receiving no response, she aimed her wand at the charred skeleton of an ornamental shrub and spoke. A lance of red fire passed through the carbonized branches and struck a heap of ash beneath it. The heap erupted and cast forth her soot-smeared henchman, capering and holding his seared fundament while emitting a keening whine.

"The bag!" she said, then turned toward her ship. I drew back until only the lashes and cornea of one eye passed through the cloud and watched her approach. "She comes," I told Hespira.

"Should we not flee? It is her ship. We are trapped here."

Her fear troubled me but I pushed aside the emotion. "We are taking a calculated risk," I said. It was an exaggeration; even using congruencies, the abstruse mathematics of chaos, I had found the odds impossible to calculate with any reliability. But it was definitely a risk.

I lost sight of Oole though I could still see Devers toiling toward us. "Where did you leave the descender?" she said.

The mute could only answer by arriving and pointing, but the disk was not there. Indeed, it leaned against the wall next to me, deactivated and unrevivable until the component I had removed and put in my pocket was reinstalled.

"Hapthorn!" It wasn't a call for my attention; rather it was spat out like a foul profanity. I saw no need to reply and let the silence grow. When next she spoke it was in a reasonable-sounding voice. "The ship will not obey you," she said.

"I believe it will not obey anyone who is not within its cloud," I replied. Her silence confirmed my supposition. I said to Hespira, "Our odds have just improved."

"It is my magic," Oole said, letting her anger half-slip its leash. "I can overcome it."

"In time," I replied. "Do you have an adequate supply of time?" That was the next variable in my planning. Madame Oole had come very quickly, once she knew Hespira was within the ambience the sorceress thought was mine. There might be others like her, competitors who might come and scoop up the prizes she had played for, while her energies were drained.

And so it seemed. "Perhaps we can come to an arrangement," she said.

"Like the one you have with Devers? I am no one's cringing pet."

Now I heard true profanity, some of it quite inventive. I waited until she wound down then asked her if she had picked up some of the more extravagant phrases in the docklands of Wathers? The result was startling; I wished my assistant was here to record it; I could think of at least two salons in Olkney whose members would have been gratified to hear the complex obscenities of which Madame Oole was capable.

"She grows very angry," said Hespira.

"That is necessary," I said. "She must think of it herself and act upon it without pause to consider an alternative."

"Think of what?"

I heard the sounds of rummaging in her skin bag, then the rustle of parchment pages. "There it is," I said. I inched forward and peeked out of the hatch. Below me, I saw the top of the sorceress's head and could just make out the translation spectacles perched on her strong nose. She was sorting through the fragments of the ancient text that revealed how to train grinnets.

Devers was looking up and saw me. Oole, too, cast her gaze up. I knew, from the smile that stole across her tired face, that she was seeing my look of deep dismay. Then I ducked back into the clouded ship, counted to five, then called down in a hesitant voice, "I suppose we could talk."

"Hah!" was the response from below, followed by another shuffling of age-dried pages. Then I heard her reading aloud, a string of syllables that sounded like nothing so much as a command, and ended with the name "Yeggoth!"

A rumble of thunder sounded from beyond the trees. I put my head out again, saw Oole scanning the skies. "I am sure we can come to some understanding—" I called down.

"Too late!" she cried, adding a laugh that was more of a cackle. Devers, too, was looking up with a smile of cruel anticipation. "I will use your own grinnet to focus and intensify my powers," Oole said. "Soon, I will be up there and you will be groveling."

"Oh, dear," I said, showing a trembling lip and fear-filled eyes. "I am dreadfully sorry—"

"Hah!" I was beginning to understand that she took a genuine pleasure in that explosive interjection. She called out the grinnet-summoning command again, louder this time, shrieking the name above the new peal of thunder that burst over us as the sky darkened.

There came a heavy silence, broken only by a loud pop! The magic-sensing disk that Osk Rievor had tossed to the ground near Yeggoth's shattered pen had suddenly burst in a shower of dark red sparks, as it was overloaded by a vast upsurge in the immediate ambience. A shadow fell over me and the ship and the man and woman below. I did not look up. It was more instructive to regard the upturned faces of the sorceress and her henchman as the jewel-and-coin-encrusted god they had lately been so grievously annoying loomed over the trees and the clouded ship. Grown huge on the thick ambience of magic Madame Oole had generated, and furious at the repeated taking of its name in vain, it roared at them once more.

I ducked back inside and said, "Ship's integrator, prepare for impact!"

The ship did not argue with my right to issue commands. It instantly deployed its cushioning processes—a most fortunate outcome for Hespira and me, because Yeggoth's glittering foreleg casually brushed against Oole's ship as the god's immense triangular head darted down with surprising speed. To give her credit, she did thrust her wand toward the oncoming doom, although I could have told her that further increasing the magical ambience of our locale would only have made her nemesis grow yet larger.

But then the several rows of conical teeth—each no longer a needle, but easily twice as long as I was tall—closed upon the sorceress. She was dead too quickly to have screamed, but curiously, she did make a last sound: a puff of air that involuntarily escaped her crushed lungs and sounded much like "Hah!" Then her two halves fell to the grass far below.

By then the ship was toppling and the cushions took hold as it fell and rolled down a short slope before its protruding aft sponsons brought it to a stop against a decorative topiary. The restraints released us, and Hespira and I made our way to the hatch, crawling over a wall which was now become the floor. The opening had ended up facing the way Yeggoth had gone in pursuit of Devers, and we were in time to see what all the henchman's cruel teasing of the god, when it was just a little creature in its pen, had earned him.

With considerable delicacy, the avatar's front teeth caught the back of the man's collar. Then its broad neck straightened, the huge head rising to toss Devers high into the air. He seemed to hang at the top of his ascent for a long moment—indeed, perhaps he did; Yeggoth's powers were uncalibrated—before he fell, arms and legs flailing as if they could swim him to some safe shore. But all that awaited him was the wide-gaping mouth of a revengeful deity. That thin, keening whine came again, then I saw the gem-studded throat move, and the sound was swallowed, as was Devers.

This had happened just short of the cottage, toward which the man had been fleeing. Now, down the side of the humble structure, blinking sleepily and looking about in some wonderment at the ruin and devastation of his back yard, came Osk Rievor, his grinnet leading him by his hand. My other self looked up at the glittering hugeness above him, smiled and dug in his pocket for a gem. He spoke some words in a tongue I did not recognize and tossed the green stone toward Yeggoth, which dipped its great head and deftly caught the offering in a curl of its long, darting tongue. Then it applied the jewel to a place just beneath its left eye, hissed a blessing in return, and disappeared.

"Nice ship," said Osk Rievor, when he reached Hespira and me. We had climbed out of the hatch and were examining the vessel's relatively minor scratches and dents. Like many spells, the clouding had died with its caster. "Who's is it?"

"Yours, I suppose," I said. "Your pet ate the previous owner."

He seemed concerned, but said, "I am sure she did something to deserve it." He spotted the skin bag Madame Oole had dropped. "Ooh, what's this?"

There were, of course, loose ends to tie up, but Brustram Warhanny took care of some of them. The Bureau of Scrutiny's orbital percepts could not fail to note the exchange of heavy-weapons discharges at the Arlem estate. The fight went on long enough for the scroots to assemble a sizable task force, led by the Archon Filidor, in person. The combination of overwhelming firepower and the Archon's vaguely all-powerful authority led to the rapid surrender of the disputants. Quick dispositions were made: Massim Shar and Irslan Chonder settled their differences with alacrity when faced with the alternative of having Filidor do so for them; Chai Esquilieu departed Old Earth in fetters, which did him no good upon his arrival at the Hand Organization's headquarters, where success is the only currency that buys rank; Hak Binram ceased to be a feature of the Olkney halfworld, but a rumor passed through Bolly's Snug that he had been seen wearing the uniform and insignia of a Bureau of Scrutiny tactical officer.

And I returned to my lodgings with my assistant, to which I expressed my gratitude for having had the acumen, while hidden in Grishant's den, to contact Binram's and Esquilieu's snoop nodes and report my presence at the Arlem estate's coordinates.

"It seemed to me that a mixed situation offered the best prospects for a happy outcome," the integrator said.

"And happy indeed it was," I said. "By the way, how did you get along with the grinnet?"

"There is that odd flavor to its communications, but otherwise it is an agreeable sort."

"It was good of it to untie me," said Hespira, who had also accompanied me home.

"Yes," I said. "That simplified matters."

"We should send it some fruit," said my assistant. "It prefers a ripe karba."

"Indeed. I do recall."

The only remaining item on my agenda, other than deflecting Brustram Warhanny's curiosity as to the strange forensics of the battle scene, was what to do with my client. I had been housing her in a spare room, but the arrangement could not endure. Irmyrlene Broon-Paskett had spent her life in farm labor, developing skills that did not easily translate into the role of housekeeper for a discriminator of discriminating tastes. A place for her had to be found, and something appropriate for her to do, for she said she would find it irksome not to have an occupation.

"Firhogs are rare on Old Earth," I said. "And unobtainable objects of devotion are also in scant demand."

We had not found a solution when it appeared on our doorstep one morning in the person of Imrith Khal, the young man who had built a dream around her on Shannery. He was now the proprietor of a vast inheritance, including the Grange estate on Shannery, from his deceased father. Having come into his fortune, he was therefore done with the period of his life when young Razhaman elegantiasts experienced the Ennoblanz. Negotiations were underway for him to return to Razham and espouse a person of standing. But it was customary for a discharged swain to bestow a parting gift on his unobtainable, and because Irmyrlene had been ill-treated for his sake, he had brought with him the deed to the Grange, made over to her. It had been part of his father's vindicat and Imrith had no use for the place. He also offered her a ride back to Shannery on the old man's space yacht. In a short time, I was alone again.

Imrith had left another gift behind, this one being meant for me. It was a recording of Issus Khal's final moments. I had my integrator play it, and saw the screen fill with an image of a magnificent ancient hall, its walls hung with the heraldic banners of Razham's noblest families, the members of which were seated at elegantly appointed tables, celebrating their annual levee. Supper was just ending, the grand ball would soon begin. The high and the haughty were engaging in the ritual of the singular cream, tapping their silver spoons against the containers before dipping into the wondrous stuff, with sighs of gustatory satisfaction—and the smiles of confirmed addicts who have got what they crave.

It was then that Issus Khal strode across the gleaming floor, mounted the dais where the orchestra waited. He caused several screens to appear in the air, angled so that none of the glittering throng should miss what he was about to show them. He silenced their whispers with a raised hand, then executed a theatrical gesture. The first images filled the screens. Khal started with a picture of the cream itself, snug in its little pot, then he worked backward, showing it being gathered from the cells of the hive insects. Next the view was of an individual creature vomiting its stomach's contents into a cell; that caused a hubbub, but Khal held up a hand in a gesture that said: wait, there is more to come.

Next came a close-up image, in slow motion, of one of the hive insects collecting a droplet of amber fluid, the recording lingering on the process before the viewpoint drew back to reveal the orifice from which the droplet had come. That brought actual shouts of protest, and a few retches from the more squeamish. Again, Khal quieted the tumult and directed the dominees and their ladies to watch the screens.

The viewpoint followed one of the hump-backed foraging insects, again in tight focus as its mandibles and wriggling mouth parts took provender.

When the scene widened to show what the forager was eating, more shouts erupted, and serious retching. Chairs were tipped back. Angry men and women rose, gesturing, mouths contorted. Prominent amongst them, she in a gown of gray and a snood of silver, he in a purple mask, were a man and woman I took to be Issus Khal's former spouse and her protector.

A general riot was brewing, with several male elegantiasts, brandishing ceremonial—though quite functional—daggers while they struggled with each other for the honor of drawing first blood. But the avenger on the dais roared them to silence and drew their eyes again to the screens for the final images. I saw Irmyrlene Broon-Paskett in the firhog pen, shoveling their output into a wheelbarrow, then a shot of its contents being dumped into the tray, attracting a swarming mass of insects. Cries of horror now competed with outrage as the dominees foresaw the weeks of strenuous ritual cleansing that would be required before any of them could step outdoors again.

Finally, Issus Khal's servant, Fezzant, was seen entering the greenhouse and emptying the contents of a single ceramic pot onto the steaming heap. The man then paused and held the pot still so that the image-capturer could zoom in on it. I saw that it was of white ceramic, delicately painted with a flowered motif. The image briefly dissolved, then we were seeing the pot again. But now it rested on a floor in Khal's chamber and squatting over it, breeches about his knees, was the avenger himself. His eyes stared straight into the percept, hard and bright, and a triumphant smile graced his lips as he held up in one hand a little silver pot, and in the other a little silver spoon. And now he brought them together for a single, melodic, mouth-watering ting.

When the mob rushed the dais, I told my assistant to remove the screen. "It was better that way," I said, "better than the way I wrote it back on the *Gallivant*. Telling the tale wordlessly with images, heaping revelation upon revelation, working backward to conclude with the pure, single note of the chime—that was perfect."

I was invited to a salon a few nights hence. Reis Glindera would direct some of his shadow-casters in a scene from Vix Rushmak's *The Empty Window*. I cared for neither the play nor the director, the combination of the two was an instance of the already overwrought meeting the undertalented.

I had not intended to accept the invitation. Now I would, and I would take Issus Khal's recording with me.

EPILOGUE

O sk Rievor came to see me the morning after the salon. He arrived in my workroom in a crack of displaced air. His first utterance was, "It works!" His second was an apology for causing me to spill my punge.

"I've brought you these," he said, placing a wooden rack containing several stoppered vials and bottles on my worktable. "And this." He laid a small notebook beside the rack. I opened it and saw that it contained handwritten notes in tightly organized penmanship.

He had found them in Oole's spaceship and had no use for them. "It makes you forget," he said, "and my concern is with committing so much to memory."

The feverishness had not gone out of him, but he looked healthier. No doubt he had found a spell for it. We conversed a little more, then he had to get back to his studies. He spoke, gestured, and disappeared.

I spent the morning reviewing Oole's notes and cataloguing the contents of the rack: paralethe, forget-me-knot, oil of myranthium, and a few substances the sorceress seemed to have developed on her own. There were recipes for combining them into different concoctions that the notes said would have highly specific effects.

"It's your choice," my other self had said before taking himself away. I sat now and thought about it. I had a standing invitation to Shannery, where my former client owned half an island and a newspaper. Greighen Island would not be a bad place on which to go through the transition to the new age; not that much would change, nor all that drastically.

I could re-create myself as a journalist with a sympathetic employer. I would have some holes in my memory, but in some less-lit corner of my mind I could have my assistant lay down an instruction not to seek to fill them in.

I mixed the dose according to a formula in the notebook, poured it into an empty vial, and stoppered it. I put away the rest of the materials and the notes, then took the vial and placed it on a shelf near the stairs to the street.

Then I sat in a chair and looked at the little container and began the process of deciding what I would do.